FINE
YOUNG
PEOPLE

FINE YOUNG PEOPLE

A NOVEL

ANNA BRUNO

ALGONQUIN BOOKS OF CHAPEL HILL
LITTLE, BROWN AND COMPANY

The characters and events in this book are fictitious. Any similarity to real persons, living or dead, is coincidental and not intended by the author.

Copyright © 2025 by Anna Bruno

Hachette Book Group supports the right to free expression and the value of copyright. The purpose of copyright is to encourage writers and artists to produce the creative works that enrich our culture.

The scanning, uploading, and distribution of this book without permission is a theft of the author's intellectual property. If you would like permission to use material from the book (other than for review purposes), please contact permissions@hbgusa.com. Thank you for your support of the author's rights.

Algonquin Books of Chapel Hill / Little, Brown and Company
Hachette Book Group
1290 Avenue of the Americas, New York, NY 10104
algonquinbooks.com

First Edition: July 2025

Algonquin Books of Chapel Hill is an imprint of Little, Brown and Company, a division of Hachette Book Group, Inc. The Algonquin Books name and logo are trademarks of Hachette Book Group, Inc.

The publisher is not responsible for websites (or their content) that are not owned by the publisher.

The Hachette Speakers Bureau provides a wide range of authors for speaking events. To find out more, go to hachettespeakersbureau.com or email hachettespeakers@hbgusa.com.

Little, Brown and Company books may be purchased in bulk for business, educational, or promotional use. For information, please contact your local bookseller or the Hachette Book Group Special Markets Department at special.markets@hbgusa.com.

Design by Steve Godwin

ISBN 9781643757001 (hardcover) / 9781643757025 (ebook)
LCCN 2025933702

Printing 1, 2025
LSC-C
Printed in the United States of America

For Leena

Who are these gods that govern us?
Is there no limit to their powers?

—ARUNDHATI ROY, *The Cost of Living*

Prologue

BY THE TIME WE found out Kyle was gone, news outlets had already reported the details: the white Tesla, the Norfolk Southern railroad bridge, the unnatural sight of the car dropping seventy feet. There was the rescue crew. The latched seat belt. The victim: male, six foot two, athletic. Pulled onto the riverbank, what was once a promising young life would soon be a collection of organs. They would be extracted, put on ice, and airlifted to people who still had a chance.

The one image I could never get out of my head was a witness account of the car levitating, suspended between bridge and river, steel and water, civilization and abyss. Standing on the riverbank with a miniature poodle in her arms, the witness was speaking to a WTAE reporter.

"I'm not a religious person, but . . ."

"But what?" asked the reporter, with a twang of genuine curiosity.

"I don't know," she said. "It was odd." The poodle leapt from her arms to sniff something in the grass.

According to the woman, the car had slowed, then stopped, suspended in air. She blinked, and it hit the water. "It was only one second, maybe more," she said. It would have been easy to dismiss her observation as magical thinking, except she went on. "I got the distinct feeling that I was watching an event unfold as if it had already happened and would happen again, like it was somehow overlapping."

"Overlapping what?" the reporter asked.

The woman stooped to pick up her dog, and the interview ended.

Of course, she could not have known that the boy dying in the ambulance was Kyle Murphy, a St. Ignatius senior. She would not have considered Colton Brooks, who was a St. Ignatius sophomore at the time of his death, four years prior. And if she'd heard about Woolf Whiting, the star hockey player, who had died under suspicious circumstances in the spring of his senior year, eighteen years before Kyle, she would not have made the connection. And yet these three deaths were almost certainly overlapping. Not just in the woo-woo, all-things-are-connected, spiritual sense. But in the sense that St. Ignatius had a problem, and we needed, finally, to acknowledge it.

Kyle Murphy took his life during my own final semester at St. Ignatius, nearly three years ago. I remember the events that followed as if they happened yesterday, only to a different version of myself. I'm home from college now to witness the end of this story—not justice, exactly, but something much more personal.

1

WHEN PEOPLE ASK where I'm from, I say Pittsburgh, or, if I feel like being precise, Sewickley, a town located twelve miles northwest of the city.

The late-nineteenth-century industrialists built their weekend estates in Sewickley, to escape the choking pollution of the Steel City. Sometimes I imagine them looking back across the river with pride, observing from a distance the clouds billowing from their mills, the bridges and buildings blackened with soot, evidence of unyielding production and profits beyond even their wildest dreams.

Then I think about their kids. They breathe their clean air. They play on their safe streets. But they cannot escape the smog their fathers created, not entirely. Because kids know what's on the other side of the river. They may not know they know, but they do. They are told, "You are so fortunate." But it's not really fortune, is it? The direction of the wind, the separation of the river, the gardens and the great rooms—it's all intentional.

While the robber barons built their Sewickley "cottages," the Jesuits built St. Ignatius on a hill above the town. Coeducational from the outset, it was a place of high ideals, a 150-acre oasis within an oasis, an institution dedicated to the formation of Character and the pursuit of Truth. At the bottom of the hill, two massive brick columns, topped with ornate ball finials, were erected to hold the iron gates to the school. The original gates remain—cast in Pittsburgh, transported by train to Sewickley, raised into place by rope and pulley. Like all gates, they are a symbol: What lies within is worth protecting.

AFTER KYLE MURPHY died, Father Michael stopped by to see my mom. When he arrived, I was sitting at the kitchen table, working on my laptop.

Father Michael didn't normally make house calls. He was my Philosophy teacher, which alone would have made the situation awkward, but the priest vibe was next-level uncomfortable. He wore a black shirt and a clerical collar under a gray tweed jacket. When he greeted me, he pulled on his beard, which had grown long and somewhat untidy—a beard that telegraphed wisdom. In other words, he looked like a Jesuit priest, which, of course, he was.

It was Father Michael who had convinced Mom to join the St. Ignatius faculty two decades prior, when she was barely twenty-five. They often had tea in the faculty lounge and discussed books in his classroom. Occasionally, they prayed together.

It didn't matter that I had grown up around him. Because he was a priest, he was intimidating, even though he was also soft-spoken and kind, and—I'm just going to say it—a lenient grader.

Mom offered to make tea and invited him into our small living room, just off the kitchen. I escaped to my bedroom but stayed there only until I heard the kettle sing. Then I stole to a dark perch at the top of the stairs, where I could see them and hear most of their conversation without them noticing.

At one point, Father Michael wept. Mom cried too, but I'd seen her cry many times. It was jarring to hear such a banal human emotion coming from a priest. Priests are often surrounded by criers—at funerals, during vigils, while performing last rites—and in my experience, they never, ever reveal even a smidgen of what we laypeople call sadness. Compassion, yes, consternation, sure, but never regular old sadness.

But there he was: a priest, a human being.

"Tell me, Alice, how can it be that we've lost another boy?"

"When Colton died, I thought, 'Dear God, not again.' But I never imagined . . ."

Colton Brooks took his life the spring before I started at St. Ignatius. Mom had tried to avoid the subject, because she'd wanted to protect her eighth grader from all things ugly and sad, but I'd sensed her distress. By the time I arrived on campus for my freshman year, everyone had seemingly forgotten about Colton. Life went on as if he'd never existed at all.

I heard Mom say something about "spiritual famine," and she asked Father Michael if St. Ignatius was still the place he'd shown her when she had agreed to teach there. If he responded, it was with a gesture I couldn't see. Then he said something about the culture, how it had tipped further from center each time deep-pocketed donors opened their checkbooks. Their conversation drifted to Woolf Whiting.

Father Michael said, "I've never told anyone this, because I couldn't admit I should have done something different. Woolf came to me a few days before he died. I'd just stepped off the ice. We sat down on a bench outside the locker room, where I always unlaced my skates. He spoke about a decision that was troubling him, with an unknowable outcome, but would not go into more detail. When he looked down at his hands, I had the sense that he was the bystander at the trolley switch. But he was blind. He could not see the bodies on the tracks. He could only hear voices, or echoes of voices, and he knew if he pulled the lever something bad would happen, but it was something he needed to do."

"Pull what lever?" Mom asked.

"I don't know," Father Michael said. "I didn't ask. Whatever it was, he carried the burden alone. I had noticed that his girlfriend had stopped hanging around outside the locker room. And his friendship with Vince had gone cold."

"Susanna." Mom said her name like it alone was a statement of fact. I assumed Susanna was the girlfriend. Would Woolf have taken his life over a breakup? People broke up all the time. I was in the middle of— I told myself not to think about it.

Woolf had been gone for eighteen years—easy to remember because he died the year I was born; Colton had been gone just four. Even though Colton had been mostly forgotten, the memory of Woolf remained evergreen. The Woolf Whiting Memorial, a bronze plaque featuring a hockey player in motion, mounted on a waist-high stone pillar, was positioned prominently near the front entrance of the hockey arena. Players touched Woolf's name for good luck as they walked by it. People still said Woolf was the best player to ever wear the green jersey, and that included the two St. Ignatius alums who were in the NHL.

But hockey stardom wasn't why Mom cared so much about Woolf. I knew she agonized over her inability to reach certain students, second-guessing whether she could have given more of herself. But was she still tormented by Woolf's death after so many years? If that were the case, I didn't see how she could continue to wake up in the morning and whirl around the house, reciting her lessons and humming to herself, as she packed our lunches.

"What was behind that big smile?" Mom said. "Whatever it was, his own mother couldn't see it. Maybe she was the least likely person to see it."

"I never thought . . ." Father Michael's voice trailed off.

"Nobody did. I worried about his sister, Madeline, sometimes. She was so . . . mercurial, I suppose. And Vince had problems at home. But Woolf sauntered around like the world belonged to him. Like he knew exactly what he wanted and how to get it."

"I keep searching my mind for even the vaguest recollection of what I said to him that day—it would have been the last time we spoke. I couldn't have offered any meaningful advice, since he was unable to tell me what was on his mind. After I tucked my skates in my bag and put my shoes on, we stood up. He extended his hand. I can still feel his palm pressed against my mine. He had huge, strong hands. When I looked him in the eye, I saw a young man looking forward. No missed opportunities. No regrets. I'd seen it before—pure potential."

Father Michael might have seen me the same way. In high school, I did everything right. I was smart and reasonably outgoing. I took care of my body. I never complained. Upon reviewing my application, my college counselor referred to me as a "model student." But potential was external, a thing other people saw. Inside lurked its less dignified germs: hunger or self-doubt; most days, both.

Toward the end of their conversation, Mom said, "Aren't you going to tell me to read Job?"

Father Michael replied, "Are priests always so on the nose?" Then he laughed a little, which broke the tension.

I couldn't fully make out their final exchange. Mom had moved closer to him, positioning her body next to his on the couch. I heard Susanna's name again, and Woolf's. Mom said, "It doesn't change what happened, but it does have something to do with the matters beyond our understanding." I thought she was talking about the mystery surrounding Woolf's death. Later, I realized she was talking about the divine mystery.

But I didn't hear what she revealed to Father Michael, and I couldn't inquire about it directly, because I wasn't supposed to be listening. When we were alone again, I did ask her about Woolf, who, until that night, I knew only as the legendary St. Ignatius hockey player who overdosed in the chapel.

"What was Woolf like?" I asked.

Mom squinted, as if she were trying to see into my soul, and said, "Sometimes, when kids are high-functioning, their parents and teachers don't know what's really going on with them."

"But his friends must have known," I said.

That's when she mentioned three other people: his sister, Madeline

Whiting; his girlfriend, Susanna Mercer; and his best friend, Vince Mahoney. They were the ones who knew Woolf best, better even than his parents, because parents can never really know their children, not fully, not the way they think they do.

To this day, I can't quite explain how Woolf went from a legend I had only considered in passing to a full-blown obsession so quickly. It had something to do with Father Michael's surprise visit. The hushed tone of the conversation. My sense that they were talking about Woolf when they should have been focused on Kyle. I suddenly saw certain forgettable moments anew: Mom crossing herself and bowing her head in prayer in front of Woolf's memorial. The time she asked if I wanted to accompany her to bring flowers to his gravesite. (I did not.) I became aware that my mom had a private life, even though it had been there, right in front of me, all along. Mothers have secrets—such a revelation to me then!

I stayed up half the night scouring the internet for anything I could find about Woolf. I landed on websites devoted to high school hockey stats. On a subreddit about NHL players who were superstars in high school, someone argued Woolf would have been the next Mario Lemieux. What a tragedy, everyone agreed.

Few details about Woolf's death were released to the public. He died of asphyxiation resulting from synthetic opioid overdose on a cold Wednesday night in March of his senior year. His sister, Madeline, discovered his body in the school chapel. She had exited the hockey rink to look for him at seven o'clock, just as the referee dropped the puck at center ice. His best friend, Vince Mahoney, was on the ice, protecting the net. The team played a period and a half without Woolf, before the coach received word of what had happened, and St. Ignatius forfeited. At the end of the season, Coach Danny Perone resigned.

No charges were filed in the case.

Woolf's mother, Monica Whiting, never wavered in her pursuit of justice, begging anyone who would listen to help bring her son's killer to account. She organized vigils on the anniversary of his death. In recent years, her announcements on Facebook garnered fewer and fewer likes.

A mother's love is a desperate thing, never prepared to let go. I knew this because Mom and I were going through something I didn't understand in my final months at St. Ignatius. All the walls between us, some hers and some mine, the things we didn't talk about and pretended weren't there, felt like they had been arranged into a maze. The only way I could get to the other side was to figure it out on my own. Why did Mom care so much about Woolf Whiting? Why was Father Michael her confidant? How well did I know my own mother, anyway?

I wondered if biological parents and their children were strangers to each other too, or if they always recognized traces of the other in themselves, even those parts of themselves they hated the most. Adopted as a newborn, I did not—do not—have that luxury. Everything Mom kept from me, from her enigmatic spiritual longings to her enduring love for a former student, felt charged, like a mystery I needed to solve.

2

AT 10:40 THE next morning, I approached McDonnally Dining Hall (a.k.a. Mickey D's, no golden arches in sight), a one-story brick building on the west side of the quad. I'm not sure how they got away with calling a meal that started during the ten o'clock hour *lunch*, but everybody had to eat, and we couldn't all do it at the same time.

A hockey player held the door for me as he hollered to a group of teammates sitting at the farthest end of the room at one of the long, rectangular tables. Then he disappeared into the lunch line.

Lunch at St. Ignatius was all-inclusive, like a cruise ship but without the crab legs. A lady at the end of the line, who remembered everyone, simply checked a box next to your name and the lunch fee appeared on your parents' bill. Didn't matter what you took or didn't take. Everyone who walked through the line paid the same. Their parents did, anyway.

Shivani had arrived first, because her second-period class was in the Ruth B. Sweetland Center for the Fine Arts, which was closer to Mickey D's. Sweets was erected our freshman year, a steel-and-brick building with large windows, tastefully modern with a nod to the past, situated adjacent to the Simmonds Center for Performing Arts.

Shiv sat by herself at one of only a few small circular wood tables, eating a bowl of raisin bran. Single-serving boxes of cereal and cartons of milk were a daily option, which might seem appropriate given that we were eating at breakfast time, but Shiv's mom had just been charged the flat fee.

I threw my bag on the floor and dropped into the chair next to her like I'd walked a hundred miles across the desert.

"I'll buy you a big box of raisin bran for your locker," I said.

"Are you also going to buy me a mini fridge for the milk?"

"You'll have to take your cereal dry," I said, pulling out a brown bag.

Before I had the chance, Shiv reached over and opened it. She pulled out the sandwich, which consisted of white bread, mayo, and two slices of American cheese, and dropped it on the table. Next, she extracted a baggie with two homemade cookies, opened it, and removed one. "Your mom's chocolate chip cookies are my favorite," she said, taking a bite.

"Why do you think I packed two?"

"But she needs to up her sandwich game," she added.

Shiv pointed with her thumb to a group of freshmen sitting at the table to her left. Their trays all looked pretty much the same. Chicken patty, white bun, fruit cup, chocolate cake. She gestured toward her bowl. "More nutrients for the money. By the way, have you ever noticed how everything is pizza?"

"Looks like a chicken sandwich to me," I said.

"Right, which is basically pizza: bread, sauce, toppings," she clarified.

"Yesterday, they served burritos," I said.

"Rolled-up pizza," she said.

"Monday was beef Stroganoff. How is that pizza?"

"Noodles are flour and water. Essentially pizza dough. Plus, sauce and—"

"Toppings—I get it. And is your cereal pizza too?" I asked.

"It doesn't hold for snacks."

"Exactly: Cereal is not a meal," I said. Shiv had ideas, and when I let them soak in, at least half of them made sense. Sometimes they were profound. She should have taken Philosophy with me, but she chose Design. "We need to talk about—"

The way Shiv braced herself against the table meant she thought I was about to bring up Ingo. I'd been talking about him nonstop, and though Shiv's patience ran deep, I feared the murky bottom. "Not Ingo," I said.

Ingo and I had started hanging out toward the end of junior year. Once we'd made it through the summer, it became obvious that we were exclusive. It wasn't something we ever talked about, because talking about relationships was embarrassing, but we both knew where we stood. For most of senior year, we were Frankie-and-Ingo, a unit. Then, out of nowhere, after a hockey game, Ingo acted like he didn't want to talk to me. He didn't say anything; it was just a body language thing, a turning away. He avoided me for about a week. When I finally confronted him, he suggested we "take a breather."

Me: "You mean break up?"

Him: "I mean a breather."

Me: "What's a 'breather'?"

Him: "A long, deep exhale, during which you figure out what you want."

I wasn't sure if *you* meant me, or if it was more of a royal *you*, meaning him.

What did Ingo want? Hard to say. He had everything a guy his age could want. What did I want? I wanted more, but I was unable to see or admit that, so I was the one being told we were taking a breather, and feeling rather hurt. Okay, gutted. Like a taxidermist had pulled out all my insides and tossed them into a metal bowl before stitching me back up and mounting me on the wall of a hunting lodge for everyone to admire on their way to supper. I imagined Ingo walking by with a buddy saying, "Ain't she a beaut."

Three weeks into our long, deep exhale, I was pretty sure Ingo was hooking up with someone else.

Shiv lifted her bowl and slurped down the remaining milk. "I'm waiting."

"What if there's a reason Kyle mentioned Woolf Whiting on his Insta?"

Kyle's account had been removed, but not before someone had screen-grabbed his final post and passed it around. Posted minutes before his car hit the water: a picture of Woolf performing a hockey stop, ice shavings flying like confetti, stick on the ice, helmet off, revealing his wide, winning grin. *If Woolf Whiting couldn't survive it, how can I? @KMurph87 (RIP)*.

"They were both hockey players," Shiv said.

"Nobody talks about it, but Colton Brooks played hockey too," I added. The rosters and stats were online. "He played in just two games his freshman year. By the next season, he was off the team. Either he got hurt or he wasn't good enough."

In the spring of his sophomore year, a security camera at the 7-Eleven captured Colton walking through the parking lot toward the railroad tracks in the early morning, before light. Minutes later, he stepped in front of an oncoming train. Fourteen years had passed since Woolf's death. Nobody saw a connection. Woolf Whiting, captain of the hockey team, was simply too different from Colton Brooks, unassuming everyman.

"Three dead hockey players," Shiv said. "Might just be a coincidence."

"What if it goes deeper?"

"Deeper how?"

"I don't know. Father Michael came over to my house last night. I overheard him and my mom whispering something about Woolf. And when I asked her about Woolf later, I could tell she was holding back."

Pushing her face closer to mine, Shiv's eyes widened slightly. I felt a part of me zipper into a part of her, our inside jokes and shared grievances operating like tiny interlocking teeth.

Shiv's parents' marriage had been arranged when they were teenagers in India, and for a long time, they seemed neither happy nor unhappy. Sometimes they fought; sometimes they laughed; sometimes they were together; more often they were not. Then, the day after

Shiv's sixteenth birthday, her dad left. Her situation made me feel like she understood me—understood how it felt to be adopted, which obviously had nothing to do with arranged marriage or separation, but it had something to do with accepting circumstances as they are and not asking too many questions.

"Check this out," I said, pulling my phone out of my bag.

A sketchy news site had run a segment on teen suicide. After a trigger warning, cell-phone footage of Kyle's white Tesla hitting the water appeared on screen. Then it cut to Monica Whiting, on set with the host. Shiv and I stared down at my phone together, our heads touching. The host asked, "What do you make of the fact that your son and Kyle Murphy were both on the St. Ignatius hockey team?"

Mrs. Whiting's expression settled into a scowl. Her natural gray hair was cropped short, which might have been stylish, but with her brow furrowed and her lips turned downward, gave the impression of austerity.

She folded her hands on her lap, adjusted her posture, and looked directly at the camera. "I'd like to express my condolences to Kyle's family. I know what losing a child feels like. I share their anguish. But—"

I hit PAUSE and said, "There's a 'but.'" Then I hit PLAY again.

"Eighteen years ago, my son, Woolf Whiting, was murdered on the St. Ignatius campus—poisoned with a lethal dose of a synthetic opioid. The investigation was not thorough. Woolf's girlfriend, Susanna Mercer, never accounted for her whereabouts that night. To my knowledge, she was never interviewed by police. And—"

"Suicide can be too painful to comprehend," the host said. "Let's talk about Kyle Murphy. For his final Instagram post, he shared a picture of your son. Why do you think he—"

Monica Whiting became agitated and walked off set. The segment cut to commercial.

Ms. Guerin, my Latin teacher, had just entered the dining hall. She approached and said, "Frankie, please put the phone away at the table." Without waiting for me to comply, she walked off.

"That mother can't face reality," Shiv said.

"But what if she can?" I put my hands on Shiv's shoulders and squared our bodies. "I mean, what if there's more to the story?"

"A good, old-fashioned cover-up?" She smiled.

I released her shoulders. "We could investigate Woolf's death for our project."

Shiv was my partner in Community Journalism. For our final project, we had been asked to pick a topic that affected the local community and explore it through the medium of our choice. A couple of the teams had already announced their projects, but we'd been struggling to come up with an idea that excited us. One team was building an interactive map to visualize gentrification and displacement in Pittsburgh, starting with the leveling of homes in the Hill District to make way for the Civic Arena. Another team was writing an exposé on a town councilman who had taken money in the form of campaign contributions from a local developer, the lucky recipient of fast-tracked building permits.

Shiv turned her body back toward the table and began tapping her spoon against her empty bowl. She said, "I'm game."

Shiv was an easy sell. Her need to solve every puzzle she was presented with probably had something to do with her inability to figure out the puzzle of her own parents.

My sandwich was untouched, the mayonnaise having lost its appeal. Shiv was working through my second cookie. She looked around. The freshmen sitting at the next table were close enough to hear us if they tried, but they were busy talking about something else. "You should eat. Do you want me to go through the line again and grab you a chicken sandwich?"

I shook my head.

Shiv stood up and walked over to the dish return, where she handed her tray to two disembodied gloved hands that appeared through the window. I always thought they should at least make us sort our own trash—like maybe always having someone clean up after you didn't build the character of future leaders, as St. Ignatius purported to do. But it was probably easier for the staff to do it right the first time.

When she returned to grab her bag, she said, "See you at track, Frankie."

I looked across the dining hall in the direction of the hockey players. One of them mimicked a robot as he stood up. He stooped over, back stiff, arms herky-jerky, and lifted his tray from the table with mechanical-pincer hands, while the others laughed and hooted. *Have you no respect?* I thought. *Kyle was your teammate!* But then, who was I to question the gods?

3

THE FOLLOWING MORNING, Mom and I arrived at the main gate. Entering the grounds meant leaving the outside world behind, which seemed like a good thing—to separate from the world to learn about it. Politicians loved to talk about the shining city on the hill, but to me, Pittsburgh was of little consequence; I had a school on a hill, and it was my city, state, and country—indeed, my whole world. For a time, it did shine.

When we reached the quad, my eyes lingered on the chapel at the crest of the hill, the center of everything, like a beating heart. The campus shimmered in the morning light, making it impossible to behold the darkness that must have been there all along. Even now, despite what I know, and having walked among ivy-covered buildings, Gothic arches, and gargoyles for two and a half years of college, St. Ignatius remains the most beautiful place I've ever seen.

We pulled into the teachers' lot and crawled toward the widest spot available. I was going to miss carpooling with Mom. I was really going to miss not answering her questions. She was always asking about Ingo, even though I never told her anything, least of all that we were taking a breather. Sometimes I reminded her about boundaries, but then she'd say something corny, like "Can't I be your mom and your friend?" and her eyes would smile with those cute crow's feet that she said made her look old but were really her best feature.

As we rolled to a stop, she evangelized the virtues of parking needlessly far away. "Those extra steps add up," she said. Really, she was scared someone would ding her fifteen-year-old lesbian car.

Mom often mentioned what a great perk it was that faculty kids got to attend tuition-free, but when she said it, she smirked, because she was so underpaid. Hence the old Subaru.

She turned off the ignition, but her seat belt remained buckled. Hands resting on the steering wheel, she turned her head to me like she had something to say, but nothing immediately escaped her lips.

"I'm fine, Mom."

"You haven't said a word all morning, Frankie." Her voice registered concern. I worried about her sometimes too. Not all the time, but whenever I wasn't thinking about myself or something Shiv said, or whether Ingo was hooking up with someone else.

"I'm just thinking," I said.

"What are you thinking about?" she asked.

"Nothing. Kyle, I guess. I feel like I don't know anything anymore."

Mom moved her hand from the steering wheel to push my hair back. She examined my face, in the way a mother does. "Oh, Frankie," she said. "You know too much. That's the problem with kids these days." She shifted her body slightly, deeper into her seat. "This is your last semester. You should be having fun."

In high school, fun was a foreign concept to me, like near-death experiences and alien abductions, and the more germane but equally elusive experience: sex. Fun was something other people had—or they said they did—but not me. Partially, Mom was to blame, because she was the least fun person I'd ever met. She did not know how to have a good time. Or maybe she did know, but she denied herself—and, by extension, me, her only daughter—the vast multitude of fun experiences available to humans in the suburban not-quite-Midwest, out of an abundance of caution coupled with the inability to apply statistical probabilities. STDs! Car accidents! Lightning bolts! Seriously, *lightning*—Mom would not allow me to take showers or baths during thunderstorms.

Mom sighed. "Come to me if it gets too hard."

We were late for assembly. In exactly twelve minutes, the bell would ring, and Mom and I would both find ourselves in class. Most days, we walked side by side from the car to Carson Hall, which everybody called HQ. That day, I dawdled three steps behind, thinking about Kyle, then trying to think about something else.

Mom hurried along the paved path. She could have saved a minute by trampling a small section of grass—shorter, as the crow flies—but she never did. In a few minutes, she would write the class agenda on the board before her students entered. Housekeeping, she called it, a humble name for the kind of planning that maintained order and created anticipation, and probably enhanced learning or did something she would call pedagogical. She's too smart to teach high school, but places like St. Ignatius exist only because of people like her.

She paused to hold the door for me, but when she saw how far behind I'd fallen, she smiled and waved, letting it shut behind her. Everyone else was already inside. I thought about what Mom had said about the problem with kids: You know too much. But nothing could have been further from the truth.

HQ WAS QUIET until everyone spilled out of the Great Hall after assembly. Soon, the lounge buzzed with a manic energy, as people grabbed their stuff in preparation for first period.

I overheard someone say what a lot of people were probably thinking: "Why would Kyle kill himself *after* getting into an Ivy?" The Ivies had released their decisions the week before, all on the same day. Kyle Murphy had been admitted to Brown, but he would never set foot in Providence.

Another guy—no need to name names—hadn't gotten in anywhere he'd applied. One of the college counselors was pulling strings to get him into a safety school for safety schools. And yet there he was, across the lounge, enjoying his gentleman's-C average, happy as a Buddha. Nobody asked, "Why didn't that guy drive off the bridge?"

People didn't talk about where they were admitted, but somehow everybody knew. Gabby told Harold, who told Lawrence—not where Gabby had been admitted but where Iris was wait-listed. People nodded at me approvingly, the prep-school equivalent of giving high fives. I was headed to Princeton.

The college counselors had instructed us that under no circumstances should we post college-acceptance videos on social media. Their concern was that these viral videos might negatively impact the mental health of the people who did not get into their top-choice school, or any school at all. And maybe because we were conscientious, nice kids, who took cues from our teachers and counselors, we came to see these videos as extra. But we all watched the ones that were posted. Some of them had millions of views. We watched to see the kinds of people who were going to our future colleges. Or we watched to see the kinds of people who were going to the schools we didn't get into. Or we watched to see how we were supposed to feel when we logged in and received news about the thing we had been working toward for our entire lives, which was, I guess, the reason I scrolled through the videos. Our counselors were worried about the kids who didn't get in, but what about the ones who did?

I acknowledge this, not to complain (I know, I know!), but to explain my headspace at the time. When I watched those strangers squeal and dance and cry tears of joy, when I saw their moms in the background egging them on—maternal expressions intoxicated with vicarious satisfaction—I thought something was wrong with me. When I found out I had been accepted to Princeton, I clicked out of the portal, closed my laptop, and went for a run. I felt numb.

The lounge emptied as quickly as it filled up. I had class like everybody else, but I stayed behind for a few minutes. Light streamed in through the east windows. It hit my face, causing my eyes to pinch shut. On the backs of my eyelids, I saw the white Tesla levitating—*one second, maybe more*. Then it was gone.

I thought about the witness on the riverbank, and the unusual word she'd used: *overlapping*. There was this thing our journalism teacher, Dr. Zapatero—Zap, when he wasn't in the room, and sometimes when he was—always said: "Without the truth, the community cannot survive."

Shiv was already in class and not looking at her phone, but I texted her anyway: *Let's make a plan.*

Later, we assigned ourselves roles. I was the scribe; Shiv was the gumshoe. I would interview the people closest to Woolf—the ones my mom told me about—assuming they agreed to talk. Shiv would track down news, reports, and other witnesses.

Intuitively, I understood something I was not able to articulate yet: I needed to see Woolf not as a hockey player, not as a dead body in the chapel, and not as a victim, but as a human being—a person who loved and was loved, who dreamed and was dreamed about, a person with a past (brief as it was), a present, and a future cut short, a person whose story overlapped with my own, both in ways that I would soon uncover, and in ways I would never understand, because they are the great mystery, infinitely complex and mind-blowingly simple, the way time can stand still for one second, maybe more. The task in front of us was clear: learn everything we could about Woolf Whiting.

4

DR. ZAP SUGGESTED we start by submitting a public records request to the Borough of Sewickley to obtain a copy of the police report. Woolf was eighteen when he died, no longer a minor, so our teacher saw no reason why we would be denied access. But when Shiv filed the request in person, she was informed the report was sealed. The reason given: The case was still open.

Shiv said, "Just spitballing here: If Woolf's death was a suicide, why didn't they close the case?"

Shiv and I debated the word *overdose* for a while. It was the word most people, including my mom, used to describe the way Woolf died. But *overdose* implied Woolf took too much of something, either accidentally or on purpose, and there was no evidence his death wasn't, as Monica Whiting called it, a *poisoning*, which—in our minds—implied someone else was involved. But these were just words. Everyone, including doctors and cops, used *overdose* to describe drug-related deaths, so we couldn't ascribe much meaning to it. We needed more facts.

Shiv also came up empty when she contacted the Allegheny County Medical Examiner's Office for the autopsy report. It was available only to next of kin.

So we couldn't get the primary source documents—not easily anyway. Shiv determined that the most efficient way to track down information would be to find someone involved with the case—a police detective or a local reporter—who would talk to her. She had online access to the *Pittsburgh Post-Gazette*'s digitized, searchable archives, which dated from the present back to the late eighteenth century. Dr. Zap suggested she also make an appointment with a librarian at the Carnegie Library downtown, which housed archives of less prominent publications. I don't know if he really thought she'd find something or he just liked the idea of her having the experience of scrolling through microfilm on one of those old machines.

The alumni database proved useful. Madeline Whiting, Susanna Mercer, and Vince Mahoney were three ghosts with email addresses and phone numbers. In my emails to them, I made sure to mention that I was Ms. Northrup's daughter. All her former students loved her, and I figured the association would engender some goodwill.

Madeline emailed me back first, within minutes: *I will tell you as much as I can.*

I could hardly believe my eyes. I hadn't really expected her to respond. Maybe our alumni network was stronger than I thought. Or maybe she'd been waiting to tell Woolf's story. Whatever her reasons, she agreed to talk on the phone later that evening.

I DUCKED OUT of track practice early and hustled home to make the call from the privacy of my bedroom. As soon as I sat down, I lost my nerve. I had no idea what to say, so I called Shiv first.

"Talk to her woman-to-woman. Start from the beginning," Shiv said. "I'll do the rest."

"The rest?" I adjusted my body in the seat of my swivel chair, which Mom brought home when St. Ignatius upgraded the computer lab. I used to like rolling around the room on it. I'd pretend it was a horse named Red, because it was covered in red fabric. My desk, a heavy wood library table with a hidden compartment that wasn't a secret, was an antique, and probably the most valuable piece in the house, a gift from my grandmother when she was simplifying, before she died. Shiv once commented that the furniture in our house was minimalist, which was her way of saying thrifty, but really there was just less of it.

When only two people inhabit a home, you don't need a ton of places to sit.

"Stakeouts. Wiretaps," Shiv said.

"Wiretaps?"

"Kidding," she said. "But I do take reconnaissance seriously."

"Are you going to wear diapers on your stakeouts?" I asked.

"I know how to pop a squat."

"On somebody's lawn? In Sewickley?"

She assured me she would be discreet. She wasn't joking.

"What should I ask her? Should we prepare some questions?"

"Ask her about Woolf, what he was into."

According to my mom, Maddie and Woolf's childhood had been idyllic, the sort of childhood people looked back on and said, "That was a nice way to grow up," after moving on to some more sparkly place, New York or San Francisco. Later, they'd contemplate returning to Sewickley to push their Uppababy strollers down Beaver Street without getting mugged.

"People all want the same thing," Shiv said.

"What's that?"

"To talk about themselves."

"Maybe you should be on the call with me," I suggested.

"You're going to Princeton next year. You can figure out how to have a conversation with another human being." This was Shiv's version of a pep talk.

A Bridge alert beeped on my phone: *Call Madeline.*

Bridge was a calendar app that most St. Ignatius people had on their phones. Shiv got me using it, and then I downloaded it on my mom's phone, mostly so I could request use of her car. One of the features was a scheduling tool, which allowed us to send each other options and vote on the best alternative. Shiv had always been really into tracking everything, including time. Even before we had phones, she kept lists—first with pen and paper, tallying by fives, then on a massive Excel spreadsheet. Shiv was an early adopter of Excel, and by early, I mean early for *her*. By twelve, she was a wizard. She could have been making sophisticated financial models, but instead she was tracking banal life experiences—how many people she interacted with on a given day, the length of the interactions, the quality. When she discovered Bridge, she put everything into the app, including sleep.

After Shiv and I hung up, it occurred to me that when I had pictured Woolf's situation, I'd imposed my own version of St. Ignatius, and Sewickley, and life generally. In my imagination, Woolf and Kyle had been virtually indistinguishable. Of Madeline, Susanna, and Vince, I'd thought, *These people are just like me*. But were they? A lot had happened in eighteen years, and I'm not even talking about earth-shattering geopolitical events. I'm talking about the day-to-day art of being human. I'm talking about Bridge.

I dialed the phone number Madeline had given me, which was different from the one in the alumni database, at 5:06 p.m., six minutes late. She picked up on the third ring, suggesting she was not eager to talk but willing. I stammered through an awkward greeting. Except for Mom and Shiv, I rarely spoke on the phone to anyone. It felt unnatural.

Immediately, she asked if she could put me on hold, because someone was in the process of delivering a new chair.

When she picked up again, she explained, "Every couple of years, they roll a new chair into my office. Apparently, chair technology operates according to its own version of Moore's law. Instead of increased processing power, the result is increased sitting time. When the maintenance guy dropped it off, he said, 'Someone must really care about you.' No, somebody cares about keeping me where they want me."

I laughed like I understood corporate angst, and then tried to crack a joke. "Everybody's talking about the government controlling our bodies, but no one's talking about the chairs!"

There was an awkward pause. It couldn't have lasted for more than a few seconds. I thought it was nothing—a reaction to my dumb joke, exaggerated by a weak connection. But it was more than that. It was Maddie thinking about something she knew, the one thing she couldn't tell me because it was a secret she'd promised to keep. I didn't know that then, though, so I hurried to fill the silence.

"Thank you for agreeing to talk to me. I have so many questions for you. Are you still there?"

"I'm here," Maddie said. "I've been here all along."

"I know talking about Woolf might be difficult," I said.

"You can ask me anything," she said. But before I could, she started talking. "I always thought his death had something to do with hockey. People were so crazy about hockey."

I channeled Shiv. "Maybe you can start at the beginning?"

And she did. Not the very beginning, but what she perceived as the beginning of the end for Woolf, which was when hockey morphed from just a game to a ticket to an alluring future. As I would soon learn, it's the journalist's responsibility to figure out the beginning of the story in order to understand the end. Madeline Whiting's version began in junior high.

I listened. I took notes. When she said she had to go, something about work, I realized the sun hung low on the horizon. We'd been talking for over two hours.

Before saying goodbye, we agreed to talk again on Sunday. She instructed me to call her work phone again, because "Corporate law does not abide the weekend." She had so much to tell me. About Woolf. About St. Ignatius.

I wanted to know everything. I thanked her profusely.

She thanked me in equal measure. Then she made a simple request. She would tell me everything I wanted to know, but I had to promise to leave her vulnerable mother alone. I recalled the first lesson of Community Journalism: Never exploit somebody's pain for the sake of a story.

I understood, I told Maddie, absolutely. Monica Whiting was off-limits.

Shiv had suggested I secretly record the call, but that seemed shady, and maybe illegal. So I had only my chicken-scratch notes to fill in the details I didn't remember. I worried, in particular, that I might not accurately recount details that might seem insignificant but would later prove important: a conversation, a shrug, a sweaty palm. But I told myself: Any errors in fact were far more likely to come from Maddie. I was impartial; she was not. My recollections were immediate; hers were eighteen years old.

I did not question her truth. And I could not have foreseen that our little project would one day attract the attention of a US attorney.

Madeline Whiting
April 2000

COACH DANNY PERONE showed up sometime in early spring.

Woolf was thirteen—Maddie, twelve—both careening through the seventh grade. Woolf was exactly ten months older than Maddie. He was a September baby, one of the oldest in their class, and she, born the following July, was one of the youngest. Their parents were always telling him to look out for her, even though he was naturally protective.

They were in the kitchen when the doorbell rang. Mo had just finished making Woolf a sandwich. Mo was short for Monica, not Mom. The nickname was Maddie's first act of rebellion, but everyone thought it was cute, and the name stuck.

Their dad, Declan, or Big D, as everyone called him, usually did most of the cooking, but he had gone on one of his trips to Michigan. Initially, he'd visited only for a couple days, sent on assignment to cover a hockey development program for the best under-17s and under-18s in the country. After years of calling himself a freelance sports journalist when he was really more of a hockey dad, the opportunity must have felt like an exotic getaway. He drank stale coffee, ate arena hot dogs, and witnessed the intricate bonds of twenty-five boys, who, for two years, spoke to their mothers only on the phone, if at all.

On the rolling hills of the Lower Peninsula, Big D discovered not a game but a religion, with its community, its rituals, its prophets. He told the stories of three boys, each believing hockey had breathed the life force into their souls. Separately, and unprompted, they all said they lived for hockey, and would die for it too. The article, titled "The

Spirit on the Ice," became a cult sensation, inspiring letters to the editor from fans and coaches and parents across the country.

Big D planned to shadow the boys, following them to the 2002 Olympics in Salt Lake, and then to the NHL. He would turn the article into a book. He was on his third trip to Michigan.

After setting the sandwich down on the table in front of Woolf, Mo spun around to go answer the door. Maddie said, "I don't see how you can be such a big feminist and a Catholic at the same time. Maybe we should be Episcopalians. At least they have women at the helm."

Mo taught Gender Studies at Carnegie Mellon. She still does. She called back, "You can't just wake up and declare yourself an Episcopalian."

"I'm pretty sure you can do exactly that." Mo was at the door, so Maddie was speaking to Woolf. "I mean, who's going to stop you?"

Maddie had declared herself an atheist earlier that year. It was something she knew with certainty, in the way some girls knew they were hot: God did not exist. Mo said she could believe whatever she wanted, but she still had to go to church.

Maddie and Woolf listened from the kitchen as a strange man spoke to Mo through the screen door. He introduced himself as the St. Ignatius hockey coach. At first, Maddie couldn't figure out what he was doing at their house. High school still seemed far off, a fairyland where people did things they would later vaguely regret, like getting their belly buttons pierced.

Coach Perone said he was aware of Woolf's considerable talent.

Mo let out a high-pitched chirp, unfitting for a feminist scholar, and invited him in, directing him to the kitchen, where Woolf sat, with his mostly consumed sandwich, across from Maddie, with the scrambled eggs she'd made for herself.

When he sat down, Maddie asked, "Do you want a sandwich? Mo's making them for everyone who pees standing up."

"Maddie, please be polite. Mr. Perone is here to talk to Woolf."

Mom touched the man's forearm. "Would you like anything? Something to drink?"

"Boys are capable of making their own sandwiches," Maddie said. "Don't you think, Mr. Perone?"

"Water's great," he said. He winked at Maddie. "I make a killer meatball sub, myself."

Mo placed a glass of water in front of Coach Perone. His fingers locked around the glass, but he didn't lift it from the table. He leaned toward Woolf as if to whisper a secret. "I've seen you play."

"You've been to my games?" Woolf seemed surprised.

"I do my own scouting," Coach said. "You're good. You could be great."

Coach Perone wore a big gold watch on his left wrist and a signet ring on his right pinky. He lifted his hands when he spoke, and each time he rested them on the table again, the ring clinked against the wood. His dress shoes and necktie seemed odd for a Saturday, and in spite of his obvious effort, he looked disheveled. He spoke fast, like a grifter plotting his next scheme.

Over time, Maddie would come to see Coach as a salesman more than anything else. An easy job, one might say: talk a kid into doing the thing he loves most in the world. But Coach Perone's particular gift was making the cost seem reasonable.

He said the development program required a substantial time commitment, not only from Woolf, but from the entire family. The predawn practices. The weekend tournaments in Buffalo and Rochester, and as far north as Montreal. Weight training and running and watching video when they weren't on the ice. He said Woolf would need to quit soccer and baseball, because he couldn't risk injury off the ice.

"He has to study," Mo said.

"Of course," Coach agreed. "He'll need a B average to play for St. Ignatius."

"He's an A student," Mo said. Woolf's cheeks turned red.

Coach expected his boys to make grades and stay out of trouble. He had no tolerance for distractions. He looked at Woolf. "Have you heard about the rink?"

Woolf nodded.

Maddie thought, *What rink?*

"You know the name Raymond Mercer?"

Woolf shook his head no this time.

"He's the most generous man in Pittsburgh. He built us the rink. St. Ignatius now has a world-class facility. With you on the team, we'll have a championship banner hanging from the rafters." Coach stuck his hand out, and Woolf shook it.

Mo told them to slow down. "We need to talk this over as a family," she said, which falsely implied Maddie's feelings would be considered.

It was already done. Their handshake was like a contract. Maddie would learn later—much later, after she became a lawyer—that a handshake between associates, like laughter between friends, was a gateway, and on the other side of it, good people ended up in positions they did not anticipate, doing things they never thought they'd do.

Woolf and Coach started talking about the development program. He had the raw talent, Coach said, but there was so much to learn. He asked Woolf if he'd ever gone to the symphony, and Woolf said he had. Mo and Big D took the family once a year so they could pretend they were cultured.

"Practice and surrender," Coach said. "The professionals don't think when they perform. Their minds go blank. By the time you're a St. Ignatius man, that's how you'll play hockey."

Mo put a salami sandwich on the table in front of Coach, even though he hadn't asked for it. He picked it up as if he'd been expecting it and took a bite. Then he pulled a piece of salami out of the sandwich and held it under the table for Jágr, who was nosing around for scraps like always.

Jágr was overweight, a fifty-five-pound dog that should have been forty. Maddie had been saving the last bite of her sandwich for Jágr since he was a puppy, but when the vet put him on a strict diet, she abided. Jágr was eight; she wanted him to live forever.

The stranger in their house, dispensing deli meat to her beloved, offended her. She did the only thing she could do. She tattled. "Mo, he's feeding Jágr."

Coach Perone lifted his hands, palms out, now empty.

"Maddie, stop acting like a child," Woolf said.

She could tell her brother wanted her to leave, but she was still eating the scrambled eggs on her plate and she had to monitor the Jágr situation. She stared down Coach for long minute, before she spoke to him. "Jágr is not allowed to eat human food."

The kitchen table was rectangular. Woolf always sat at the head of the table, and Maddie sat on the far end, by the window. Mo and Big D sat across from each other on the long sides, so they could pass food and settle disputes. Woolf and Maddie were in their usual spots now, force of habit, and Coach was in Mo's usual seat. When she joined them, she sat in Big D's spot.

Coach consumed his sandwich quickly, in four of five bites, leaving a large piece of crust. He pushed the plate toward the center of the table.

Mo said, "We've always agreed Woolf and Maddie would go to public school. Quaker Valley is—"

"I'll see to it that Woolf receives a full scholarship, of course," Coach interrupted. He glanced at Maddie, smiling, offering her nothing.

Woolf said, "I want to play for St. Ignatius."

Mo repeated, "We'll talk it over as a family."

Woolf started to argue. "The rink—"

Coach Perone slapped his hands down on the table and leaned in to push himself out of his chair. "I'll leave you to discuss the opportunity." Looking at Mo, he added, "Of a lifetime."

Woolf and Mo both stood up from the table, turning to walk him out. Coach petted Jágr on the head. Then he reached back across the table and lifted the remaining piece of crust from his plate. Before holding it down for Jágr, he looked at Maddie and winked. Cooing at Jágr, he said, "A little piece of crust won't hurt you. Good boy. Good boy. Don't let them take away your bread. Good boy."

No one said anything as Woolf, Mo, Jágr, and Coach wound through the hallway to the foyer. Maddie listened from the kitchen.

Before Coach departed, Woolf made a bargain; even then, when he was a kid, he understood his power. He wanted Coach Perone to offer Vince a spot in the program too. Coach must have agreed to consider the request, because the last thing she heard Woolf say was, "Thank you, sir. You won't regret it."

Maddie had spent the better part of her childhood trying to avoid hockey. But now she found herself on the family computer, looking up Coach Perone and St. Ignatius. A press release announced he'd recently been hired. An article gushed about the construction of the Raymond J. Mercer Arena on the school's campus. In the featured photo, Coach shook hands with a man in a suit and an overcoat, his hair combed back and gelled—too flashy for the Burgh.

If she'd found anything else on Coach Perone, she would have brought it to Mo and Big D. Even something small might have been enough to convince them that this so-called opportunity of a lifetime wasn't what it seemed and Woolf should go to Quaker Valley with her, as they'd always planned. But there was nothing. The only records in Coach Perone's name were of wins and losses from his former school—mostly wins.

She turned off the computer, went to the den, and turned on the TV. She suffered through a game of single-player *Punch-Out!!* to remember the way things used to be, and then, with a shrug, she resolved to grow up alone.

5

"THAT'S ALL YOU got?" Shiv asked.

We were sitting on the Lawn, eating lunch the next day, Friday. Kyle had only been gone since Monday, but that week felt like an eternity.

The weather had turned warm early, summer putting the squeeze on spring. I'd taken my shoes off to feel the soft green grass between my toes. St. Ignatius grass was luxurious, bright and plush, free of the prickly unevenness of other people's grass. Mom liked to say, "The grass is always greener inside the gates."

Shiv chewed the last pretzel from her fun-size bag and tilted her head back to dump the remaining salt and crumbs into her open mouth.

"What do you mean? 'Start from the beginning,' you said. It's interesting that she started with Coach Perone, don't you think? We should see what we can dig up on him."

"Coach Perone gave an overweight dog a bite of his sandwich. Not exactly a federal crime. I've done worse than that." Shiv wasn't a bad kid. She drank, on occasion. Somebody's dad once caught her smoking weed on the golf course. He called her mom. In fact, she got caught almost every time she did something she wasn't supposed to, which seemed more indicative of innocence than delinquency.

"Why would Coach Perone resign after Woolf died? He lost a player, tragically, but why resign unless he did something wrong? Especially after all those championships," I said. "Meanwhile, how's your sleuthing going?"

"So far, nothing," Shiv said. "Those *Post-Gazette* archives are amazing. I looked up everything that happened in Sewickley in the past twenty years. I searched for Woolf's name, and also, out of interest, I searched for Colton Brooks and Kyle Murphy. I had no idea high school sports were covered in major newspapers, but I guess people *care*. So Woolf's there, but most of the coverage is about hockey championships. The headline when he died was 'St. Ignatius Hockey Player Dead from Overdose,' and the article is mostly about hockey. A Detective Faron is quoted saying they are interviewing friends and family, chasing all leads—I googled him. He died of natural causes in 2012. Dead end."

According to Shiv, Colton Brooks received zero coverage. Apparently, if you are not a star athlete or a beautiful girl, nobody cares about you, sorry.

Kyle's death was different. Like Woolf, he was an extremely photogenic hockey player. But also, teen suicide had become a trending topic. According to the news, teens were in crisis. Parents were worried about suicide clusters—especially rich parents, who realized their money couldn't protect them when they read about those kids in Palo Alto who stepped in front of a Caltrain.

Shiv was thorough. She expanded her search back through the '90s, to make sure no incidents were reported in Sewickley that might have foretold trouble, though she knew, of course, that bullying, and even abuse, would have likely gone unreported. She did find one article that quoted two Sewickley mothers, Nanette Van Buren, and—get this—Monica Whiting. The article was about how local mothers were banding together to effect change on gun safety. Nanette Van Buren claimed her thirteen-year-old daughter had been "shot by a neighbor in a nonfatal incident." Monica Whiting was quoted as saying, "When you live in a place like Sewickley, you don't think you have to worry about guns. You think, 'Not in my neighborhood, not my kids,' but guns in the hands of children do not discriminate."

Maddie hadn't mentioned the Van Buren girl when we spoke, and any connection to Woolf's death in high school seemed beyond remote. But the story did crack our perception of what my mom had referred to as their "idyllic childhood." At the very least, a gun-related incident was worth looking into.

"I'll ask Vince Mahoney if he knew the Van Buren girl." I would have my first opportunity to talk to Vince later that evening. He had responded to my email and suggested we meet at Eat'n Park, which seemed like an odd choice for a grown man who was recently named one of Pittsburgh's most influential leaders in the *Business Times*, but maybe he was low-key cool. I agreed to meet him after track practice.

Shiv was all about "being present," or at least she was in a phase, so she'd started turning off her phone during the school day. If she had been Catholic, she would have been really good at Lent. So it was notable that she was looking at her phone that day. I figured she was probably tracking down some detail pertinent to our investigation. Like a jealous boyfriend, I demanded, "What's on your phone?"

"Nothing," she muttered. "An email from my dad." She handed me her phone so I could read it, and then tried to change the subject, "Do you think it's sad that your mom is a Catholic and a lesbian?"

I wasn't sure what she meant by *sad*. But it wasn't like I hadn't thought about it.

She added, "I guess what I'm asking is: Why is she Catholic?"

"She's known she's Catholic longer than she's known she's a lesbian," I said.

"Right, okay, but being Catholic is a choice."

But it wasn't a choice. Not really.

The question every person raised with religion must eventually ask is: Does my church do more harm than good? But then you could ask the same question about Starbucks, or the Pittsburgh Pirates, or recycling, or marriage, or democracy. If you asked the question enough, you'd end up alone, naked in a forest, without worldly attachments, confident you are doing no harm. Then you'd realize you were a Zen Buddhist, and you'd come full circle.

"I think her lesbian side and her Catholic side are like an old married couple at the dinner table. They eat together in silence."

"Have you ever talked to her about it?" Shiv asked.

"Catholic girls don't talk to our mothers about that kind of thing," I said. "We push everything under the rug and pray it stays there."

"Until when?"

"Until our mothers die."

"By then, it's too late," Shiv said.

"For what?"

"To have a relationship."

"The relationship happens on top of the rug," I said.

After her dad left, Shiv told her mom everything, including—and I cannot fathom telling someone related to me something like this—about the time she tried to have sex but made the guy stop because it hurt like hell. Her family life had always struck me as conservative. She was not allowed to do all the things I was not allowed to do, and she was also not allowed to date Muslims. Her mom once had the lock on her bedroom door reversed, because every time Shiv was grounded, she snuck out. She still found a way out—she crawled out her window and shimmied down a tree. But when her dad went to West Virginia, everything changed. Something cracked open between Shiv and her mom, and they started to have a real relationship, an adult relationship, one that was not based on rules and punishment.

My relationship with my mom was also not based on rules and punishment, but not because we told each other everything. Quite the contrary. We told each other as little as possible. We understood implicitly that part of our Catholic identity was breaking the rules and carrying on, because, well, *life*. At no point in time did we discuss changing the rules.

"Why are you asking about my mom?"

"My dad gave up everything for ISKCON." Shiv was referring to the International Society for Krishna Consciousness, better known as the Hare Krishnas. "His family. His money. Everything. And I thought maybe your mom did the same thing. Not her family and money, obviously, but her identity."

"His money?"

Shiv nodded. "Now he's on the board."

"Your mom let him give away your money?"

"They kept separate accounts. Mom doesn't care. Dad's the one who told me he donated 'lavishly.'" She used air quotes when she said the word *lavishly*.

Mr. Badlani was an entrepreneur who grew a small manufacturing company into a large one. I think he made valves for the oil and gas industry, which sounds simple, but I never really understood it. He sold the company before he joined the Hare Krishnas.

I thought about saying more but decided against it. Shiv's mom was an anesthesiologist in Pittsburgh. If she wanted, she could buy a boat and cruise it down the Monongahela.

Her dad's email described daily temple activities, starting with Mangala Aarti at 4:30 a.m. He wrote that he was sometimes unable to attend—presumably, he overslept—but he always went to 7 a.m. Worship. There were six Worships throughout the day. He capitalized *Worship*, which reminded me of the note my mom had left on the counter that morning: *Gone to Mass, back to pick you up for school.* Daily Mass was not part of her typical routine. I pictured her kneeling in the pew, praying for Kyle's soul. Or, more likely, Woolf's.

He closed the email with *LOL Shayana*. I asked Shiv what it meant.

"He writes 'LOL' all the time. He means 'Lots of love.' Ha ha! 'Shayana' is a term of endearment."

"The temple is only like an hour and a half away," I said, as if she didn't already know. I thought the fact that her dad emailed her weekly meant he had not abandoned her, as she claimed he did, but later I understood you can abandon somebody without disappearing entirely. You can even abandon someone while living under the same roof.

In high school, I lacked the imagination necessary for true empathy. I, too, had been abandoned, but I felt simultaneously less aggrieved, because the people who'd abandoned me didn't know me, and more so, because Shiv's dad had been there for the first sixteen years of her life and she had grandparents in India whom she'd actually met, and aunties and uncles, and a million other people who were always stopping by her house. Mom and I had each other but no one else.

"Just makes it worse," she said. "He could come home whenever he wanted, but he hasn't been back to Sewickley since the day he left."

"You could visit him there."

She crinkled her nose, lifting her upper lip. "I could. He invited me. But it feels wrong. Like a betrayal."

"Of your mom?"

"I don't think she cares. I mean, maybe she does. But she's like, 'Go, beta. Do what you want.'" Shiv mimicked her mother's accent and her mannerism, the way she waved her hand in the air when she spoke.

"So go," I said.

"I'm thinking about it," she said.

The Hare Krishna commune was in rural West Virginia. It was as if Shiv's dad had stepped into a wardrobe and exited into another world. By the spring of our senior year, he'd been gone two years. He claimed he was ready to enter his third stage of life, which meant he would begin detaching from family, according to Vedic tradition. Essentially, he took an early exit from grihastha, the householder stage, which would have otherwise ended when Shiv and her sister were both educated and married. I guess you could say he'd modernized an ancient value system.

Tweaking religion is risky, though. Best case, it gets a little watered down. Worst case, it's used to serve some nefarious purpose, imagined by people in power, motivated by self-interest.

Shiv certainly wasn't getting married anytime soon. As early as high school, she had a plan: Straight out of college, she would focus on wealth creation; money sooner was better than money later.

Compound interest and all that. In her mid to late twenties, she would freeze her eggs. By thirty-five, she would meet her life partner. At thirty-eight, she would semiretire, and they would travel the world together. The trip would be first-class. Only the best hotels and restaurants. Exclusive locales. A year, maybe two. By forty, she'd pull those eggs out of the liquid nitrogen and make babies.

You could roll your eyes and say "Best-laid plans," but I was reasonably confident she would execute them. Shiv was a mastermind. She viewed life as one big sudoku puzzle. Complicated, sure. Long. But the thing about sudoku is you can solve it. You can win. And Shiv was a winner. She'd never admit it, but in this way, she was exactly like her father. They just had different puzzles. His ended with a commune in West Virginia. Or maybe it was just getting started. Who knew?

Mr. Badlani wasn't a bad guy. The timing of his departure was simply convenient for him. He'd sold his business. Shiv's older sister, Anisha, had moved away for college, and Shiv seemed more independent than she really was. Maybe we all did.

"Don't judge me for not going to visit," she said. "I've been busy."

"I thought you didn't believe in busyness," I said. Shiv thought no one was actually busy. People simply chose one thing over another.

"True," she said. "I'm prioritizing our project."

Next period started in five minutes.

Shiv dropped her phone into her backpack and slung it over one shoulder. She said, "Maybe I should go see my dad. Maybe you're right. But you've been avoiding your family too." A true statement, depending on the definition of *family*.

I didn't respond, and Shiv started walking away. Then she stopped and turned around, now walking backward in the direction of HQ. "Not sayin' you should do anything different."

My adoption had been confidential. Mom signed a nondisclosure agreement. My birth parents' identities were sealed in the vault of her uncompromisable integrity. However, there was a clause that stated that when I turned sixteen I could initiate contact, if I so chose. Until I was about twelve, I was obsessed with figuring out who they were. I snooped all over the house, including in a locked box that my mom kept hidden in a crawl space. (The combination was my birthday.) But I found no relevant paperwork. Eventually, I gave up. By the time I turned sixteen, I employed the tactic my Sewickley neighbors used on the chronically unhoused: NIMBY zoning laws and lack of public transit. The zoning law in my head kept out everything I didn't think I needed. How else could I continue to stroll down Beaver Street and grab a Frappuccino without having a panic attack?

It was no different from how the parents dealt with climate change and corporate malfeasance and public corruption, all manner of environmental and social ills. They talked about these things, at book clubs and poker nights, on the sidelines of our games—I know they did because Mom was always reporting what so-and-so said about this and that—and the bleeding hearts wrote emails to city council, and the ones who were really committed organized campaigns, so greater numbers of emails flooded the inboxes of our so-called representatives. Then everyone went about their lives.

So, yes, Shiv was right, I could have known the identities of my birth parents, but I hadn't asked, because I was terrified the information would ruin my life.

I see now that the thing I feared most was that Mom and I would have to face the fact that our shared history went back only to the time of my birth. Seventeen years was but a blink in the grand scheme, and what if a blink wasn't enough? What if, in my birth mother, I recognized something deeper, something generational, something that because it had no beginning would also have no end?

I ARRIVED AT Eat'n Park that evening wearing St. Ignatius warm-ups over my track shorts. Vince was already there, waiting for me in the corner booth. I recognized him from his headshot on the

Mahoney's Produce website. When we made eye contact, he waved like he already knew me.

I'd planned to eat at home later, but Vince insisted I order something, and I didn't want to appear ungrateful. When the waitress came by, I asked for a vanilla milkshake. As soon as it arrived, I regretted it. The heap of whipped cream topped with a cherry made me feel like a kid. I offered the cherry to Vince. To my surprise, he reached across the table and plucked it off the top, dangled it into his mouth, and pulled it off the stem with his teeth.

Looking around the restaurant, he said, "This was our spot. Woolf, Maddie, Susanna and I used to come here all the time. One of us could fire off a text with three letters, 'ENP,' and the rest of the crew would show up. We always sat in the corner booth."

Everyone else in the place was old. Two guys sat alone at separate ends of the counter, and the tables surrounding us were occupied by couples, eating in silence. It was hard to imagine Eat'n Park as a St. Ignatius hangout.

Vince smiled warmly. He looked young for his age, almost angelic, with smooth skin and chiseled features. Even then, still pining for Ingo, and generally attracted to boys my age, I could see he was a hottie. He wore a button-down shirt and slacks that day, which was basically what he wore every time we met thereafter, swapping in checked, solid, and plaid button-downs and the occasional golf shirt. He sat with his legs spread and crossed, his right ankle supported by his left knee, as if someone, presumably his father, taught him that men were supposed to sit that way. He was a little bit uncomfortable in his own skin, as if he did not know he was handsome. He put his hands in his pockets too frequently, and when he broke eye contact he looked down at the table or the floor.

A father came in with his daughter. They sat at a table on the far side of the diner, so I couldn't hear what they were talking about. It couldn't have been anything particularly interesting—she looked about seven or eight, probably concerned about a dance recital or a soccer game. But her father looked at her with such intensity. He leaned over the table toward her. If you could only see his side, you might think he was in an important business meeting. I thought, *I've never had that.*

The feeling was fleeting. Occasionally, I slipped into a gender-essentialist thought spiral about paternal absence, and I had to remind myself I was free-spirited and cool. I didn't need a dad. If anything, I was loved too much. I sometimes wished Mom had another outlet for her affection. Watching the dad and his little girl was simply cute.

My attention quickly returned to Vince. Under different circumstances, I might have developed an unrequited crush. But my feelings toward him were more or less defined by a single slip of his tongue. Once, during that first encounter, Vince called me by the name of his little sister, Laura. He quickly corrected himself, but I didn't need to be Freud to understand how he saw me. I was four years younger than Laura. We had barely missed each other at St. Ignatius. Unbeknownst to Vince, with that minor slip, the nature of my attachment to him became almost familial.

Of course, he wasn't my brother, but I did feel like we could be friends someday.

I asked him if he knew a girl named Van Buren who took a bullet on the rough-and-tumble Sewickley streets of his youth.

Vince Mahoney
October 2000

VINCE'S BABY SISTER, Laura, was born a month before his fourteenth birthday.

His parents had given up on having another baby. "We tried," his mother had said, "It didn't happen." When it did happen, his mother was in her midforties. She said the pregnancy was "God's will." His dad gulped down his gin and tonic and cleared his throat. It may have been God's will, but it was his mother's responsibility.

"I'll help change diapers," Vince offered, and he did when he was around, which wasn't much. When he wasn't at school, he was usually at the Whitings' house, avoiding his own.

Maddie liked to tag along. Vince didn't mind. Woolf was a good big brother, but there were times when he didn't want her around. The day they found Paris Van Buren was one of those days.

Vince and Woolf sat cross-legged on the floor in front of the TV, playing *Punch-Out!!* on the Nintendo. Woolf hit pause when he noticed Maddie hovering.

"Can I play?" she asked.

"We're playing two-player. One. Two," Woolf said, pointing first to himself, then to Vince.

"But I'm good at *Punch-Out!!*" She really was good. She beat them both, more than half of the time.

Woolf tossed the controller on the ground. He looked at Vince. "Let's go find her a friend."

Before she could protest, they were out the door on their bikes. In those days, neighborhood kids were abundant. They played outside on weekends and after school; they had nothing better to do.

Woolf and Vince returned to the house with a girl trailing them on her bike.

"I'm Paris," she said, extending her hand toward Maddie like a management consultant. "Like the city." Her family had just moved to town, so she didn't know anybody.

"Paris, Texas?" Maddie asked.

"What? No. Paris is a city in France."

"You look more like a Paris, Texas," Maddie said. "There are multiple places called Paris."

"But only one of me." The girl smiled, pointing at herself with her thumb.

Paris said something to Maddie about a dance she had choreographed. "You can be one of the backup dancers—"

"Want to kick the soccer ball instead?" Maddie asked. It was pretty obvious she didn't like Paris.

Woolf and Vince began lacing up their Rollerblades. By the time they had them on, sticks in hand, more kids had showed up, ready to play. They skated away to set up the nets and pick teams. It never occurred to them to invite the girls to play.

Maddie flicked the soccer ball to Paris, not hard, but it hit her in the face. Her body crumpled to the ground, and she cried.

Woolf skated over to them. "Maddie, we found you a new friend to play with, and you made her cry already?"

"I want to hang out with you and Vince," Maddie said, looking down at the ground.

"Maybe after the game," Woolf said. They always played street hockey in front of the Whitings' house, because it was the flattest part of the neighborhood and there was very little traffic. If a car approached, they had to stop the game and move the nets to the side of the road. Woolf was the best player, even then, even on the street. The game would go all afternoon, until Mr. Whiting called them in for dinner.

Woolf helped Paris to her feet. "She's sorry. Maddie, tell her you're sorry."

"I don't need a friend," Maddie yelled.

Woolf said, "I'll get your bike, Paris. Don't take it personally. Maddie's bitter."

PARIS CAME AROUND a couple more times that month. The last time Vince saw her anywhere near the Whitings' house was the day Maddie shot her in the butt.

Mr. Whiting had invited Vince to dinner when he picked them up from hockey.

They were pulling into the driveway when it happened. Paris screamed. Maddie dropped the gun.

When Paris stopped crying, Mr. Whiting took her home. Vince probably should have headed home too—dinner was off—but all his gear was in the Whitings' station wagon, so he went inside with Woolf.

By the time Mr. Whiting returned, Mrs. Whiting was already on the phone with Paris's mom. She kept repeating statements like "We do not have guns in this household," and "We are not the type of people who own guns," and "We are anti-gun." At one point, she even said, "We're liberals, for goodness' sake!" She hung up. "You are so lucky you didn't break skin. Paris has a welt on her back."

"Thought I got her in the butt," Maddie said. The BB had torn through Paris's shirt, which hung below her waist. Somehow, the deed would have been funnier if she'd hit butt.

Mr. Whiting said, "Were you aiming for her butt?"

"I told you, it was an accident," Maddie said. "I didn't think it would go off."

"So in your infinite wisdom, you pointed a gun at a little girl because you didn't think it would go off? We are not gun people, Madeline," Mrs. Whiting said. "You are going to tell me where you got it," she demanded.

"It's not even a real gun," Maddie said. "It's a BB gun. Lots of kids have them." The gun was in the middle of the kitchen table. Mr. Whiting emptied the remaining BBs from the magazine.

"Not in Sewickley," Mrs. Whiting said. She assumed everyone in town shared her particular value system, when in fact the only thing they shared was a mutual affinity for restored houses and organic produce.

"It doesn't even have a safety," Maddie said. "How dangerous can it be?"

Vince lurked quietly on the other side of the kitchen, trying to make himself invisible. Woolf ate a drippy pear over the sink.

"Who gave you the gun, Madeline?" Mrs. Whiting repeated.

"Some kid," Maddie lied. "He doesn't go to our school."

"What's his name?"

"I don't know," Maddie said. "I only met him once."

"Where did you meet him?"

"Down by the railroad tracks, I think. Or maybe in the park? He was visiting his aunt. Or his grandma. I don't know, okay?"

"Woolf," Mrs. Whiting said, and then, "Vince. Do you know where Maddie got the gun?"

They shook their heads.

"I assured Nanette Van Buren we would dispose of the BB gun," Mrs. Whiting said, finally clarifying that she knew it wasn't a semi-automatic assault rifle. "Tomorrow, we are going over to her house to apologize in person."

Mr. Whiting picked up the gun, pointing it toward the ground.

"You are not to leave this house, unless it's for school, until you tell us who gave it to you," Mrs. Whiting told Maddie.

"But you said we are going over to Paris's house tomorrow. How can I—"

Mr. Whiting cracked the slightest smile before his face went straight.

LATER, THEY FOUND Maddie outside on the back deck, dropping a Superball and catching it on the way back up. She closed her hand around the ball and dropped it again.

Jágr followed, close to Woolf's heels. He ignored the ball and chased a fly.

"Hey," Woolf said, his eyes on the ball. "Thanks for not telling."

A space between boards shifted the trajectory of the ball. She leaned forward to grab it. "I don't tell secrets," she said.

"What are you doing out here?" he asked.

"What does it look like I'm doing?" After a brief pause, she bounced the ball again. "Mo said I can't leave the yard."

"At least you're allowed outside. Vince and I will keep you company," he said.

She bounced the ball off the deck into the sliding glass door. Woolf grabbed it on its ascent and tossed it gently onto the deck to return it to Maddie. "You guys are going to get bored and start playing video games."

"So play with us," Woolf suggested.

"You don't have to hang out with me. I'm not going to tell Mo," she said.

"Hit me," Woolf said, holding out his hand. She tossed him the bouncy ball. "Let's get our gloves and play Pitch'em." Pitch'em was Woolf's made-up name for a game where one of them stood on a makeshift mound and threw a baseball as hard as he could at the other, who crouched in a catcher's stance. When Woolf pitched, he'd bring his knee all the way up to his chin, like El Duque, or he'd go submarine style with his throwing arm, like Chad Bradford.

Woolf rattled off stats like Billy Beane, and he knew all the pitchers. He might have liked baseball even more than hockey, but he didn't have the talent for it.

Sometimes Vince would laugh so hard at Woolf's exaggerated windups, he'd miss the ball. In Pitch'em, if the ball was in the strike zone and got by the catcher, the pitcher won a point.

"The cherub is heavy," Maddie said. "It looks like it's anchored into the ground like a gravestone. No one would ever think to move it."

"I'm careful about putting it back so it looks like it hasn't been moved. How'd you find my hiding spot?" Woolf asked.

The cherub statue had been on the property longer than the Whitings, and it was half hidden in the shrubbery that crawled along the skirting on the underside of the house. "I followed you guys out a few weeks ago. Does anyone else know about it?"

"We'd have to shoot them if they did." Woolf chuckled.

"Just us three?"

"Not even Jágr," he said, bending down to scratch the dog's ears. Jágr licked his hand. "Just us. It's our secret."

"Maybe we should bury something else there," Maddie said. "Like a time capsule."

"How about my signed Jaromír Jágr puck?" said Woolf. "We can bury it tonight after Mo and Big D go to bed."

Woolf and Maddie shook on it. Vince placed his hand on top and held it there until they all let go. Maddie never told her parents she'd found the BB gun under the cherub. They never found out it had belonged to Woolf and, before that, Vince had taken it from his own garage, where it had been stored for years. His dad had used it to shoot at squirrels in the wooded area behind their property, until he eventually upgraded to a real gun, which his mom made him keep in a safe in their bedroom.

Maddie was grounded for months. She missed birthday parties and sleepovers. She didn't go anywhere other than school, sports, and piano, unless you counted Woolf and Vince's hockey games, which Maddie did not. Still, she never told. Eventually, Mr. and Mrs. Whiting dropped it. Maybe they figured she had done her penance. Or maybe they admired her persistence. Maddie could keep a secret, for sure.

6

THE ST. IGNATIUS library held yearbooks dating back to its founding. Shiv had checked out the four that featured Woolf Whiting.

"No Madeline Whiting," she said, pointing to the picture to the left of Woolf in his freshman yearbook. Maddie was in the same class as Woolf.

"Maybe she missed picture day," I suggested. But Maddie was not anywhere in the yearbook. Not in the track team photo. Or the debate club. Or the jazz band.

In the other three yearbooks, she was pictured in all three.

"So she transferred in after freshman year," Shiv said. "Wonder what she did that made her switch schools."

"We don't know that she did anything. Maybe her parents wanted her to have the best education in Pittsburgh. Maybe they thought she should be with her brother. I'll find out when I talk to her again."

"Holy shit," Shiv said. "I can't believe Maddie actually shot that girl."

"With a BB."

"Still an assault," Shiv said.

"It was an accident."

"She'd obviously tell her parents it was an accident."

"You don't believe it?"

"Do you?"

"Vince seemed pretty convinced it was an accident."

Shiv pulled up the notes I'd sent her after meeting with Vince. After several minutes, she looked up from her computer and said, "The cherub statue is still there in the Whitings' yard."

"You saw it?" I asked, adding, "Remember, Monica Whiting is off-limits. I promised Maddie."

She nodded. "It's hidden behind some bushes, but easy to spot from the side of the house."

"See anything else?" Her stakeouts weren't yielding much intel.

"Mrs. Whiting comes and goes. I don't think she has any friends."

When Shiv's parents arrived in the US, they found people with Indian last names online. They sent connection requests to strangers and became friends with them. These friends became a large part of their support system. For as long as I'd known Shiv, she had been surrounded by family friends. A woman like Mo Whiting must have seemed incredibly lonely to her. Mom and I were lonely too, compared to Shiv's family.

"You must have better things to do than surveil an old lady," I said.

"I really don't." She was taking senioritis to a new level.

"I wonder how Maddie felt about her brother going to St. Ignatius on scholarship," I said, thinking about my own scholarship. If my mom hadn't been a teacher at St. Ignatius, I'd have gone to public school, and I was self-aware enough to know that I wouldn't have been accepted to Princeton then.

"If their parents had different expectations for them, maybe Woolf felt the pressure," Shiv said.

I didn't need a sibling to understand the lack of parity, but Shiv probably felt it more acutely. Her sister was premed. Shiv was headed to Northwestern, where she planned to study psych and other business-adjacent subjects, so her mom viewed her as a wild card.

I wasn't sure what I'd ask Maddie when we spoke later that evening. The thing I really wanted to know was whether Woolf was happy. By all accounts, hockey had been taking him where he wanted to go. But was it just a "ticket," as Maddie had claimed? Maybe he also loved the game. Or he'd loved the game when he was a kid, and at some point he'd stopped.

"What is this you are listening to? It is not music," Dr. Badlani called to us from the kitchen. I had put *The Wall* on Spotify. The house had an amazing sound system, so the synthesizers felt like they were hitting from inside my head. None of my peers listened to Pink Floyd or really anything old. When I arrived at college, angst would become a shared sensibility, in certain circles. "Run Like Hell" would slap. But not so much in high school.

Shiv was too immersed in what she was doing on her computer to care about the music that day. I couldn't really explain to Dr. Badlani why I was so into Pink Floyd. Something about their lyrics spoke to me. Their songs weren't about speaking truth to power. They were about the nature of power. The inevitability of it. I was really into stuff I considered deep, because it made me feel special.

In college, I have started to see that the deep girl is just as superficial as the hot girl. I read books and think thoughts and try to be smarter than everybody else, but I will never know more than the woman on the riverbank, watching Kyle's car levitate.

Dr. Badlani walked into the living room with a bowl of pistachios. She didn't ask why we were looking at old yearbooks.

"Frankie said she didn't want anything," Shiv said.

Her mom waved Shiv off. "People always say they don't want anything, but they really do."

Dr. Badlani always served delicious food, most of it homemade. The house, which she hired an architect to design, had an open plan for entertaining, with a central atrium extending all the way up to a skylight in the roof.

When Shiv and I were in fifth grade, my mom started going on silent retreats at a Catholic monastery on the South Side. Every few months, she would turn off her cell phone and place it in the kitchen drawer, before dropping me at Shiv's house for the weekend. "But what if I need to reach you?" I would ask, and she'd say Dr. Badlani had the number for the main office at St. Paul's, in case of emergency. "But what if I need to talk to you and it's not an emergency?" I would ask, and she'd tell me I would have to wait until she returned. And then I'd start, "But what if," and she'd tell me everything would be fine.

Quickly, I got used to the ritual of putting the phone in the drawer, and I actively looked forward to Mom's retreats. I gorged myself on the junk food in Shiv's pantry, and we had no bedtime. We'd sit on the second-floor balcony with our legs dangling through the rails and watch the adults play bridge late into the night, worried they were having more fun than we were.

I did feel Shiv's pain when her dad left for West Virginia, but mostly I felt relief that my mom disappeared only for a few days at a time. If spirituality was an act of abandonment, then I'd take the Catholic version—spirituality lite—because I knew Mom would turn her phone on as soon as she got back. She was there when I needed her, and even when I didn't.

Our relationship was about to change, though. For my whole life, Alice Northrup had been Mom because she had mothered me, but soon I would leave for college. The mothering would come to its natural end, or it would take on another form. I couldn't wrap my head around it.

I cracked three pistachios, tossing the broken shells, one by one, into the bowl with an exaggerated hook shot. One of the halves bounced off the side and landed on my phone. I picked up the phone and let the shell slide off. The physical experience of its fall—the downward pull of gravity, the quiet clink of shell on shell—pulled me from the real world into the phone world.

Barbara Bertrand had posted an Instagram Reel about the March for Climate Action. It all seemed grand and hopeful, like our generation had something to say, and the old men in Washington finally had their over-the-counter hearing aids turned on. The videos in the Reel were from the previous year's march. Barbara and I had shared a hotel room on that trip. After we turned off the light, she in the king bed and I in a cot, I asked her if she cared about whether people liked her, because it was something I cared about a lot. I'll never forget what she said: "It feels so much better to be worshipped."

Barbara was my generation's cheerleader equivalent—the modern queen of our progressive little kingdom. It was a new kind of social capital, measured not by the span of one's thigh gap, but by the distinction of one's achievement. Barbara earned straight A's and had near-perfect test scores. She played viola, which was slightly more interesting than violin. She was the captain of the varsity tennis team—not the best player, but the best sportswoman. Her stewardship of the Climate Action Club had catapulted her past some trombone prodigy or dogsled champion or spelunking enthusiast to get into a college she was unwilling to name. If someone asked where she was going, she'd first say, "California," and if you took the bait, she'd clarify with "Palo Alto," and only after you said, "Stanford?" would she confirm with a nod.

Shiv looked over at my phone. "What are you doing? You're not thinking about going back to DC this year?"

"Shiv, our planet is dying."

"You watching Ingo get in Barbara's pants is not going to save the polar ice caps."

"I thought you said she was 'just a shoulder'!" We'd seen Ingo stretch his arm around Barbara during assembly. He whispered something into her ear before sinking down in his seat and resting his head on her shoulder, in the way a child might comfort himself against a mother. Shiv had said, "Maybe Ingo feels bad about Kyle, and Barbara's just . . . a shoulder," which briefly reminded me that my problems were infinitesimally small.

"Yeah, you know, a 'shoulder,'" Shiv said now, using air quotes and winking with one eye, then the other. "Comforting. Sturdy. Available. Okay, fine—a vagina."

I reacted to Barbara's story with a fire emoji to show her we were cool. Or maybe that our planet was on fire. Solidarity.

The laws of our universe dictated that we would not compete for a boy's attention. We would not submit to the indignity of a catfight that was so obviously a remnant of our patriarchal past. We were evolved enough to view Ingo for what he would eventually become, after his hockey career ended and he gained weight, and male pattern baldness stole his virility and his confidence: a relic. Barbara and I, we were the future! We were powerful! Together, even more so. A silly hockey player could not obfuscate this reality. Barbara and I had something more enduring than a high school hookup: We had a network. Five, ten, twenty years down the road, I could ping her. She could give me a job. Or an injection of capital. Or we could cohost a luncheon to bring together powerful women, where we could give each other awards for elevating the voices of other women.

"Anyway," Shiv said. "We've got more important things to do."

I didn't end up going back to DC that year. Not because Shiv and I were busy with our investigation. And not because I didn't think I could save the polar ice caps. I didn't go because I knew Ingo wouldn't be there; the hockey team was playing an invitational in Buffalo that week.

How cringe I was in high school! I knew better. All those girls who'd come before me had cried enough, pined enough, handed over their self-respect enough. My generation was supposed to be over boys. We knew their antics and bravado were flimsy cover for their delicate egos and Oedipal desires. We knew they were needy. They needed to feel big. They were puffer fish, those boys.

At least I can admit it now: I was so smart, but so basic.

Madeline Whiting
October 2001

THEIR PARENTS' DECISION had been made when they were both out of the room: Woolf would go to St. Ignatius on scholarship, and Maddie would remain in public school. To justify the decision, Big D said, "You have so much to offer, Madeline. Your classmates will benefit from your intellect. Your mother and I believe kids like you should participate in the social infrastructure of public schooling."

Though she spent her freshman year in the cramped, Soviet-style corridors of Quaker Valley High, Maddie never missed a St. Ignatius hockey game. As soon as her presence was no longer compulsory, she'd stopped resenting watching her brother play.

Three weeks into the season, everyone was already talking about the superstar Woolf Whiting. The team had played their previous two games away, returning to home ice undefeated. Mercer Arena was packed on a Wednesday night.

From chests to lips to ceiling to ice and back up again, the collective howl reverberated throughout the arena. Mo had chosen the name Woolf. She and Big D had agreed on Christopher, but empowered by twenty-four hours of labor, Mo made a game-time decision and had the surname of her personal feminist icon printed on the birth certificate instead.

Virginia Woolf may have been his namesake, but when Woolf checked a player into the boards or slammed the puck into the back of the net, everybody lifted their heads and howled, and his name became nothing more than a sports cliché. Mo didn't seem to mind.

A group of St. Ignatius students clustered near the glass at center ice. They stood for the entire game. Maddie sat with her parents, higher up in the bleachers and to the right. She knew the names of the other parents, which player belonged to each of them. Mrs. Mahoney, Vince's mom, sat two rows below, his dad a no-show. She spent most of the game minding Laura, now crawling and pulling herself up on the bleachers. Some of the students—Woolf's friends—occasionally offered a friendly wave or a polite nod, but no one asked Maddie to stand with them. It was strange, being in a place with people her age, cheering when they cheered, heckling when they heckled, but remaining apart.

Woolf probably took more hits that game, but two would play in Maddie's head on repeat:

Halfway into the second period: The game is tied 2–2. A shot is deflected wide from the St. Ignatius net. The puck is passed up ice to Woolf. Before he clears the blue line, he looks up. Number 27 skates full bore in his direction. Woolf is big, but this guy is bigger. Sticks clack on ice, skates scrape, people cheer, hands slap on the back of the glass. The wallop of the hit cuts through the noise. And then silence.

It is the silence that alarms Maddie. Mo reaches down and grabs her hand.

Woolf is down: One. Two. Three. Four. Five seconds. Vince covers the puck at the net to stop play. Woolf gets up on one knee. Fans yell for a penalty. None is given. Woolf skates to the bench with his teammates. A doctor checks him for concussion.

Mo lets go of Maddie's hand. Woolf is back on the ice for his next shift.

Third period: Still 2–2. The puck is dumped into the corner. Woolf is the fastest man on the ice, so he gets there first. His opponent trails—number 13 this time, even bigger than 27. Woolf corrals the puck and turns away from the boards toward the net. He advances. Number 13 raises his stick across and out from his body, spreads his legs wide. He appears to leap off the ice. Woolf can't dodge him. They collide. The stick thrusts into Woolf's chest pads.

The whistle stops play. This time, Woolf is slower to get up. He holds his chest. He is helped off the ice by the trainer, the doctor, Coach Perone.

Number 13 receives a five-minute major and a game misconduct. The referee escorts him to the rubber, and he walks in the direction of the visiting locker room.

Woolf returns for the power play. He scores. St. Ignatius goes on to win 5–2. Later, an x-ray will reveal he played out the game with a fractured rib.

After the game, most of the students dispersed. Maddie waited outside the locker room with the parents and the girlfriends. Woolf emerged, and immediately a small group of fans, or maybe friends, mostly girls, formed around him. Five minutes later, Vince walked out, leaning slightly to his left to support the weight of the backpack slung over his right shoulder. Now a St. Ignatius man, he no longer had to haul his hockey gear in and out of the Whitings' station wagon. Mercer Arena had a place for it.

When he saw her, his expression changed. When someone is happy to see another person, people always say "His face lit up," but for Vince, when he saw Maddie, she recognized the inverse, a kind of relaxing of the muscles.

"Let's walk home," he said, exhaling a long, deep breath, like he'd been holding on to it for the entire game and only now could he let go. They both lived about a mile from the school, easily walkable, although the Whitings' house was a detour for Vince.

Outside, he kicked up a small pile of fallen leaves. She swung her foot into the ground, about ten times more forcefully, kicking the leaves toward him.

"You're such a little sister," he said. "Always one-upping everything. I wasn't even trying to hit you. I was—"

"Skipping?"

"I was going to say *thinking*," he said. "I was thinking about the game."

"You won," she said. "What's there to think about?"

"Those two goals I let in," he said. "We should've won 5–0."

"Man, your dad did a number on you. You go undefeated, and you're still beating yourself up over a couple goals."

He put his arm around her neck, pulling her into a headlock. She squirmed out and kept walking. He followed, right on her heels, like Jágr often did. "Sometimes I feel like the whole team relies on Woolf to score a hat trick every game. Without those goals, our record wouldn't look so hot."

"I thought that was how hockey worked," Maddie said. "Someone on the team—not the goalie—scores enough goals to win."

He bumped his shoulder into hers. "You know what I mean, though, right?"

"Oh, like what it feels like to live in Woolf's shadow. Yeah, I think I have some experience with that."

They slipped off the lit road into the darkness. Maddie slowed her pace, and Vince moved next to her, shoulder to shoulder, close enough that she could smell him. He had the same musty-sweaty-hockey-gear stench that Woolf always did after a game, but Maddie didn't mind it on Vince.

Campus was quiet, save the occasional car headed toward the front gate, stragglers from the game. A black SUV swept by, catching them in the headlights, and the driver laid on the horn three times. Vince flipped his teammate the bird, smiling, and then used the same finger to tuck his hair behind his ear.

Until high school, Vince's hair was short—thicker but otherwise similar to his dad's style. The only thing that could be said in favor of replicating Mitch Mahoney's crew cut was that it was a good frame for his strong jawline and Roman nose, features Vince had inherited.

The Mahoneys looked like they belonged in beer ads from the '50s. But around the time he arrived at St. Ignatius, Vince grew his hair long enough to push back and flop over and tuck behind his ears, the same way Woolf wore his hair.

As they crested the hill, Big D and Mo rolled up next to them in the station wagon. Mo waved through the open passenger window. Looking at Vince, she said, "It's a school night. Please walk her straight home." Big D hit the gas, and they were gone.

"Did you notice how she told *you* when to walk *me* home, as if I don't control my own person?"

"Take it easy, Gloria Steinem." Vince flicked her on the side of the head. "You can control your own person, but you shouldn't walk alone at night."

"This is Sewickley. What's the worst that could happen?"

"Serial killers love places like this." He locked his hands around her neck and then let go.

Maddie's mind drifted back to the game. "Those guys were gunning for Woolf tonight."

"It's part of the sport," Vince said. "Woolf's our best player, so there's a target on him."

"He'll get hurt."

Maddie only worried about her brother right after a particularly violent game. She'd see the plexiglass heave on impact. She'd hear the crack of the pads. She'd feel a jolt of fear. But it would begin to dissipate as soon as he was back on his skates. By the next morning, the feeling would have vanished.

"Coach put McCabe on his line to protect him. He's our enforcer."

"You mean goon," she said.

Vince proceeded to recite several lines of dialogue from *Slap Shot*.

"What about you? Are you doing okay?" she asked.

Vince looked tired. It might have been all the weed he smoked, but even before all that, he was always in his own head. You'd think he wasn't having fun at all, and then, suddenly, he'd flash a smile that made you realize he was having the time of his life.

His gait slowed. She had assumed he wanted to walk so he could blow off steam from the game, but now she realized he was killing time. He didn't want to go home, which was okay with her—she didn't want to go home either.

SUCH WAS THEIR dynamic, and so it would have remained, except for something that happened between Woolf and Vince the following summer, before sophomore year. Woolf wanted to earn some extra capital (his word), which he planned to invest in the stock market. He asked Mr. Mahoney for a job at the warehouse, where Vince had been working summers since he was fourteen.

Because public transit to and from Sewickley was essentially nonexistent and neither Woolf nor Vince yet had a driver's license, Mr. Mahoney picked Woolf up on his way downtown every morning, Vince in the passenger seat. Maddie was always asleep when Woolf left the house, because of the ungodly hour. Despite his drinking, Mitch Mahoney was an early riser, which probably had more to do with the produce business than the man.

Half the summer passed this way. Maddie woke up to a quiet house. By nine, Big D was in the basement writing. Mo was in her windowless office at CMU, contemplating the patriarchy.

Then sometime in late July, Maddie woke early in a pool of sweat. Mo and Big D were too environmentally conscious, too frugal, or both, to run the air conditioner. Maddie shuffled into the kitchen and put her head in the freezer, groggy from sleep. Jágr let out a gleeful bark and spun around at her feet, his tail wagging rapidly. She closed the freezer door and stepped toward the pantry. It wasn't until she swung the door shut that she noticed the form of a person at the kitchen table. Startled, she dropped the Milk-Bone box.

"Shit," she said, pushing Jágr's nose away. "No, dog, no." He scarfed up three or four treats before she could put the rest back in the box. "Why aren't you at Mahoney's?"

"I quit yesterday."

"You did?" Woolf never quit anything. Even when Mo signed them up for tennis, which he hated, he went to every lesson. While they sat waiting to be picked up, he pretended his racket was a guitar and sang the tennis bubble blues.

"Too much lifting." He stretched his muscular arms toward the ceiling. "My body is an asset." He really talked like that sometimes.

"I don't believe you," Maddie said. Something was wrong. She tried to pull it out of him. She pledged secrecy. Assured him he could trust her. "Is Vince okay?"

"He's the one who made me promise not to tell anyone. Even you."

"Why would he care if you told *me*?"

"He cares what you think about him, I guess. He's embarrassed."

"But he didn't do anything, right?"

"Right."

Neither Woolf nor Vince ever told Maddie what happened that summer at the warehouse. Vince insisted it was nothing. Woolf never spoke of it again. For a long time, Maddie had been under some illusion that Vince was family, but whatever had happened at the warehouse that summer exposed the limits of friendship.

7

ON MONDAY, SHIV and I were on our backs next to the track, alternating sets of crunches and leg lifts. Coach had us running 200-meter repeats for the first half of practice, before letting us go for strength training. We figured he'd leave us alone.

"The report was supposedly public, but I had to practically wrench it out of that weasel's hands." Shiv was talking about Headmaster Campbell. She had been trying to track down more information about Coach Perone's resignation. Dr. Zap told her that personnel files would be private, but she should talk to the administration anyway. Someone might let something slip.

When Woolf played on the team, Chad Campbell was just an English teacher with a talent for schmoozing. According to my mom, Father Michael had been next in line for headmaster, but when the position turned over, the school was in the middle of a fundraising campaign. The board leaned into what they called a "talent for selling the vision," and Chad got the job.

The *Report on Player Safety* had been commissioned after Woolf's death. The St. Ignatius board hired a law firm to investigate team policies. Headmaster Campbell had probably handed over the document to Shiv to get her out of his office.

According to the report, a team doctor, whose name was redacted, had been injecting some of the hockey players with an anti-inflammatory drug, commonly prescribed to athletes to reduce pain. This course of treatment had been approved for Woolf by his parents and Coach Perone. No wrongdoing was uncovered. But it must have been enough to force Coach Perone's resignation. FOR PUBLIC RELEASE was printed on the cover, though it was never made available online. Shiv called it "CYA legalese."

The report also made one other thing clear: Woolf had never been prescribed opioids, and though players were not drug tested, there were no signs of illicit drug use or addiction.

Shiv and I counted out thirty scissor leg raises together before dropping our feet to the ground, to show Coach we were working hard.

"So what happened at Mahoney's warehouse?" Shiv asked, verbalizing the question that had been on my mind all day. At two o'clock in the morning, I'd texted Shiv about Maddie's claim that something had happened at Mahoney's Produce, knowing she'd respond immediately. Shiv claimed insomnia so she could justify occasionally popping Ambien, but really, she loved staying up late and sleeping in. "And does it matter?"

"Could Woolf have been killed because he witnessed something?" I asked.

"Two years later?" Shiv shook her head.

"Maybe he stayed quiet all that time and then threatened to tell?"

"Let's say he witnessed the worst possible thing," Shiv said.

"A murder?" I suggested.

Shiv turned her head toward mine on the grass, incredulous.

"Okay, probably not a murder."

"Maybe Mr. Mahoney was having an affair," Shiv said. "Think about it. Mrs. Mahoney was stuck at home with a toddler. She was probably cranky from all the tantrums and whatnot. Midlife crisis, anyone?"

"An affair just makes Mr. Mahoney a douche. Woolf wouldn't have quit his job because his boss cheated on his wife."

"So a murder is too hot, and an affair is too cold," Shiv said. "What did Woolf witness that was just right?"

We did a set of crunches, knees to elbows, again counting to thirty.

"When are you talking to Vince again?" Shiv asked.

"He said to call him whenever."

My wishy-washy response visibly annoyed Shiv. "Text him and ask him if you can drop by Mahoney's after school tomorrow."

"What about track?"

"Skip it," she said.

"Mahoney's is in the Strip," I said, meekly protesting. The Strip District was a half-hour drive, on a good day, and parking was annoying. Mom and I occasionally made the trek to buy fish from Wholey's, but only when we needed a girls' day out.

"I know where it is," Shiv said. "Ask him for a tour. You might notice something there. Or maybe it's just a big, boring warehouse. Act impressed. He'll open up to you more if he feels like a big deal." Shiv was all about Jedi mind tricks: People want to talk about themselves.

"Do you want to come with me?" I asked.

"I have an appointment with a librarian at the Carnegie Library," she said.

I pulled out my phone and texted Vince about meeting at Mahoney's. Then I sent a second text, explaining I had to run an errand in the Strip for my mom, so I would be nearby, which was a lie.

Honestly, I would have done whatever Shiv told me to do. I couldn't talk to my mom about the project, but Shiv and I shared everything. In her, I felt a kind of permanence. Even when St. Ignatius was over, even if Ingo and I had broken up for good, I'd still have Shiv. I could text her in the middle of the night. I could crash at her house. I could laugh at her awkwardly timed jokes. I could tell her that getting into my dream college didn't make me happy. And she wouldn't roll her eyes at me.

"When are you talking to Maddie again?" Shiv asked.

"Day after tomorrow."

"Don't space out the calls too much. You're giving them the opportunity to craft the story. Better if they blurt it all out."

"Better?"

"More honest, I think."

"I want to know what happened as much as you do, Shiv, but I can't force the conversation."

Coach looked over at us, and yelled, "Frankie and Shiv!" He stood on the track using a stopwatch to time the girls running the mile.

We pulled our heads off the grass simultaneously, resting our weight on our elbows.

"Strengthen your cores, not your jaws!"

I gave him a thumbs-up.

After practice, Shiv dropped me off at home. Before she pulled out of the driveway, she texted me: *Maybe Mr. Mahoney hit Vince?*

It could explain the time lag. If the abuse had escalated, Woolf might have later threatened to expose it. Maybe he was worried about what would happen to Mrs. Mahoney and Laura, after Vince left for college. Or maybe Mitch Mahoney was a harmless drunk, who'd once been arrested because he shot a bullet into a snowbank and it ricocheted into his neighbor's garage, a fact that Shiv had discovered in a court docket sheet online.

THE NEXT DAY, after last period, I borrowed Mom's car and drove downtown to the Strip District. I picked up a pepperoni roll at Mancini's for Vince. Then I drove to a small employee lot, located beyond the loading docks, where Vince had instructed me to park.

A couple guys were unloading a truck. One of them saw me walking toward them and said, "Now that's the way a skirt is meant to be worn." I was wearing a plaid skirt and a white button-down shirt, because I hadn't changed after school. He started to whistle, but abruptly stopped when Vince appeared.

The other guy said, "She here to see you, boss?"

Vince waved them off. "She's in high school. Get back to work."

I wished I'd worn pants.

"Please ignore those guys," Vince said. "Would you like a tour?"

As we walked around, Vince talked about his dad. "Before he died, my father converted the old facility into a modern, climate-controlled warehouse. He hired new people in purchasing and sales. He worked nights and weekends—around the clock—and business boomed. He drank during the day at work lunches with investors, and at night in seedy bars with truckers."

"I'm sorry," I said.

"For what?"

"Your dad died."

He shrugged. "It was a long time ago. Dad was a real yinzer. Always talking like those idiots on the loading dock. But he was Penn State–educated, and he sometimes read books, especially if they were about American history. Smarter than he let on. He loved hockey more than anything. That's why I got into it. But I was too slow. Forward and backward, I skated lines, figure eights, crossovers. I practiced turns and stops. No matter how hard I worked, I didn't move faster."

We stopped next to a crate of tomatoes, and Vince picked one up and handed it to me. "Go ahead," he said. "Try it."

I took a bite. It tasted like a tomato.

"Hydroponic," he said. "We never used to get local tomatoes this time of year, but we do now. We're doing all sorts of stuff with local growers."

The profile I'd read about Vince was about how he'd reimagined produce distribution. On-demand software allowed Mahoney's to balance producers' output with buyers' needs. If a Pennsylvania-grown tomato was available at the same cost or less, you got a Pennsylvania-grown tomato.

He offered me a seat in his office, and I handed him the greasy bag I'd been carrying around.

"Mancini's? Thanks. How'd you know?" He dropped the bag on his desk.

"Your dad would be proud of what you've done with his place," I said.

He looked at the floor. "You read that stupid article, didn't you? Mitch wasn't really a proud-dad type guy. He was too angry."

"Did he ever hit you?" I asked, feeling brazen. Vince disarmed me. The way he moved was slow and methodical, like he didn't need to be someplace else.

"Never," he said. "But he was thrown out of a Peewee game because he walked out onto the ice and punched my coach, mad because I'd been riding the bench."

"People around here take hockey really seriously," I said.

"It was Woolf who suggested I try goalie. We practiced on the ice when we could, and on the concrete when we couldn't. By stopping Woolf's shots, I learned to stop every shot. Then I never left the ice, not for a single shift."

"Did that make your dad happy?" I asked.

"The thing about a twelve-year-old's logic is you understand everything except the most important thing. For the rest of that season, my dad was banned from attending the games. By the following season, he was technically allowed in the rink, but my mom kept him away. He might have been happy, but he wasn't there."

Some years had passed since Mitch Mahoney died, but his spirit still resided in that warehouse. I was there for a couple hours, long enough to learn the details of what happened the summer after their freshman year, when Woolf took a job at Mahoney's. As Vince told the story, I could feel Mitch in the room with us. It's not like I mistook the chill of the refrigeration units for the breath of his spirit. But I got the sense that everything Vince had accomplished was for the sake of impressing a ghost.

Vince Mahoney
June 2002

VINCE HAD BEEN spending weekends at the warehouse during the school year, until one of his teachers claimed he wasn't living up to his potential and his mom decided that learning to operate a forklift wasn't the best use of his time. When he wasn't playing hockey, he was supposed to be studying.

He didn't actually use the time to study, but he did read books written by Bret Easton Ellis, Michael Chabon, and the like, which his mom mistook for studying. When he read *The Mysteries of Pittsburgh*, he practically wrote himself into the plot. Not in a meaningful way, but as a bystander, smoking a bowl in Art's Museum of Real Life.

His closest friend at the warehouse was a guy named Wayne. He was a tall, lanky seventeen-year-old, who'd dropped out of Allderdice to work at Mahoney's full-time and deal drugs on the side.

When Vince returned to work the summer after freshman year, he thought Wayne had changed, but he later understood that, now a St. Ignatius man, *he* had changed and Wayne had stayed the same—which was what made him attractive, that backward pull of the familiar.

Woolf showed up that summer for a job, and two realities collapsed in on each other. School and hockey were one reality; work and weed, the other. Woolf occupied the former, Wayne, the latter.

"When you win the Stanley Cup, I'll be able to tell people 'I knew you when,'" Mitch Mahoney said to Woolf on his first day. Woolf extended his hand to shake on ten dollars an hour, same as Vince earned.

On their break, Vince and Wayne smoked a joint in the vacant lot next to the warehouse. They were flicking a Frisbee back and forth when Woolf vaulted over the Jersey wall. Wayne tossed the Frisbee his way, and he leapt to grab it over his head.

Woolf tossed it back to Wayne, on target. Wayne caught it and threw a forehand.

The Frisbee sailed over Vince's head. He turned and ran. He almost caught up, stretching to grab it, but he lost his footing on the loose gravel and landed face down. He brushed the gravel off his body and examined his skinned arms.

Wayne pulled a can of Yuengling out of his backpack and passed it to Woolf. "Only got one more—you want it, dude?"

"I should probably go rinse this," Vince said. His arms were scraped but not bleeding.

"Nah, man, you're fine," Wayne said. "You wan' another hit?"

Woolf cracked the Yuengling, trying to act like he'd been there before, but his shoulders were stiff. A siren, a block or two away, moved closer.

"Don't worry, DubDub. Cops roll by on Penn Ave all day. No one comes back here." Vince had been calling Woolf "DubDub," short for his initials, since second grade. But with Dubya in the White House, it had taken on new meaning. Vince used it more frequently, and with greater gusto.

"What about your dad?" Woolf asked.

Vince pointed at the can in Woolf's hand. "Not his drink of choice."

Wayne took the half-smoked joint out of his stash case and relit it. He started rambling about *Slap Shot 2*: how the film never should have been made, how the original was one of the best sports films ever, and how watching 2 is worse than Guantánamo, because no one voluntarily goes to Guantánamo, but you can't not watch *Slap Shot 2*, even though you are theoretically free to do as you please. "I'd rather be waterboarded," Wayne said. "And I've seen *Slap Shot 2*—twice."

Even stoned, Wayne spoke fast, and most of what he said was

unintelligible. There was no point in asking obvious questions like "Why'd you watch it a second time?" He'd look at you like you were an idiot.

He continued to talk about how the dialogue was atrocious, and how there were bad films that were good if you watched them stoned but this was not one of them, and how it was impossible to watch without descending into a pit of despair, because he couldn't even believe something this bad was not porn. He wished it could be permanently eradicated for the benefit of the culture, and he thought the government should take out an entire data center in Nevada to make sure the last backup could not be recovered. This would be a good use of the military, he suggested, better than what Cheney had planned.

He then spiraled into a tirade about how the soundtrack was even worse than the dialogue. And—whoa—maybe the government used *Slap Shot* 2 to torture people, and maybe that was why the movie was made and unleashed on the public in the first place.

Vince wanted to put Woolf and Wayne back into their separate realities, where he could manage them. He thought about his mom, who asked about Woolf often, and referred to him as "a very nice young man." She would say no such thing about Wayne. She would call him "a bad influence."

Wayne reached out to pass the joint. The sirens sang in the background. "Not today, man," Woolf said.

WOOLF THOUGHT WAYNE was a dumbass, but they were cool. Or maybe not cool, but Woolf tolerated him. He didn't want Wayne around his sister, but he didn't object to his presence otherwise. Woolf knew there was a world outside the Sewickley bubble. Anyway, Wayne was harmless.

Wayne did not cause the rift between Woolf and Vince, but he was there for the incident that did. Later, after they made peace with each other, neither one of them ever discussed what happened at Mahoney's again, and Wayne became collateral damage, not persona non grata necessarily, but someone of the past.

The incident at the warehouse shook some people up. Vince's dad had been drinking. He was always drinking, but that day, he was drunk, more so than usual. He'd been gone all afternoon at a long lunch. He didn't return until around four. He was in good spirits, celebrating some big new investment, talking about expanding into Maryland and Ohio. He asked Jan to go buy a couple thirty-packs for all the guys. But when he opened the petty cash box, he thought it looked light, so he counted it. It was short. Only a few people had access to the box—Jan, who was his admin, and Freddie, who supervised the guys on the floor.

Nobody expected him to lose control, but his mood shifted fast. Mitch Mahoney was smiling one minute, and the devil took him the next. He grabbed a metal stepladder, which had been folded up and absently propped against a stack of pallets. Gripping it with both hands, he swung it like a bat. Before anyone could react, they heard the clash of metal on bone. Freddie crumpled to the ground.

One of the guys took Freddie to the hospital. He had surgery—broken nose, jaw, and cheekbone. Lawyers got involved. Freddie went on disability. Never had to work another day in his life. Sometimes Vince wondered if Freddie did steal the petty cash—not that it mattered.

Witnesses were paid off or threatened—maybe both. In the end, everyone agreed a load fell on his face from the dock. Workplace accidents happened all the time.

Woolf refused to take hush money. Vince begged him not to tell anybody. He never did. But he ascended to some moral high ground that Vince could no longer access. Woolf stopped calling; stopped inviting him over. They didn't see each other for the rest of the summer.

In the fall, they returned to St. Ignatius and took the ice in their green jerseys. By then, they'd both cooled off. Things weren't the same, but they seemed better for a while.

8

KYLE'S FUNERAL WAS held on Saturday at St. Mary's, an imposing Romanesque imitation of the European cathedrals of the eleventh and twelfth centuries, situated just south of Starbucks. How many times had Mom driven by it, crossed herself, then waxed on about the architectural history? On the day of the funeral, she paused briefly on the steps, as if to take in the stolid girth of a sleeping giant, hung her head, and entered without saying a word.

Kyle had been dead twelve days. When I saw Mrs. Murphy standing in the back of the church, I pictured Mo Whiting's face as she walked off the set in the middle of her interview. Then I looked at my own mother. The saddest thing about dying young is all those people have mothers.

ON MONDAY, INGO skipped third period so he could have lunch with me off campus. Ditching class was out of character for him. He suggested we grab sandwiches at Klein's Deli. By the time we ordered, paid, and retrieved our food from the counter, we only had about fifteen minutes before next period. We shared a large Reuben at a table by the street. He did most of the talking. I may or may not have been using Shiv's Jedi tactic: Everyone wants to talk about themselves. When he started profiling the Cornell hockey coach, I nodded like the bobblehead doll on Father Michael's desk.

Did having lunch off campus mean we were no longer taking a breather? Did he want to get back together? As Ingo blabbered on about hockey, these questions receded into the background. I wasn't sure why I couldn't ask them. Maybe because I didn't want to hear the answers. Or maybe because I sensed Ingo didn't have any. When we got up to leave, he put his hand on my butt and squeezed. I kept walking, pretending it hadn't happened, acting like I didn't care.

He parked at the far end of the student lot and cut the engine. Then he leaned over and kissed me. I didn't ask if he'd been hooking up with Barbara, because I knew he had. I didn't ask if Barbara knew he was making out with me, because I knew she didn't. I didn't ask if he planned to hang out with Barbara again. Or what he was doing with me. Or who he liked better. I didn't ask why he thought he could get with both of us. Why he didn't care how much it hurt. Was it because he was a guy? A hockey player? Just because he could?

I kissed him back. I let him put his hand up my shirt, and then between my legs, his fingers pressing through my tights. The way he kissed me, the desire, the ache: I forgot I deserved so much more than Ingo was offering. In lieu of acknowledging my self-worth, I worshipped the god in front of me.

Finally, I said, "Someone might see us," but never that I didn't want to kiss someone who didn't care enough about me to not kiss somebody else.

WHEN SHIV NEGLECTED to show up for track, I didn't think much of it. Sometimes she skipped practice. We'd joined the track team to hang out together and stay in shape, and because sports were required. Unlike, say, girls' lacrosse, which was nationally ranked and scouted by D1 colleges, track was the snot-nosed little sibling in the family of St. Ignatius athletics, ignored by everyone. Our coach taught sophomore English, and, as far as we knew, his qualifications to lead us were limited to his fondness for a novel called *Brewster* and the whistle in his right hand. Shiv and I didn't exert ourselves. Mostly, we killed time. Shiv was obsessed with the steeplechase, but she usually brought up the rear.

Back in the locker room, I found a Bridge invite: *470, strictly business.*

The first time Shiv sent an invite labeled *470*, I showed up unannounced at Holly Wyatt's house—470 Spruce Lane—at the specified time. Mrs. Wyatt answered the door, confused and somewhat worried, because Holly had told her we had an away track meet across town. "Why aren't you with the team?" she asked. She pulled up the app and looked at Holly's calendar. Shoving the phone in my direction, she said, "See. It's right there. Avonworth today."

I shrugged.

Right then, it hit me: *470*. Shiv was always talking about how a Venti Mocha Frappuccino had 470 calories. I was due at Starbucks. I didn't even try to cover for Holly, who was probably vaping in Riverfront Park; Mrs. Wyatt was already dialing her cell.

I stopped using Bridge when I left for college, not out of some post-nostalgic longing for the inefficient olden days, but because no one at Princeton uses it. Sometimes, I miss it. Or I miss the way Shiv had turned it into a game.

BY THE TIME I arrived, Shiv had already consumed an entire Venti Mocha Frappuccino. I asked her if she wanted another. Occasionally, she let me pay for something so we could pretend money wasn't the thing her family had and mine didn't. But before I could turn toward the counter, Shiv pushed her phone into my hand with the Starbucks app already open. Her balance automatically reloaded with her mom's credit card, so it was essentially a bottomless pit of money.

"Hurry back. I have some ideas to run by you," she said. I marveled at her ability to consume approximately one thousand calories of beverage and still be the skinniest person I knew.

The place was pretty empty, so I lingered by the pickup spot, figuring I wouldn't have to wait long. Then my nose caught the weed stank wafting off the guy working the blender. After what felt like twenty minutes, he reached down into the fridge for the whipped-cream canister and began to move his arm in a slow circular motion. The result was symmetrical, each rotation leaving a slightly smaller circle of cream, reaching a singular point at the top. He then placed the canister back in the fridge, grabbed two dome-shaped plastic lids, one in each hand, and pushed them over the cream, smooshing his perfect exercise in futility.

I took the drinks from the counter before he called my name.

"I should have warned you," Shiv said. "By the time Stoner Dave is done with the whipped cream, you could have a complete translation of the *Aeneid*." I'd been working on translating the *Aeneid* for the entire semester. Shiv couldn't imagine anything more pointless.

"So?" I said, placing her Frappuccino in front of her, like the good cop in an interrogation room. "Why'd you ditch track today?"

Before I sat down, Shiv started talking. "Check these out." She pushed over printouts of four articles from a defunct paper called the *Sewickley Argus*. "I found these in the microfilm archive at the Carnegie Library. Who knew our little borough had its own town crier? Jody D'Angelo! You can keep those. I have my own copies."

Shiv informed me that the *Sewickley Argus* had been one of the longest-running newspapers in Western Pennsylvania, dating all the way back to 1902, while I scanned the headlines: ST. IGNATIUS HOCKEY PLAYER FOUND DEAD IN SCHOOL'S CHAPEL. INVESTIGATION INTO HOCKEY STAR'S DEATH STALLS. MOTHER OF LOCAL HOCKEY PLAYER CAMPAIGNS FOR JUSTICE. SEWICKLEY FAMILY DIVIDED OVER SON'S DEATH.

Shiv had skipped track that afternoon to drive to Sheffield Street, on Pittsburgh's North Side, where Jody D'Angelo lived and maintained an office. After the *Argus* was shuttered, she began working as a private investigator. Finding D'Angelo was Shiv's first real break. She practically vibrated with the thrill of it.

Shiv had spent nearly two hours with D'Angelo. Apparently, the case still haunted the woman. According to D'Angelo, Mo Whiting believed her son's death was not self-inflicted for three primary reasons.

D'Angelo dismissed the first: A mother knows her son.

The second might have also been discounted due to maternal bias, except the medical examiner's findings supported it: A puncture in the skin indicated the drugs had been injected, not ingested orally. Mo Whiting didn't think her son had access to drugs or needles. Even D'Angelo thought it was unlikely that an upper-middle-class kid from Sewickley, with no history of illicit drug use, would shoot up.

And finally, Monica Whiting was obsessed with a missing St. Christopher amulet that Woolf never took off. He certainly wouldn't have removed it from his neck when he needed it the most, she claimed.

"St. Christopher is the patron saint of safe travels. He's known as the protector," I explained to Shiv. "Half the hockey team wears those things under their jerseys. Ingo has one."

Shiv said, "Mo was naïve about access. Drugs are everywhere. Although—"

"Sewickley kids mostly take pills," I said.

"Right. Would've been true in 2005 too."

"Maybe he wanted to control the timing," I suggested. "If he'd taken pills, someone might have found him in time."

"But he could've just done it where no one would look for him. Why the chapel?" Shiv wondered.

"Did D'Angelo have the autopsy report?" I asked.

Shiv shook her head. "As a PI, she's more thorough. Back then, she was just trying to tell a family's story."

"You should be writing everything down," I said.

Shiv tapped her finger on her forehead. "It's all in here."

"At some point, we're going to need to write the essay," I said.

"We haven't found anything good yet," she said.

But what was "good"? And how would we know when we found it?

Jody D'Angelo's reporting on the Whiting case bothered me. She had clearly gained Mo Whiting's trust. A desperate mother searching for answers was an easy mark. The fourth article in the series read like a tabloid account of a celebrity divorce. But Monica and

Declan Whiting were not celebrities. I just didn't see the point. Did their Sewickley neighbors need to know that after the death of their son, they started sleeping in separate bedrooms? That they no longer ate meals together or worshipped together or attended their living child's debate competitions? That Declan Whiting moved out, first to an apartment across town, then to Florida?

Shiv wanted to talk to Mo Whiting. She thought her pain was inevitable. It didn't matter if we involved her or not, because either way, she'd still be a mother who'd lost her child. But I'd made a promise to Maddie, which I intended to keep. We were walking a fine line, as real journalists do every day, and maybe that was the point of the class—to learn how to stay on the right side of it. Shiv didn't agree with me, but she promised to leave Monica Whiting alone.

While Shiv googled "synthetic opioids," I checked Bridge on my phone. I could see when Ingo was busy, based on whether his calendar was blocked off (it was), though the contents of his calendar were private. I assumed he was with Barbara. Maybe he was in the weight room or, I don't know, taking a dip in the cold plunge that had just been retrofitted into Mercer Arena. But my mind's eye saw Barbara straddling him in his Range Rover, her back up against the steering wheel, accidentally laying on the horn.

IN THE NOT-SO-DISTANT future, during a late-night bitch session with my college roommate, she would ask why I had been so hung up on Ingo in high school, and I would have no good answer.

Ingo was a terrible conversationalist. He could solve an equation, but when I tried to talk to him about something interesting, he'd say, "I don't want to think about that"—which I guess meant he'd rather be thinking about his last hat trick, or how much he could bench, or whether Klein's pastrami was better than their corned beef. He also wasn't the best-looking guy at St. Ignatius. Adam Ali held that title, with his dreamy mop of dark, curly hair and the unfathomable depths of his chocolate brown eyes. His eyelashes were so long, someone made a meme of him drying them with a miniature hair dryer. Ingo was more average. He had the look of a nice Catholic boy—clean-cut, shirts starched, well trained in the art of firm handshakes and sincere smiles.

And yet Ingo was my ideal. I thought he was perfect. Probably because subconsciously I'd bought into some old-timey value system, dictating that I attach myself to another Catholic so we wouldn't drift away from separate religious traditions out of conflict or ambivalence. Not that plenty of Catholics didn't drift away together, but with two, obligation multiplies.

Ingo had another thing going for him that I would have never admitted being attracted to: His family was rich. Not as rich as Barbara's family, but not far off. Rich enough to drive a Range Rover. And, okay, I liked riding around in his Range Rover. I liked being kissed in his Range Rover. I liked imagining that one day, I would walk into a showroom and buy myself a Range Rover. Or someone would buy one for me. St. Ignatius had so conditioned me to believe in my own excellence that any last vestiges of the princess fantasy had been deleted from the subcortical structures of my brain. I didn't want to be a princess; I wanted to be a Renaissance (wo)man.

A guy like Ingo fit into this fantasy quite well, because while he was on Wall Street making gobs of money, I could be studying religion and philosophy and language, and, generally, thinking deep thoughts. Thinking deep thoughts was the one privilege I believed I was entitled to, and maybe the only benevolent byproduct of wealth. I think about this a lot, even now: how we still need philosophers, even though society absolutely does not value philosophers, unless they find a way to appeal to some political agenda.

My point is that at St. Ignatius, I was surrounded by wealth, even though Mom and I didn't have it. So I pictured myself spending years holed up in academia, writing some magnum opus about the meaning of life, while—sigh—driving around in a Range Rover. It was only once I got to college that I realized the world is full of Ingo equivalents, and now I can also see how devastatingly boring most of them are—how boring Ingo was—and I quickly lose interest. Knowing what I know now, I'd rather drive around in an old Subaru, like my mom. At least she isn't forced to have conversations about equity-to-asset ratios, or whatever those guys talk about.

But in high school, I was powerless to Ingo's nice Catholic future-finance-bro charm. I thought I was in love with him. And maybe it was love. Maybe high school is the only time you really feel love with your whole soul, like when it's over you think there's nothing left. Because you don't know any better.

AN OLD-MAN COFFEE klatch had posted up at the table in the corner. They were talking about Franco Harris's "Immaculate Reception" in the 1972 NFL playoffs. My mom hadn't been born yet when he grabbed that tipped ball an inch above the turf and ran it in for a touchdown, but Pittsburghers still spoke about it like it happened yesterday.

Bushy Brows said, "If I make it to heaven, I want to shake Franco's hand."

Flat Cap barked, "Fat chance."

Bushy Brows replied, "I don't know about you guys, but I'm not taking any chances. Even started going to daily Mass at St. Mary's."

Chubs interjected, "Say an extra Hail Mary for me, will ya?"

"Pascal's wager," I said to Shiv. I'd just read William James's "The Will to Believe" for Philosophy, so the wager had been on my mind.

"That's the thing I'll never understand about you Christians—why put your money on a god who would toss your ass in hell for not believing?" Shiv smiled. "But if the old man thinks he's gonna meet Franco Harris in heaven, then by all means."

She looked down at her cup, thinking about something she did not share.

I pointed to the siren logo. "Your dad has Krishna, and we have Her."

She laughed. "When we die, the barista can compost our ashes with the old coffee grounds."

I crossed myself and said aloud. "In the name of the Father, the Son, and the Holy Spirit."

"What is the Holy Spirit, anyway?" Shiv asked.

"When you feel God in your gut, it's the Holy Spirit," I said.

"How do you know it's not *God* God?"

"You mean God, the Father?"

"The one who made the world in seven days."

"Six."

"Right. You know what I mean."

"It's all one god, so it doesn't really matter. Might not be God at all. Maybe it's indigestion."

"So why make the distinction?"

"I don't know, okay. It's a made-up thing."

"Arguably, all of it is a made-up thing," she said.

"Touché," I said. "The key to religion is not to think too hard about it."

Joking around with Shiv reminded me of Woolf and Vince. Their bond went all the way back to kindergarten. It crossed state lines for hockey tournaments. It brought their families together for early mornings and late afternoons and weekends. Everybody knows friendships fade. People change. But Woolf and Vince seemed like boys who would grow up to be each other's best man, who would sit together in old age and talk about the past. The incident at the warehouse wouldn't have been enough to come between them. Naturally, I thought, *Maybe it was about a girl.*

"Vince and Maddie haven't mentioned Susanna yet," I said.

"Maybe she's not significant," Shiv said.

But my mom wouldn't have told me about her unless she was. It was time to ask Maddie about Susanna Mercer.

Madeline Whiting
September 2002

    MADDIE WAS THE new girl sophomore year. Woolf was the guy everyone, upperclassmen included, said hello to and slapped on the back, as if they were best friends.

Maddie might have been happy at public school—or at least not unhappy—but Mo and Big D cracked at the slightest hint of trouble.

Trouble was a blow job. Ninth grade was almost over. Hot in late May, tank tops and cutoffs were the girls' uniform. Summer sang her siren call.

The recipient of the blow job was a boy named Tyler. They were behind a dumpster near Quaker Valley's football field when the coach caught them. Nothing happened to Tyler. Well, something happened; he probably got high fives in the locker room. But Madeline was called to the principal's office, and they weren't punishing her; they were "just concerned."

Her parents decided it would be best for everyone if she got a fresh start. A fresh start meant no one at St. Ignatius knew she'd given Tyler a blow job; it also meant no one knew her at all, except, of course, as Woolf's little sister.

Mo and Big D took out a second mortgage, and they became a St. Ignatius family.

    BECAUSE PUBLIC SCHOOL did not offer dead languages, Maddie enrolled in Latin I as a sophomore. Studying the classics was like stepping into a cryotherapy chamber—good for rich people, useless for everybody else. Maddie didn't want to be everybody else.

Latin met in a small classroom on the third floor of Carson Hall. A bust of a curly-haired Roman atop a pedestal greeted her when she entered. Later, she learned it was the flat-nosed face of Virgil, whose poetry she would spend her entire senior year translating.

Everyone else in the class was a freshman. Susanna chose the Latin name Ursula ("little bear"), which made Maddie regret her choice, Augusta ("magnificent"). She was trying too hard. Outside of class, Susanna would joke about throwing Virgil's bust out the window. She would consistently refer to Latin class as the burning building, as in "Hey, are you headed into the burning building?" or "I'd rather be almost anywhere else than the burning building."

But Susanna belonged there; she belonged everywhere. St. Ignatius was made for her, with her effortlessly erect posture, the slouchy sweater that fell off her shoulder, and those two delicate gold chains around her neck. She didn't need to learn a word of Latin to be granted access.

When the bell rang, Susanna said, "Mickey D's?" First day of school, and the freshmen were already calling the dining hall Mickey D's.

Maddie thought it was presumptuous that Susanna acted like they were already friends when they had just met in class. But that was how Susanna was about everything: preternaturally confident.

"Can we stop by the lockers? I need to grab my lunch," Maddie said. The lockers were located in the underbelly of Carson Hall. Juniors and seniors enjoyed the privilege of the lounge upstairs. They tossed their coats and bags up there on hooks and shelves and chairs, negating the need for lockers altogether, so the basement was mostly occupied by freshman and sophomores.

Susanna dropped her Latin book and notepad into her unlocked locker. If Maddie had left her locker unlocked at her old school, most of the contents would have been either taken or destroyed within minutes, but at St. Ignatius people respected each other's property.

On the walk to Mickey D's, Maddie waited for Susanna to say the first thing everybody did when they met her—"You're Woolf Whiting's little sister"—but she didn't mention him.

"Here good?" Susanna said, stripping off her sweater and throwing it on a chair.

Maddie dropped her brown bag on the table. "I'll be here conjugating Latin verbs until you get back."

"Don't learn anything without me," Susanna said. For girls, the standard school uniform was a plaid skirt and a white polo with the St. Ignatius seal. Khaki or dark slacks and white button-down shirts were acceptable substitutes. If the shirt had a collar, a girl could get away with it. As Susanna walked away, most of her back was covered by the thick, wavy golden hair that she was always moving from side to side, tying up and letting down again. Her dark-blue bra, faintly visible under her thin white shirt, matched her plaid skirt. In class, she wore the cardigan over the ensemble. Subtlety was her best asset. When Maddie peeled her eyes away, Woolf was sitting at the table.

He pointed to Susanna's sweater. "Guess you don't need me to find you a friend anymore. Maybe no one will get shot this time."

Maddie rolled her eyes. "You know that was an accident."

"Paris was a nice girl," Woolf said. "And you wanted nothing to do with her. Why are you so bitter, Mads?"

Susanna returned to the table carrying a wrapped cheeseburger in one hand and a carton of milk in the other. No tray.

"Hey," Woolf said, in the way boys do.

"Hey," she said, looking from his face to Maddie's then back again. Lifting a finger off her milk carton, the nail polished blood red, she pointed from one to the other and back again.

"I'm Woolf," he said, extending his hand.

"Susanna," she said, taking his hand. Then, as if to mock decorum, she immediately unwrapped her burger and took a bite so big she had to work to keep it in her mouth.

"Can I have a bite?" Woolf said.

Susanna handed it to him, and he took a big crescent-shaped bite from the same spot she had, unconcerned with the idea of her saliva on the bread. He handed back what was left and said, "Mustard, nice. Well, I'll leave you both to it."

Maddie said, "Sorry."

"That Woolf Whiting took a bite of my burger?" Susanna said. "I'm not sorry."

"Gross," Maddie said. But they were kind of perfect for each other.

By spring semester, Susanna and Woolf were a couple. When they became official—holding hands in school, going to dances together, calling each other saccharine pet names like Sweet Pea—Maddie thought of Woolf and Vince hopping on their bikes to find her a friend, returning with Paris in tow. All these years later, she had been the one to invite Susanna to join their crew. The novelty of her presence quickly turned to intimacy. Only Vince expressed awareness of the risk, too casually. "You sure about Susanna?" he asked Maddie once, shortly after Woolf announced his romantic intentions. The question had seemed insignificant. Maddie could not remember her response.

9

THE IDEA OF Susanna Mercer made me nervous. I studied every picture I could find online: the honey highlights in her hair, the length of her neck, the height of her cheekbones, the symmetry of her face. She was objectively, unequivocally beautiful. But beyond her appearance, something else was evident—restlessness, or maybe soulfulness. Whatever it was, a photographer could not have manufactured it. In an interview, she claimed she'd been scouted by a modeling agency but had chosen nonprofit work instead, to help people.

FaceTime was her suggestion. I thought I'd prepared myself, but when she appeared on screen, my level of intimidation went from about a seven to a ten. As she spoke, her cheekbones seemed to lift further, her brown eyes became more mysterious, her wavy hair, more voluminous. She seldom smiled.

As our conversation progressed, her intensity persisted. She never took a sip of water or glanced at another screen, or moved from her position in front of a tranquil painting of a cobalt-blue river winding through a ravine. Her eyes searched my face, like she was trying to determine whether she could trust me.

Not at first, but with increasing conviction, I sensed that she, too, was intimidated. I wasn't sure why. I was a high school student, powerless, a nobody.

Susanna wouldn't talk to Mo Whiting or anybody else after Woolf died, but she was talking to me now. Either she was trying to control the narrative or she wanted to know if Shiv and I had discovered something we weren't supposed to. Or both.

She told me she planned to return to Sewickley the following week for ScoreFest. The event was, drum-roll-please . . . a hockey thing. Everything that happened at St. Ignatius was, in one way or another, a hockey thing, but we were all too busy winning to see the way the sport coursed through us. Eventually, after we bled and bled and bled, we looked down at the floor and saw it: a puddle of forest green, the color of our jerseys.

I didn't love hockey, but I didn't hate it. Even before I met Ingo, Shiv and I went to most of the games. Entertainment in Sewickley was a scarce commodity.

Initially, I couldn't figure out why Susanna was involved with ScoreFest, which was a celebration of the arena's renovation and twenty-five years of St. Ignatius hockey on campus (and an opportunity for wealthy alumni to open their checkbooks). Of course, her family's name was on the rink, but St. Ignatius hockey seemed far removed from Susanna's nonprofit work with the unhoused in San Francisco. When I asked her about it, she told me about Kenny.

She didn't know everyone her organization served by name, or even most people, but she knew Kenny. He was always popping by, like a busybody aunt. She thought he looked a little bit like Woolf—tall with broad shoulders, a hockey build on a man who'd never set foot on the ice. His smile beamed, which was the other thing that reminded her of Woolf, whose smile always came quickly and lasted longer than other people's smiles.

She wrote a story for the newsletter about Kenny. Her boss had helped him secure a below-market-rate apartment in one of SF's new mixed-income buildings. The development had been covered extensively in the press. Susanna had no interest in quoting the mayor or the developer, or the San Francisco Housing Authority. Her story was about where Kenny came from and where he was going. He liked his new digs, and he had a steady job, busing tables at a hip fusion restaurant in SoMa. He told her, "It's the dream, man. I'm livin' the dream."

One day, she offered Kenny a free backpack on his way out of her office. A local sportswear company had donated several boxes of them. But he refused it, insisting he didn't need it.

When her father called to ask her to manage the twenty-fifth-anniversary celebration for the arena, he'd just wired money to cover her monthly expenses, which did not include rent, because she lived in a Pacific Heights condo that he owned. Her "emergency" credit card, which she used when she went out to eat with her venture capitalist and techie friends, was linked to his account. He paid her therapist directly. Kenny wouldn't even take a free backpack.

Ray Mercer had been pushing Susanna to quit the nonprofit and join the family office for some time. He didn't see the point of working for a salary that left her below the poverty line. He'd pay her "real money," he'd told her, and she could establish an office in San Francisco, managing public relations and philanthropy for the family. ScoreFest was just the first event on their calendar.

She gave her two weeks' notice at the nonprofit, and told herself that, with her family's resources, she could do even more for people like Kenny.

I wondered if it ever occurred to Susanna that she had agreed to work for her dad so she could be financially independent from her dad. It was the kind of circular logic that only made sense to rich people.

"Can you tell me about your relationship with Woolf?" I asked, reluctantly adding, "Did you love him?"

She didn't answer the second part of the question. Even over FaceTime, I could tell she was being evasive. She kept asking questions about me, changing the subject. Was I excited about college? Was I ready to leave St. Ignatius? How was my mom?

Susanna had been Mom's student at St. Ignatius, and over the years they kept in touch. It would take some time to piece it together, but I came to understand how much she admired my mom. Occasionally, Susanna would drop some non sequitur—about how Alice Northrup seemed to know every historical fact off the top of her head, or how she'd spent a hard-earned weekend chaperoning a school trip, or how she'd carried two mugs of hot tea from the faculty lounge back to the classroom and they'd chatted until sundown. When I heard these stories, I felt jealous—or not exactly jealous, but grumpy—because Susanna and the rest of Mom's students had never experienced how often she said no, which felt like always: *No, you can't go out. No, you can't get in a car with so-and-so. No, you can't wear that, or buy that, or say that.* And when I called her a fascist, she'd just say, "When you're a mother, you'll understand."

I steered the conversation back to Woolf.

After everything Susanna told me, I believe her feelings for him were limited to a time and a place, and, more importantly, to a specific function of her heart. It was love—I would call it that—but it was destined to end. Not because of what happened, which was unknowable to her then, but because her attachment to Woolf held her back, and she knew to sever it.

Susanna Mercer
September 2002

WOOLF'S REPUTATION PRECEDED him. Susanna's dad and Uncle Danny (Coach Perone) had been talking about "the kid" for a long time. Susanna knew him as the hockey player who would take St. Ignatius all the way to a championship.

Susanna met Woolf through Maddie, though the girls were practically strangers themselves. Woolf was a sophomore; Susanna, a freshman. The second time she spoke to him, a few weeks after they met, he approached her on the Lawn. "Watch out for Maddie," he said.

"Why?" she asked.

He just laughed and said, "You should come over sometime."

"When?"

"How about tonight? After soccer practice." He knew she played soccer, though she hadn't mentioned it.

"Will Maddie be there?"

"Don't think so. Maddie and Vince go to Eat'n Park on Thursdays to do math together." He smiled and winked when he said "do math."

"They don't really do math?"

"No, I mean, I think they do. They're in Algebra II together. Maddie likes hanging around Eat'n Park. Our dad used to take us there as kids whenever Mom had to work late. Maddie always ordered the same thing—fries and a milkshake. Now she goes with Vince every Thursday. Big D—my dad, we call him Big D—cooks on Thursdays. You can stay for dinner."

AFTER SPORTS, THEY rendezvoused at the rink, which made more sense than the hallway outside the girls' locker room in the gym. The hockey team had won their first game of the season the night before.

Hockey practice that day had been off ice. The players spent time in the weight room and reviewed footage of the team they were playing next. The hockey team had their own weight room at the rink. Every other athlete at the school, including the football players, shared the weight room in the main gym, near the basketball courts. The girls' soccer team didn't use the weight room at all, but for some reason, the amenities enjoyed by the hockey players irked Susanna. Everything they used was in some way superior—newer, bigger, and exclusive—all paid for by her father.

As Woolf climbed the stairs, she saw the sweat in his hair. He'd thrown on his St. Ignatius tracksuit over a T-shirt. He hadn't showered; neither had she. He didn't notice her standing there until he was almost at the top, and when he did, his arm flew up into the air. He waved too enthusiastically, like a sailor returning to port after a long voyage, catching a glimpse of his patient lover.

She turned away from him, toward the exit. He gently placed his hand on the center of her back as he opened the interior door for her. She handled the second door herself, and they slipped out into the brisk fall air together.

He carried only his backpack. Her backpack, heavy with books, was strapped on both shoulders, and her soccer bag was slung over her right.

"Let me take that for you," he said, lifting the bag by the strap. "We're walking to my house. Big D will drive you home later."

He pointed to her green St. Ignatius warm-up pants and then zipped his track jacket to his neck. "Dressed like this, maybe we should jog."

"I'd smoke you," she said.

"Or a quick skate before we go?" He looked back at the rink.

"You'd win on the ice," she said. "I'm hopeless on a slippery surface. Ray Mercer loves hockey, but he never once took me skating as a kid."

Woolf shrugged and then looked up to the sky. "Huh," he said, as if he understood.

The Whiting house was a fifteen-minute walk from campus. When they turned onto his street, he pointed to a single-story house with a double front door, unusual for the neighborhood. "Wanna hear a story?" he asked with gleaming eyes and a charming smile. "Maddie . . ." he started.

It was the way he started many of his stories. Woolf talked about his family more than anything else—even hockey. His house, which they would soon enter, was like a kingdom: Maddie, Mo, and Big D, the royal court; and Jágr, the lazy king, perched on his throne. Such a common and sentimental idea, that one's family life might be his whole life, was new and surprising to Susanna, whose own kingdom had always been distributed across time zones and continents, on trips that mixed business with pleasure, and at parties hosted by the colleagues her parents called friends.

". . . poisoned the neighbor's dog," he continued.

"No way."

Just yesterday, Maddie had gleefully reported that when she left the kitchen to go to the bathroom, Jágr had snatched the last piece of lemon meringue pie from the table. Maddie thought the combination of his guilty eyes and meringue-covered whiskers was the cutest thing she'd ever seen. She was a dog person.

Woolf told the story from the beginning, starting with the ant infestation in his hockey gear, which then spread to his teammates' gear. Maddie had collected the ants in the woods and lured them into the gloves with brown sugar. On the hook for exterminator and professional cleaning fees, Maddie took over Woolf's paper route on

Mondays and Wednesdays, which led her straight to the jaws of a vicious little bull terrier, Pickle.

Paperboys paid for the papers in advance and collected cash once a week from their neighbors to cover the costs, plus delivery. Maddie hated collection day, which added an extra thirty minutes to the route. On her first Monday, Mr. Martin paid her in rolls of pennies, claiming he was otherwise out of cash. One of the rolls was two pennies short, and the other included a Canadian penny. On Wednesday, his bull terrier bit her on the ankle.

According to Woolf, the bite was pretty minor. He had warned her about Mr. Martin, who liked his paper folded in half and placed on the right side.

Mo suggested she take treats to distract the dog. Maddie came up with a better idea.

"She was the Godfather of paper duty," Woolf joked. "She made Pickle an offer she couldn't refuse."

"What kind of offer?" Susanna asked. They slowed their pace while Woolf finished the story.

"She gave that little dog a peanut butter sandwich laced with raisins. Pickle ate about half the sandwich. A few hours later, she threw up on the doorstep. Mr. Martin discovered the other half of the sandwich in the yard."

"Raisins?"

"Raisins landed Pickle in the hospital, sick, not dead. Maddie knew what she was doing."

Susanna laughed. "Maddie is such a badass."

"On top of the money she owed for the ants, my parents tacked on a grand for the vet bill. She's still paying Mo and Big D back. In the end, she only hurts herself."

The front door was unlocked. Pushing it open, he announced, "D, we're home," as if it were Susanna's home too.

The house smelled divine—a mix of lemon and fat.

"Let's hang out in the den." He called their recreation room the den, which struck Susanna as adorable, like something you'd hear on a rerun of *The Wonder Years*.

Mr. Whiting poked his head in through the French doors. "I'm roasting a chicken over carrots, onions, and potatoes. Dinner will be ready at seven." Then he made eye contact with Susanna and said, "Can we count you in?"

She nodded, "Smells amazing, Mr. Whiting." It was the first time she'd met him, so this exchange served as an introduction.

Mr. Whiting looked at Woolf, "Set the table for four, please. Maddie's out tonight, but Mo should be home any minute."

Susanna sometimes set the table at her house on the nights that her family ate together, which had become increasingly rare. One evening, she was reading *Cosmo* at the table with her feet up on the end chair, when she looked over and noticed Esther—the woman who had practically raised her—juggling two pans and a pot of water on the stove. She asked if she could help; Esther gestured with her chin toward a stack of silverware. Susanna copied Esther's form. If her parents noticed a difference, they didn't say so.

Stopping in front of the vintage yellow wall oven to feel its warmth, Susanna said, "Retro."

Big D chuckled, "It's retro all right. Doesn't get a degree over four hundred. Only the bottom coil works, so when I need the broiler, I use the lower oven."

Woolf offered her a glass of water, placing it into her hand without waiting for a response.

"Can it be fixed?" Susanna asked.

"We probably need to replace it at some point," Mr. Whiting said. "But I built the pizza oven out back. Buying a new oven for the kitchen seems extravagant."

"You should come back for pizza night," Woolf said.

After they finished setting the table, they retreated to the den, where he left her while he went to change.

Susanna poked around. Under the TV, she found one of those boxy old Nintendo gaming consoles.

Woolf returned in jeans and a flannel, and she briefly wished she'd brought a change of clothes for dinner. The skirt, tights, and white button-down that she'd worn to school were folded in her soccer bag, but she had no intention of pulling tights back onto her legs, which still smelled faintly of shin guards.

Woolf dropped to his knees next to her, lifted the little plastic door on the console, and pushed down on the game cartridge to pop it out. He handed her *Super Mario 3*. "Wanna play?" he asked.

"How old is this thing?"

"Mo and Big D weren't big on video games when we were kids. Maddie found this beauty at the consignment shop and bought it for me for my twelfth birthday. The 'rents were so tickled by her gesture of sisterly love they let us play it together for hours." He picked up a game called *Punch-Out!!* from the stack. "This one is Maddie's favorite."

"Let's play it," Susanna said.

Woolf removed the game from its plastic case and blew on it before pushing it into the console.

He sat next to her on the floor, cross-legged, their knees touching, and handed her a controller. She unlaced her Chuck Taylor high-tops, her go-to street shoes when she pulled off her cleats after practice. After she'd tossed them aside, Woolf said, "Nice kicks. You are so *Blonde on Blonde*." She wasn't sure what he meant, but the compliment made her feel okay in her warm-ups, even sexy in her sports bra.

She couldn't identify what she felt that day, but she would decide later it was envy. The tan sectional was so worn its skin had begun to peel, and in certain spots, especially near the seams, the dull underside of the leather was visible. Someone had made a slipcover out of a heavy striped material for the armrest on one end, which was worn through itself, tatters upon tatters. It was a couch one would expect to find on the street at the end of the semester, with a cardboard sign—FREE—scrawled in black Sharpie, a treasure for a college student furnishing a temporary rental.

But the couch and other furniture—a recliner and a coffee table—offered so much more than their flea-market aesthetic. Jágr rotated in circles to find a comfortable position at the end of the sectional, in the spot where the seam had split open to reveal white foam stuffing. He jumped up with a start when a delivery truck drove by, and darted across the entire length of the L shape to the other end, where he raised his front legs onto the striped fabric, and bounced up and down, barking hysterically—a guard dog, if only in his own mind.

Many of the Whitings' possessions could be similarly categorized. Their station wagon, the one that Mrs. Whiting had just pulled into the driveway, made a racket that could be heard from inside the house, which Woolf affectionately referred to as a purr (the vehicle may or may not have had a working muffler), and the brakes were loud enough to irk the neighbors. Its doors had been dented and nicked by hockey pucks, baseballs, and bicycles. But Susanna would come to see the wagon the way Woolf did, as sturdy and reliable, the vehicle that transported the family to every hockey tournament in the tri-state area. When Susanna turned sixteen, Maddie would give her driving lessons in it.

Things that might be considered kitschy, like a heart-shaped basket hung atop an old telephone wall mount, or the tarnished brass table transecting the standing floor lamp, where she had placed her water glass, were homey and functional.

Any of these objects, alone, without context, would be undesirable, but together, operating as a system, along with Jágr and the rest of the Whiting clan, they were evidence of a life well lived, maybe even a happy life—impossible to know for sure.

Woolf's entire body moved when his thumbs pushed down on the controller to make his little dancing boxer punch her guy. When he lifted his arms to the height of her face, she glimpsed the skin of his elbow, visible through a hole in his flannel. She reached over and poked two fingers through the hole and pinched his funny bone. He peeled his eyes off the game to look at her, gently nudging her in the side with that exposed elbow. Then he returned to his avatar, delivering three quick uppercuts, which resulted in a TKO.

She thought, *Of course Maddie's favorite game is the one where she can punch her opponent until spit flies from his mouth.*

Susanna and Woolf punched the stars out of each other until dinner, a wholesome way to spend an evening.

Years later, in her late twenties, Susanna would find herself lounging blissfully on a lover's houseboat in Sausalito. She would ask herself if she loved the man or his circumstances, and if the latter, whether she could replicate them on her own. If she could, the man was unnecessary. And that would be the end of that.

10

THE NEXT DAY, Shiv didn't show up at Mickey D's for lunch. I kept looking at my phone, waiting for a text, even though we weren't supposed to have our phones out at the table. On another day, I might have slipped into a group of seniors. At St. Ignatius, we liked to say *We're all friends here.* But I wasn't in the mood for conversation that day. After about ten minutes, I picked up my lunch bag and headed outside to eat by myself.

I sent her a text: *WHERE RU?*

Her silence stung.

The daytime moon shone pale against the cerulean sky. I loved the moon as a little girl. Mom would take me on moon walks, sometimes well past my bedtime, and I'd point to the glowing orb and shake with glee. It must have seemed like a window into the heavens, mysterious and magical but right there in front of me. A celestial body that required no faith.

I'd been a quiet child, pensive, with a habit of spacing out. Mom always wanted to know what I was thinking, and on several occasions she offered to arrange for me to "talk to someone." I declined every time. For all those years, I'd assumed that the prospect of therapy was simply progressive parenting, and I suspected we could not afford it. Her offers became more frequent, her pleas for access to my brain more intrusive, following the suicides—first, Colton's, the spring before I started at St. Ignatius, and now, Kyle's. Maybe all parents worry about their children's mental health, but I felt like she didn't trust me. Like she thought every bad mood or moment of self-doubt was indicative of some predetermined malfunction of the mind, and one day, out of nowhere, my reality might fracture.

Ingo texted: *Out early, u free?*

After replying, I sat up and waited for him. He exited HQ and descended the steps, pushing his hair back on his head. Then he put both hands in the pockets of his slacks and walked slowly. When he saw me, he smiled out of one side of his mouth. His demeanor—the easy confidence that came from knowing the world was rigged in his favor—made me think of Woolf, how Susanna had described him, and Maddie's insistence that his death was neither suicide nor accidental overdose. Then I thought about Kyle, about how I knew him but didn't *know* him.

When Ingo sat down I asked, "How are you?"

"Good. The exam was easy." He'd completed his Linear Algebra exam quickly, which was why we had this time together.

"No, I mean, how are you *really*?"

"I'm fine. What's up with you?" he said.

"Would you call yourself happy?" I asked.

"Why are you being so weird?" He put his arm around me and pushed his fingers into my waist to make me squirm. "I aced my exam. I'm sitting on the grass with the hottest girl in school. Of course I'm happy. What are you doing tonight? We can hang out at my house. My parents have a thing in the city."

"Are you still hanging out with Barbara?" I asked.

"What? No. Barbara and I are just friends," he said.

"I can't tonight," I said. When he looked at me, seeking a reason, I added, "Plans with Shiv."

"Shiv can come over too," he said. "I'll invite a couple of the guys. Not a party."

I had planned another FaceTime with Susanna that night. "Can't tonight," I repeated.

Ingo squinted at me with the earnest cluelessness of a boy who'd never had to make his own sandwich. I could not help but compare Susanna's and Woolf's relationship to mine and Ingo's. Based on everything I'd learned about Woolf, he and Ingo seemed eerily similar. They both wore the C on their hockey jerseys. They were better with numbers than words. They each had a sister (though Ingo's was a couple years older, already off at college).

The bell summoned us to class. Standing, Ingo reached down with two hands to pull me up. As soon as I was on my feet, he threw his arms around my neck and hugged me, which was completely out of character. We never hugged or kissed in public. I wanted someone to witness our intimacy. Barbara was still living rent-free in my head. And I, the heartless landlord, wanted it to cost her. But when I extracted my face from Ingo's chest, there was no one around.

Then he said, "You look good today."

Ingo was so simplistic, but I couldn't see it. Hockey: fun. Girlfriend: hot. Hungry: must eat. My love was like a political affiliation. It let me down, and I went back for more. At no point did I consider leaving the party.

Susanna Mercer
November 2003

SUSANNA TOOK US History with Alice Northrup sophomore year. Ms. Northrup was known for focusing her exams on a single minute detail. People crammed for days, sometimes weeks, memorizing names, dates, and places, to avoid the nightmarish scenario of opening the blue book only to scribble total bullshit onto the empty page, because the morsel offered in the question was unrecognizable to the palate.

On the day of the fall exam, Ms. Northrup projected the image of a postcard, penned in August 1945, addressed to the Federal Works Agency in Washington, DC. The message was written in what was clearly the penmanship of an adult, but it was signed *CLARA AND MOM* in a child's capital letters, the *R* backward, along with a tiny stick-figure illustration of what could be interpreted as a girl and her friend. The note was brief but compelling: *The Lanham Act changed our lives.*

Under the postcard, Ms. Northrup's prompt read: "How did the Defense Housing and Community Facilities and Services Act of 1940 (colloquially known as the Lanham Act) change the lives of women, and why is it relevant today?"

Susanna read and reread the cryptic message projected on the screen, and then fixed her eyes on her empty blue book. Some of her classmates were already scribbling feverishly. Susanna knew what the legislation was, what had led to it, and why the government had cut the funding after the war. She stared at the postcard for a minute, wondering where Ms. Northrup had found it, and why it held particular significance to her.

In the corner of the front whiteboard, to the left of the projector screen, Ms. Northrup maintained a few items that she never erased, including her name and email address, the school motto, *Nominatim non generatim*, and her liberal translation of the Latin: *We experience particular events, not universal truths.*

Clara and her mother were Ms. Northrup's particulars, the lens through which the class was meant to analyze a sweep of history.

When time ran out, Susanna was the only student remaining in the classroom. She placed her exam on the top of the others on Ms. Northrup's desk.

"How'd it go?" Ms. Northrup asked.

"Is it possible that, as a country, we're regressing?" Susanna asked.

Ms. Northrup pointed to the stack. "I look forward to reading your exam."

"I love this class," Susanna said. "But sometimes I think no matter how much we learn from the past, we'll still make bad choices."

"Do you want to see something?" asked Ms. Northrup. She slid her laptop and the blue books into her messenger bag and fastened the buckle.

"Sure." Soccer practice didn't start for forty-five minutes. Woolf and Vince would be down at the rink until six. She'd planned to text Maddie, but that could wait. "Where are we going?"

"Upstairs."

They made their way to the third floor. Susanna followed Ms. Northrup down the corridor. There was nothing up there but classrooms, most of which belonged to the language department, each door offering a greeting: HOLA! BONJOUR! GUTEN TAG! The Latin classroom was adorned with a sign that read CAVEAT EMPTOR! ("Let the buyer beware"), which pretty much summed up Ms. Guerin's sense of humor.

Ms. Northrup opened the door to the classroom across the hall and held it for Susanna. The boards were covered with matrices and equations, which Susanna recognized from Woolf's math homework.

"Stand right here," said Ms. Northrup, guiding Susanna to stop in front of the window.

Natural light entered the third floor through a series of dormer windows, five across on the front of the building. The central window was arched, while the other four were rectangular, which, if a person cared to notice, was aesthetically pleasing from the outside, a study in symmetry, drawing the eye to the white-framed central window as if it were a doorway in the sky, granting passage to angels.

Susanna leaned forward and looked down. Paved walkways criss-crossed the verdant grass, meticulously groomed, blemished by only a small number of stray leaves. The trees had been stripped bare early that year by unusually strong winds. She looked back at Ms. Northrup, who gazed straight ahead. Beyond the quad, the grounds gently sloped upward to the peak of the hill. Everyone called the section of grass in front of the chapel "the Lawn," and it was where Susanna knew to find Maddie at lunchtime. She was always perched in the same spot, eating turkey on white or salami on rye, happy to put down whatever she was reading to commiserate.

"Do you see?" asked Ms. Northrup.

Having never set foot in this particular classroom, Susanna had always assumed the architect's intent had been fulfilled in the building's exterior beauty, but standing behind the window with Ms. Northrup's hand on her shoulder, she realized she had missed the point. The arched window created a perfect frame. The entire chapel was visible, the top of the steeple kissing the crest of the glass with a dot of blue sky above the cross; the steps leading to the chapel door appeared to rest on the bottom of the window frame, and the two stained-glass windows, on either side of the door, fell within the window grids.

The chapel had been built first, in the prime spot on the far edge of the Lawn. All paths led to it; all sight lines had been designed around it.

"Father Michael brought me up here after I'd met with the hiring committee," Ms. Northrup said. "The interviews had taken the whole day, and I was exhausted. I'd spoken with teachers and administrators, even the headmaster. Father Michael had just started teaching here, but he was all in, fully committed. I hadn't been given the job yet, but that was a formality. Whether I would accept the offer was less obvious. I was only a few years out of college. My life could have gone a million different ways."

"What'd he say to convince you?" Susanna asked.

"He instructed me to view the chapel from this exact spot, and he said, 'St. Ignatius will undergo some changes in the next few years, but it is, first and foremost, a Jesuit school.' He knew that meant something to me, even though we hadn't discussed it explicitly in my interview. Back then, and still, I was in awe of Father Michael, humbled by the idea of him—that a man like him existed in the modern world. Not because of his knowledge of language, of the classics, of history and literature—and religion and philosophy, of course—but because of all those years he had given to the foreign ministry.

"During the interview, he had referred to himself as a social worker. I got the feeling he hadn't planned to return to the US until his retirement, if at all. Despite his credentials and experience, he was so nice. Boldly, I asked him why it mattered so much that St. Ignatius was a Jesuit school, and he said, 'Because the Jesuits have always understood that the quality of the education is not determined by the endowment or the buildings, or even the agreed-upon curriculum. The people matter most.' I reached out and shook his hand, and said, 'Indeed,' which was as good as signing a contract. So here I am, and here I will remain."

Susanna admired her teacher. But while Ms. Northrup felt the magnetic pull of the place, Susanna felt an equivalent force repelling her from St. Ignatius, Sewickley, her infinitesimally small life. Father Michael's piety had been enough for Ms. Northrup. Susanna was more skeptical. What if it was a con?

The postcard penned by "Clara and Mom" referred to the legislation that funded universal childcare during World War II. Mothers wrote in from all over the country, requesting that the government extend funding after the war, to no avail. Because why fund childcare centers, which provide such obvious benefits to women and children, in peacetime?

Susanna observed her teacher, still looking in the direction of the chapel. "Why don't you have kids, Ms. Northrup? Is it because this country is hostile to women?"

She chuckled, then blurted out, "I've always wanted a child."

"I guess you have us—your students," Susanna said, attempting to walk back her stupid question. Everybody was always asking women if they wanted kids. Talk about hostility.

Ms. Northrup had something on her mind. "I love my students, but I'll never hold them, or dance with them in the kitchen, or watch them sleep."

"I don't get why people like watching babies sleep."

Her teacher laughed again, finally turning away from the window to make eye contact. "One day, you'll understand."

Susanna knew she would never want children. As a little girl, she'd hated dolls. Having to brush their hair and pretend to feed them seemed menial and depressing. She would never feel what other women described as the ticking of a biological clock. She would never view milk-production as a miracle. (Were cows also miracles? I mean, maybe.) She would never try to create meaning through the act of child-rearing. And, most of all, she would never ever become her mother, Patricia Mercer, who treated her only child as a territory in the narcissistic empire of ego.

But on the day Ms. Northrup took her up to the third floor, what Susanna did not yet know was that her biggest fear was not, in fact, becoming her mother, but something worse: becoming the product of everything her parents had given her, and then having a child. In a moment of anger, the mother might call the child ungrateful, and then, having seen through the mother, having seen everything that had made her, the child would feel pity and maybe even disdain. The mother would say, "But I've given you everything!" and the child would say, "What about love?"

No way. She had no interest in becoming a parent. Maybe Ms. Northrup could teach a child to love the world, but Susanna would find her purpose elsewhere.

11

ON THURSDAY, I saw Shiv briefly at assembly. Later, she texted, saying she was going off campus for lunch, and she wasn't in the lounge during her free period, so I didn't see her again until chapel.

Seniors attended Mass in the chapel at three o'clock, after last period, on Thursdays. Juniors went Wednesdays, sophomores Tuesdays, and freshmen Mondays. The 156 people in our senior class fit shoulder to shoulder in the pews, barely.

I found Shiv about halfway toward the front on the left side. Sitting down, I had to scooch her body over with my hip to make room. Shiv never complained about Mass. Attendance was mandatory for everyone, but non-Catholics were not required to stand or kneel, and they didn't take Communion. Shiv liked shaking hands when we offered the sign of peace. It was the Catholic kids who begrudged Mass. As part of our identity, holy obligation was harder to accept.

When I asked her about it, she said it was like waiting for the bus. The longer you waited, rationally, you knew the bus must be closer, but with every tick of the clock, the bus seemed farther away. I'd been waiting for the bus longer than she had.

According to Shiv, lots of things in life worked this way. I remember asking her what the "bus" was, metaphorically speaking, and she shrugged and said, "It's whatever you're waiting for: enlightenment, God, to be dismissed with the words 'Go in peace.'"

Religion was all about waiting, and Catholics were in a rush for the exit.

"What'd you do at lunch?" I asked.

"Waste of time," she whispered.

"Next time, I'll go with you," I said.

"Then I would have wasted two people's time."

I started paying attention when Father Michael began his homily. His presence at the lectern did not *command* attention; it was more of a request: *I beseech you by the mercies of God.*

He began: "Eighteen years ago, a student entered my classroom. We sat down at the same table I now share with some of you. We spoke for less than an hour, and I thought we were talking about goaltending and set plays, the mechanics of the game. Honestly, the conversation was unremarkable. Analyzing St. Ignatius hockey games had, by then, become a hobby, my small way of contributing to a team that never, or rarely, lost.

"Later, a boy on the team died. His name was Woolf Whiting. In the aftermath, my mind kept cycling back to that visit from his teammate, as if searching for a clue. You see, we didn't know why Woolf had died. We understood the mechanics—the how—and we could analyze them, much like the details of the game. But we did not understand the more important question. And I began thinking about that question—Why?—as it relates to the loss of young life, and I realized it is generally not the question we ask each other, precisely because it is unanswerable. It is the question we ask God: 'Why, God, why? Why have you forsaken me?'"

Shiv grabbed my hand, holding it down firmly on the pew between us. The tenderness of the gesture made me think about the way a person takes the hand of someone on a gurney.

Father Michael continued, "The Jesuits have a way of thinking about unanswerable questions. We call it 'casuistry.' The St. Ignatius motto, *Nominatim non generatim*—through the particular, not the abstract—is based on this mode of reasoning. When you cannot apply broad principles to a question, you must understand it completely, in fine detail, and only then can you begin to draw comparisons with other questions that are, if not answered, at least understood.

"I began thinking about autoimmune disease. It didn't need to be autoimmune disease. It could have been cancer or some other ailment that overtakes the body. But autoimmune disease seemed appropriate because it is *of the body*. It is the body turning on itself.

"And, perhaps due to my Jesuit training, I could not help comparing what happened to Woolf with such a disease. Something, or someone—perhaps Woolf himself—attacked his body, the thing *he* was meant to protect. It is impossible to think this way—to go down this spiral—without understanding something fundamental about losing someone with so much promise.

"After we lost Kyle, one of you approached me with a question—a very Catholic question—about suicide and mortal sin. And when the question was posed, I could not help but think about that most pertinent analogy, and how if one of our students died of autoimmune disease, no one would inquire about the fate of his soul. But is not suicide simply the mental equivalent of autoimmune disease? And if so, who has the responsibility to suppress it? Certainly, the responsibility did not fall to Kyle, whose own mind was attacking itself. And by this way of thinking, suicide is *not* a mortal sin, and could never be.

"But here's the thing about casuistry: In recognizing these details, in giving them power, we are forced to grapple with our own complicity, and the complicity of this community, our beloved St. Ignatius—a beautiful place, a sacred place, but a place that has, on multiple occasions, failed its fine young people."

Father Michael paused, and—I could have sworn—he looked right at me. Did Dr. Zap tell him that Shiv and I were investigating Woolf's death? I pictured Father Michael huddled on the couch with my mom. What were they hiding? What would happen if Shiv and I found out?

He continued, "I have been trying to understand what happened eighteen years ago. To own up to it. To make peace with it. I can still see the grimace on the face of the young man in my classroom. I can hear his voice falter, ever so slightly. I remember, after all these years, the way his leg shook under the table. Was he there to warn me? Was I too distracted to notice? Could I have saved Woolf Whiting?

"Those of you who knew Kyle may be overcome by similar questions, and before today, I told myself I should not say anything that might give those thoughts more power, because they can be unproductive and, worse, damaging. But when I sat down to write this homily, I understood that not talking about them will not make them go away. And as young people, you should not go on with your lives and ignore what has happened, only for it to surface later, in a conversation with a priest or a therapist or a bartender.

"So let's talk about it now—our own complicity—my door is open to you."

Father Michael had called us "fine young people." How a priest could know what was hidden in the recesses of our teenage hearts was beyond me, but I had no doubts about our collective character.

What troubles me now, after reading Shakespeare and Tolstoy for my humanities sequence at Princeton, is not that he was wrong about us, but that he was right. We were fine young people. But one day, in the not-so-distant future, we might find ourselves in the midst of some business transaction or political maneuver, in service of someone or some profit, only to find that we have quietly, and perhaps unknowingly, turned a corner and become the adults we had once dismissed with contempt.

A senior named Emily read the General Intersessions. After each petition, she lifted her hand to prompt the response "Lord, hear our prayer." When she said "We pray for students who suffer with mental afflictions," I joined in. Mental illness didn't make the cut every week, but it was like gravel on an old country road: Sometimes the dust blew up.

After Communion, I climbed over three people who hadn't left the pew to get back to my spot. The last one was Shiv. Only about 60 percent of us came to St. Ignatius Catholic, and exactly the same percentage left Catholic. Occasionally, someone jumped ship, claiming burgeoning atheism or disillusionment, but no one bothered to update the stats. Once a Catholic, always a Catholic. The door didn't swing the opposite direction either.

When Woolf went here, the school was more like 90 percent Catholic. I imagine it must have felt claustrophobic, everyone's sameness like a well-insulated house—cozy at first, then stuffy, until someone finally opened a window.

As we walked out, Shiv asked, "You think the kid in his classroom was Vince?"

Father Michael had not given any indication, but it seemed plausible.

"When Father Michael came by to see my mom, he told her that Woolf had come to him for advice right before he died. It'd be strange if Vince also went to see him. Like, why are all these hockey players talking to a priest?" I made a mental note to ask Ingo this question.

Shiv added, "Father Michael left something out. Whatever it is, he feels guilty about it."

"I think his point is that we all feel guilty."

"Do you feel guilty?" Shiv asked. "About Kyle, I mean."

The answer was no. Maybe Ingo did, a little bit, because they were teammates. Maybe he thought he could have reached out in some way, or recognized a sign, as if Kyle's lethargic skating or errant slap shot might have predicted what was to come. If Ingo had these thoughts, he didn't share them with me, and I had a feeling he would easily dismiss them.

I resolved to call Vince as soon as possible.

WE SPOKE LATER that night. When I told him about Father Michael's homily, Vince confirmed he was the student in his classroom that day. The clarity with which he remembered their meeting astonished me. I couldn't remember details from conversations with my teachers that had occurred within the year, and here was a guy recounting an hour of his life, eighteen years in the past. His recall alerted me to the possibility that memory operates like a detective, identifying and prioritizing clues, creating a narrative. Hindsight is not 20/20; it selects what to see, even as it remains unclear.

Vince Mahoney
February 2004

THE GREENWOOD ACADEMY game was a turning point for Vince and Woolf. The game, against their archrival, had not gone well.

Vince's mom was in the stands, though she always left after the first period. Laura had to be put down by eight, which meant his mom had to be home, because his dad wasn't—and even if he was, he was anything but a modern man.

Either because it was Greenwood, or because he was too drunk to stop himself, his dad did the one thing he promised he wouldn't do. After his mom and Laura had gone home, he showed up.

Vince didn't know he was there until the third period. He made a high glove save off a ricochet, the puck impossible to see until the last second. The crowd cheered and then quieted, and a lone, gruff voice stammered, "It's gonna be a shutout toooo-niiiite!" When Vince looked up, a light from overhead glinted off the metal flask in his old man's hand as he brought it to his lips.

Vince let in three consecutive goals.

Somebody, a parent of one of the players on the other team, yelled, "Sieve," and then yelled it again and again. Unimaginative, miles from poetic, the chant was familiar to every goaltender in the history of the sport, white noise that Vince wouldn't have registered, except in his peripheral vision, he saw movement. He turned his head up to the place where his father had been standing. When he didn't see him there, he scanned the crowd. Then he heard one last "Sieve!" before he watched his dad push through, in the direction of the heckler.

Play at the other end had stopped when the opposing goalie covered the puck. Every head turned up to the stands. Several men became entangled, working to hold Mitch Mahoney back, bending over to pull the heckler off the ground.

Mr. Houser, the St. Ignatius athletic director turned enforcer, a slight man who nevertheless, commanded authority, put a hand on Mitch Mahoney's back and coaxed him toward the aisle. St. Ignatius had a way of handling indiscretions swiftly and quietly, and, depending on the parties involved, without formal acknowledgment. It had never happened, even though everyone knew it did.

Vince's dad had tried his best to overcome his demons, though his efforts were never enough. He was better than his own father, who was probably better than his father. Maybe that was the goal of being a son: to be a little bit better than your old man. Then the world would be less painful.

Someone must have called his mom. By the time Vince got home, she knew what had happened. He listened to his parents argue about it late into the night. Eventually, Laura woke up screaming, as she often did during that period, and his mom disappeared into his sister's room and didn't come out for the rest of the night.

VINCE ARRIVED EARLY for practice the next day. The rink was mostly deserted. The Zamboni was on the ice. Coach's door was open, which meant he was in his office. Father Michael, who always warmed up with team, their unofficial cheerleader/mascot, donning skates and a priest's collar, was lacing up on a bench near the glass. He was on the ice before every game and most practices. He loved hockey, and the players loved him.

The locker room was silent. With the door closed, he couldn't even hear the Zamboni. Briefly, he thought, *So this is why Woolf likes being here early.* But he knew better. Woolf liked the camaraderie of the place, not the quiet.

Vince surveyed the gear-filled cubbies, the spotless benches, and the gray-flecked rubber floor. He thought about how new everything looked, not like the spaces of youth hockey, gum under the benches and scuff marks on the walls. He loved the sport back then, everything about it, even when he rode the bench. All week, he looked forward to game day. And the tournaments, especially the tournaments. Before Laura was born, his mom drove him everywhere, the two of them on the road before the sun came up.

He and his mom had gotten into it that morning. Laura had one of her bloody noses, and his mom was doing three or four things at once: cleaning up the blood and picking up toys and grinding coffee. She always made sure coffee was up by the time his dad came down, even though she preferred tea or water or juice for herself. Something about it, the effort of it, after what his dad had pulled the previous night, set Vince off.

Over time, he'd grown accustomed to his parents' dynamic. He generally felt a low-grade despair when he thought about relationships, the way one probably feels when living comfortably under the rule of a despot, fully aware someone else is suffering and the situation is untenable, but unsure if anything can be done or who ought to do it.

He could have made the coffee himself, while his mom tilted Laura's head back and pinched her nose with the tissue, but instead he yelled something, or maybe just raised his voice to a decibel higher than Laura's shrieks. Then he dropped his empty cereal bowl into the sink and left.

The spring on the storm door was broken. He flung it open, and it clapped shut. He didn't intentionally slam it—his mom must have known—but the sound was loud enough to make an impression. Later, sitting in class, and then again, as he picked through the lunch she had packed for him, he tried to remember what he'd said to her, but he could not.

When the door of the locker room swung open and hit the doorstop, he heard the clap of the storm door again, like an echo.

Woolf wasn't alone. Before Vince raised his head from his hands, he heard the boisterous laughter of Walker and McCabe.

McCabe fist-bumped Vince before sidestepping to his cubby. Walker nodded and said, "What up, man."

Woolf walked over and took his hand, as if to help him to his feet. Vince stood, an act of compliance, though it seemed convivial. Woolf's expression was tense, maybe *in*tense—not game-time-let's-get-fired-up intensity but the kind of intensity Vince saw in his mother's eyes when his dad came home from the bar (as if *she* had done something wrong). But then Woolf smiled, and he looked genuinely happy, like there was no place on Earth he'd rather be.

"You're here early," Woolf said.

"I wanted to talk to you."

"Yeah? What about?" he asked, surprise evident in the inflection of his voice.

"About last night." Vince broke eye contact.

"Last night?"

"The game."

"Oh," Woolf said, putting his hand on Vince's shoulder. They sat down on the bench next to each other.

Walker and McCabe had started to undress. McCabe put his earbuds in, and Vince could hear the pulsing of hip-hop from across the room. Walker was digging through his bag looking for something.

Vince hesitated.

Woolf said, "Forget about the pucks that got past you last night. We'll still make it to the state championship."

They had lost the game by one, 3–2. Both St. Ignatius goals were scored by Woolf's line. He'd left the ice with a goal and an assist.

The door swung open again, and a young guy, muscular like a weight-lifting coach, dressed like an EMT, entered, carrying a soft black case. He didn't say a word until he reached the far corner of the room and unzipped the case, opening it like a book. Walker, McCabe, and Woolf lined up next to him. He asked them, together, how they were all feeling, though he didn't expect an answer. Face to face with Woolf, he told him to rate his pain.

Woolf rocked his head back and forth, like he had no idea, and then said, "Maybe a four," and then turned around toward the bench. He bent over and pulled down his pants. The guy leaned over him and wiped the exposed area with an alcohol swab before pulling out a prefilled syringe. Then he injected something into Woolf's upper glute.

He did the same for McCabe, and then Walker, asking each of them to rate their pain before the injections. One said four and the other said five, suspiciously similar to Woolf's answer.

Before the guy left the room, he disposed of all three syringes in the stainless-steel bin, labeled biohazard, which was mounted on the wall next to the trash can.

Woolf returned to his position on the bench next to Vince, a big sheepish smile smacked across his face. He reached to grab his lower back. "I won't feel pain till tomorrow."

"What is it?"

"Helps with the inflammation," he said matter-of-factly, as if he'd just popped an Advil.

"How long have you been getting the shots?"

"Not as long as you've been smoking weed." Woolf laughed.

Vince forced a smile.

Walker and McCabe started putting on their pads. McCabe had his earbuds back in. His lips moved with the lyrics, and he tapped his foot. Walker occasionally glanced over at Woolf and Vince, but mostly minded his own business. Vince was overcome by the sinking certainty that his presence was irrelevant, which was worse than intrusive.

Woolf changed the subject. "Have you talked to Susanna lately? She never wants to hang out."

"Ask your sister," Vince said. "They're always together. I think they formed a girl band. No instruments. Just personas."

"Maddie's big on loyalty. She'll tell me to go talk to Susanna myself." Woolf winced a little as he got up from the bench, and then again when he reached down to pull the gear out of his bag.

"Body like an old Buick," Vince said, tossing a roll of tape at him.

But by the time Woolf glided onto the ice, his body would be a high-functioning machine, German quality and precision.

Vince looked at the clock mounted above the door. In a few minutes, the rest of the guys would file in. "Hey, DubDub—"

"Yeah?"

"Never mind." He stripped down to his underwear, moving slower than usual, unintentionally, as if his joints had found a way to fill the time. He thought about the guy who had administered the shots and wondered if he was the doctor who prescribed them or some lackey.

Head down, lacing up his skates, Woolf said something Vince couldn't make out. He asked him to repeat it. "You belong on the ice," Woolf said, tugging on the laces as he worked his way up, "as much as me, or anyone else."

Briefly, Vince felt like they were talking as kids, like they did that day Woolf decided Vince should play goalie so he'd never have to leave the ice.

He liked putting his pads on next to Woolf; he liked pretending it still felt the way it used to feel. "Maybe it's not a good idea to keep playing through pain."

"The college scouts are watching," Woolf said. "I need a scholarship."

"You could take out loans," Vince said.

"Why would I want to do that?"

"No more shots in the ass."

"I told you, man. It's an anti-inflammatory. Every pro athlete in the world takes this stuff," Woolf said.

"You're not a pro," Vince said. "We could talk to someone."

"Dude, forget about the shots. Don't worry about me. It's not like

I'm downing a handle of gin and smashing in some guy's face with a stool, like your old man."

There it was, how Woolf really felt: superior. Vince was so stunned his jaw clenched shut. He could not respond—not even with the rote "Fuck you" repeating in his head.

Vince knew how some of the guys saw him. It wasn't about money. His family had that. It was because his dad spent his days in a warehouse and his nights in dive bars. When he told stories, his Pittsburgh accent was perceptible; when he drank, it was obvious.

But Woolf wasn't like the other guys. Vince had practically lived at the Whitings' house when they were kids. After Laura was born and his parents stopped coming to his games, he rode with Woolf's family to all their tournaments. How could status come between brothers?

"Maybe you're jealous the scouts aren't here to see you."

In that moment, Vince's anger clouded how unlike Woolf that comment was. Later, he would wonder if Woolf had changed or if he was just struggling to figure out who he wanted to be. Vince muttered, "Dude, if you weren't a self-obsessed asshole, your girlfriend might still be into you."

Their friendship never recovered from that conversation. It wasn't like one of them said, "We aren't friends anymore." It was more of a slow drift. Perhaps, given more time, the wind would have changed direction again, righting their course.

THE NEXT DAY, after last period, as everyone dispersed to cars and buses, or to locker rooms in preparation for various sports, Vince peered in through the window on the door and saw Father Michael sitting alone in his classroom, writing something on a yellow legal pad. He opened the door wide enough to stick in his head.

Father Michael motioned him in. "Vince," he said. "To what do I owe this afternoon visit?"

Father Michael looked more natural on skates than in shoes,

especially the brown oxfords he favored in the classroom. Maybe other people saw him differently; for Vince, the ice was their contextual environment.

They sat at the large communal table in the center of the classroom. It was the only room in the school where the students sat facing each other. The other classrooms had individual chair-desk combos, arranged in forward-facing configurations.

Vince was pulled into a conversation about the Greenwood game, as if by gravitational force. On the legal pad, Father Michael drew the opponent's set piece after a face-off: The center dropped the puck back to their defenseman, who found a man open on the goal line, who fired it across the ice to their other defenseman, who went backdoor. When he saw the positions of the players, stick figures on paper, and the direction of the puck, arrows to dots, the goal appeared to be virtually unstoppable from a goaltender's perspective.

Using pen and paper to analyze plays was something Vince's dad had done before he stopped coming to games. Father Michael's motives were different, though. He wasn't chewing Vince out; he was showing him why it wasn't his fault.

Father Michael pulled a sandwich out of his lunch sack, ham and Swiss. He offered Vince half. The man was a scholar. He spoke several languages, including Bengali, because he ran a school in Bangladesh before relocating to Pittsburgh. In his presence, it was easy to forget all that. He was just a guy who loved hockey and packed his own sandwiches.

Vince had eaten earlier, but he didn't mind a second lunch. Holding the half sandwich out in front of him in the direction of Father Michael, he said, "Cheers." Father Michael reached out with his half, and they tapped them together like champagne flutes before taking their first bites.

Vince settled in and looked around. There were the books, of course, but a philistine could fill a bookshelf if so inclined. "If you really want to know a person," Vince's mom once said, "look at his knickknacks."

The St. Ignatius crest and motto, engraved on a wooden plaque, was mounted on the rear wall. Next to it was a shield above the name ST. JOSEPH'S HIGH SCHOOL, with an address in Dhaka. Below the address was the Latin motto, the same as the St. Ignatius motto, and below that was something else, written in what Vince presumed was Bengali.

Vince stepped closer to the crests, holding his sandwich in one hand, and recited the Latin aloud. "*Nominatim non generatim.*"

"I wrote the motto for St. Joseph's when we erected the school," Father Michael said. "When I came here, St. Ignatius was in a rebranding phase, removing its old mascot and rethinking its values. The administration decided to adopt the motto as a governing principle."

"Sister schools," Vince said.

Father Michael smiled at the idea.

Vince asked him how many Bengalis had converted to Catholicism while he was there, not expecting a number exactly, but a vague percentage of the students under his tutelage.

Father Michael said, "Zero," and Vince repeated, "Zero?" Father Michael nodded. "I can't think of a single person who converted to Catholicism while I was there. That wasn't our purpose."

Framed photos of former students sat atop the ventilation unit under the windows. They were arranged in no particular order, the St. Joseph's students in their powder-blue uniforms mixed among St. Ignatius students in khakis and white button-downs. Next to the bookshelf, there was just enough wall space for a single relic of Father Michael's glory days: a Minnesota men's hockey NCAA national championship pennant. In the corner of the room, at the front, sat two bronze giraffes, maybe two and a half or three feet tall. A T. J. Oshie bobblehead doll adorned the desk, wedged between books and papers. There was a crucifix on the front wall, above the whiteboard, as there was in every classroom.

Inspecting a giraffe, touching its ears, Vince asked, "Are these from Bangladesh?"

"Bloomfield," said Father Michael.

Vince walked back to the table, still holding his half sandwich, now half gone, and sat three chairs down from Father Michael. Sun streaked through the windows, flooding their side of the table. Father Michael stood to lower the blinds. The room dimmed. Vince squirmed in his chair, aware of the intimacy of the situation, feeling much like he did in a confessional—like something was expected of him and he wasn't sure he could deliver. Briefly, Vince thought about what he would say if he had to confess his sins, and the truth, which pleased him, was: not much. He should help his mom more and pay more attention to Laura. Every Catholic kid goes to confession, because they are led to, but kids don't really need it, and it's not one of those habits, like healthy eating or voracious reading, that sticks around in adulthood.

"You know," Vince said, "the pope should consider moving reconciliation back in the sacrament queue."

"How do you mean?"

"Like, maybe after marriage," he said, thinking of his parents. To be fair, his mom was a saint, but his dad could use a little absolution. "That's when people could really use it."

Father Michael laughed. "It will be there when you need it."

Vince had resolved to state his concern about Woolf and the other guys emphatically, as an objection that ought to be reported to some higher authority—the headmaster or the board—but by the time he shoved the last bite of sandwich in his mouth, the conversation had settled into an uneven silence, which Vince attributed to his own sobriety. He was overcome by the youthful limitations of the pupil. And Father Michael wasn't just a teacher; he was a priest.

"Do you remember the hits?" Vince asked, gesturing to Father Michael's Minnesota pennant.

"The ones I took? No."

"But you remember the guys *you* hit?"

"One or two of them," he said. "The guys who didn't get up right away."

Vince waited for him to say more, then asked, "Were they okay?"

"As far as I know."

"But you *don't* know?"

Father Michael finished chewing and swallowing before he answered. "Sometimes it's difficult to assess the harm we cause, or the good." He started to say something, stopped, then started again. "Once, after a clean hit, a guy left the ice with a concussion and didn't come back. He didn't play again that season, and he was off the roster the following year. I kept track of him. He's a scientist now. He lives in Boston with his wife and three kids."

"Sounds okay."

"His work is on neurodegenerative conditions."

"Not a coincidence."

Father Michael searched Vince's face, looking, maybe, for some acknowledgment that his answer was satisfactory. Then he added, "Things have changed. Helmets are better. Concussion protocols—"

"Some of the players are getting shots," Vince blurted out. When Father Michael didn't react, he added, "For pain."

Father Michael turned his head away and rolled it back. He stroked his beard. "For inflammation. Yes, I'm aware," he said.

"You're aware?"

"I've spoken with Coach," he said. "The players are under the supervision of a doctor, and all their parents have given consent."

"You mean the EMT guy?"

"He's a doctor."

"What's his specialty?"

"Sports medicine."

"A chiropractor?"

"A physician. Vince, I understand you're concerned about your friends, but they have a right to privacy."

"I don't want to talk about my friends," Vince said, but he didn't say what he did want to talk about, which was an idea that wasn't yet fully formed in his mind. Then something came out of his mouth that he hadn't thought about in advance. "Coach Perone will win at any cost."

"For now," Father Michael replied, "the cost is not too high."

Vince believed Father Michael knew everything there was to know. He trusted Father Michael. Only later, long after he graduated from St. Ignatius and quit the game, would he ask himself why. Because he was a priest or because he was a hockey player? Love of the game is like a kaleidoscope, all color and refraction. All you see is beauty.

Vince stood up, but he couldn't shake the desire to linger, so he walked to the back of the room to examine the photos again. He picked up the one that captured Father Michael standing in the middle of a group of students in Dhaka. He had a trimmed beard and dark hair. He towered above the kids. In almost all ways, he had the appearance of an outsider: white, Christian, and, owing to the serenity of his expression, not simply foreign, but otherworldly. He looked happy, in a way Vince had never seen him look at St. Ignatius, except on the ice.

"Why'd you leave Dhaka?" Vince asked.

"I published an article about underage workers—young girls—working in garment factories. It upset some people."

"You were deported?"

"Around that time, I had to travel back to the US. My brother had been diagnosed with cancer, and we didn't know how much longer we had with him. As it turned out, we didn't have long. He died two months later. All I wanted to do was go back to work. But by then I couldn't return to Bangladesh. My visa was denied, and there were threats against my life.

"I was never suited for diocesan work," he continued. "I had entered the priesthood because I was attracted to the foreign missions. I assumed I would be reassigned somewhere else. But then the opportunity at St. Ignatius came up. Father Gregory was planning to retire soon, and he thought the school could use another Jesuit."

"You knew him before?" Father Gregory had retired two years before Vince arrived at St. Ignatius, but the man was a legend.

"From seminary, yes. He was my teacher. A force. He taught evolutionary biology at St. Ignatius before any of the other Catholic schools did. Suffice it to say, I had big shoes to fill. But I felt I could do some good here. St. Ignatius had come a long way, but it was in the midst of another shift—this time, cultural, as opposed to theological, having more to do with the parents."

Vince put the picture back down on the air unit.

Father Michael said, "If you'd like, we could talk to Coach Perone together about what's troubling you."

"That's okay. Thanks, though."

Father Michael stood up and walked over to the enormous floor-to-ceiling bookshelf, which covered the entire wall on one side of the classroom. He ran his finger along a section on the second shelf from the top until he came to *The Spirit on the Ice* by Declan Whiting, which he pulled down.

The book had been released not long after Canada defeated the US in the 2002 Winter Olympics; hockey was having a moment. The *Pittsburgh Post-Gazette* ran a profile on Declan Whiting, and the book was reviewed in *The New York Times* and a few other places. Vince didn't read it when it was first published, one of many things he didn't bother to do. But he did attend a local reading with Woolf and Maddie, where they both exhibited equal parts pride and embarrassment because their old man was receiving public recognition.

A woman in the audience asked about violence, and before answering, Mr. Whiting paused deliberately, as if he'd been expecting the question but didn't want his answer to appear rehearsed, and then said, "To a certain extent, violence will always be in sport, because it is in humanity. And sport is just humanity onstage." The woman still held the microphone in her hand, so she pressed, "But what about your son? How is it that we have come to worship a game so much that we will sacrifice our own children to it?" Mr. Whiting deflected with something about injuries and deaths resulting from car accidents. "But we hand over the keys, do we not?" he said. The woman didn't respond because the microphone had been seized and handed to the next person—who was already asking if Pittsburgh would ever have another Mario Lemieux.

Soon after the book was published, something happened that proved Declan Whiting's point. One of the three featured players, Albie Harris, took a hard hit to the chest in the third game of his second season in the NHL. He popped up quickly but immediately fell backward onto the ice. Medics performed CPR and used a defibrillator to restart his heart. When he was taken off the ice in a stretcher, there was no movement, no thumbs-up, no indication that he was breathing. His teammates and their opponents stood still; time stood still. The game was called off.

When Albie Harris woke up from the coma two days later, he said he had seen God. Then he asked who won the game.

Doctors weren't sure if he would ever play again. But Albie did return the following season. Good as new. Better. Analysts said he was no longer watching the game as it happened. His passes anticipated his teammates' speed and direction; his shots sought out holes before they existed; his skating dodged bodies before they struck. He could see the future. When asked how he did it, he said God had visited him when he lost consciousness and had never left. When asked if hockey was worth almost dying for, he said it was. Not *almost* dying but actual death. He had died, so he knew.

Father Michael passed *The Spirit on the Ice* to Vince with his left hand and then reached out his right. Vince tucked the book under his arm, looked him in the eye, and gripped his hand firmly, which made him feel like a man, or at least like he was becoming a man, or trying to, anyway.

He didn't return *The Spirit on the Ice* to Father Michael until graduation. By then, the pages were dog-eared, and all of Vince's favorite passages were underlined in red pen. He hadn't planned to give the book back at all, but it seemed like the right thing to do in the end.

St. Ignatius went 18 and 1 in the regular season and won the state championship that year. Raymond Mercer and Danny Perone had built the hockey program from nothing to something, with grit and the great American dollar, the combination of the two promising deliverance.

12

WHEN FATHER MICHAEL greeted me in Philosophy, first period, I thought about *The Spirit on the Ice*. Vince had said he'd dog-eared and underlined Father Michael's copy, like it was his personal Bible. I wanted to know why it mattered so much to him.

I tried to pay attention in class. Deep breath, in and out, in and out. As Mom tells it, by the age of two, I would lie in bed, soothing myself with deep breathing. She'd lie next to me and listen to me inhale and exhale every night until I fell asleep. I thought that sounded like a bad use of her time, but she says it relaxed her too. Her toddler's loud breathing was the one thing that quieted her mind. One day, I would understand.

We were reading Kafka's *The Metamorphosis*, and we were all worried we'd become Gregor. Life was binary: Either you were the man or you were a tool of the man. And if you ended up the latter, poor fool, then you'd already woken up as the vermin.

There were twelve of us in Philosophy. It was available only to upperclassmen, after completion of required courses. Other electives included Community Journalism, which Shiv and I had chosen together; Economics, which was popular because St. Ignatius was full of Gregors; Organic Chemistry, which all the kids who wanted to be doctors took for obvious reasons; and Design, where they invented things like knit caps with ponytail holes and reusable to-go cups that looked exactly like disposable to-go cups. Not everyone had time for these electives. Some people ended up repeating courses they'd dropped, and the sporty kids took Weight Lifting. They didn't get credits for that, just toned bodies.

Father Michael had the weary look of a man who was previously handsome. He joked that his demise would not be precipitated by the various dysenteries, roundworms, and other exotic illnesses he'd suffered in Bangladesh, but rather the common cold. Then he coughed into his curled arm before steadying himself on his desk.

Later, I relayed the comment to Shiv, and she said, "Chad will stab him in the back long before a cold gets him." She was referring to Headmaster Campbell. Shiv believed if your name was Chad, you were either a bouncer at a biker bar, a gym teacher, or a white-collar criminal. Chad was not behind door number one or two, which left only one possibility. He just hadn't been caught.

The class discussion on *The Metamorphosis* continued to unspool. A guy named Brian talked too much, his voice squawking from the other end of the table. His skin was so clean and shiny he looked like he'd been squeegeed. He called Grete a psycho. He kept repeating that word: *psycho*. "What kind of psycho plots to kill her own brother? The poor guy was planning to send her to music school, and this is how the psycho thanks him," he said. Everyone agreed: Grete behaved badly.

Without raising my hand, I blurted out, "Grete is the one with the talent!"

After a while, I lost interest in the dumb bug. I started thinking about all the hours I'd been spending talking to Maddie, Vince, and Susanna. They were all so open. Initially, I hadn't even thought they'd email me back. Their willingness to talk confirmed that they owed something to this place, to teachers like my mom. At least, that's what I told myself.

After class, I lingered in my seat. When everyone else was gone, I stood up and walked over to the bookshelf. The books were organized alphabetically by author's last name. I scanned the W's. Many years had passed since Vince had returned the book. I had no idea if I would find it.

But there it was: *The Spirit on the Ice* by Declan Whiting. I ran my finger to the top of the spine, tilted it toward me, and slowly extracted it. I tried to look nonchalant, like I hadn't been looking for anything specific.

"Take it with you," Father Michael said. He hovered near the front of the room, erasing the writing on the board.

"Thanks," I said. "I'll return it when I'm done."

A brief silence fell over us. I wanted to leave but felt like I should say something first.

He held eye contact. I could not look away. "When Ms. Northrup told me she was adopting a baby, I was so happy for her," he said. "I knew she would make a wonderful mother. Because you lived on campus, I would see her walking you in the carrier and, later, in the stroller, and then holding your hand while you skipped. You were always together. Some of her expressions—'Goodness gracious' and 'Well, well'—became yours. Now, when you speak in class, you remind me of her, always drawing connections that other people don't, and seeing people before ideas. You've grown into a fine young woman, Frankie."

Looking down at the book in my hand, I said, "You gave this to Vince Mahoney. That day he came to your classroom, he left with it."

"Yes," he said. "You've been talking to Vince?"

"Why this book?" I asked.

"I thought it would help him," he said. "Vince was sensitive. Most people didn't know that, because he never wanted anybody to know. He didn't really belong on the ice. Not because he wasn't good. He was. But he didn't want to be there. He wanted to be somewhere else."

"Did Woolf belong on the ice?" I asked.

"Woolf was born a hockey player," he said. "He might have made it to the NHL."

"I thought he wanted a career in finance," I said.

"He could've done both. He had the talent. He had the mind."

"Do you think hockey killed him?" I asked. It was the wrong way to phrase the question. I wasn't sure exactly what I was asking, but I thought it had something to do with Father Michael's complicity. His guilt.

"No," he said. "Honestly, I don't believe his death had anything to do with hockey."

"But his pain—"

"It was never severe. He played through it." Father Michael inched closer to the door. "His physical pain," he clarified. "I have no idea what was going on in his head."

"He didn't take his own life," I said, aware of how much I sounded like Maddie. Was I trying to convince Father Michael or myself? I had started to doubt my instincts. As I'd learned about Woolf's aspirations, I recognized something we had in common: the more we questioned our purpose, the harder we worked to convince everybody we were unstoppable.

Father Michael pressed his lips together, pulling them inward. He held the door for me as I exited the classroom. Alone in the hallway, I realized it had been *my* body moving toward the door; Father Michael had simply followed my lead. Deep down, I must have known he could not, or would not, tell me what happened to Woolf.

THAT NIGHT, AFTER FaceTiming with Susanna, I read *The Spirit on the Ice* in one sitting.

The book ended with a passage that seemed like it could have been written about Woolf:

> *In their youth, all three of the boys had worshipped the spirit on the ice in separate but equally transcendent ways. They had given up their childhoods, their mothers, their friends. They had traded their boyhoods for something better. They were little hockey players, destined to become big hockey players— famous players, who hoisted the Stanley Cup over their heads, took it home to their mansions for a night at a time.* <u>*They lived for the game, and they were willing to die for it. Is that not religion?*</u>

Someone, maybe Vince, had underlined the last two sentences in red pen.

Declan Whiting had not intended it, but the book was a eulogy. Not for the son he didn't know would soon die but for a boyhood given over to hockey.

And yet I wasn't convinced hockey was the only god Woolf worshipped. Most of what he had done appeared to be an investment in his future: a top college, a career in finance, wealth, status. When someone is good at everything, people don't consider what underlies the confidence, the charisma, the *achievement*.

If Woolf was struggling, Susanna might have been the only one to see it, because for her, unlike almost everyone else around him, hockey did not create a massive blind spot. I looked back through my notes from our conversation earlier that evening and noticed: Susanna only cared about what Woolf was like off the ice.

Susanna Mercer
November 2004

SUSANNA PREFERRED SPENDING time at the Whitings' house, but when Woolf asked to come over to her house, she agreed.

He cut through the neighbor's yard, approaching the back of the house through a small opening in the hedges, which was the fastest way to get there from the east. She observed his arrival from her bedroom window. He came into view, then approached her dad, who was outside on the patio, where he sat most evenings. They shook hands.

By Susanna's junior year (Woolf's senior year), their families had grown enmeshed. A fifth chair had been added to the Whitings' dinner table. Mr. and Mrs. Whiting had invested their nest egg with Raymond Mercer Capital. They were so pleased with their returns they sent the Mercers a fruit basket.

Woolf still hadn't come inside after twenty minutes, so she went out, carrying two glasses. Woolf and her dad were sitting next to each other in chairs facing the covered pool, separated by a small table and a bottle of whiskey that her dad used to replenish his glass.

The night air was warm for early November, light-jacket weather. Woolf balanced a Mexican Coke on his armrest, which had come from the fridge, indicating he had entered the house while she was upstairs, retrieved it, and gone back out without alerting her to his presence.

Picking up the whiskey, she said, "You don't mind, do you?"

Her dad gestured toward the bottle, palm open. "Pour them small, okay?" he said. "Your mother would not approve."

Woolf blushed, as if he didn't deserve a jigger of Ray Mercer's fine whiskey, but he took the glass without a word.

"Do you two need more alone time?" Susanna asked.

"Stay," Woolf said. "I'm trying to figure out what to study at Notre Dame so I can be as successful as your dad."

Her father moved his glass away from his lips. "You've got so much ahead of you, kid. Fifty years, maybe sixty, unless you retire early."

"But what I do next matters," Woolf said.

"Every move you make matters in some small way. In the end, all you have is your reputation."

Susanna rolled her eyes. The boys were not looking at her.

Her father continued, "If you want my advice, study something that works your brain muscle. Think of your education like drills on the ice. You skate lines, you shoot, you rehearse set plays. When game day comes, you're ready to go, even if you don't know it yet. It's all about hard work, day in and day out. And your teammates. It's about them too, the guys who back you up." He glanced at the empty, lit house, like he was looking for his confidant, but her mother was not home.

Woolf mirrored her father's posture, the way his hand absently wrapped around his glass, his gaze, even his trademark expression (the corners of his mouth turned slightly downward). Maybe Woolf didn't want to be exactly like Ray Mercer, but he wanted his life, or he thought he did—why else would an eighteen-year-old boy convince himself to the point of certainty that he wanted a career in finance?

Woolf was proof you could live in a place like Sewickley and still feel poor. You felt that way because your girlfriend's family lived in a house designed by Louis Sullivan, which was a relatively minor holding compared to their summer home on Nantucket, and her father had a temperature-controlled room designed to store bottles from Kentucky, Japan, and Scotland, because his whiskey of choice was Old Weller, but the Japanese stuff was in vogue and sometimes the occasion called for Scotch.

"—private equity or hedge fund?" Woolf asked. Susanna had missed the first half of the question, but she got the gist.

"As an intellectual exercise? Hedge fund. But you should look at private equity. Here's what you do right out of school: Buy a business that's been family-owned for years. Not hard to find. Some old guy wants to retire and doesn't have a kid to take it over."

"Like Vince's dad," Woolf started.

"Funny you should mention it. He's been approached, but he's holding out. Thinks Vince will get his act together and run it someday."

Woolf laughed. Vince sold weed to their classmates and avoided schoolwork at all costs, but he was smarter than almost everybody.

"I know the guys who tried to buy him out," her father said. "They worked up a plan to expand into seven states. Anyway, that's where you get your start. You find one of these companies no one thinks twice about because they sell something forgettable but essential, and then you strip out the fat—get rid of the uncle or brother-in-law who hangs on but doesn't do anything—get a loan, leverage the business, expand. Build it into a multinational. It's not rocket science. A smart kid like you could do it." Her dad winked at Woolf, who appeared enthralled.

"Maybe Woolf should enjoy a party or two first. Stay up all night talking about David Foster Wallace or whatever college guys talk about." Susanna stood up. "Where's Mom, anyway?"

"St. Ignatius board meeting," her dad said.

"At nine o'clock?"

Her mother's influence over St. Ignatius's sizeable endowment intrigued Susanna. There was something entirely normal about it and yet unseemly, in the slick way that all business is unseemly.

Raymond Mercer Capital managed money for several of her mother's charity contacts. Her dad occasionally joked that Patricia Mercer was his rainmaker, which was more true than funny. Her parents' dealings were as unremarkable as Sewickley's clean air. Nobody noticed what they couldn't smell.

Taking Woolf's hand, Susanna said, "Let's go upstairs and talk."

"Uh-oh," Woolf said, looking at his mentor. "When she wants to talk—"

"You better listen," Mr. Mercer said. "The women are always right." His chuckle was either self-deprecating or condescending, possibly both.

"I love you, Pops," she said, "but please get your head out of the fifties, or the *women* will walk out on you."

"I have no female employees," he said, which wasn't true. He employed Esther. And his administrative assistant was an old church lady who looked like Bea Arthur. Presumably, he did not consider her a woman.

Susanna nodded toward the house. "Are you here to see *me* or my dad?"

Her father had started calling Woolf "the intern." On weekends, when Woolf wasn't playing hockey, he worked downtown at Raymond Mercer Capital. He'd be at the office for several hours at a time. Sometimes he bailed on plans with Susanna because the projects were time-sensitive. Once, she'd asked him what exactly he did for her dad. He pushed his laptop in front of her face and showed her a massive Excel spreadsheet. She clicked around for a few seconds before she pushed it back to him, bored.

Most girls would find him adorable. He *was* adorable, the kind of guy everybody's mom called a "great catch," which was also his primary deficiency: Susanna did not want anything her mother wanted. She occasionally thought about breaking up with him, but she worried about hurting him; under all his happy-go-lucky hockey-star-today-mogul-tomorrow charisma was the fragile heart of a boy who had been loved too much by his mother.

Her dad said, "I have to make a call," and he shook Woolf's hand like he was a business associate, not her boyfriend.

DOOR OPEN, FEET on *the ground* was her mother's rule. Lately, though, she hadn't been around much. Rules did not interest her father. Susanna closed the door and locked it, for good measure, even though her father would be out back on his phone for the remainder of the night.

They sat down on the edge of the bed. Woolf kept his feet on the floor. His hands were at his sides, supporting his weight, and he looked at the chalkboard wall, which Susanna had insisted on when she went through a doodling phase, though she'd never been much of an artist. Now the wall was blank but for a single Borges quote, which she had altered by adding a suggestive clause, like one does to the end of the message in a fortune cookie: "We do not exist in the majority of these times; in some you exist, and not I; in others I, and not you; in others, both of us. In the present one, which a favorable fate has granted me, you have arrived *in my bed*."

Up on the wall, the words felt more subversive than the sex itself, waiting for her parents to get over themselves long enough to notice them. But they never did. A week passed, then two. If Esther appreciated the passage, she didn't say anything.

Woolf wasn't looking at the words. He'd seen them before, and they'd talked about their forking paths. She climbed up and straddled him. Touching his chin with her thumb and forefinger, she squared up their faces. "Do you want to talk about it?" she asked.

He put his hands on her hips and looked her in the eye for the first time since he'd arrived. "Your dad has given me this opportunity to be his apprentice, and I can't waste it. Imagine what he's doing for all those people. Regular people—my folks. They'll be able to retire because of him." Woolf had become an unapologetic fanboy.

She swung her leg off him. He walked over to the chalk wall, acting like someone trying to calculate a tip and hold a conversation at the same time. Using different colors, he drew two line graphs. The first sloped downward, with a few peaks and troughs. The line on the second graph started at roughly the same place but sloped gently upward, never descending. He pointed to the second, "That's your dad," and then to the first, "And that's everybody else."

Want to know how to kill a mood? Hero-worship a girl's dad with a couple of pink-and-purple line charts on her bedroom wall. "Don't be so obsessed with money," she said. "It will ruin your life."

"Money is good. Your parents are philanthropists," he said.

"Can we talk about something else? Anything. Whatever. Hockey?"

"Sorry," he said, finally getting it. And then another Woolf, boy of every mother's dreams, perked up. "Hey, guess what? I talked to Coach, and he agreed to delay practice on Wednesday so we can cheer you on in the semis."

"The hockey team is going to watch a girls' soccer game?"

"Well, the first half at least. As much as we can."

"Wow," she said, "How'd you convince Coach Perone?"

"Fan support really helps," he said. "The guys will be loud."

"Don't make it about the *guys*, okay?" she said.

"We're just cheerleaders," he said.

Susanna went to the hockey games like everyone else, but she didn't make signs or howl when Woolf scored or checked someone hard into the boards. She made out with him after games, but not because they'd won, which was almost always. In fact, she would have liked Woolf better if he hadn't been a hockey star, because then she wouldn't have been the hockey star's girlfriend, which somehow diminished her as a soccer player, which seemed to matter only to her. Even her parents were too busy to attend her games.

The sound of the garage door opening meant her mom was home, which was fine, because they weren't doing anything anyway—not tonight. Susanna flung open the door. "You guys can come to the game if you want," she said. "Doesn't matter to me."

But it did. She played her worst game of the season. When the hockey team left at halftime, St. Ignatius was down by three. They scored twice in the second half but never hit their stride.

Later, the boys were praised for cutting practice to cheer them on. Heroes, regardless.

13

THIRTY-SIX HOURS AFTER my FaceTime with Susanna, she was due to arrive in Sewickley for ScoreFest. We'd made no plans to see each other, but I awaited her arrival with the fluttery anticipation of a paparazzo about to snap a photo of a celebrity. I'm not proud of how I felt. In general, I tried to maintain the steely nonchalance of a cool kid. But the truth was that I cared. I *wanted*. I wasn't rich enough not to.

Looking back, I'm not even sure what I wanted from Susanna. To be worthy of her time? For her to like me? Maybe I knew, deep down, that she was withholding something from me, and I wanted her to reveal the truth.

I arrived at the rink with Ingo. His plan was to put his gear on early, so he could listen to the speeches, ready to lace up his skates and play. The current players were scrimmaging the alumni after the presentation.

Before Ingo could dash off, I grabbed his hand. "Can I ask you something?"

"Shoot."

"What does Father Michael do for the team exactly?"

"Why?" Ingo had the bewildered expression of a guy who'd never thought about the organization that favored him.

"Just curious," I said.

"Guys go to him when they're off their game—missing shots, feeling slow, whatever. He analyzes opponents and strategizes set pieces. Sometimes he prays for us, and that's enough. People are superstitious about Father Michael. They don't think we can win without him. I don't really believe that, but whatever works, right? He's like a mascot, strategist, and spiritual advisor, all in one dude."

"Sounds like he has a lot of power."

"Not really," Ingo said. "He's like a mirror. He helps us see what's already there." He pounded his fist on his chest, unironically. Then he disappeared into the locker room.

WHEN I LOOKED up, I found myself in front of the Woolf Whiting Memorial. Woolf's presence occupied the cold, hollow building, and the chill of the place was as otherworldly as it was corporeal. Bowing my head, I thought about how people always said some variation of the same: "So tragic"/"So senseless"/"So young."

I made my way over to the bleachers, where I could hide out until everybody else arrived. I liked the quiet of the empty rink. The smell was familiar, rubber meets musk. I texted Shiv to let her know I was already down here.

Someone from maintenance had placed the podium and microphone in the foyer. It had been positioned in the center of the space, close to the memorial, which was the natural place for a speaker to stand.

Peering over the handrail, I saw her. She wore heels and a skirt suit, professional chic. Her wavy hair was down. She shook it out and flipped it back over her shoulder, like she'd just come up from the beach. Susanna Mercer belonged in a magazine, not in Sewickley.

I crouched down so she wouldn't see me and watched her drag the podium about six feet to the left, directly under the add-a-year banner that hung from the ceiling, displaying the years St. Ignatius had won the state championship. The five years following Woolf's death were often referred to as "a rebuilding period." After that, St. Ignatius started winning championships again. Several years appeared on the banner consecutively, followed by a two-year gap and then another series of wins through the prior year. The current year was conspicuously absent—we'd lost the quarterfinal game in a shootout—a disappointment Ingo would probably carry into old age.

Susanna placed three glasses on the shelf on the inside of the podium and filled the crystal pitcher at the water fountain. Placing the pitcher on the concrete ledge behind the podium, she paused to look down at the empty rink.

Before disappearing from sight, she left a stack of glossy programs on a table near the entrance. I hoisted my body over the rail and grabbed two, because I knew Shiv would forget to pick one up for herself.

The agenda was straightforward. The headmaster, Chad Campbell, would give the opening remarks. Predictably, he'd extol the ways in which fierce competition on the ice shaped the hearts and minds of young men (and women!). His speech would be the stuff everyone had heard a million times before but occasionally needed to be trumpeted by the voice of a charismatic lifer with eyes that smile and a flop of hair parted on the side—his pretty wife watching with their two toddlers in the back of the crowd—to remind themselves why they care about hockey more than, say, the *Summa Theologiae*. In the world of sports, there are no twists, only cliché, Queen's greatest hits blaring in the background.

St. Ignatius currently had two alumni in the NHL, but neither was on the agenda. An alum who played for SC Bern in Switzerland was listed next. I'd never heard of him. Naturally, he would talk about how St. Ignatius formed him as a pro hockey player, and as a man.

Finally, Raymond Mercer would take the podium. He'd explain that he didn't have an education from a place like St. Ignatius. He'd say words like *bootstrapped* and *self-made*. He'd thank God for his (implied) genius. Then he'd talk about his legacy. After his remarks, the VIPs would head to the new press box for cocktails, and the rest of us would make our way to the stands to watch the alumni take the ice with the St. Ignatius team.

Father Michael was listed as the referee for the game.

On the back of the program, Mercer was given credit for donating the capital for the expansion and modernization of the arena. Seating capacity had doubled; a state-of-the-art sound system boomed; a Jumbotron hung over center ice; a press box, perched above the stands, promised a heavenly view; the home locker room now boasted a cold plunge.

BY THE TIME Shiv arrived, the foyer was full and bodies spilled over into the stands. I handed her the program and watched her slip it into her bag without looking at it.

Headmaster Campbell delivered his remarks, as expected, and received polite applause.

The SC Bern player's speech was an overly long sports history lesson on the early-'90s Penguins, their back-to-back Stanley Cups, and Kevin Stevens's role. "Lemieux, Jágr, and Stevens," he said. "A line like that doesn't come along so often." He perseverated about Stevens—his injury, his addiction. I wasn't sure where he was going with it. He pointed up to the championship banner. "I don't know—I don't know if any of it matters, if the game matters. But on my deathbed, I'll look back and see the moves, the shots, the hits, the goals, and the wins!" He gestured at the facility. "Thanks, Mr. Mercer. Thanks for giving us home ice."

The crowd erupted into applause. Ray Mercer walked up to the podium, grasped the SC Bern player's hand and shook it vigorously before pulling him in for a hug, and then began clapping himself.

After their embrace, the hockey player leaned back to the microphone and said, "It is my pleasure to introduce the man who has made all of this possible. Without him, St. Ignatius would not exist." Again, the crowd cheered.

It was an interesting choice to give Mercer credit for the existence of not St. Ignatius *hockey*, but St. Ignatius. One could easily write these words off, coming from a moonstruck hockey player, but the underlying truth was undeniable. Without Raymond Mercer, St. Ignatius would have existed, as it had for over a hundred years, but it never would have become quite like the place we inhabited. Some other, imagined version—a Catholic school, a prep school, but not a hockey school—seemed less *itself*.

Mr. Mercer lifted the microphone out of its stand, pushing down the air with his empty hand to settle the crowd. "Now this is a party. A ScoreFest! A quarter century of hockey on campus—and a whole lot of goals!" he bellowed, extending his index finger as if it were a conductor's baton in conversation with the hollers and whistles, which grew louder as his arm rose higher until he closed his hand into a fist. He had everyone's attention.

Raymond J. Mercer: financier, philanthropist, man of the people, maestro of his own legacy. His voice swelled, as he spoke about himself—born and raised in Altoona by a single dad, a rep for Beech-Nut, who stocked grocery store shelves with jars of baby food. By age nine, he started hanging around the hockey rink after school, because no one was home and he had nowhere else to be. By age ten, he was sharpening rental skates in exchange for free ice time. He taught himself how to skate. He practiced stickhandling on his cul-de-sac. For a while, he thought he was pretty good. Then he met Danny Perone. Danny was better. He had the edge.

Mr. Mercer emphasized the importance of "building an edge." When he realized he'd never do it in hockey, he did it in finance. The hockey team was St. Ignatius's edge. Or rather, the endowment was the edge. The former begot the latter. He didn't say this expressly, but it was there, like a layer of permafrost, close to the surface.

He paused. It was a long pause, long enough for the crowd to fall silent again. Then he said, "A quarter century. It's been a real humdinger, hasn't it?" People cheered. "California burned. Texas flooded. A sinkhole swallowed a bus right here in Pittsburgh. We survived a deadly virus—downright biblical, 'the pestilence that stalks in the darkness, the plague that destroys at midday.'" His voice boomed. "And you know what we're still doing? Playing hockey. Winning. Winning. Winning! We've been to hell"—his way of acknowledging Woolf, Colton, and Kyle—"and you know what we did when we got back? We put the puck in the net."

A voice from the back of the crowd interrupted. "Are you suggesting winning hockey games forgives the deaths of three boys?"

Caught off guard by the interruption, Mr. Mercer winced and dropped back on his heels. He turned his head toward the heckler. I couldn't see her from where I was standing.

He looked down at the podium, as if to find his place on a note card. His head began to shake, too vigorously. He might have ignored her and rolled on, but something made him address her. "Excuse me, but if you are suggesting what happened to those boys has something to do with what we've built here"—he paused to rotate his arm like a cantor soliciting a response from the congregation—"you do not understand causation. Our boys are leaders, on and off the ice. They're in the NHL, pro leagues in Europe. They are captains of industry—executives and lawyers and politicians. Do you have any idea who is about to take the ice for the alumni? I'll tell you. A CEO of a Fortune 500 company, a congressman, a surgeon, a pro hockey player." He winked at the SC Bern player. "So don't tell me there's something wrong with winning."

A few people clapped.

"Say his name," the woman shouted. "Say my son's name. Woolf Whiting!"

I felt Shiv's hand on my arm. Mo Whiting was in the room with us.

"Monica. This is not the time." He knew her. Red veins in his eyes were now visible, even from the middle of the crowd, where I stood. Either he had a mild case of conjunctivitis, or he was about to lose control.

"When is 'the time'? Your family has never publicly acknowledged my son," she shouted.

Mr. Mercer looked at Susanna and smirked. "Do we need to call security?"

St. Ignatius did have a security guard. His name was Rob. He was friendly if spoken to but mostly invisible. He rode around campus on a bicycle, and he could get up the hill in under twenty seconds. His most memorable attribute was the size of his calves. People said he used to be Secret Service for Obama, or maybe CIA. When asked about his past, he always said "classified," his expression blank, like he'd been properly trained to keep a secret. No one knew if he was joking. Whatever he did before, his job at St. Ignatius must have been a vacation. He only worked during school hours—I'd never seen him at a game or any other evening event—and his role mostly involved optics. The parents felt better with him there.

So even though I knew better, because it was after five o'clock, I looked around to see if Rob was standing silently in the back. He was not.

Mo Whiting had made her way through the crowd and now stood near the front, a few feet from the podium.

Suddenly, she lunged toward Mr. Mercer, grabbing the microphone from his hand. Her body immediately lurched backward, as if she had anticipated a more difficult extraction. Mr. Mercer steadied himself against the podium.

Turning to the crowd, she brought the microphone to her mouth, close enough to lick it. "I had to see it for myself," she said. "ScoreFest. My God. The invitation came from *Susanna Mercer*, asking us to celebrate twenty-five years of St. Ignatius hockey, six seasons undefeated, seven state championships. And here you all are. Well, let me tell you why I'm here. Eighteen years ago, my son, Woolf Whiting, didn't take the ice for the face-off." She approached Susanna. "How dare you celebrate!"

Everyone in the audience looked on, rapt.

"Are you done?" Mr. Mercer demanded.

"The only explanation for all this—*this* ridiculous public relations campaign for the purpose of putting Ray Mercer in the public eye, to take credit for a hockey program that, while it might be considered successful on the ice, has failed these boys time and again—is that it is part of an elaborate—" She continued to talk, but the mike cut out. Father Michael had disconnected the receiver.

Suddenly, Monica Whiting rushed forward, arms outstretched, palms up, in what could only be described as an unathletic Wonder Woman dive. Susanna couldn't keep her balance on those high heels, and she fell back, catching herself on the concrete floor with her arms.

Shiv leaned over to me and said, "Catfight." But neither woman was really fighting. Hair was not pulled. Punches were not thrown. They clung to each other, like each was trying to stop the other from hurting herself.

Susanna pulled herself away. She stood up and adjusted her skirt, smoothing it back into place with her hands. Ignoring everyone else, she looked down at her attacker on the floor. "Please, let me—"

"You killed my son. I can't prove it, but you had something to do with it. Where did you go? Why wouldn't you talk to me? Explain yourself!"

Susanna scanned the crowd, looking from side to side, front to back, until finally her eyes rested on my face. Her hand covered her mouth.

Even now, after thinking about what happened next for some time, it is difficult to describe. It happened in that one second, maybe more—enough time to perceive a car levitating. When Susanna moved her hand from her mouth, my eye was drawn to the slight cleft in her chin. From there, I traced the sharp line of her jaw, the height of her cheekbones, the wide almond shape of her eyes. It was like looking in a mirror, wondering: *How can this be my face?*

Before she opened her mouth to speak, I was overcome with a feeling of transcendence, a deep understanding that goes beyond reason and requires no evidence. I understood why she'd been so nervous to speak with me on our first FaceTime call, why she'd acted like I was the one with all the power, why she'd asked so many questions about me. I understood that she'd known me before I knew her. We were connected.

In that moment, in front of a crowd of people, Susanna gasped, "I was pregnant."

When the water pitcher shattered on the floor, everyone froze. Mr. Mercer stood over it, his hand still outstretched. "That's enough," he said.

The crowd fell silent. All eyes were on him, the great benefactor, standing over broken crystal.

The athletic director, Mr. Houser, helped Mo Whiting to her feet, turning her body in the direction of the door. She didn't pull away. He said something in her ear as he escorted her out.

Susanna stood still, a pool of water from the broken pitcher running under her heels.

Father Michael must have turned the microphone back on, because his melancholy voice came over the speaker, apologizing for the interruption. He said, "Brothers and sisters, please put your phones away." For the first time, I realized people had been recording. When they didn't immediately comply, Father Michael added, "There is nothing to see here. Please, show compassion for a grieving mother. Respect the privacy of those in our community. I shouldn't have to remind you that you are all St. Ignatius men and women."

Nothing to see here? Au contraire, Father Michael. People may not have known what they'd just seen, but they knew it was something.

The last thing I heard him say was, "Play on."

The skaters took the ice. The world may be on fire, but the game must go on.

14

AFTER SCOREFEST, I assumed Susanna hopped the first flight back to San Francisco. She made no immediate attempt to contact me. To explain. Did I deserve an explanation? Did I want one? When Mom confirmed it—Susanna Mercer was my birth mother—she wanted to know how I felt. She asked in a million different ways.

I had no answers for her. I'll be honest: I felt like a fraud. Like *I* was a fraud. Like I'd been one person for seventeen years, Frankie, and now I was someone else—let's call her Francesca. I thought I wanted to know this Francesca so I could reject her, but I see now that it was more complicated.

According to my mom, only a handful of people knew the story of my birth parents. Susanna, her parents, their lawyer, and Mom were contractually bound by the information. But Susanna also told Maddie and Vince she was pregnant, because she needed their support. If Susanna had asked permission first, Mom would have advised her not to tell anybody. For years, she feared that Monica and Declan Whiting would find out and file for custody.

For her part, Mom never told a soul. That is, until the day after Kyle Murphy took his own life, when Father Michael visited our house. She confided in him then that the tragedy of Woolf's death had led, indirectly, to her ability to adopt me.

I asked if she had considered telling me when I started digging into Woolf's death. I felt like she owed me that. She reminded me that I hadn't wanted to know the identities of my biological parents. I had been clear about this decision when I turned sixteen. But she also admitted that she worried our relationship would change when I found out. And it would change, of course. But not in the way she'd feared.

When Susanna blurted out the words "I was pregnant," I saw her as the girl she was when she carried me—afraid, vulnerable, so obviously alone—but I also saw her as tired. Tired of the secret, tired of keeping the secret from Mo Whiting, tired of keeping me from Mo, *my grandmother*, or maybe of keeping Mo from me, and, most of all, tired of not knowing if her decision was right or wrong. I think it was the exhaustion that broke her, not the secret itself. And when she finally spoke those words, she appeared to regain some strength, as if she'd received a jolt of adrenaline and, after all this time, she was ready. Ready for what, I did not know.

The pregnancy was Susanna's secret to tell, but my identity was not. Mo now knew she had a grandchild, or at least, that the possibility had once existed inside Susanna's womb. Armed with this new information, Mo immediately filed a petition seeking a court order to release my information. I might not have learned of the petition until later, but Maddie had just reviewed a copy of the document, and she could not avoid the topic when we spoke on the phone.

MADDIE WAS MY aunt; I was her niece. There were questions I wanted to ask her. Did she consider reaching out at any point? When I turned sixteen? After I contacted her, why didn't she tell me who she was? Who *I* was? How did she keep the secret from her parents for so long? Why did she agree to it in the first place? All these questions and more were like static noise in the background. I tried to ignore them so I could maintain my composure and keep talking. The talking felt like the most important thing.

Her voice quivered when she asked, "How are you?"

I didn't answer.

After a long pause, she said, "Mo's attorney is a hack."

I had no idea what she was talking about.

She continued, "No ethical attorney would go along with this. Mo wrote it: her theories, her demands, her syntax. I can't believe he agreed to file it. He should be sanctioned by the court."

"What does it say?" I asked.

Maddie's description of the petition was convoluted. Later, I could only remember a few of the details she offered, and even those, I did not fully understand. "Baseless claims with no evidence," she repeated. One of those claims was about my existence. Mo knew only that Susanna had been pregnant. She did not know I had been carried to term. She did not know about my adoption. She had no way of verifying the identity of my father. But the entire petition was predicated on these facts.

According to Maddie, Mo's petition detailed the wrongful death of her son and claimed the motive behind the murder was the elimination of his paternal rights. Was Mo grappling in the dark for something that wasn't there? Or was something there and just out of her reach?

"My God," Maddie said. "I can't believe she went there. I thought she'd moved on from making wild accusations."

"Would it be easier if we told her who I am?" I asked.

"Don't worry about the petition. The Mercers' attorneys will handle it," Maddie said. I could tell she was sorry she brought it up. She was unable or unwilling to give me advice on the possibility of meeting my grandmother.

I asked her, "Could it hurt?" But I already knew meeting Mo would hurt. I just didn't know how much.

"When you're young, you look at your parents and think, 'How can you go to church every Sunday and then do that?' But later, you realize they were simply interacting with the world as they found it. Hypocrisy starts looking a little more like exigent circumstance." Maddie was endearingly oblivious to her own lawyerspeak. "When I finally understood that being alive is just the experience of one exigent circumstance after another, I forgave Mo for her obsessions, and Big

D for leaving, and I started to forgive Woolf for dying, which I'll probably be doing in one way or another for the rest of my life."

There was a lull in the conversation, and then Maddie quickly transitioned to the past, to where we left off the last time we spoke. Her voice mellowed.

Looking back, I believe her reaction to the petition was connected to the choice she made to keep the secret of Susanna's pregnancy from her own mother. Blaming Mo and her attorney for their desperation was easier than reckoning with her own betrayal of her mother. I did not yet understand the magnitude of that betrayal. I had not considered what my mom and I owed Maddie for keeping Susanna's secret—which was everything.

Madeline Whiting
February 2005

WOOLF AND SUSANNA broke up in the most public way possible: at a school dance.

The Clipper, St. Ignatius's winter dance, was held on the eponymous boat that cruised the three rivers of Pittsburgh. Unlike prom, the girls asked the boys to the Clipper. Maddie took the tradition seriously enough to avoid it altogether sophomore and junior year. Now a senior, she decided attending the dance was a small humiliation, less pathetic than not going.

She asked Vince to the dance as they smoked a bowl by the railroad tracks. "As friends," she emphasized. Without a word, he dropped his lighter into his pocket and extended his hand to shake on it. Just friends.

When she got home, she found Woolf and Big D sitting at the kitchen table together.

"I need a dress for the Clipper," Maddie proclaimed.

"Don't go overboard," Woolf said. "Vince will be wearing his Patagonia."

"How'd you—"

"I know everything," he said. Susanna had told him.

Maddie pictured the pea-green fleece that Vince wore over his button-down shirt every day. "I still need a dress. Susanna bought hers at Saks." In addition to the Clipper, which was open to all students, St. Ignatius held a junior/senior prom. If a girl went to all four Clippers and two proms, she would need six new dresses that no one else had.

"Great idea," Big D said. "Borrow one from Susanna."

They did not wear the same size.

"What are you wearing, Woolf?" Maddie asked.

"Jacket and tie, purchased with my own money."

Big D said, "Mom will take you shopping," leaving out the obvious: *Not at Saks.*

"Susanna said she'd help me find something. I just need a credit card."

"Ask your mother."

Woolf said, "I'll need the car for the dance."

"Everyone's going to be jealous of your sweet ride." Maddie nudged Woolf with her elbow.

"What's wrong with the wagon?" Big D said. "We drive American cars."

"American *car*," Maddie said. "Singular. We drive *an* American car, which was made overseas and assembled here."

"You can take the car, but you'll have to drive your sister too. I don't trust Vince behind the wheel."

Big D was right about that. Vince would be high at the dance.

Woolf said, "One day, I'm going to buy Big D his dream car."

"A used Chrysler minivan?" Maddie suggested.

"1977 Ford Bronco in tangerine orange," Big D said, without lifting his head from the newspaper he'd been reading intermittently throughout the conversation.

THE NIGHT OF the dance, Maddie and Woolf left home together. When they arrived at Susanna's house, Woolf knocked on the front door, holding a corsage in one hand and straightening his tie with the other. Maddie trailed a few feet behind.

Mrs. Mercer stood at the door, motioning to her: "Come in, Madeline. Let me see how beautiful you look." Maddie and Woolf followed her through the house to the kitchen, where Mr. Mercer sipped whiskey. Susanna was still upstairs getting ready.

Woolf asked a question about rates on CDs, and Mr. Mercer muttered something about taxes and overhead. Big D never said it outright, but he felt superior to men like Mr. Mercer, whom he called "chronically tax-avoidant" as if it were diabetes. Raymond Mercer Capital operated out of Antigua, a known tax haven.

Woolf had mastered a powerful technique of preparing questions that made him look intelligent and informed but, more importantly, made adults feel admired. Watching Woolf operate, Maddie had learned simple flattery was not enough—to really win people over, you had to make them feel like you wanted to become them.

Her brother prematurely possessed the thing that most people acquire at some point between MBA programs and making unholy sums of money: a self-fulfilling sense that the world belonged to him. He was really American in this way—able to overlook obvious character flaws in favor of productivity. When he teased Maddie, he often called her "bitter." It was his favorite insult, because it was the thing that separated them.

Calling her bitter just made her more bitter.

Mrs. Mercer handed her a Coke in a glass bottle—cap already removed—and put out a series of small crystal bowls filled with nuts and pretzels and chocolate-covered espresso beans. Olives were presented in a long, skinny boat with a matching bowl for pits. The hors d'oeuvres would have been more elaborate, but it was a Saturday, and Esther didn't work weekends.

Woolf held a Coke bottle in one hand and grabbed a handful of cashews with the other. He thanked Mrs. Mercer with the sincere nonchalance of a guy who'd been there before. Of course, Maddie had been there too—she'd spent most of last summer with Susanna, in bikinis by the pool. But Mr. and Mrs. Mercer had been mostly absent. On one lazy afternoon, Maddie asked if they ever came home, and Susanna shrugged and said, "I can feel when they're close, because my cortisol spikes."

For fun, Maddie looked at Mr. Mercer and said, "Woolf wants to be just like you, but our dad thinks paying taxes is an ethical imperative."

"Maddie—"

"It's okay, Woolf." Mr. Mercer stepped back and looked at her. "Lawyer, right? You want to be a lawyer one day? Then you'll learn to do your due diligence. My clients trust me as the custodian of their life savings. If not for regular people, like your parents, I'd have sailed off on a yacht a long time ago."

Maddie marveled at how someone so rich could see himself as a martyr. The man was a Capitalist. He drank expensive whiskey and smoked cigars. He supported politicians who opposed taxes. But he was not a hypocrite. The best thing about assholes is their consistency.

Susanna appeared, holding the silk skirt of her dress as she carefully descended the stairs. It was a two-piece, which was the hot trend among St. Ignatius girls, because the floor-length skirts were classy, but depending on the way their bodies moved, their midriffs showed.

Mr. Mercer stood up and put his hand on Woolf's shoulder. Following their eyes, Maddie looked at Susanna too. Her thick golden locks fell halfway down her back. With delicate fingers, she tucked her hair behind her ears. A tendril dislodged and fell over her eyes. She formed her lips into an O and blew it off her face. The hair flew up and fell right back down. She tucked it behind her ear again.

They took pictures in various configurations—the girls, the couple, the siblings, and all together. Woolf smiled for the camera, but in nearly every shot, his eyes were on Susanna. If Vince had been there, the whole situation would have been more bearable, but Woolf had strategically planned to pick Vince up after Susanna. He did his best to keep the Mercers' world separate, which Maddie thought was a desperate, try-hard thing to do.

Maddie imagined what it was like to be Susanna, but to do so she had to disassociate what she saw—perfection—from what she knew: Susanna envied *her*. How many times had Susanna said, "Let's go to your house," where there was no pool, no surround sound, no Mexican Cokes in the fridge? How many times had she curled up with Jágr on the couch, stroking his head, asking him to be her "therapy animal"? Once, she'd even hypothesized that Woolf would make a better brother than boyfriend.

But she couldn't possibly know what it meant to have a brother, all those puny torments, like the way he'd rub his hands in her face when they stank from his hockey gloves. The first time he did it, the joke was a little bit funny. The second and third time, it was slightly less funny. But he knew that if he kept it up, again and again, Maddie would go a little bit crazy, and then the joke would become downright hilarious.

On the way out, Mrs. Mercer observed Maddie touching one of the tiles on the wall above the counter and said, "Reclaimed from an Italian palazzo." After closing her eyes for a moment, Mrs. Mercer opened them to look out the window over the sink, as if she'd just returned to Sewickley.

WHEN HE CLIMBED in next to her in the back seat of the wagon, Vince said, "Hey, DubDub, drop me and Mad Dawg at Eat'n Park." He looked at Maddie. "My van's parked there. We can grab a burger, and then I'll drive us to the dance."

"I told Big D I'd drive you guys," Woolf said. "Reservation for four at Monterey Bay."

"Why's your van at Eat'n Park?" Maddie asked.

"Long story," Vince said.

"Lemme guess," Woolf said. "You left it there last night because you were too messed up to drive home."

"I was fine," Vince said. "But there were two cops sitting in a booth by the door, and I was pretty sure they were waiting to follow me out, which was shady. If you're a cop and you think a guy's not good to drive, why not say something before he fucking drives? Wouldn't that be better police work? More civic-minded or whatever? I was not going to be entrapped, so I walked home."

"That's not entrapment," Woolf said.

Vince looked to Maddie for corroboration. She said, "He's right. It's not."

"Whatever, Stabler and Benson, that's not the point."

"Woolf, it's fine," Maddie said. "I won't tell Mom and Dad."

"No," Woolf said. "I'll pick up the tab, okay?" His hand was on Susanna's headrest, and he turned around to look at Maddie to show her he was serious.

"Sure," Vince said. "I'll eat overpriced fish on top of a hill, as long as you're paying." He pulled out his pipe, but Woolf said he couldn't smoke weed in their parents' station wagon.

"Why are we in this heap, anyway?" Vince asked. "Couldn't Susanna's dad hook us up with the Ferrari for our special night out?"

"The wagon will get us there," Woolf said, petting the dash as if it were Jágr's head.

Maddie handed Vince a flask filled with vodka. He took a drink and passed it up to Susanna, who cocked her head and let the alcohol drop into her mouth without touching her lips to the rim.

The drive from Sewickley through downtown Pittsburgh was about twenty minutes. After circling through the three passengers twice, the flask was empty. Reaching down into a canvas tote, which Mr. and Mrs. Mercer hadn't noticed being smuggled out of their house, Susanna pulled out a bottle of whiskey from her dad's collection. Three Japanese characters and the English words small batch were printed on the label.

Vince held it out in front of his face, as if he could read the characters. "A thing of beauty," he said.

Susanna responded, "Only the best for my friends."

- - - - - - - - -

THEY DECIDED TO park at Station Square and take the Duquesne Incline up Mount Washington. It would have been easier to drive all the way up, but they hadn't been on the incline since they were kids, and nostalgia had taken hold, thanks to Susanna's whiskey.

By the time they arrived at the restaurant, Woolf's sobriety was the chasm between them. Maddie stared bleary-eyed at the menu. Vince asked the waiter which fish was the freshest. He replied condescendingly, "It's all fresh, kid." Without flinching, Vince ordered the fifty-dollar Wagyu rib eye.

Maddie consumed about a quarter of her arctic char and pulverized the rest, pushing it around her plate. Vince obliterated his steak, leaned back in his chair, and placed his hand on her lap. He caressed her upper thigh a few times before pushing his hand between her crossed legs. Only the thin silky fabric of her dress and a couple of inches separated his fingers from her underwear.

He'd never touched her like that before. She didn't know if his hand operated by his own will or at the whim of the alcohol, but she didn't care. He removed it when his phone buzzed in his pocket.

"Ouch." Vince looked up from his phone toward Woolf, who had kicked him under the table.

"Dude, put away your phone," Woolf said. "We're not meeting up with Wayne to buy weed before the dance."

"*You're* not meeting up with Wayne," Vince corrected. He gestured toward the girls. "We'll do what we want."

"If you want to hang out with my sister and my girlfriend, Wayne's not invited."

Vince put the phone in his pocket. "Fine. You guys are all snobs."

Susanna ordered the toasted coconut pot de crème, which was basically Eat'n Park's coconut cream pie deconstructed, and the flourless chocolate cake, not because she planned to eat any of it. She always overordered and graciously picked up the tab.

When the desserts arrived, Woolf insisted that Susanna have a bite, but she refused. He loaded up a fork and forced it toward her. She refused again. He told her how delicious it was. She said no again, firm and annoyed. Finally, he asked her what her problem was, and she said she wasn't hungry. "You ordered it," he protested.

This went on for what seemed like a long time. During the argument, Vince's phone buzzed again, and he silenced it.

Maddie said, "Woolf, drop it. She ordered these for us." She shoved a huge spoonful of the pot de crème into her own mouth. She scooped up another and shoved it toward her brother's mouth. He turned his head away. In an effort to grab the spoon from Maddie's hand, he flung the coconut cream into Susanna's lap.

"Are you going to apologize?" Maddie snapped.

"For what?"

"Being a dick."

"She's always ordering stuff she doesn't want," Woolf said.

"I'll pay for it," Susanna said. "I'll pick up the whole tab. Don't worry about it."

Vince pulled out his phone to text Wayne back. A clump of cream landed on his face, and he looked up and saw Susanna's raised hand covered in the stuff. He wiped it off and licked it. "Not bad."

"You're making a mess," Woolf said.

"You need to chill out, or Susanna's gonna dump you," Maddie said, though she didn't mean it.

"We're not her charity case," Woolf said.

Susanna rolled her eyes. "Why? Are you on Heather's dad's payroll now?"

Heather was a St. Ignatius sophomore and the daughter of Joseph Mackey, the famous Penguins player, who had retired and become a Hollywood financier.

Everyone looked at Woolf.

Susanna was drunk but coherent. "One internship isn't enough? Does my dad know you're moonlighting with Joe Mackey?"

"You don't get it, Susanna. You couldn't possibly understand. Everything is given to you. Oh, you want a summer internship? Ray Mercer can make a phone call. Well, my dad can't make phone calls. I do things myself. I need to network. Heather's dad is helping me. What's the big deal?"

"Heather is in love with you, Woolf. You're using her."

"I'm not using anybody!" he yelled.

"Woolf," Maddie whispered, "Maybe take this outside?"

"No," Woolf said, "She needs to understand."

Susanna said, "We're in high school, Woolf. You don't need to network."

"No," he said, "*You* don't need to network. You don't need to do anything. You can lie by the pool all summer. Who cares? When you decide you want a job, it will be there."

"That doesn't give you the right to lead Heather on," she said.

"What are you talking about? You're crazy."

But Susanna wasn't crazy. She was right. Over the last few weeks, Woolf had been at Heather's house more than he'd been with Susanna. He'd flirted with Heather at Mickey D's. They'd been hanging around the hockey rink together.

After Woolf paid the tab, Susanna looked at him and said, "We need to talk."

Their foursome parted ways outside the restaurant. They had to take the incline back down to Station Square, where the Clipper ship was docked. Woolf said they'd meet Vince and Maddie on the boat.

"Don't be late," Maddie said.

A BREEZE TOUSLED Vince's hair. He pushed it back with both hands, tilting his head to the sky. Leaning against Maddie weightlessly, he said, "Killer night."

It was cold but clear, and the view of the Pittsburgh skyline was magical.

Maddie looped her hand through Vince's arm and held on to the crook of his elbow.

They found a deserted park nearby, a postage stamp of green grass with an old playground, badly in need of maintenance. Two swings beckoned, and without saying a word, they moved toward them. Vince sat down next to her and wrapped his arms around the chains. He packed his pipe with a little nug and complained he couldn't get more before the boat departed. After testing it, he passed the bowl with his lighter.

Looking out beyond the precipice of Mount Washington, Maddie witnessed her city as if in a time-lapse. First, the rivers cut through the hills of Appalachia, untouched except by those who fished from their waters and lived on their shores. A vast wealth of coal and gas, buried in seams and trapped in strata of shale and sandstone, awaited extraction. Next, the coal barges came, floating downstream beyond the smog of the city. Then, tracing the winding corridor of the Monongahela, her eyes descended to the Cathedral of Learning in Oakland, a short walk from Mo's office. In the foreground, the US Steel Tower arose, dominating the skyline, a monument to a bygone era. Now, Carnegie and Frick and Mellon were ghosts floating through the clean, clear air of the present, their names adorning the city's museums and symphony halls and mansions, the illusion of human decency purchased through the generous support of the arts.

The time-lapse ended where it had begun, at the convergence of three great rivers, forming the Golden Triangle. For many years, in her most obliterating moments of grief, Maddie would imagine herself back in this place, next to Vince on a swing in a dilapidated playground at the top of the world, less than an hour before the Clipper ship set off down the river—when Woolf was still alive and her family hadn't yet fractured, with Jágr, home on the couch, anticipating their return—Pittsburgh revealing itself all at once as the center of an American empire and the modest town where she grew up. And she would be released from the unbearable present to that dimension beyond, where she could have a brother again.

WHEN THEY'D FINISHED smoking, they took the incline back down to Station Square.

They ended up alone in the cable car. Vince plopped down, facing the skyline, his arm outstretched on the back of the bench. Maddie nestled into him, resting her head on his shoulder. "This isn't the worst place we could be," he said.

He seemed unsure of himself. She could smell weed on his breath and his clothes, and in his hair, which mixed with the scent of his cologne.

For no reason, they laughed hysterically. She wanted him to kiss her then, which may have been because of the weed or because she'd wanted it since she was twelve.

He said, "We could blow off the dance, you know."

"Where would we go instead?"

He shrugged, "Nah, we better go. Woolf would kill me if I ran off with his little sister."

She wanted to be anybody other than "Woolf's little sister."

"The view's okay," he said, looking down into her face with his glassy eyes. "I like your dress."

"Thanks," she said. "Susanna bought it for me."

The cable car inched downward.

By the time they arrived at the dock at Station Square to board the Clipper ship, Woolf and Susanna were already there. As soon as Susanna saw Maddie, she grabbed her arm. "Come on," she said. "You can be my date tonight." Ms. Northrup, one of the chaperones, greeted them as they climbed on the boat. The boys trailed behind.

The DJ played a mix of pop and hip-hop, and a few late-twentieth-century classics canonized by the high-school-dance industrial complex. Woolf spent the entire night dancing with Heather Mackey.

Everybody noticed. One after another, people kept coming up to Maddie and whispering, "Did Susanna and Woolf break up?"

If Susanna cared, she didn't let on. Vince was too awkward or too cool to be seen on the dance floor, so the girls spent most of the night dancing with each other.

Woolf dropped off Vince first. Then he pulled into their driveway and let Maddie out before taking Susanna home and circling back.

Maddie never discussed the breakup with Woolf, but she knew how much it had hurt him. Brothers and sisters are especially loath to admit their true feelings. Theirs is the most cryptic of all bonds. Sisters talk things out. Brothers fight them out. But a brother and a sister can only *know*, and it is the knowing that reinforces the connection.

For this reason, Maddie would never tell her brother the truth: She loved him more than anyone in the world. Her silence on the matter was not among her regrets. She assumed he knew. Somehow, through the circuitry of their sibling brains, he knew, as she knew.

15

A FRENCH BAKERY had recently opened on Walnut Street, around the corner from the bookstore. On rainless days, the aroma of yeast, butter, and vanilla wafted down the block. Maybe smelling like a French bakery had always been Sewickley's destiny, and knowing, finally, who I was, granddaughter of an industrialist, the kind who dealt in interest and leverage, rather than iron and steel—the modern kind—made me feel at once repelled and more at home.

Shiv picked me up at my house. Mom was using our car, and riding my bike wasn't practical, because it had been raining for eight consecutive days.

"Should I start calling you Francesca now?" she asked when I climbed into her car. "It's actually a decent name for an heiress."

"Shut up, no."

"Why aren't you better at sports?" She continued to probe my biological inheritance.

"I'm on the track team."

"We lost every meet this season," she said.

"So far," I added.

"What?"

"We've lost every meet *so far*. Losing is not a foregone conclusion."

At the intersection of Broad and Beaver, a pickup truck pulled up on our tail. The light turned green, but Shiv wasn't paying attention. She said, "They were all so willing to drop everything to talk to you. All three of them, holy shit, they knew all along. I mean, obviously

Susanna knew, seeing as you arrived in this world through her vagina. But Maddie and Vince? They knew too. But Mo Whiting didn't. Which means her own daughter kept this whopper of a secret from her for like eighteen years. I mean, she has a *grandchild*."

I pictured the look on Mo Whiting's face when she learned Susanna had been pregnant. It was the look of someone who had lived for years in one reality and then, out of nowhere, saw a ripple in the fabric, a doorway into another reality. She had come to speak her mind, but she'd left speechless.

I was the living, breathing remnant of her dead son. I shared his DNA. But, for all those years, I could have sat down next to my biological grandmother at Starbucks and she would not have given me so much as a sideways glance.

"You can go," I said, pointing at the green light.

Up ahead, a woman with a good parking spot unlocked her car. Shiv flicked on her turn signal. We stopped a few feet behind the spot, in front of the partially boarded-up storefront of a gourmet dog bakery called Howl.

It had been one of those minimalist designer shops that displayed its products—dog treats—on shelves like crystal figurines. A sign hanging in the web-cracked window read: INDULGE YOUR BEST FRIEND WITH A CUSTOM BIRTHDAY CAKE! Shiv always thought it was a money-laundering operation.

The store's vandals stole nothing. The treats were taken from their pristine shelves, piled in the large open space in the middle of the store, and set ablaze—each five-dollar item burned to oblivion, sending the message that people love their dogs more than they love each other.

Shiv turned to look at the guy behind us, who honked politely, then less politely. "Is that the same truck? Why doesn't he go around us?" she said.

He honked again.

Ignoring the torrential rain, Shiv unlatched her seat belt, lowered her window, leaned out, and flipped the guy the bird. She put the window back up and repositioned her body in the seat.

The guy laid on the horn like Kenny G playing the saxophone. At home, I could walk all the way up the stairs and shut my bedroom door, and he'd still be holding one note. My mom's taste in music was unconscionable.

Shiv proceeded to calmly parallel park, like a horn wasn't blasting inches from her bumper. If parallel parking were a personality test, Shiv would have gotten an A+ for her confidence and can-do attitude. Most people think young women are bad drivers, because they are easily distracted and lack depth perception, but most people don't know Shiv. She's always had excellent depth perception.

The guy put down the passenger-side window of his truck as he passed. He motioned to Shiv, rotating his arm in the air like he was cranking an old manual window. A rosary hung from his rearview mirror. He had a mustache and a mullet. She obliged, cracking her window. I worried he would say something offensive to the brown girl who had taken the good parking spot, but he flashed a friendly smile and said, "Wanted to alert you ladies that your taillight is out." A Taylor Swift song blasted from his speakers.

"Huh," Shiv said. Then we shared a belly laugh, which of all intimacies was the one that made me believe nothing could ever come between us.

Before we got out of the car, Shiv told me she'd reached out to Heather Mackey. Based on her IMDb page, I was confident Heather would have no interest in talking to her. She was basically famous. She had produced several sports documentaries and anthologies, taking home multiple Emmys. Her first project listed was a documentary on the Pens in the '90s—her dad's team. "Still no word back," Shiv said.

"What could she tell us anyway?" I asked.

"Maybe she was the last person to see Woolf alive."

INSIDE THE BAKERY, the owners were in the open kitchen, absorbed in conversation about the price of butter or QuickBooks, or whatever people who owned bakeries discussed, but because they were speaking in French, it sounded like they were passionately in love. Shiv loved love. She also loved croissants made by French people.

The woman approached the counter, wiping her hands on her apron. Shiv ordered a chocolate croissant. I asked for the ham and Gruyère. "And two chai lattes," Shiv added, pulling out her credit card and swiping it before I could protest. The chai lattes were five dollars each. I worked summers and holidays at a boutique for eight dollars an hour, so it was not lost on me that Shiv had just burned through the equivalent of approximately three hours of my labor, without giving the sum a second thought.

The woman handed us our croissants on plates that looked like they had been hand-painted in France and told us she would bring our lattes to the table.

"I went by the Mercers' house last night," Shiv confessed.

"Did you—"

"No. Calm down. What would I say anyway? I snuck into the backyard, which is, by the way, obscenely nice, even for Sewickley. Mr. Mercer was sitting by the pool. It was weird."

"Why is it weird to sit by your obscenely nice pool?"

"The pool was covered." Shiv pulled her sweater closed and shivered. "I mean, let's say the guy likes being poolside, even though it's like fifty degrees outside at night, fine. But he didn't have a cell phone or a newspaper. He held a glass of whiskey in his hand and stared into the abyss—not the pool, which was covered—the metaphorical abyss, for over an hour."

Depressed rich guy sips whiskey alone: Not exactly national news. "You were there for over an hour?"

"I almost left several times, but I kept thinking something would happen. Like Mrs. Mercer would come out and talk to him about what happened at ScoreFest, or his phone would ring in his pocket and he'd answer it. But no."

"So you crouched behind a bush and watched Mr. Mercer do nothing?"

"Frankie, the man is a zombie. He looks nothing like the Raymond Mercer on the internet—the one with the Robert Downey Jr. man-of-the-people vibe. He's more like—"

"Ben Affleck?"

"I was going to say a vessel of self-loathing, but sure, Ben Affleck, sans back tattoo. The whole time, I kept thinking: 'Why is this man so lonely?' He has a daughter. And a *granddaughter*, right here in Sewickley."

"Who he's never met."

"Right, but why? It doesn't make any sense. He knows you exist. Why is he not doing completely obvious things, like paying for college? You're all stressed out about loans and scholarships, and your grandparents are literally the richest people in Pittsburgh. Half the hockey team doesn't pay St. Ignatius tuition because of the Mercer scholarships, and they don't drop a dime on their own grandchild?"

"I'm not their grandchild. I'm no one's grandchild." Mom's parents both died before my twelfth birthday.

"Genetically, you—"

"I'm not asking them for anything. I don't need their help."

"Of course." Shiv reached across the table and pinched my cheek using her thumb and index finger. I hit her hand away.

As we polished off our croissants, I showed *The Spirit on the Ice* to Shiv, pointing out the underlined passages and marginalia. I told her Vince had called it a love story, but the love was for a game.

"All stories are love stories," she said, in precisely that moment when both our hands were on the book. She added, "What's it really about?"

That's when I realized it was about pain. Maybe pain and love were one and the same. Avoidable, to a certain extent, but the more you lived—really lived—the more you received.

"If Woolf was murdered, it was by someone he trusted," Shiv said, changing the subject. "No one else could have injected the drugs in the side of his neck without a struggle."

"His neck?" I repeated, raising my voice. It had been reported only that the drugs were delivered by "intramuscular injection." When I pictured it, the needle always entered his upper arm, below the shoulder, like a shot at the doctor's office.

"Or whatever. Just sayin' he would have fought off a stranger. Imagine Ingo in the same situation."

"You said his *neck*," I pressed. What did Shiv know that I didn't? And why was she keeping secrets from me? I'd left nothing out. Nothing of importance. Nothing I remembered, anyway.

She blinked for a beat too long, then pinched the bridge of her nose. When she opened her eyes, she looked down at the table. "The base of his neck," she clarified. "His trapezius muscle."

"How do you—"

"I read the autopsy report," she admitted.

"How did you?"

After a long pause—too long—she said, "Mo Whiting showed it to me."

"What the hell, Shiv?"

"We've had a few conversations. Honestly, I didn't intend to talk to her. But she saw me on her property. Did you know she flies a planet Earth flag in her front yard? I think she hates aliens." Shiv laughed at her own joke.

"Or she believes in science," I said, momentarily distracted.

"These days, one must take a side," Shiv said.

"You promised you'd be discreet," I said.

"Remember when we talked about the cherub statue. How it's . . ." Again, she paused to think.

"Yeah?"

"Well, I wanted to see if anything was still buried there."

"The Jágr puck?"

"Who cares about a stupid puck. Think about it. Woolf might have hidden other stuff there too."

"Like what?"

"I don't know. I thought it was worth looking."

"And did you?"

"I didn't have the chance. Mo Whiting pulled into the driveway."

"And asked why you were creeping around her property?"

"She asked me who I was, so I told her my name, and that I was a St. Ignatius student. When I said the name of the school, all the color drained from her face. I almost ran, because I thought she might call the police, but then she leaned against her car door, too weak to stand. I helped her inside. She said, 'Every time another boy dies, someone comes around here trying to make a connection that doesn't exist.' So I told her I wasn't sure Woolf caused his own death either, and I was investigating. Don't worry—I didn't mention you."

"And?"

"Well, I realized the conversation was an opportunity."

"To peruse the autopsy report?"

"It's huge, Frankie." Shiv reached across the table toward me as I slouched back in my chair. "I saw a blown-up picture of the puncture wound. The medical examiner noted that it was not a natural spot for a self-injection—not impossible, but unlikely."

The police had treated Woolf's death as a run-of-the-mill overdose by a heedless kid. Mo Whiting had concocted a conspiracy theory about the Mercers paying off the police to deflect attention from their daughter, which, okay, maybe. But, after learning what was in the autopsy report, Shiv figured the local cops at the scene had just been incompetent. It's not like people get murdered in Sewickley all the time. The officers probably had no idea what they were doing. And later, when they learned of the puncture wound, and that self-injection was "not impossible," they might have been biased toward their initial assumption. Worse, they might have worried their shoddy police work would be exposed. So they stuck to their story: self-inflicted overdose; nothing to see here.

Shiv stood up, walked around our table, and positioned her body behind me. I turned to look at her, but she gently placed her hand on my jaw and guided my head back into a forward-facing position. Then she jabbed a finger into the muscle at the base of my neck on the back-right side. Her nail was sharp enough that I could still feel it even after she slid back into her seat. Without thinking, I found myself holding an invisible syringe, my thumb cocked to push down on the plunger. In order to reach the spot where Shiv had poked me, I had to point my elbow to the ceiling, rotate my shoulder backward, and then twist my hand awkwardly, pointing the phantom needle to my skin.

"See!" Shiv said. "According to Mo, the site of the injection was the key detail only the killer would know. It would have been used to establish the veracity of a confession, if the police had ever elicited one. So it was never released to the public. Nobody, outside the family—"

"Not even the reporter from the *Argus*—"

"Right," Shiv confirmed. "Jody D'Angelo only knew the drugs were injected. Mo couldn't tell her anything that might have interfered with the investigation. It makes more sense now—why Mo and Maddie have always been so sure it wasn't a suicide. Everyone assumed they just didn't want to believe it, but there's actual evidence! Anyway, I had to give Mo something in return. Again, don't worry, I did not tell her you are her granddaughter."

"What did you tell her?"

"I told her Woolf witnessed something at Mahoney's Produce before he died. I may have mentioned I was talking to Vince and Susanna, which is kinda true, because you're talking to them, but, like I said, I didn't bring you into it. When she asked me if Susanna *had* the baby, I said I didn't know."

"You shouldn't have done that, Shiv."

"I didn't want to lie to her, but what was I supposed to do?"

"You shouldn't have talked to her at all."

"I'm sorry, Frankie."

Anger swelled inside me. Until that moment, I didn't know I had the capacity to be so mad at Shiv. But I was mad at everybody. Mad I didn't know the grandmother who lived less than ten minutes from me. Mad I'd been talking to my biological mother on FaceTime and she didn't tell me who she was. Mad my mom knew I was investigating Woolf's death for a school project and she hadn't informed me I was related to him. My own dad! The dad I never knew. And never would. Gone before I was even born. Oh my god, I was so fucking mad. Mad my aunt had always known about me but she'd been too busy becoming a big-shot attorney to meet her dead brother's kid. Mad at myself for not asking where I came from the minute I turned sixteen, when I was entitled to the information.

"Sorry isn't good enough, Shiv. You can't just expect to be forgiven. Your mom always forgives you when you mess up and get caught. But I'm not your mom. I don't have to forgive you."

"I'm sorry," she repeated. "I didn't mean for her to see me. She wasn't supposed to come home until later. Is it really a big deal? Now we've seen the autopsy report. And Mo Whiting is no better or worse off. So she knows something happened at Mahoney's. To be honest, I didn't get the impression she cared. She's still convinced Susanna killed Woolf, and her family covered it up. Now she thinks the secret pregnancy could have been the motive."

"You don't get it, do you?" On the verge of tears, I raised my voice. "You can't even see the line you crossed. This is my life. Mo Whiting is my *grandmother*. You had no right to talk to her." All my anger was directed toward Shiv for doing something that was, frankly, very much in her character: trying to solve the puzzle.

"Well, I mean, it's a free country. If she's willing—"

Then I said something I would regret. "Just because your dad left your family doesn't give you the right to meddle with mine."

Shiv stood up and walked out. She didn't say goodbye or ask if I had another way to get home. Through the window, I watched her flip up her hood and walk with her head down to her car. If she was crying, I would never know. Her hood obscured her face, and even if it hadn't, any tears would have been swept away in the rain.

16

I WOKE UP on Sunday to a text from Shiv: *Decided to go to West Virginia.* She didn't say when she'd be back or why she'd changed her mind about visiting her dad. I felt shame for saying the thing about her dad leaving. I knew I couldn't take it back.

I'd assumed Shiv had been so invested in our project for the thrill of solving the puzzle, but her eagerness may have come from a more vulnerable place. Maybe she needed to know why the people we love leave us. Maybe she wanted to prove Woolf hadn't abandoned his friends and family willingly.

Mom and I had a Sunday-morning ritual. We made large, elaborate breakfasts, the kind you might find at a popular brunch spot: eggs Benedict, huevos rancheros, French toast, sourdough pancakes, steak and eggs. Whatever it was, we made it together.

She was halfway through a pot of coffee, with the *Post-Gazette* spread out across the kitchen table, when I finally descended the stairs, in gym shorts and a hoodie.

Homemade biscuits were rising on a cookie sheet lined with parchment paper, ready to bake. Biscuits and gravy with eggs was my favorite.

When the doorbell rang, Mom jolted forward in her chair. People had stopped coming to the door during the pandemic, and, for the most part, they hadn't returned.

"I'll get it," she said. "Set the oven to 450, please."

Maybe the Mormon was back. The last time he came to our door,

Mom was too polite to immediately send him away, but every time he opened his mouth, she responded with some version of "We're Catholic," like Mormonism was a vampire and Catholicism was garlic. Each time, he responded with something like "That's good, because you already know Christ." And then she repeated herself, as if he hadn't heard her. After he was gone, I said something like "You know he's trying to convert us, right? He thinks his religion is better." Mom said no religion was better. That better was not the point. I did not ask the obvious question: "Then why are we Catholic?" I already knew the answer.

Before my grandmother married James Northrup, a Methodist, she was Marta Baldocci. Marta's parents (my great-grandparents), who had immigrated to America from Italy as children, were strict Catholics. When James asked for Marta's hand in marriage, her father would not agree until James converted and promised to raise any children in the Catholic faith. Marta and James Northrup had one child, Alice. A man of his word, James took his wife and daughter to church every Sunday and holy day. Each night, he sat by little Alice's bedside as they prayed the same prayers my mom would eventually pray with me. I never met my mom's father, but apparently, by the end of his life, his devotion to the church far exceeded my grandmother's, who simply accepted Catholicism as her inheritance. As it was mine.

Mom returned to the kitchen with an envelope and said, "I've been served."

The Mercers' attorney requested that my mom provide a written deposition, on condition of anonymity, in response to Monica Whiting's petition to disclose any and all information related to "the pregnancy, possible birth, and subsequent adoption of Woolf's biological child."

For Mo's petition to be granted, a judge would need to be convinced of a "compelling reason to disclose identifying information," and that reason had to "outweigh the expectation of confidentiality." Initially, this struck me as empty legal jargon. But the more I thought about it, the worse I felt. A judge would weigh the facts: Monica Whiting's dead son was my biological father. His life had been taken before he could consent to my adoption. And maybe, just maybe, he would have wanted me to meet my biological grandmother.

"Was it wrong to keep her from knowing about me all these years?" I asked.

Mom said, "There isn't always a right or wrong, Frankie."

"But isn't there a 'compelling reason' for her to know who I am?"

"I suppose," Mom said. "But Susanna and her family thought there was a compelling reason not to tell her."

"So I could be your daughter," I said.

Mom nodded. "You'll be eighteen soon, and you're about to leave for college. I'm not sure if meeting Monica Whiting would be such a bad thing anymore. I honestly don't know."

"What are you going to write?"

"Depends on the questions," she said. The oven beeped when it reached 450. Mom slid the pan of biscuits inside and set the timer.

I reached for the cast-iron pan, heated it on the stovetop, and began cooking the sausage. We worked silently for a while, maneuvering around each other in our small kitchen.

When the gravy was ready and the biscuits were out of the oven, Mom fried the eggs. I stepped outside to the potted herb garden to pick chives, which I chopped and sprinkled on top.

Mom suggested we say grace after setting the plates on the table, which we typically only did at dinner. That morning, I understood her desire to give thanks.

After grace, without pausing, her head still bowed, Mom continued. "I'll tell them the decision should be yours, and yours alone. I'll tell them there is no better person to make such a decision, because you are a wonderful young woman."

"Amen," I said. I felt closer to her in that moment than I had for a long time. All those times I'd called her a fascist fell away, discarded like a snake's old skin, and I saw her not as a mother but as a person, Alice, maybe for the first time in my life.

She asked about Ingo. Either she was trying to change the subject or I was giving off a vibe that only she could identity as not my usual self. When I told her Ingo was fine, she asked about Shiv.

I didn't want to get into it, so I said, "Shiv went to West Virginia to see her dad," and shoved a huge forkful of biscuit into my mouth.

My chewing was interrupted by a second knock on the front door.

"What is it now?" Mom said, standing up again. "Was I supposed to sign something?"

But it wasn't the process server. When Mom opened the door, she said, "Come in, dear," like she was talking to a child. Then I heard sobbing, and a muffled apology.

I swallowed the food in my mouth and checked my teeth using the camera on my phone. By the time I walked into the living room, Mom and Susanna were sitting side by side, embracing.

Mom commented that the couch was embarrassing, because the fabric was faded and worn. Susanna said it was comfortable, and that her mother had an excellent upholsterer, whom she would refer. Our roles—teacher, student, mother, daughter—became blurred. We were three women in a room together. Sometimes when I think back on this period of my life, I hold on to that feeling. We were present. We were equal. We loved each other.

The moment didn't last long. Susanna stood up and smoothed her blouse. She extended her arms. I stepped toward her. We hugged, keeping our bodies distanced. I let go quickly, with all the coolness I could muster. We exchanged pleasantries. How nice it was to finally meet. How beautiful I was. By this time, we'd been talking over FaceTime for nearly three weeks, but neither of us was capable of acknowledging the magnitude of the secret Susanna had kept from me on those calls.

Part of me was glad I hadn't known. Each time we spoke, I had grown less intimidated.

Susanna wore a soft, oversize cardigan in neutral oatmeal over a silk blouse that tied at the neck, paired with high-waisted jeans. She'd traded her usual heels for pointed-toe flats. The tears streaking down her face made her look young, and when she sat back down, her proximity to my mom made an odd impression on me. Her lips parted, and she turned her head, pushing her hair behind her ear.

How had I not seen it? We looked so much alike. Seeing her there on my couch, the couch I'd been slouching on for my entire life, was like watching a version of my future self. Except it wasn't. She was stiffer. More erect. She was a Mercer. I was a Northrup. We had the same features. Even some of the same mannerisms. (How could that be?) But we did not have the same pedigree.

And here's the thing about pedigree. My time at St. Ignatius had fooled me into believing it didn't matter. The other kids—the rich kids—were all so nice. Really inclusive. The vibe wasn't so much *I don't see class*. It was more like *I do see class, but we're all friends here*. I never felt like people were talking behind my back about the dresses I wore to dances twice, or whether having a mom as a teacher at the school was an advantage or a disadvantage, or if Princeton viewed me as some sort of low-income diversity case.

Not only were people not saying these things; they weren't even thinking them. To think them was passé. To think them was to admit that being rich was better than being middle-class—hell, poor, even— and not only were people unwilling to admit that, but they actively deluded themselves into not believing it.

The teachers were probably aware that being rich was better. Mom must have thought about it sometimes, like when she shopped at the budget grocery store, which was farther away than the organic store, or when her teenage daughter commandeered her old car for an entire afternoon, so she couldn't run a simple errand. But she never complained to me.

When I saw Barbara with Ingo, I did not understand how she was so sure of herself. I didn't get it, because I had not considered the power of the we're-all-friends-here delusion. I thought, *It's good to be friends with these people who like me and don't judge me, and who have disproportionate access to most of the world's capital.* The college counselors worked hard on my behalf, as they did for everyone. My teachers wrote me glowing recommendations. And Shiv paid when we went out.

But looking at Susanna, I saw that I was not like her. I finally understood why I would never be a Susanna or a Barbara, or even a Shiv. The reason Barbara had the confidence of a time traveler who had already seen her incomparable future was because she *had* already seen it. It didn't matter if her startup went bust. Or if she decided to take a year off and backpack in Nepal to restore her mental health. Or if she accidentally got pregnant.

I shared in some of these privileges. St. Ignatius gave me access. You could say I didn't speak the secret language or know it existed, but, guess what, the secrets aren't so secret anymore. Wealth is not that complicated. People know that meritocracy is compromised, and that being friends with everyone allows the rich kids to feel okay about being rich.

I didn't begrudge Susanna her wealth. I didn't ask why Mom and I had been sweating about scholarships and grants and loans and part-time jobs when the Mercers' charities were funding the education of people they didn't know. Maybe I should have. But I was grateful Susanna had chosen my mom and handed me over to her, no strings attached.

Was I being naïve? Had I been so indoctrinated by the we're-all-friends-here culture that even when I recognized it as a smoke screen, I didn't care? Maybe. But I had to get on with it.

Susanna talked about what happened at ScoreFest. About Monica Whiting. About the decision to allow my mother to raise me without interference. She told me what it was like to find out she was pregnant at sixteen, how she confessed to her parents, how they reacted. At some point, I realized Mom had left the room. She'd probably made an excuse, like putting on a fresh pot of coffee, but I had no recollection of her departure.

Apparently, every year, on my birthday, Mom sent Susanna a letter about me and often included a picture. Susanna called their correspondence a "window into my world." Those letters would have been her only window. My social media was private, and personal online activity was discouraged by the college counselors at St. Ignatius. I wondered what Mom had written about me. Who did Susanna think I was? Was she right?

I'm not sure how long she stayed that day. Long enough. She never looked at her watch or her phone, and she made no attempt to leave until she'd answered my questions. As she stood up from the couch, she said, "Your life may not be what you expect, but it will be yours." Susanna Mercer was not above a meaningless platitude.

Laughter escaped through my nose in the form of a sniffle. She laughed too. A hearty laugh. A laugh that was long overdue. Then she told me she was leaving for San Francisco the next day, and I was welcome to visit her anytime. She offered to fly me out.

And just like that, she was part of my life.

We said goodbye at the door. Before she pushed through the screen, she turned and embraced me. This time, she enveloped me with her whole body. We held on tight. It was like a drunken hug between old pals. I smelled the subtle perfume of her expensive shampoo (oakmoss with notes of rose and pomegranate, I would later read on the bottle in her bathroom). I felt the heat of her breath in my ear. Our bodies swayed together. I was transported.

First, to the old house on Faculty Row that no longer exists, where Mom and I lived until I was ten. I'm a toddler, standing on Mom's feet as she dances down the hallway and tosses me on my bed. Then I'm on an airplane, my first flight, my small body stretching across the seat onto Mom's lap. Then I'm at the scene of the accident where

Shiv wrecked her first car. Mom arrives before Dr. Badlani. She takes our hands—I on her left, Shiv on her right—and we walk across the street to look at the totaled car. She isn't mad. She wants us to see what we could have lost. Then I'm in our town house, making biscuits and gravy with Mom that very morning. Our arms brush as we slip past each other in our small kitchen. Then I feel her tears on my cheek when she kisses me goodbye in front of my college dorm. This hasn't happened yet, but it is so real. Then I hold the fleshy crook of her arm as she walks me down the aisle at my wedding. Then her tough, knotted hands lift my firstborn from my arms. Finally, I lay my head on her chest as she takes her last breath.

Somehow, Susanna is present in each of these moments. Or maybe each moment occurred simultaneously between us as we stood in that threshold, granting us the permission to hug each other with abandon until the temporal order was restored. It was maternal touch in its totality. It was beautiful.

The thing that had terrified me about finding my birth mother—that I would no longer belong to the mother I loved—receded after Susanna's visit. I could be the baby that came from Susanna's womb *and* the woman my mom raised at the same time. Woolf could be part of me too. It was okay for me to want, as Woolf had wanted. The wanting was necessary. Without it, life was just accumulation.

MOM RESPONDED HONESTLY and thoughtfully to the questions in her written deposition. Reading her answers helped me understand why my identity had been kept secret. Mo Whiting wasn't a bad person. She just loved her son.

The judge ultimately dismissed the petition, and my identity remained sealed. But in the end, the decision delayed our meeting by only a few months. I would introduce myself to my biological grandmother when I learned the truth about what happened to Woolf. Then, I was ready.

Susanna Mercer
March 2005

PATRICIA MERCER HAD been too preoccupied to notice the ways her daughter's body had started to change. To be fair, it looked much the same at first. But Susanna had changed the moment she found out, and then changed again when she decided what to do about it. So maybe the problem was not that the mother hadn't noticed her daughter's body, but that she hadn't noticed her daughter at all.

Esther stocked the kitchen with groceries, and every week a new quart of ice cream appeared in the freezer. If she wondered why it was so quickly vanishing, she didn't ask.

"Please set the table, dear." Her mother's voice was unusually chirpy.

"Why?" They hadn't shared a meal together at the dinner table in weeks.

Esther had cut up vegetables and stored them in separate Tupperware containers. Her mom stood at the island, tossing the contents of each one into a salad. She pointed toward the sliding glass door. Her dad was out back on the patio, firing up the grill. He had installed heat lamps so he could be outside by himself year-round.

"Chimichurri steak," her mom said, adding, "Esther made the chimichurri."

"Why?" Susanna repeated.

"Stop asking that. We're eating together as a family tonight," she said.

Though they'd tried for years, her parents had failed to produce a sibling for Susanna. Two miscarriages preceded her birth, and two more followed. When Susanna thought about the five pregnancies, her mind almost exploded. Five positive pregnancy tests. Five cycles of hope and dread. Five periods of morning sickness and cravings and bloated insides, followed, in all but one instance, by cramps and bleeding and passage. Four D&Cs.

Her birth was a miracle, as all births are miracles. Her parents never stopped telling her as much. Twelve hours of labor: Not bad in the scheme of things. And then there was Susanna, named after a great beauty in the book of Daniel, pure and righteous.

Fatigue rolled through Susanna's body like a slow-moving fog. She thought about how different it felt from the routine tiredness she had once felt with early risings. She was tired in her bones.

"Can we get a dog?" Susanna asked. "I think we need one."

"Who would take care of it?"

"I would, until college. Then you and dad will need the company."

"You're never here. And your dad and I both work."

"Not to split hairs, but you *volunteer*," Susanna said.

Her mom sat on the boards of St. Ignatius and a Catholic charity. She took these roles seriously, dressing up in colored skirt suits and nylons, full makeup, and gold jewelry, always hurrying to meetings, often pictured in the local society pages. Susanna wasn't sure if her mother had power or the illusion of power, but when she observed her parents hosting dinner parties or came across pictures of them at charity events, it was obvious that, between the two of them, her mom dominated.

Recently, her dad had started to look frail, like a strong wind could easily topple him. Every now and again, he would say things like "I'm paying a fortune for . . . ," and Patricia would correct him with "You mean, *we* are paying a fortune." Then she'd finish his point by telling Susanna "You better apply yourself," which was the Catholic parent way of saying "Don't have sex or do drugs."

Too late.

The enthusiasm with which many of her father's clients greeted her mother made it clear who had brought them into the fold. St. Ignatius's chief investment officer, Robert Grealy, had recently been at their house for dinner with his wife. Susanna had eavesdropped from the living room and caught enough of the conversation. Grealy was considering investing a not-insignificant portion of the St. Ignatius endowment with Raymond Mercer Capital. Susanna assumed this had something to do with the multiple-fork dinner they were about to enjoy in celebration.

"Woolf and Maddie have a dog. The Whitings seem so . . . happy. Happier."

"One day, you'll understand that people only seem happy because you are not privy to their private matters."

"The dog could be a therapy animal. I'll get him a vest."

"No one in this house needs therapy, honey. Your father just closed a big deal."

Her dad had slipped in from the back and was now hovering. "Market volatility means big risk but big opportunity—"

"We can name him Nasdaq."

"Name who?" he asked.

"Susanna wants a dog, because the Whitings have one and they seem happy." Her mother's intonation was a verbal eye roll.

"Who's going to buy the dog food?" he asked unironically.

"The same person who buys all our food," Susanna said. "Esther."

"But who's going to pay for it?"

Susanna pointed to the raw beef on the platter. Esther had purchased it from a local farmer. "Mom demands only premium cuts from cows raised in Western Pennsylvania. Are you seriously suggesting we should be worried about the cost of dog food?"

Her dad stepped closer to her mother, placing his hands on her waist from behind. It wasn't a romantic gesture—more like *We're in this together.* Then he picked up the platter of raw beef and returned to the grill.

"I'm not saying a dog will make us happy," Susanna told her mom. "But if we were happy, we'd have a dog."

"Let's talk about it later. We have too much going on right now."

"You mean like next week? Or after you're dead?"

"Sure, when I'm dead, you can get a dog."

"Jesus, Mom, I'll be a senior citizen by then."

"Please don't say 'Jesus,' Susanna."

"What are we celebrating anyway?"

"The St. Ignatius board voted to invest the endowment with your father." *The board voted* apparently sounded more ethical than *I convinced the board.*

"What happened to working for the little guy?" Susanna asked. Her dad's fixation on teachers and plumbers and auto mechanics, people from places like Altoona, where he grew up, was more than a brand. It was his identity. He never spoke about finance without mentioning these people, how he'd given them financial security.

"He's pivoting." Her mom dropped business jargon with a straight face, like a white rapper. "If he does what he says he can do, the St. Ignatius endowment will be bigger than Deerfield's. Bigger than Andover's. St. Ignatius *is* the little guy. But not for long."

"Sounds risky." Susanna tapped her fingers together like an evil genius. "What if he loses the money? Will St. Ignatius have to cut the water polo team's travel schedule?"

"Failure is not an option."

Susanna felt a flutter. For a Catholic girl, she had failed in the worst possible way. She felt like a monster. How she had mustered the courage to tell her parents, in that precise moment, would always remain a mystery to her.

"Better fill up that glass," Susanna said, pointing to the half-full wineglass in her mom's hand. "I also have news."

Patricia Mercer must have assumed her daughter's news was something banal—a class project, weekend plans—because she didn't react. She inspected Susanna's place settings and took another sip of wine.

"I'm pregnant," Susanna said.

The wineglass dropped from her mother's hand.

Without a word, she retrieved a new glass, filled it, and carried it to the table with the salad bowl. She sat down and put her napkin on her lap. The shattered glass and a small pool of red wine remained on the floor.

"Do you want me to get that?" Susanna asked.

Her dad entered, carrying the empty platter, dirty from raw meat, in one hand and the grilled steaks on a cutting board in the other. He put the platter in the sink and began to slice the steaks at the kitchen island, mumbling something about having already let them rest. Then he carried the cutting board to the table, not bothering to clean the platter or transfer the meat. The board blocked his view, so he did not notice the shattered glass and the wine on the floor.

He served the steak. Her mom passed the salad.

Susanna observed her father slather chimichurri on his meat. Without looking up, he picked up his knife to cut a bite-size hunk, which he brought to his lips.

Her mom said, "Let's say grace first."

He smiled, as if he'd forgotten who he was, and put his knife down so he could fold his hands. He began: "Bless us, O Lord, and these Thy gifts . . ."

It was the same grace every Catholic said—the one Susanna's family had stopped saying when they'd stopped eating at the table together. Mom joined in midway. Susanna chimed in for the amen.

Her mom stabbed a dainty bite, pulled the steak off the fork with her teeth, and began to chew with deliberate calm. By the time she swallowed, Susanna could have sworn the earth had completed a rotation on its axis.

Her father ate like a king at a feast in his honor, aware only of his own pleasure. He still thought they were celebrating.

Finally, her mom said, "Susanna, how could you?"

"What?" her dad asked, looking up from his steak for the first time.

"We've given you everything. All you had to do—"

Her mom was always saying some version of "We've given you everything" or "Everything we do is for you." For a while, Susanna had assumed she was simply the object of some inner complex associated with being an only child. But she later learned Maddie and Woolf's parents said the same things to them.

There is a fine line between doing everything for one's offspring and doing everything for oneself. What parent doesn't want a perfect child? And if everything her parents did was really for themselves, and Susanna deviated from their expectations, then they weren't really *giving* everything; they were taking everything away. In that sense, her parents were slowly killing her.

"We are *Catholic*. You are a St. Ignatius woman. Does that mean anything to you? You have no regard for what your father and I have sacrificed for you. What is the board going to say when they find out—"

"What are we talking about?" her dad interjected.

"The *board*? Are you serious, Mom?"

"We convinced them to place the endowment with a firm that shares the values of the institution. Catholic values. They will not tolerate a scandal," she said.

"Paranoia getting to you much, Mom?"

"We'll take care of it," her mom said.

"*Take care of it?*"

"You have your whole life ahead of you," she said. "This is not the time—"

"You just said we're *Catholic*. St. Ignatius. Your charity. Oh my god, you don't even let me wear jeans to church. You are such a hypocrite. Are you seriously suggesting— Can you even say the *word*, Mom?"

"What is everybody talking about?" her father demanded.

"Mom's talking about an abortion," Susanna said.

"Susanna, please," she started.

"A what?" Her dad was clueless. He had always liked to say "Don't tell me your problem; tell me your solution."

A FEW WEEKS earlier, Susanna had confirmed she was pregnant in the Eat'n Park bathroom. She'd driven all the way to a Rite Aid in Moon Township to purchase a pregnancy test, because she couldn't risk being recognized at the 7-Eleven, or any other place in town. She didn't have the guts to take the test until she returned to Sewickley.

She was sitting on the toilet at Eat'n Park, waiting for the results, when she noticed a message etched on the back of the stall door. Actually, there were three messages. One read CALL ME FOR A GOOD TIME and included a phone number. The second was NOMINATIM NON GENERATIM, the St. Ignatius motto. She closed her eyes and pictured Ms. Northrup's classroom, those same Latin words handwritten on the board. The third, either a response to the pretentious act of scrawling Latin on a bathroom stall or an independent expression of a simplistic inner life, read FUCK YOU.

Her hand shook with fear when she picked up the test from the top of the toilet paper dispenser and chucked it in the sanitary bin. *Nominatim non generatim*: In general, the positive result was catastrophic, but in her particular situation, it didn't have to be. Later, she would understand that her family's wealth meant she would always have options, but as a scared kid, she thought the motto etched on the bathroom stall was a sign from God.

Maddie was there at the diner that day. When she asked what had taken so long in the bathroom, Susanna lied. They shared a plate of fries.

After they left, Susanna couldn't go home. She didn't remember getting in her car, turning the key in the ignition, or driving to the

St. Ignatius campus. When she opened her eyes, she was parked on Faculty Row. Alice Northrup lived in the cute white bungalow, next to an almost identical one at the end of the street. Her name was on the mailbox.

Entering her teacher's home felt strangely intimate: The teakettle whistled in the kitchen. The smell of dryer sheets wafted from the basement. The unfolded blankets on the couch and dishes in the sink begged to be tidied.

When Ms. Northrup bent over to place two mugs of hot tea on the coffee table, Susanna noticed the smoothness of her olive skin. Her brown hair was pulled back in a ponytail, making her round face and big brown eyes appear doll-like. The boys sometimes called her hot—people speculated that she was a lesbian, which probably made her more desirable in their eyes. When Susanna asked her age, Ms. Northrup said twenty-seven, which struck Susanna as somehow both younger and older than she had imagined. Susanna told her she'd just taken a pregnancy test and didn't know what to do.

Ms. Northrup said, "If you decide to carry the baby to term, you could consider allowing me to adopt her." She'd said *her*, and Susanna would later remember that as significant, though Ms. Northrup used the feminine pronoun as the default in class.

Before this moment, Susanna hadn't known why she'd come here, why she needed to see Ms. Northrup, why she trusted her. But she had known Ms. Northrup wanted a baby, hadn't she? They'd spoken about it before. And she recalled thinking Ms. Northrup could teach a child to love the world. If she couldn't, nobody could. Susanna had gathered that Ms. Northrup had probably considered adoption before, maybe she had even researched agencies and timelines.

So, yes, there was that feeling of kismet, but when Susanna thought about it later, she realized it was simply a matter of two people listening, learning each other's deepest wants and needs, and coming together to meet them.

SUSANNA LIFTED THE spoon from the chimichurri, letting the green sauce slowly drizzle back into the bowl. "Dad, do you know Ms. Northrup? She's a history teacher at St. Ignatius. I had her last year. She wants a baby."

Her mother interrupted, "A bit personal for history class, don't you think?"

"What decade do you live in, Mom? People talk about stuff."

Her dad pushed the last piece of steak around his plate, mopping up the sauce. "Well then, she should have one," he said dumbly.

Susanna said, "I mean, maybe she *should*. She's not married. And I could be making this up, but I don't think she likes men. She's also Catholic, devout or whatever."

"Or whatever?" Patricia hated nonspecific language, which she considered irritating. She especially hated the word *stuff*. *Whatever* was a close second. "So you've told Ms. Northrup about this, have you? We'll need to take care of her."

"Mom, are you seriously worried she's going to tell everybody?"

Her dad finally looked up at her as he soaked a piece of crusty bread in the soup of sauce and blood on his plate. "You're not eating," he said.

"Dad, I'm pregnant, and Ms. Northrup is going to adopt the baby."

He looked at Patricia. "How long have you known about this?"

Her mother tipped her head back and polished off her wine before pouring another glass. "Have you told anyone else, Susanna?" she asked.

"You think I want to be the girl from school who everyone talks about?"

"Woolf? Your friends?"

"I haven't told Woolf. Not yet. We sort of broke up a couple weeks ago."

"You did?" Her dad seemed genuinely surprised. He looked at the full plates on the table and then down into his own clean plate, as if he'd suddenly noticed the incongruity.

"So he doesn't know," her mom confirmed.

"Good," her dad said.

"Good for who?"

"Good for everybody, Susanna," her mom said—or maybe it was her dad who said it. Ray and Patricia were suddenly in lockstep.

"People at school are going to notice."

"You'll finish junior year at home. Dr. Bryant will be discreet."

"This isn't *Ireland*," Susanna said. "You can't lock me up in a convent."

"Ms. Northrup will need to sign a confidentiality agreement," her dad said.

"She's not— I trust her," Susanna said.

"She'll sign an NDA. One day, you'll understand," he said.

Her mom nodded in agreement.

"Do you even care about the baby?"

"We care about *you*, Suz," her mother said. "Your life—"

"This is my life." Susanna had anticipated a different reaction, but her parents were too diabolical to succumb to overt anger. Saving face was their default setting.

"Let us help you."

"What about Woolf? He deserves—"

"We can keep this secret, as a family. But Woolf can never know," her mom said. "You must know that, or you would have told him already."

"What about Esther?" Susanna asked.

"I'll handle Esther," her mother said.

Esther had been working for the family for years. She'd taken out their liquor bottles. She'd emptied the paper shredder. She'd cleaned up the blood when Susanna turned ten and decided it was time to shave her legs. Her parents never found out.

Susanna's dad walked over to the bar and poured himself a glass of port. The corners of his mouth turned downward as he placed the bottle back on the shelf.

"No one ever has to know about this, honey." Her mother reached across the table. "Trust us: We're your parents."

The touch was gentle, programmed to protect the child as an extension of the self. It was possible for Susanna to conflate her assurance with love, because it was the only kind of love she'd ever known.

Susanna turned her hand over and let her mother hold it.

BY THE FOLLOWING evening, her mother's only mention of the pregnancy related to the NDA their attorney had drawn up. Most Fridays, her dad came home early, around six o'clock, carrying a large pizza, half pepperoni, half mushroom. They referred to pizza night as a "family tradition," but the impulse was neither communal nor celebratory. Esther took off at noon on Fridays, and, left to their own devices, her parents hadn't prepared a meal since the late '90s.

That night, her dad came in with two bags from Mister Chicken. Susanna stuck her nose into one of the bags and inhaled. "What's up with this?"

"Decided to do something different tonight," he said. "Uncle Danny's coming over."

Danny Perone wasn't Susanna's real uncle, but he liked to hang around on holidays and tell stories with her dad.

Growing up, they played hockey together on an outdoor rink in Altoona. They'd rooted for the Pens long before they won back-to-back Stanley Cups. A couple of gritty Rust Belt kids, both dreamers.

Uncle Danny's father was unemployed, but he'd won some kind of settlement money, enough to live on. He chauffeured them to hockey games in his abundant free time. Their stories featured icy roads and fog so thick the old man was afraid to pull over.

Mostly, Susanna's dad and Danny talked about the games, recounting details that men their age should have long forgotten. Their grievances were plentiful—a cross-check, a high stick, a trip. They reminisced about good plays too. The mere mention of a particular slap shot could shift the mood in the room.

Sometimes, Susanna wondered why her dad gave up the game. He must have figured out he was never going to be great, and greatness was his only ambition. In high school, he saved all the money he made working at the ice rink and caddying at a local golf course. He bootstrapped his way into college.

Uncle Danny didn't go to college. He would have gone pro, except he'd had one concussion too many and his doctor said another might kill him. Death was the only thing that scared Danny Perone, so he gave up playing and started coaching.

"Why's Danny coming over?" Susanna asked.

"What is with you always asking 'Why'? Because Uncle Danny is our dear friend," her mother said.

"He's Dad's friend, not yours. Also, not my uncle."

"You can call him Coach Perone then, Susanna." She added, "Show some respect."

"I still don't get why we're eating Mister Chicken."

"Like home cookin'," her dad said, riffing off their slogan. "You remember Craig."

"Craig Busack?" her mom asked.

"That's him—Busy."

Her mom smiled like his very existence was an inside joke. "Busy gave us a nine-dollar salad spinner for our wedding. Turned out to be the best gift we received. We're still using it."

"Esther is still using it," Susanna corrected.

Her dad continued, "Busy owns a Mister Chicken franchise in Altoona, one of over a thousand locations nationwide."

"You didn't drive all the way to Altoona to get—"

"Of course not," he said. "I picked this up downtown. I wanted to see one of the locations with my own eyes. Try the product."

Susanna picked a little piece of chicken skin off and stuck it in her mouth. "Like KFC minus the *F*."

"The chicken isn't the problem. It's the—"

The doorbell chimed.

Uncle Danny trailed her dad into the kitchen. Eyes on the table and hands on his paunch, he said, "Patricia, you've outdone yourself."

Susanna stood up and shook his hand when he offered it to her.

"Didn't lift a finger," her mother said.

"Oh, Mom, give yourself some credit. You transferred the food from one container to another," Susanna said.

"You, my dear, can do the dishes," she said.

Dad pulled out a chair for Uncle Danny. "Remember Craig Busack?"

"Busy? Never liked that jagoff."

"He's the proud owner of a Mister Chicken franchise. We are enjoying this fine meal in his honor." Her dad was in a good mood.

"Why the hell would we do that?" Danny asked.

"Guess how much Busy is paying for these napkins?" Her dad reached into the Mister Chicken bag on the counter and pulled out an enormous stack of paper napkins. Susanna had set the table with cloth napkins.

Everybody acted like the question was a completely normal topic of conversation.

"A sixty-five-percent premium. On napkins. In my hand, I hold twenty-three overpriced napkins."

"You counted them? Could you have delegated that task to the intern?"

"Woolf no longer works for me. Anyway, Busy is hemorrhaging money, and I have it on good authority that his location is not the exception but the rule." Her father cupped his hand around his mouth and whispered audibly, "I'm shorting the stock."

Uncle Danny wanted to get in on the action.

Her father handed him a broker's card. "Call this guy, and he'll arrange a transfer. But, Danny—"

"I owe you," he said.

"A big one." Her father raised his glass, "To Mister Chicken."

Uncle Danny was her dad's only true friend from before he was rich—before he was anything. Her mother had no friends. Maybe after a certain age, people made only convenient acquaintances or trusted colleagues, but not friends who hung around each other for no reason, like she and Maddie did. But if friendship had its season, like a ripe tomato plucked from the vine, it would eventually rot.

After the Mister Chicken dinner, Danny Perone didn't come around much. Susanna didn't know why, exactly, but she suspected it had something to do with her dad letting him in on the deal and the favor he owed in return.

17

ON MONDAY MORNING, Shiv didn't show up at school. Her name was on the board outside the dean's office, which meant her absence had not been excused.

When I looked at my phone after first period, I had a series of texts from her.

Shiv: *Thinking about Pascal's wager*
Shiv: *We make a similar wager with our parents*
Shiv: *We have two options: love them or hate them*
Shiv: *Someday we'll understand them*
Shiv: *If we hate them we gain nothing*
Shiv: *The family wager*

Her trip must have been difficult. I hoped that she was making peace with her dad, and herself.

If heaven and hell weren't real possibilities, there was no reason to make Pascal's wager. Shiv's family wager didn't have the same problem. People may not like their families, or even want to be a part of them, but they are unavoidably real.

The upside was not infinite, but maybe it was enough to forgive her dad for leaving.

Shiv: *I'm sorry about Mo*
Shiv: *Something's been bothering me*
Shiv: *Where was Susanna the night Woolf died? Why wasn't she at the game with Maddie and everyone else?*

I put my phone in my bag without responding.

On my way to class, I pictured Susanna going to see my mom

after she took the pregnancy test in the Eat'n Park bathroom. Alice Northrup was such a magnanimous figure in Susanna's mind. I bet it never occurred to her that my mom had acted selfishly that day. Susanna knew she had options ("This isn't *Ireland*"), but when the lovely, young teacher suggested adopting the baby ("her"), the pregnant sixteen-year-old saw only one possibility. Mom's interests were also served by keeping the adoption confidential. The secrets surrounding my birth certainly weren't in the Whitings' interests; I wasn't entirely sure they were in mine.

Even though my mind was elsewhere, my body made it to class on time. Finals were the following week, so we spent the entire period reviewing material for the exam. Mercifully, Calculus was my only class with an exam. Philosophy had a paper. Latin required a translation. Shiv and I had the project for Community Journalism. Messing up at the end of senior year was pretty hard. To fail, I'd have to disappear altogether.

Even Mom had loosened her grip. I'd started hanging out with Ingo again, and we stayed out late on school nights with impunity. Were we back together? Had we ever been together? We never said "I love you." We were smart enough to know people who said the L-word in high school would come to regret it. Caring too much about anything, most of all a person, seemed hopelessly sentimental and uncool. Trying to be cool was also uncool. Aloofness was the cigarette dangling from our teenage lips.

Shiv was the exception. When her dad left, she decided she was going to say the L-word and "best friend" and "forever" and everything else that oozed out of her goo-filled heart and exited her body in the form of verbal affection. I see now that she was the cool one. The rest of us were rubes.

THAT NIGHT, VINCE and I met again at Eat'n Park. While he was considering what to order, I told him what happened with Shiv:

that she'd been secretly meeting with Mo Whiting, and that we hadn't spoken since before she left for West Virginia.

"Listen," he said. Reaching across the table, he pinched the top of my pen in his fingers, lifting it slightly off my notepad. We locked eyes. "St. Ignatius will fade away. All the books, most of your teachers, the glory of sports—"

"Not exactly glory."

"The embarrassment of sports," he edited. "The dances, the dramas, all of it. Either you'll forget, or you'll remember and none of it will matter. But you know what you'll always have?"

"The ability to think?"

"No," Vince said. "You'll always have Shiv. You'll lose touch with everyone else. Boyfriends, teammates, everyone. But you'll have her. I should have had Woolf. God knows, I've needed him." Then he cried. Right there in front of me and everyone else at Eat'n Park. People probably thought I was breaking up with my much older, inappropriate boyfriend. *Man*friend.

Our waitress had dropped off the check and stopped refilling our waters long before we left. Time slowed the way it does only in a diner. The evening crowd dwindled. The night-shift waitress ambled in and tucked her purse behind the counter.

It wasn't until months later, during office hours with one of my college professors, that I realized why I liked Vince so much. My professor sat ponderously, awaiting an insightful comment that reflected whatever idea he had in his head. I was there to stroke his ego, and he was there because office hours were a requirement of his employment. On the contrary, Vince expected me to surprise him.

When he went to the counter to pay, I noticed the flyer for MindTwister, which was happening the next evening. I fanned my face with the paper. Shiv loved puzzles and games. For my last birthday, she made a poster-size crossword, laminated, and gave it to me with a dry-erase pen, in case I messed up. The clues were things like "Where

I called you from when my parents grounded me in seventh grade." After sneaking out of the house, she had run to Quaker Valley High School, which was basically in her backyard. The school had an old pay phone, still operable. I had been impressed Shiv knew my number by heart. The answer was eight letters across: payphone.

Before pushing the door open to leave, Vince looked back and pointed at me. The gesture was distinctly not a wave. It was more like *You got this.*

This was high school. Or maybe life.

My Calculus book was out on the table. I had planned to stick around for a while and study for my exam, but I never cracked it open. I wanted to text Shiv, but I didn't know what to say. I couldn't ask if she'd returned from West Virginia, without first acknowledging the twenty texts she'd sent while she was gone. When I considered responding to those, I knew it was too late.

Instead of crafting a message, I snapped a picture of the MindTwister flyer and sent it to her. Three dots appeared on my phone. I waited while she thought and typed and deleted and thought and typed and deleted again.

Eventually, she responded: *I'm in.*

Vince Mahoney
March 2005

AFTER SEEING WOOLF, Walker, and McCabe getting pain injections before a game, Vince never showed up early to the locker room again. Whatever was happening in there was easy to ignore, if he wasn't there to see it. By senior year, he hardly ever thought about it, and when he did, he told himself, *Woolf's probably done with it by now*. But he never forgot the fundamental truth of hockey: Pain was part of the game.

He hadn't spoken about Woolf's pain to anyone except Father Michael, and it might have stayed that way, but for a chance encounter with Coach Perone. It was after a rare loss. Vince had allowed two goals, a high slap shot just inside his stick-side post and a deflection from the top of the crease. These goals were anomalies—St. Ignatius had controlled the puck for most of the game, and they should've won, they would have won, except the other team had somehow neutralized Woolf, who was scoreless. The final score was 2–1. Their opponents had gotten lucky, but as Coach liked to say, "A win is a win." Of course, a loss is also a loss, but Coach favored positive tautologies and chest-pumping platitudes.

The mood after the game was glum. Coach accompanied the team to the locker room. When everyone was inside, he said, "Tomorrow, we start preparing for next week." Then he turned and walked out. The guys dispersed quickly. By the time Vince left, the place was deserted.

He sat in the stands looking down at the ice, imagining what it was like to be a spectator. He pictured his mom, her hair streaked with new grays, her eyes tired, after long days of chasing Laura around the playground. Kissing Vince on the cheek, she had said, "I can't wait to be a grandparent one day, so I can have my fun and then give them back." Vince wanted the same thing—maybe everybody did—exuberance, adversity too, with the ability to let go and walk away. But there were pucks in the back of his net that would haunt him for the rest of his life.

It was late when he exited the rink. He dropped his backpack on the steps and walked around to the rear of the arena toward a wooded area at the edge of campus. Pulling his collar tight around his neck with one hand, he reached into his pocket with the other. He lit up a half-smoked joint, which he'd been carrying around all day. Normally, he didn't smoke on campus, but he didn't feel like driving down to the tracks on his way home.

He sat down on a bulging tree root, lowering his head to shield his face from the wind. The hum of the ice chiller drowned out the crunch of footsteps on frozen grass; he had no warning. Right up until he saw the toes of black dress shoes under his nose, he'd been certain he was alone.

"Put it out," said Coach.

He did.

"Are you stupid?"

"What?"

"I asked if you're stupid."

"I dunno. Maybe?" Vince said.

"If you get caught, you'll be suspended," Coach said.

"I did get caught," Vince said. "You caught me."

Coach shook his head. "You can't play if you're suspended."

"So, I haven't been caught?"

Coach stepped forward and snatched what was left of the joint. He held it up between their faces. "Is this all you have?"

Vince nodded.

Coach slipped the roach into his pocket. Vince stepped back, unsure if the confrontation was over. The weed must have dulled his reflexes, because he didn't move when Coach advanced toward him, reached into his coat pockets with both hands, and pulled out a small aluminum stash jar. Holding out the jar in the direction of the lights on the back of the rink, Coach asked, "What's in here?"

"Just weed," Vince said.

"I can see that," Coach said. He put the jar into the same pocket as the roach.

"Where'd you get it?" Coach asked. He was wearing a black overcoat, leather gloves, and a skullcap, which covered his comb-over. Vince didn't have a hat or gloves.

It was a simple enough question, but answering it would make him a snitch. Vince shrugged. He could feel Coach's warm breath on his face.

Coach put both hands on Vince's shoulders, like a father, and dug his fingers into the muscle, like a threat. "One more time," he said. "Where did you get the drugs?"

"The guy doesn't go here."

"Is he selling to anyone else on the team?" Coach asked.

"No," Vince said.

"Are you?"

"No, sir." He'd never called Coach *sir* before. He never called anybody *sir*, not even his dad.

Coach stepped back. Looking Vince in the eye, he said, "I need a name."

What would Coach do with the information anyway? He'd already played his hand. He had no intention of telling the headmaster or anybody else. The tournament started next week, and he needed his goaltender. Emboldened, Vince said, "How about you give me that back instead?"

"Now why would I do that?" Coach snickered.

"I need it," Vince said. "Like Woolf, McCabe, and Walker need shots in the ass."

Coach didn't immediately respond. He rested his weight on his back foot and folded his hands in front of his body. Then, like a shark catching the scent of blood, he said, "You can either tell me where you got the drugs, or I'll call your father."

Wayne used to disappear from the floor at Mahoney's, sometimes for hours at a time. If Vince asked where he'd gone, he'd say, "Had to run samples to the lab. No one wants E. coli in their romaine."

Which was bullshit. There was no lab. Texts came through on his burner, and he'd leave for pickups and drop-offs. None of the other guys seemed to know or care what he was doing, and word never got back to Mitch Mahoney.

Vince sang. "His name is Wayne. Like I said, he doesn't go here."

"How do you know him, if he doesn't go here?"

"Can we go inside?" Vince asked. "It's freezing out here."

Coach waited for his answer.

"From the warehouse," Vince said, hanging his head. "He works for my dad."

Coach nodded. "I'm not going to catch you with drugs on this campus again. I'm not going to see you high again. If I run into you in the hallway and your eyes look even a little bit—"

"So, you're not going to tell my dad?"

"If I find out anyone else on the team is smoking weed and it came from you, or Wayne, well then, Mitch Mahoney will be my first call."

Coach extended his hand. Vince pulled his hand out of his pocket, sweaty even though the rest of him was cold. His damp skin stuck to Coach's leather glove, so when they finally let go, the handshake wasn't quite over.

Vince watched him walk away, up the hill toward the faculty lot, which was in the same direction as the student lot. Briefly, Vince thought about lighting up again to take the edge off. Coach had cleaned out his pockets but somehow managed to ignore the backpack, which Vince had thrown down absently on the steps in front of the rink. If Coach had bothered to look there, he would have found a dime bag. He walked over to collect it, swinging the pack over his shoulder. Coach was right: He was stupid.

18

BY TUESDAY, SHIV'S name had been erased from the dean's board. She must have slipped into assembly late, because I didn't see her until she hooked her arm into mine on the way out. I pulled away, caught in a momentary state between apprehension and affection, that eerie dissonance of the mind remembering a shared history before the body reacclimates, the same feeling you might get when someone you love picks you up at the airport. She mumbled something about lunch in the art building and her Design project. Track season had ended with a loss the previous week, so I didn't see her again for the rest of the day.

After school, she texted to ask if I wanted a ride to Eat'n Park, but the rain had stopped, so I told her I'd bike.

When I arrived, Shiv had already secured a booth and ordered two Cokes and a plate of fries. When the drinks arrived, she slurped out some of her soda. Under the table, she topped off her cup with Jack Daniel's.

MindTwister wasn't a typical trivia thing—it was a series of deductive-thinking puzzles that teams completed at their own pace. The winner was the first team to finish.

The MC-slash-DJ, the male equivalent of a Burgh babe—a Burgh *bro*—hosted the event at various locales across Pittsburgh. With his Steelers track jacket and his '70s-style tortoiseshell aviators, he was probably well on his way to becoming a hometown celebrity, one of those people who blurs the line between reality TV and real life.

Burgh Bro handed each group a slip of paper with the first MindTwister, along with a notepad to jot down answers.

It went like this:

Imagine you are driving in a blizzard. You pull off the turnpike and find a remote inn. When you arrive, the only people there are the innkeeper and two lovers in room 3. You are given a key to room 2 and told not to lose the key, because the innkeeper does not have a duplicate. You decide to spend the evening by the fire in the lobby, locking your door behind you. The innkeeper informs you that the turnpike is now closed, so entry and exit from the inn by car is impossible. When you wake up in the morning, you discover a bloody murder scene in room 2. The lovers are both dead, and the innkeeper is gone. How did you survive the night?

I immediately suggested that "you" are the murderer. After all, you were the only one with a key to room 2.

I handed Shiv my cup under the table. She said, "Let's role-play for a minute. You and Ingo are the lovers in room 3. I'm in the lobby by the fireplace, with the key to room 2 in my pocket."

"We'd probably be in the lobby with you," I said.

"Okay," Shiv said. "We're together in the lobby. So that leaves the innkeeper—"

"How do we know there wasn't someone else there that the innkeeper missed?" I asked. "Or it could have been a murder-suicide. But why would they be in room 2?"

"The question is odd," Shiv said. "How did you *survive*?"

I drew a diagram of an inn on a napkin. Shiv grabbed the pen out of my hand. "This isn't your Calculus final," she teased. "I just figured it out."

"You did?"

"Remember how the puzzle started: 'Imagine' . . . The blizzard is imagined, so the murder is too."

I raised my cup and said, "To question one!"

Shiv skipped over to the MC with our answer scribbled on the little yellow sticky note.

We were given the second puzzle. Buoyed by solving the first, Shiv was really into the game. She read the puzzle aloud:

"A killer drives northeast on I-376. He avoids the airport but stops at Primanti Bros. in Moon Township. From there, he drives southeast until he crosses the state line, driving the speed limit so he does not call attention to himself. He is pulled over in Steubenville for a broken taillight. The officer runs his plates and lets him off with a warning. Why isn't he arrested?"

Shiv initially thought it had something to do with crossing state lines. But if the authorities in Pennsylvania were looking for him, why would he stop at Primanti's? "Yinz gotta get 'em Primanti's n'at," she said in her best Pittsburghese.

"How was West Virginia?" I asked.

"My dad joined a cult," Shiv said, "but, like, a harmless one."

"Does he seem happy there?"

She tilted her head, as if she hadn't considered his happiness. "Yeah, I think he is," she said. "People kept coming up to me, saying stuff like, 'Krishna sent your dad to us.'"

"Really?"

"Some kind of shake-up is underway. The guy running the place has been making shady deals. I met him. He looks like Gandhi. My dad's calling for more transparency."

"I take it the guy doesn't get along with your dad?"

She shrugged. "My dad claims he went there because our temple was too political. But it's so political down there. Everywhere you go, it's political."

Burgh Bro broke the lull in the room with an announcement. "Yinz ready for a halftime break?" he yelled into the mike. At this arbitrary midway point, Eat'n Park offered half-priced pies.

"Do you want to talk about Mo Whiting?" Shiv asked. When I didn't respond, she continued. "After I spoke with Jody D'Angelo, I started to wonder why Mo had always been so sure Susanna was involved in Woolf's death. Jody told me it was because Susanna had been like family. She was over at the Whitings' house all the time, until right before Woolf died. She ate dinner there multiple nights a week. Then, suddenly, she disappeared. Mo tried calling. She stopped by the Mercers' house. She went by the school. No Susanna. So Mo started to get suspicious. And maybe she crossed a line by returning to the Mercers' house too many times. The Mercers sent their lawyers to threaten her. Which, fine, that's probably just a rich-person thing. But they were aggressive, which made Mo even more suspicious, like 'Why are you trying so hard to get rid of me, when I only want to talk?' Still, her certainty never made sense to me—and not just because Susanna was a pretty, rich girl. Why would Susanna kill Woolf? Why was Mo Whiting so stuck on her, from the beginning?"

"Did you ask Mo?"

Shiv nodded. "The St. Christopher amulet. She told me Woolf's godmother gave it to him when he was baptized. His dad bought him a chain for his confirmation in eighth grade, so he could wear it around his neck. After that, he never took it off. Not to shower. Not to sleep. Not to play hockey. In fact, Mo had only seen him without it once. She arrived home from work early—Woolf hadn't expected her. He was up in his room with the door closed—Mo knew what was going on. She didn't want to embarrass her son, so she called out to warn him. Woolf and Susanna hurried downstairs, their hair messy and their faces flush. They'd straightened their clothes, but the amulet hung around Susanna's neck. She had taken it when they were messing around and forgotten to give it back in their rush to get dressed. When she thought Mo wasn't looking, she slipped it back over Woolf's head. Mo didn't ask her son if he was having sex. She deferred that conversation to Declan. She tried not to think about it. But she never forgot about the amulet. Mo said the experience of finding her son dead without the amulet felt like déjà vu. The two moments were overlaid in her consciousness. She was overcome with absolute certainty that Susanna had taken the amulet."

The waitress came by with fresh sodas, and Shiv instructed me to drink up to make room for the good stuff.

"*Arriba,*" she exclaimed. We raised our cups.

"*Abajo,*" I sang. We touched our cups to the table.

"*Al centro,*" Shiv responded. She pushed her cup into mine, and the plastic made a dull sound.

"*Pa' dentro,*" I said, and we sucked down our drinks through straws. Kings of the diner.

Shiv said, "I figured out the puzzle."

"Why didn't you say something earlier?" I asked.

"The toast was more important," she said. But she was really talking about our friendship. "He was killing *time*. The police weren't looking for him, because he wasn't guilty of anything."

"Except what we're doing right now," I said.

"We're not killing time." She pulled up Bridge on her phone. In her calendar, we were in the middle of a block called FIGURING SHIT OUT, coded in red. The only other red in the recent past was Kyle's funeral.

It was getting late, and I had planned on calling Maddie again, so we didn't stay for the third and final MindTwister. Shiv turned right out of the parking lot, and I trailed her on my bike for a block before heading toward home. She still hadn't gotten her taillight fixed, and I worried she might get pulled over after drinking. She texted me when she got home safe, a tacit acknowledgment that she shouldn't have been driving.

I guess we made up that night. I can't even remember if I was still mad about Mo Whiting. But I needed my best friend.

Sitting at my desk, I wondered what the final MindTwister might have been. All we had to do to solve the puzzles was listen. Could we solve Woolf's mystery by simply paying attention?

When Maddie described the night of Woolf's death over the phone, I hung on every word.

Madeline Whiting
March 2005

THE HOCKEY GAME was at seven o'clock on a Wednesday. By six thirty, Maddie sat in an aisle seat, her coat saving the spot next to her for Susanna. Everyone else was there—students, teachers, parents, even a scout from Notre Dame. No one missed a St. Ignatius hockey game, especially not the week before playoffs.

Later, the police would create a timeline—pinpointing who'd arrived and when, down to the minute.

Maddie knew it was 6:48 when the announcement came over the speakers, because everyone looked up at the scoreboard, where the game clock counted down, twelve minutes till start. The calm voice belonged to the athletic director, Mr. Houser. He said, "Declan and Monica Whiting, please report to the locker room."

Woolf hadn't been himself lately. Twice, Maddie caught him bent over, holding his back. He claimed it was nothing, that he was just stiff. The doctor had cleared him to play.

If it were possible, she'd have taken his pain, at least half of it, as much as she could bear. She left her coat on the bench, covering two seats—one for her and one for Susanna—and asked Brad, a shy kid whom she hadn't spoken to since Latin I, sophomore year, to make sure no one took her spot. He told her he'd fight anyone who tried to take it, and she almost gave him the satisfaction of a smile, but she turned and rushed away before he could see her face.

Her body tumbled through the locker room door. Mo and Big D were already there, talking to Mr. Houser.

"Good, you're here," said Mo. "Have you seen Woolf? He's not with the team." She gestured to the closed door, in the direction of the ice, where the rest of the team was skating in circles and shooting a barrage of pucks at the net.

"Not since right after school," Maddie said.

Mo hadn't yet entered full-on panic mode, but she blinked rapidly and shook her head repeatedly. She looked at Mr. Houser and said, "How could you lose him?" as if he had allowed a toddler to wander off from the merry-go-round at Kennywood.

"I'll run up the hill and check the chapel," Maddie said. Woolf always went to the chapel to pray before games. Everyone knew not to bother him there. He was superstitious about it. Other people were too, and even if they weren't, they figured, let the kid do what he needs to do. They wanted to win, so they left him alone.

THE DOOR WAS unlocked, as usual. When Maddie entered, the chapel was lit only by outside lights. She could barely make out Woolf's form on the wooden steps of the altar. In the dim light, from where she was standing, he looked like he was praying, laid prostrate, and she called out, "Hey, moron, did you lose track of time?"

She flipped up all five switches on the control panel next to the entrance. Ceiling fans whirled to life. Sconces lit the walls between each of the stained-glass windows. Drop lights over the pews illuminated God's house. When the backlights next to the tabernacle came on, Maddie saw what she would eventually describe to the police as "complete stillness."

She ran to her brother. She shook his body. She put her ear to his chest, feeling lungs without oxygen, listening to a heart with no beat. She picked up the syringe, moving it away, as if it could still hurt him. "Wake up, wake up!" she yelled, beating on his chest. She pulled his shoulders off the steps. He was heavier than she remembered, solid muscle. "Everyone is waiting for you. The game just started. Hurry! Where is your helmet? Your pads? Lace up your skates. Why aren't you on the ice already?" His body fell back to the wood. She pushed her legs under him, holding his head on her lap. "Get up! You are going to Notre Dame. Get up! You are going to be rich one day. Get up! Call me 'bitter.' It's okay. It's going to be okay. You are my brother. You are my only brother. I only have one brother. Get up! I need you to get up. I need you."

Grunting, shouting, she wrapped her arms under his and yanked him up again by the armpits, their bodies splayed on the steps, his head on her chest. As reality seeped through the crevices of her panic, she noticed something: The St. Christopher amulet that he always wore, underneath his shirt, hanging from a long chain around his neck, was not there. He'd worn it for as long as she could remember. She lay back, her head at the foot of the altar, holding her brother's body on top of her. The detective would later call the scene "compromised," but he would also say it is impossible not to compromise the body of someone you love.

Maddie looked up at the hanging crucifix and tried to fathom what Woolf said when he prayed. Unaware of how much time had elapsed—it could have been a minute or an hour—she lifted her phone out of her back pocket and called Mo. Someone else must have called the police. By the time Mo and Big D made their way up the hill and yanked open the chapel door, Maddie heard sirens approaching.

For years, every time she heard a siren in the distance, she relived that moment. Out of breath from running up the hill, what came out of Mo's mouth was the sound of a dying animal. On his knees next to Woolf's body, Big D performed CPR, forcefully, urgently, as if grit could bring back the dead.

Maddie touched her own face, surprised to find no tears.

When the paramedics arrived, Big D was told to stand back. Three bodies swiftly encircled Woolf. Mo said, "Please save him. He's not gone. He's not gone. He's not gone. Save him, please."

But he was gone. The paramedics determined death, and the cops got on their radios. Maddie and her parents were led out of the chapel. Nobody asked if the police were following protocol or if they had any idea what they were doing.

Outside, one of the medics, a woman who looked so young that only her uniform set her apart from the students, asked Maddie if she was okay. Maddie didn't know how to answer, so she said, "This isn't real."

Mo cried into her hands. Big D held her up, and also back, in case she tried to make a break for the chapel. Eventually, a police officer informed them that Woolf's body would be taken to the coroner's office, and there was nothing they could do tonight.

They were told to come to the station the next day. The cop's demeanor was lackadaisical. Maddie had discovered her brother's body and disturbed the scene, and yet, she was told to go home. The lack of investigation should have been a red flag, but no one was looking for flags that night.

Mo screamed something about staying with her son. The cop told Big D he would drive them home, and they could pick up their car tomorrow. Maddie said she would stay and get a ride home later. Big D started to say no, but Mo squirmed out of his embrace and started moving toward the police tape.

The officer stopped Mo and guided her to his SUV. Maddie watched her mother's body go limp as he helped her into the back seat. Big D hugged Maddie, and said, "Okay, stay with your friends. We'll talk when you get home." Then he slid in next to Mo, and the cop closed the door.

Sitting behind the cage, her parents looked like they were being arrested. In a way, they were, and they'd remain in a prison for the rest of their lives, the kind people can leave by their own free will but never do.

Some of the hockey players had made their way up the hill. Maddie hadn't noticed them until Vince kneeled next to her. When he placed his coat over her shoulders, she remembered she'd left her own on the bleachers at the rink. She hadn't noticed the cold, though she was shivering and her fingers were numb. Vince said, "I'll take you home." He helped her to her feet and held her as they walked to the parking lot. If he had been anyone else, she would have sent him away. Vince was the only other person in the world with the right to call Woolf the thing she had just lost forever: brother.

AFTER VINCE TURNED the key in the ignition, he would put the van in reverse and his foot on the gas, and then they would be on the road, and then they would say goodbye in her driveway—a series of motions that would inevitably lead to the state of being alone. Instead, they sat still, watching their breath fog the windshield. She stretched her body over the space between the seats, placing her head on his shoulder. He adjusted his body to put his arm around her and pull her into his chest, his chin on her head.

Sitting in that van was like wading in shallow water, gentle waves lapping rhythmically against her body. She closed her eyes and felt buoyant, almost calm, but aware that at any moment a rip current might pull her out to sea. She tried to remind herself, *If it happens, don't panic; swim parallel to shore.* But what if it was already too late? What if she'd been swimming against the rip for a long time and she'd exhausted her body without knowing it. She would almost certainly drown.

What followed was a righteous and unshakable sense that, considering her present circumstance, she could act however she wanted. She could say anything to Vince—intimacies she'd thought about for years, with no intention of articulating. Later, regret could be ignored in the face of that other, more urgent state: pain. For now, she was invincible.

"You should kiss me," she said, pressing her cheek against his chest again.

"Are you sure?" he asked.

She pulled back, settling into her seat, and looked at him. His lips parted slightly. His skin looked smooth in the white light from the parking lot. He broke eye contact and looked at his hands on the steering wheel.

"I'm sure," she said.

They stayed in the parking lot for a long time. After a while, Maddie understood that there was no rip current. Desire was not a force pulling her out to sea; it was a lightning rod, taking everything—every thought, every emotion, every synapse—to the ground.

SHE DIDN'T CRY until later that night. Eventually, a therapist would tell her it was normal for a person in shock not to cry.

The house was dark when Vince dropped her off. She picked the hidden key out of the hanging flower basket before noticing the door had been left cracked open for her. Vince waited in the driveway until she waved him off.

Jágr greeted her, tail wagging. Big D descended the stairs and told Maddie her mom was in bed.

"Asleep?" Maddie asked, though she knew better.

"I'll sit with you," he said. "Do you want to eat?"

Maddie crouched down on the floor with Jágr. His was the only presence she could bear. "You can go take care of Mo," Maddie said.

Instead, Big D went to the den, where he slept that night. One day, Maddie would realize that once her family retreated to separate corners of the house, they never lived together again.

In the kitchen, Maddie found a partially eaten lasagna in the fridge. On game nights, Big D always made comfort food. He and Mo would eat before the game, and Woolf and Maddie would feast on the leftovers late at night. She pulled the pan out and cut a piece big enough for herself and Woolf combined. Standing at the counter, she ate the food cold, gulping it down, each mouthful bigger than the last.

With one bite left, stabbed onto the fork, she dropped the plate, ran to the bathroom, crouched over the toilet, and threw it all up. She held her position until she was sure her body was done, and then she stood up to wash her hands and rinse her mouth. If she hadn't needed the sink, she probably wouldn't have looked at herself in the mirror that night—she didn't want to—but no one can stand in front of a mirror and not look.

She thought, *If it were me and not him, Woolf would take care of Mo and Big D. He'd shake all the hands at the funeral. He'd channel his grief into a life of discipline and hard work. He'd become a captain of industry. And when the newspapers and magazines profiled him, they would say: "The death of his sister was the pivotal moment of his life."*

But it wasn't her. It was him. And what had she done? She'd hooked up with Vince.

Back in the kitchen, the broken plate remained on the floor where she'd dropped it, remnants of sauce and cheese on the surface, pasta still twined in the prongs of the fork. Odd, because Jágr usually ate everything within reach.

She found him sitting upright, eyes fixed on the front door, waiting expectantly for the one person who would never come home again. Jágr knew their rhythms. He was anticipating the late return of his favorite person.

On any other Wednesday, Woolf would have walked through the door by now. He'd bend down so Jágr could lick his face. He'd go directly to the kitchen, dog at his heels, heat his dinner, and sit down at the table. When his plate was empty, he'd serve himself another portion. Jágr would wait patiently, quiet until Woolf stooped to give him the scraps. After licking the plate clean, Jágr would accompany Woolf to the dishwasher and watch him place it in the rack. Together, they would ascend the stairs. Jágr would wait outside the bathroom door, listening for the sound of the shower, then he'd amble to Woolf's room and jump up on his bed, where he would rest until they could be together again.

Maddie kneeled on the floor next to Jágr. She told him, "Woolf's not coming home, boy. He's never coming home."

This time, she didn't have to touch her face in search of tears. She could taste them on her lips. Jágr turned his head toward her face and licked the salt water from her cheek.

She was already on her knees. That might have been why. Or maybe it was because she was out of other options. Whatever the reason, Maddie did something she hadn't done since she declared she was an atheist in junior high: She tried to pray.

She *wanted* to pray. She wanted to ask God, "Why?" She wanted to ask for forgiveness. She wanted to say Hail Marys and Our Fathers. She wanted to feel something, even if that meant feeling the presence of something she didn't believe in. So she folded her hands, fingers interlocked, and bowed her head. And then—

She felt nothing.

Maybe feeling nothing wasn't proof of anything except the depravity of her own heart. But her brother was dead, and she felt the Absence, and she understood the truth of her conviction: God did not exist.

19

SHIV SLAMMED HER Frappuccino on the table so hard a little slush emerged from the straw. "So why wasn't Susanna at the rink that night? Where was she?"

I didn't need to ask Susanna where she was the night Woolf died, because I already knew.

Susanna and Patricia Mercer *were* on the St. Ignatius campus that night. They weren't at the chapel, where Woolf died, and they weren't at the hockey rink with everyone else. They were at the second house from the end, on Faculty Row. It's gone now, but back then it was my mom's house.

No attorneys were present. Patricia Mercer had apparently had some ideas about dispensing with formalities and coming to an understanding "as women," which my mom had viewed as a tactic. Not that it mattered. They could have told her she had to cut off a limb upon receipt of the child, and she would have signed the papers.

When I asked my mom if she thought about Monica Whiting after Woolf died—as a woman, as a mother, as a human being—she said she did. But she had signed a contract. What else could she do? She found the situation regrettable, but if she had to go back and do it all over again, she'd do the exact same thing.

"I'm not sure if that's really regret if you'd do it all again," I said.

"I think it is," Shiv said. "I regret the burrito I ate for lunch, but I'd eat another one."

"Sure it wasn't pizza?"

Shiv's face went deadpan. Reaching across the table, she put her hand on my shoulder, the gesture of a proud father. "Everything *is* pizza. Sauce, cheese, toppings . . ."

We stopped talking and looked toward the door when we heard familiar chatter. I don't know why I was surprised—Starbucks wasn't the place to go if you didn't want to run into somebody—but Ingo's presence briefly took the wind out of me. He was with two other guys, both hockey players, and three girls. Not a triple date, more of a six-person crew. Still, one of the girls was Barbara.

When he saw me, his face contorted in the way one does when a smile is cut short. He approached our table and had the gall to accuse me of doing something untoward. "You said you had to work tonight."

"We are working on a project," Shiv said. "A really important one, so you can go now."

Ingo looked at me.

"Community Journalism," I said, which seemed to satisfy him. "Looks like you found someone else to hang out with anyway."

He rolled his eyes. Few things aggrieved Ingo more than the implication of impropriety when he believed he had done nothing wrong.

I had channeled enough self-respect to ask Ingo to tell Barbara to stop texting him all the time. She could text someone else's boyfriend. If feeling that way made Ingo my boyfriend, then I guess he was.

While I was thinking about how much I hated Barbara, Ingo excused himself and returned to his crew. I couldn't outwardly acknowledge how I felt about her, because, well, *sisterhood*. But I kept fantasizing about existing in a Barbara-less vacuum. In the vacuum, Ingo and I were blissfully happy.

Barbara caught me looking at her and waved. She smiled with her whole face, eyes aglow, dimples pronounced, teeth slightly parted. A small gold cross dangled suggestively against her breastbone, visible just above the button of her shirt, inches from her perky, little breasts.

Shiv said, "Ingo definitely has a type."

"What are you talking about?"

"I'm not saying you're the same as Barbara. I'm saying you're the same type."

I shook my head in disbelief.

"Oh, come on, Frankie," she said. "Gorgeous-slash-ambitious."

"But I'm nothing like Barbara," I said.

I wasn't exactly protesting. Deep down, I wanted to be more like Barbara. She seemed so . . . Happy? Uncomplicated?

Like Barbara, I was headed to a top college. Unlike Barbara, I questioned my purpose. Something was missing. Or I was missing something. Or everybody was, and most people just didn't care. Kyle had cared, I guess. As a result of this—let's call it insecurity—I feared I would never achieve Barbara's level of success.

St. Ignatius didn't have a popular crowd, in the way people mean when they talk about high school social dynamics. But certain people were at the center of everyone else's orbit. Barbara was one of these people; I was not.

Before I started hanging out with Ingo, I was usually either with Shiv or alone. I liked to take walks around campus by myself. The campus had been home for the first ten years of my life, before our bungalow on Faculty Row was demolished to make way for the new dorm and we moved to the town house off campus. Nobody else walked the grounds unless they were going somewhere specific. Sports teams ran circuits around campus, but those were mandatory.

I WOULDN'T SEE Barbara as anything other than a boyfriend-stealing perfectionist automaton until my sophomore year of college, when I ran into her over Christmas break. I had heard she'd dropped out of Stanford to found a tech startup, something involving AI, for which she'd secured a $50 million A round. I'd immediately pictured her on the cover of *Forbes*: the white button-down, the gold cross still dangling against her breastbone. Maybe she'd ditched the Catholic-schoolgirl look, in favor of a turtleneck or a hoodie, but that's not how I saw her in my mind's eye. And here's the thing: What I saw, or what I thought I saw, was entirely wrong.

I ran into her on Beaver Street. She was looking down into her phone and about to walk right past me. With perhaps too much enthusiasm, I stepped in front of her body and exclaimed, "Barbara! I heard about your company!"

For some reason, we agreed to take a walk together, which ended on a bench in Riverfront Park. She told me her story.

Toward the end of frosh year at Stanford, she'd gone to a fraternity party on campus, and she'd ended up alone with one of the brothers, in his room. She didn't have to tell me exactly what went down; I already knew, because I'd heard the story a million times before. I'd read the same crime alerts from the Department of Public Safety at Princeton. The assault was always perpetrated by an acquaintance. It always occurred in a residence hall. The only person responsible was the perpetrator. And so on.

Barbara had been on her period that night. The next morning, the guy pushed the blood-stained mattress out his window, evidently disgusted with *her*. So when she walked by the house on her way to report the incident, she saw her humanity reduced to menstrual blood on a rapist's shitty campus-issue mattress, discarded in the bushes.

There was an investigation. In the end, the cost of the mattress was assessed against the balance of the guy's university bill. The punishment for his crime: $350, charged to his parents.

She left Stanford, because staying was unbearable. Meanwhile, her dad had secured funding for his new project, KlaraAI. Her parents decided dropping out of college to found the next unicorn was better than dropping out because you'd been raped.

Barbara's gaze was fixed on the river as she recounted these details. She did not once look me in the eye. And yet, for the first time in my life, I saw her as a human being. Oh my god, her humanity had been there all along, and I'd never gotten out of my own head long enough to recognize it. Barbara had to be violated in the worst possible way, literally raped, before I could finally see her as more than the sum of her achievements.

How had I never understood the limitations of sisterhood? Were we all little Ayn Rands running around minding our own business until one of us was assaulted, prompting the rest of us to care?

And if so, how much do we have to suffer before we finally see each other? Maybe it's worse for men. I don't know. Maybe men don't see each other at all.

Barbara is still the CEO of KlaraAI. She hasn't graced the cover of *Forbes* yet, but I heard she closed a B round for a couple hundred million. Maybe she's doing fine. But now, when I think about her, and when I think about Susanna, I understand what their families took from them by cloaking their humanity with NDAs and fake origin stories: the one thing that would allow them to be seen, really and truly seen.

I CLOSED MY eyes and listened to the hum of the milk frother. Mercifully, when their drinks were ready, Ingo and his crew took them and left. The net result of this unfortunate encounter, in our unfortunately small town, was that I felt sick to my stomach and could not finish my Frappuccino.

"Too bad Woolf can't tell his side of the story," I said.

"Let's go back to the Whitings' house," Shiv suggested. "If we dig under the cherub, we might find something there."

"Are you going to alert your buddy Mo before digging up her yard?"

"I'm sorry," Shiv started.

"I don't care anymore," I said, and I meant it. We both nodded in agreement, though I wasn't exactly sure what we were agreeing on. "You really think we might find something?"

"I don't know," Shiv said. "A drug stash?"

"Or the only thing there is an old hockey puck."

"Maybe," Shiv said. "If Woolf has something to tell us, we might find it under the cherub." We locked pinkies, something we never did, but it felt right in that moment. "Monica Whiting doesn't get home till after six on weekdays."

"We should go next week, when exams are over," I said.

Shiv rolled her eyes, because she wanted to go sooner, then agreed to my terms.

I also had plans to talk to Maddie and Vince once more to learn about the aftermath of Woolf's death. The only thing left to do after that was to write up our essay and turn it in. Neither Shiv nor I cared about the grade. The implications of our investigation extended well beyond the class, a fact that would please Dr. Zap to no end.

Madeline Whiting
March–April 2005

RECALLING THE IMMEDIATE aftermath of Woolf's death, Maddie could still smell Detective Faron's deodorant: Old Spice. Whenever she smelled that particular brand on a man—during sex, on the subway, in an elevator—it jerked her back, leaving her with the feeling of whiplash.

During the interrogation on the day after her brother died, Maddie had been the one to bring up the neighbor's dog. In a daze, she wasn't entirely sure why she mentioned something so minor. Later, she realized how intimidated she felt in that cold, gray room, without her parents present (a lapse Big D would condemn). She must have figured the cops would find out about what she'd done to Pickle and think she was crazy. When she mentioned the raisins, Faron nodded knowingly. "I get it," he said. "I would resent doing my brother's paper route too."

She wanted to tell him she hadn't resented the paper route—not really—but he had already moved on. He asked about Vince, whether Maddie had seen him with drugs. When she said they occasionally smoked weed—only weed—the detective winked at her.

"Did Susanna break up with Woolf, or was it the other way around?" Faron asked.

Susanna had broken it off, but Maddie couldn't explain why. "People break up," she said, as if it wasn't something they chose to do, but something that had happened to them.

Woolf's mental state was the primary topic of the interview. Faron wanted to know if Woolf had difficulty balancing hockey and school and his other commitments. "Did he seem overwhelmed?" She remembered that question specifically, because, if anything, Woolf always seemed underwhelmed, ready for his next big move: college, a career in finance, a family. He acted like a grown man in a teenager's body.

Detective Faron only apologized for one question: "I'm sorry I have to ask you this, Madeline. Do you think Woolf intentionally hurt himself?"

She watched his face crinkle into a grimace, in anticipation of tears, but her eyes were dry. She said, "If you knew him, you'd know how stupid that sounds."

"Stupid?" He raised one of his fat-caterpillar eyebrows, as if he'd caught her in a lie.

She folded her hands together on the table. Her freckle, the marker she'd used as a child to learn left from right, had faded over the years, but she still looked at it sometimes. How could she explain the obvious? Faron had asked her opinion, but he needed evidence. "I can prove it," she said.

"Prove what?"

"Woolf had an aggressive portfolio," she said. "He talked about it all the time—about having a long time horizon, no plans to withdraw the money. He had a scholarship to college lined up. He used to say that with enough time, he could recover from any loss, ride out a bear market, or whatever."

Faron was no financial genius.

"Don't you get it? Woolf was planning for ten, twenty, maybe fifty years down the road. He was planning for retirement."

"Eighteen-year-olds don't plan for retirement," Faron said, shaking his head.

"My brother did."

Then Faron asked her the question she'd been thinking about but did not expect: "How well did you know your brother?"

She was hit by one of those mental sequences that people describe after near-death experiences. When her life flashed before her eyes, she saw Woolf, always there, from the moment she was born until the moment he died. When they fought as kids, Mo would always say, "You only have one brother," insinuating that the sibling relationship would eventually supersede the parent-child relationship. That Woolf and Maddie would bury their parents one day. At least, that was how it was supposed to work.

And then she realized something else: Her brother was unknowable to her.

FRIENDS AND NEIGHBORS dropped off casseroles and baked goods. Big D shoved everything he could into the freezer. When the freezer was full, the food went directly into the trash.

The kitchen table was covered in papers, which included autopsy and toxicology reports, newspaper clippings, and business cards from private investigators.

The table's function no longer involved eating. Occasionally, Maddie would spot Big D spooning cereal into his mouth over the sink. Sometimes Mo would slather peanut butter on bread. She'd eat three bites and push the rest into the disposal. People started telling Mo she looked good, obviously referring to her thinness, but they were wrong. Her skin was gray. Her concealer did not hide the bags under her eyes.

Maddie needed her best friend. But in the weeks after Woolf died, she and Susanna traded phone calls only a few times. When Maddie asked to meet up the first time, Susanna said she wasn't feeling up to it. When she asked again, Susanna said she needed to be alone. Maddie didn't ask a third time.

By April, Susanna had stopped coming to school. People assumed she couldn't handle being on campus after Woolf died, and many were busy with their own grief. Maddie heard the Mercers had arranged for Susanna's schoolwork to be dropped off at home, so she wouldn't fall behind. Ms. Northrup proctored her exams and returned her papers personally. Susanna had taken the SAT early, so she didn't have to worry about it in the spring.

So Maddie was surprised when Susanna called out of the blue, asking her and Vince to meet by the railroad tracks at midnight. Maddie had been sneaking out of her house since junior high, and Vince's mom went to bed early with Laura when his dad was out drinking, so arranging a rendezvous wasn't a problem.

Maddie and Vince were already there, passing a joint, when Susanna approached. Maddie didn't notice her best friend's body until she saw the shock on Vince's face. He squeezed his eyes closed, and then opened them wide. "What the—"

"It's Woolf's baby," Susanna said. The night was warm for April. Susanna needed only a fleece, which she could still stretch across her belly and zip up, and a beanie pulled down over her ears. Her long hair blocked the night air from entering her open collar.

"How long?" Maddie asked.

"About halfway," Susanna said.

They stood facing each other in a tight triangle, close enough that Maddie or Vince could reach out and touch her belly without moving their feet. Neither did. "Put that out," Maddie said to Vince. "Can't you see she's pregnant?"

"Oh, I can see," Vince said. "That day in Advanced Bio, when you puked your guts out, you were—"

"I've learned the hard way that morning sickness isn't relegated to the morning. How unfair is that? For a while, it came and went in waves. The smell of the lab must have triggered it."

Maddie became conscious of her inability to look away. It was like Susanna had jumped out from behind a mirror in a fun house.

"Now you know why I've been laying low," she said.

"Did Woolf know?" Maddie asked.

"I didn't have the chance—"

Maddie took a small step back.

"The truth is, I wasn't going to tell Woolf. Now all I want to do is tell him. So I'm telling you instead. Promise you won't . . ."

"Won't what?" Maddie asked. "Tell the whole school?"

Susanna nodded. "And you can't tell your parents either. Because they'll want the baby—you know that, Maddie."

Maddie tried to envision a version of their lives with Woolf's baby crawling around the floor. Mo and Big D had stopped speaking, unless they were fighting about the police not doing their job, or how the open investigation was affecting Maddie, or whether they could stay in the house Woolf once occupied without doing themselves in.

Mo talked about nothing but Woolf's murderer. She didn't talk about his life. She didn't share memories of his childhood. She didn't cry while watching home videos of his first time on ice skates or blowing out candles on a cake, or all those long afternoons running around the neighborhood. She didn't cry at all. She was too busy.

When the police investigation stalled, Mo's engagement with the circumstances turned into an obsession. Even Big D could no longer rein her in. Could a baby fix them?

A train approached, the short blasts of the horn still distant.

Vince kicked the gravel at his feet. "It's their granddaughter."

"DNA isn't what matters," Susanna said.

Maddie covered her face with her hands. "Why tell us now?"

Susanna was quiet for a minute. "I can't keep this secret alone. It's too big for one person."

"Nobody else knows?" Maddie tried to wrap her mind around how the Mercers planned to hide a baby.

"Ms. Northrup agreed to keep it quiet. And my parents obviously know, but they're more embarrassed about it than I am."

"You told Ms. Northrup?" Vince asked.

Susanna started to explain. "Ms. Northrup is going to adopt her. We agreed to—"

"It's a girl?" Maddie asked.

"Unconfirmed. When I told Ms. Northrup, she immediately started talking about 'her.' She wants to call her Francesca." Susanna described the plan for a confidential adoption. Francesca would be able to decide for herself whether she wanted to know the truth after she turned sixteen.

"So one day, my brother's kid might show up out of nowhere? Like, she could ring the doorbell?"

"By then, everything will be different." Susanna's hair looked thicker and more beautiful, if that was even possible. "I shouldn't have told you," she said. "Not telling your parents—it's too hard. But I need you to swear . . ."

Maddie said, "I won't tell anyone."

"But—" Susanna had started to say something, then stopped. She cupped her belly with her right hand. "If Mo finds out, she'll want her."

"Yes, she would," Maddie said.

A scenario played out in her head: What if Ms. Northrup raised the child, and Mo and Big D helped—had her over after school, fed her cookies, taught her how to tend the garden, like normal grandparents.

But Mo would do everything she could to change Susanna's plan. She'd argue the child would be better off with two parents who are genetically related to her. She'd try to take down Ms. Northrup.

Time had stalled the day Woolf died. Everything had unfolded, but nothing had changed. Their house was no place for a baby. It would never be. The kitchen table would always be covered in papers that belonged somewhere else: in a drawer, or a fire. "I won't tell," Maddie repeated.

"You seem distant," Susanna said. She tossed her hair over one shoulder, eyes shimmering.

"Everything is not about you, Susanna. I lost my brother, and my parents lost their son. We have other things to *not* talk about."

The train was close now. The rumble of the wheels on the tracks was audible, the steady percussion echoing the way they felt, maybe the way everybody their age felt.

"It's the right decision," Susanna said, like she was still trying to convince herself. "All the attention on us—on St. Ignatius—it's all bad. People are calling Vince a drug dealer."

Vince looked to the ground. "I sold a little weed to a few people," he said. "That doesn't make me a dealer."

"People are saying you were having sex in the student parking lot," Susanna said, "*the night Woolf died.* Is it true? Did you guys do that?"

"Who cares what they say about us," Maddie said. "How are you hearing this stuff? You haven't been at school."

Susanna rubbed her belly. "Francesca still has a chance to be happy. Someday, if she wants, she'll learn the truth, not the lies about us."

Maddie pointed at Vince and Susanna, before turning her thumb on herself. "Three prime suspects," she said.

"Four," Vince said, "Don't forget about Woolf."

"There's no way Woolf would've injected those drugs into his own body. That is insane," Maddie said.

"It's actually not that crazy," Vince said.

"How would you know, Vince?" Maddie snapped. "You stopped—"

"Woolf was playing through pain. Coach—everybody—wanted him on the ice."

"And?" Susanna asked.

"And I wanted him to stop going along with it. I said he should take some time and let his back heal. He had no idea what he was doing to his body. Maybe he was taking more than those shots the doc was giving him. I don't know. Woolf brushed me off."

Maddie sat down on the ground, pulling her knees to her chest.

"Why didn't you tell anybody?" Susanna pressed him.

"I told Father Michael," Vince said. "I thought he'd know how to help Woolf without, like, ruining his life."

"You mean ruining *your season*," Maddie said, tears and snot all over her face.

"Give me a break. You know I don't give a shit about hockey." Vince stepped away and relit his joint. "Maybe Woolf talked Father Michael out of reporting it. The championship was coming up—"

"Someone murdered him," Maddie said.

"Woolf wanted to play hockey. People didn't stop him, because they wanted him to play. Maybe he took it too far. He must have thought he could handle it."

"Not true, Vince. Hockey was his ticket. A thing he was good at. Got him into St. Ignatius. Got him in with certain people. Woolf wanted to be more than some kid on the ice." Maddie had to raise her voice almost to a yell to project over the passing train.

The earth vibrated. Time passed, maybe a couple minutes, but it felt longer. No one spoke again until the train had disappeared.

"Look." Vince's voice broke. "I don't know, okay. I don't know why he did it. But I think he did. I mean, what's the alternative?"

Maddie shook her head.

"I'm not saying he did it intentionally," Vince added.

"We don't know what happened," Susanna said. "We need to stop talking about it. Police, fine—if they make you—but no reporters. No TV shows or whatever they try to make, okay? That's why I asked you to come out tonight, to make a pact. We're all in this together now. Think about Francesca."

"Let's call her Frankie," Maddie said.

Vince pointed at Maddie. "Should we call you Aunt Madeline?"

"I'm too young to be an aunt."

Susanna sat down next to Maddie and put her arm around her waist. She said, "I trust you." They put their foreheads together and promised never to tell anybody about the baby. Vince went along with it.

BEFORE SNEAKING BACK into her house, Maddie stopped by the cherub statue where they had buried the hockey puck. She considered digging it up, but she didn't have the strength to move the cherub. What would she do with an old puck, anyway? Carry it around like a talisman?

She started to tell Woolf that she planned to keep Susanna's secret, but standing there, she felt the Absence, and she knew she would never again be able to tell her brother anything. It was a decision she'd have to make on her own, and she would be the one to live with it.

That night was the last time she saw Susanna before Mo went public with her personal vendetta. Susanna's hibernation fueled Mo's conviction that she was the killer. The police received statements from Susanna only through her lawyer. The media had no access to her. Mo organized the first of many vigils for Woolf, each time begging anyone with information to come forward, as if he were missing, not dead. Susanna's absence was noted each time.

Maddie was unable to tell Mo the one thing that would explain Susanna's behavior. She knew Mo well enough to predict that knowledge of the pregnancy would only amplify her animosity. Maddie did the only thing she could do. Nothing.

In the midst of all this, Maddie received her acceptance package from NYU. Confronted with the message "You've made it!" she pictured Woolf in his Notre Dame sweatshirt, his face nuclear with self-satisfaction. She had wanted to go to NYU because it was the opposite of Notre Dame. Now that he was gone, the thing she'd thought she wanted no longer appealed to her.

She enrolled at Carnegie Mellon instead. It wasn't a choice she remembered making. She kept waking up in the morning to find she was still in Pittsburgh.

But keeping Susanna's secret was a choice.

20

THE NEXT MORNING, Shiv texted: *Impressive that Maddie never told Mo about the pregnancy. It's a big secret to keep for so long.*

When she was in high school, Maddie seemed to view most interactions as sentimental, trite, and generally beneath her—gifting carnations, passing notes in lockers, wearing corsages to dances. She was too complicated for boyfriends, too aloof for parties, too smart to care what people thought of her. I got the impression that the things Maddie considered embarrassing were the things that would have made her feel less alone. Her stubbornness was born out of a desire to avoid the pathetic trappings of high school, which most people enjoy because they are too inexperienced to know that one day they will regret them. But if you take this kind of reasoning all the way to its end point—inevitable death—every decision, incident, and interaction is pointless, so the fact that people care just makes them human.

Was Maddie able to keep the secret of my existence because she was prematurely independent? My heart broke for her.

OUR LAST EXAMS were that day. Shiv's Bridge invite for 4 p.m. was labeled *Forgive us our trespasses*. We planned to go to Monica Whiting's house and dig up whatever was buried under the cherub, before she was due home from work.

The first thing I noticed when we stepped onto the property was the quality of the grass. No dandelions, no crabgrass, no creeping Charlie: the lawn of a person who did not tend to it herself.

Mo Whiting's lawn was the only part of the property that was well maintained. The house was small, not much bigger than the town house Mom and I shared. The forest-green paint was peeling off the shutters on the front of the house to the extent that I could see that they were, at one time, eggshell. Black mold appeared to be growing on the beams that held up the porch roof. The house screamed, *The owner has given up.*

"Side of the house," Shiv said. We made our way across the yard to the cherub, which was partially hidden by a bush.

We stood next to it for a minute, eyeing each other. "Are we really doing this?" I asked.

"Why not?"

"We're trespassing, for one thing."

"Pshhhh." Shiv looked in the direction of the shed. The wood door, which was rotted through, hung open. "If we don't find anything useful, we'll put the cherub back, and no one will know we were ever here," she assured me.

The cherub was heavy, maybe fifty or sixty pounds, and, over the years, it had settled firmly into the ground. Shiv took one wing, and I grabbed the other. We lifted it high enough to clear the depressed earth and dragged it onto the grass a few feet away. The ground was compact, but Shiv had had the foresight to bring a trowel.

While she dug, I watched the road. It was now after five, and though Shiv claimed Mo Whiting never returned home before six, there was always a chance she might deviate from her routine.

Before I could tell her to hurry, Shiv said, "Got something here." She unearthed a Ziploc bag, dirty but fully intact, and handed it to me. Lifting a second clear bag out of the murky outer bag, we could see immediately that we were looking at Woolf's signed Jaromír Jágr puck in its plastic case. Without opening the interior bag, I slid it back into the dirt-covered bag with the intention of returning everything exactly as we found it.

As I pressed my fingers along the seal, anticipation morphed into disappointment. Doubting we'd find anything else, I felt like a kid waking up on the day after Christmas. Shiv continued to dig up the entire area where the cherub once rested.

Several minutes passed. I kept my eyes on the road while briefly considering whether we should have done this work at night. I didn't really care if the neighbors saw us—we could run—but I did not want to cause my biological grandmother more pain. I wasn't in a position to reveal my identity to her yet, especially not while my best friend was digging up her side garden.

When Shiv reached the edge of the ground compressed by the base of the statue, she pulled out another, larger, plastic bag and handed it to me. My heart palpitated. Again, there was a second bag, which, this time, I opened. Within that bag, I found a plastic folder, and I thought we might be in an environmentally unfriendly Russian nesting doll scenario, but there was no more plastic. Inside, I found a set of documents and Woolf's St. Christopher amulet, still on its chain, the one Mo insisted he never took off.

We crouched down over the dirt pile and flipped through the papers. They appeared to be financial statements. "Too bad he didn't leave us a flash drive with a crypto key," Shiv joked. Crypto didn't exist when Woolf was alive. "It's been right here in her yard all along," Shiv said, pointing to the amulet.

I nodded, swinging the amulet in front of my face like a pendulum.

A car passed on the otherwise-quiet street. Back when Woolf and his friends played street hockey, the neighborhood must have been alive with the clamor of kids and their games. But they had all grown up and moved away, leaving their old stomping grounds to the empty nesters, who would eventually downsize for better views or less maintenance, making way for a new set of young families. The turnover hadn't happened yet, evidenced by the eerie quiet.

"What kind of car does Mo drive?"

"Stop worrying." Shiv looked at her watch. "She's probably at Whole Foods, poking her way through the hot bar."

I looked at the time on my phone. "I need to get going anyway. I'm supposed to meet Vince in twenty minutes."

"Let's take the folder and the amulet with us," Shiv said. "I'll put the puck back."

Squatting by the hole in the ground, Shiv used her trowel to rebury the puck and smooth the dirt. "Grab a wing," she instructed. We placed the cherub back exactly where we found it. If Mo were to walk around the shrubbery and look closely, she might see that the dirt had been disturbed, but that seemed unlikely. And whoever maintained the lawn wouldn't notice or wouldn't care.

"Why would Woolf bury this stuff?" I asked, tucking the papers back into the plastic folder.

"Maddie said he had a long-term financial plan. Maybe he was working on some big investment. Maybe he thought this place was safer than a filing cabinet," Shiv suggested. The documents were marked confidential. "At least we know Mo was wrong about Susanna taking the amulet."

We were glad to tie off that loose end. But it did not feel like an ending. "Should we show it to Mo?" I dropped the amulet into the folder before resealing it and tucking it under my arm. "How would we explain digging up her yard?"

"For eighteen years, she's believed that amulet is evidence of Susanna's guilt. She'd want to know about it," Shiv said.

"But she—"

"Frankie, she won't care. We can explain the situation to her."

"I need to think about it," I said.

We climbed into Shiv's car, which was parked on the street, two houses down. She turned the key in the ignition and put down the windows but didn't start the engine right away. The silence between us felt almost religious, like the in-between moments in Mass when no one is talking.

My phone vibrated with a Bridge alert. I pictured Vince sitting at the corner booth at Eat'n Park, waiting for me.

Vince Mahoney
July 2015

AFTER THEY GRADUATED from St. Ignatius, Vince didn't hear much from Maddie. Occasionally, he saw something funny that made him think of her. When he ran into her South Bend doppelgänger, dressed in a hot-pink velour track suit, double buns atop her head, he texted Maddie a picture, and she wrote back, *You should ask Muppet-me out.*

He knew she'd gone to CMU, even though she'd always talked about NYU—her "great escape," as she had called it. Four more years in Pittsburgh only delayed the inevitable: law school in New York, and a big, prestigious firm after that. He also knew her parents had split, and her dad was living somewhere out of state—Florida, or maybe Arizona. Some of this information came from his mother, who was still friendly with Monica Whiting, even if they weren't friends.

So he was surprised when Maddie showed up at St. Mary's for his dad's funeral. He saw her sitting in the back of the church and turned around twice to make sure it was really her. The third time he turned to look at her, his eye caught Wayne, standing behind the last pew.

When the organ stopped, most people filed out quickly. His mom, who had steadied herself by Vince's side, slunk out of the pew, flanked on one side by Uncle Harry, her brother, and Laura on the other. Vince had expected Laura to reach up and take their mother's hand, but she was fifteen then, ready to enter St. Ignatius in the fall, no longer the little girl of his imagination.

A few of the guys from Mahoney's nodded in his direction, shook his hand, gave him a half hug over the pew. "Mitch never stopped boasting about ya, kid. All he ever wanted to talk about was Notre Dame hockey," one said, putting his hand on Vince's shoulder with the false familiarity of an acquaintance who calls himself a friend. Vince tried to smile, but his face contorted awkwardly. He felt his cheeks lift, but, against his will, the sides of his mouth turned downward into a frown. The last time his father came to a hockey game, he was asked to leave the premises.

Vince had played for two years at Notre Dame. Then, in a moment of clarity, which the team counselor called a "mental breakdown," he quit. He didn't see the point anymore. He lost his scholarship as a result, but his parents didn't mind paying tuition for a couple of years, a small price to have a kid with a degree from Notre Dame.

As the church emptied, Vince found himself unable to move. Before long, Maddie sat down next to him in the front pew.

"Do you ever look around and think, 'This is strange'?" she asked.

"The world, you mean?"

"No, church. And, yeah, maybe the world too." She reached into the tan leather bag that hung from her left forearm, pulled out a steel flask, and passed it to him, tapping it against the side of his leg. He took it, holding it up in front of his face before lowering it to his lap and twisting off the cap.

"Same flask," he said.

"It has served me well," she said.

"Only you would bring a flask to the funeral of an alcoholic," he said, laughing. He put it to his nose. "Whiskey? You were always more of a vodka girl."

"I grew up," she said. "And I'm sorry about your dad."

He took a swig before putting the cap on and handing it back. "Dad would appreciate the gesture."

She nodded, sliding it into her handbag.

"You should have told me you were coming," he said. He rubbed his chin with his thumb and forefinger as he turned toward her. "I would have shaved."

"I've never been much of a phone person," she said. "It's good to see you, Vince."

He smiled at her, and then, as if he'd given her permission, she smiled for the first time since she'd arrived. After all the years, her smile was exactly the same; it felt the same to receive it.

She wore a fitted black dress that fell just below her knees, and black high heels. The only color on her person was the tan bag, which was probably worth more than Vince's car. She looked like a New York attorney, which she was, obviously, but she was also the punky little girl standing behind the screen door in her underwear, and the gangly teenager with limbs too long for her torso. The beauty on display now had always been in her possession, even if she didn't know it. She had simply grown up, and moved away, and become the person she was meant to be. Maybe she hadn't even changed all that much, but she no longer belonged in Sewickley.

Sitting next to her, Vince became overly conscious of the wrinkle-free dress shirt and the black slacks he'd purchased from Banana Republic when he arrived in Pittsburgh three days prior. He'd been working on an organic farm in Vermont, and he didn't have anything to wear to the funeral. Now, he felt like he'd picked the wrong thing, or maybe the right thing wasn't available at Ross Park Mall.

She faced forward, looking at the altar. She'd renounced the church long ago. He went to Mass every Sunday and every holy day. He suffered from a lack of creativity, enjoyed the simplicity of being told what to do. But there were also moments when he considered himself a person of faith. Maybe it was possible to find God under a rock, but he wouldn't know which rock to turn over, because, again, the creativity thing. So he came back to where he was raised, to *how* he was raised. Catholicism was, for Vince, principally a religion of familiarity, which he supposed was the same reason many Muslims, Hindus, Buddhists, and Jews returned to their traditions. Keep coming back, and the mystery becomes a natural state, easier to abide.

He watched Maddie pull the flask out of her bag again. She tilted her head back and closed her eyes as the whiskey touched her lips.

When her eyelids fluttered open, she jumped. Wayne stood inches away from her in front of the pew. He reached out toward the flask. When she released it into his hand, he said, "Don't mind if I do."

Vince took it before Wayne could put it to his lips.

"That's no way to greet an old friend," Wayne said. "Aren't you glad to see me?"

"Must have forgotten my manners," Vince grumbled, extending his hand. Wayne shook it without taking his eyes off Maddie.

Wayne wore a black suit that hung loose on his tall, lanky frame, which he'd probably picked up secondhand, maybe for this occasion. Vince had never seen Wayne in anything but baggy jeans and hoodies.

Wayne's effort to pay his respects to Mitch Mahoney annoyed Vince, though it should have had the opposite effect. All those Mahoney's guys, pretending to love his dad—maybe they did love him, maybe they loved him more than Vince did—made the situation feel like a farce. *Remember when Mitch hit Freddie with a stepladder?* Vince wanted to yell. But nobody yells at a funeral.

Maddie held out her hand in the position of a handshake, thumb up. Wayne released his hand from Vince's grip, and in a single scooping motion, grabbed Maddie's long, elegant fingers, and turned her hand so he could lean forward and kiss it. Then he laughed, like kissing the hand of a beautiful woman was a big joke.

Wayne gestured in the direction of the framed picture of Mitch Mahoney, which was on a table near the altar. "How'd you know the boss?"

"I'm here for Vince," Maddie said.

"Ohhh, it's like that." He whistled.

"It's not 'like that,'" Vince said. "She's Madeline Whiting."

A look of recognition flashed across Wayne's face. "I knew you reminded me of somebody," he said.

"You knew Woolf," Maddie said. She had never met Wayne in person before, but she'd chided Vince for texting him all the time back in high school. Woolf's distaste for Wayne had transferred to her, like sibling telepathy, but instead of knowing the same thing, you hate the same person. "The warehouse," she started.

"Beautiful *and* smart," Wayne said.

"Buddy, you have no idea," Vince said.

Wayne's feet were in the same spot, but his upper half was now leaning over them, a close talker with bad breath. In an attempt to say goodbye, Vince stood up and offered his fist, a vestige of their adolescent relationship. Wayne gave him a bump but remained planted.

"Sorry to lose the boss," Wayne said.

"Sure." Vince sat down again.

Maddie crossed her legs and pushed her body back in the pew. She didn't look uncomfortable, but stiff and generally unapproachable, a necessary pose for a professional woman: *Don't fuck with me.* Such body language was familiar to her but didn't suit her. When she was a kid, she used to drape herself over furniture, spreading her arms across chair backs, kicking her legs up on tables. She took up as much space as possible; she made herself big. But those endearing habits of a little sister were now gone. Her hands were folded on her lap, the handle of her purse still looped around her arm. Her eyes were fixed on the stained-glass window, or she might have been looking at a station of the cross—or nothing at all, just away from Wayne. Her expression reminded Vince of someone in a waiting room whose patience hadn't yet worn thin.

Wayne swung around the side of the pew and slid in next to Maddie. "Woolf never mentioned a little sister to me. I was surprised when I saw you on the news, standing right there, next to your mom, as she pleaded for information."

Maddie did not respond.

Wayne carried on like he'd run into them at a popular brunch spot. Normal people did not act this way in the presence of the bereaved.

"Well, Madeline Whiting, you have certainly added an element of grace and sophistication to an otherwise dreary occasion," Wayne continued with false charm, convincing only when under the influence of narcotics, which Vince was not.

"You mean this funeral?" Maddie compelled him to dig his own grave. It was a lawyer's trick.

"I mean your return to the second-grayest city in the country," Wayne said.

"Pittsburgh is actually fourth in gloom," she said.

"Well then, let's grab some piña coladas and hit the Monongahela," Wayne said.

She laughed, briefly entertained by his banter. To end the conversation, Vince could have simply exited the pew, but he believed any movement would kick off a chain of events that would ultimately lead to Maddie's departure. If she got into her car and drove off, he might not see her again, for months or years. Wayne's ongoing presence felt like a theft.

Because his father had died and they were at his funeral, Vince felt entitled to his wishes—like a child on his birthday who wanted the cake and the ice cream—but he also knew, deep down, that he hadn't done anything to deserve what he wanted. He wasn't even sure whether he'd loved his father. He picked at the farm dirt that was still lodged under his fingernails.

"Are you praying?" Maddie asked. "Should we give you a minute?"

"What? No."

Maddie reached over, took his right hand in her left, and held it out. "The hands of a farmer," she said. He thought, *More of a homesteader*. And then, *I haven't done anything with my life*.

Wayne chuckled and looked at Maddie, whispering as if Vince couldn't hear. "He's all permaculture, pigs in the pasture, yada yada, but Mahoney money comes from produce grown on real big farms."

He leaned toward her, close enough that their heads almost touched, then danced away, using his torso. Extending his palms, he waved jazz hands, and sang "Pesticides," like a tone-deaf cartoon character.

Vince knew Maddie didn't care what Wayne had said, but there was a time when what he was doing up in Vermont made him feel good, even if it didn't anymore, and to hear Wayne belittle his work over the last five years enraged him.

"I'm a corporate attorney," Maddie said. "My clients make the pesticides." She might have been speaking metaphorically, or maybe she literally worked for Monsanto. Vince had no idea.

"You guys want to grab a drink?" Wayne suggested.

"I need to get to the house," Vince said. "People are expecting me."

"I'm with him," Maddie said.

"Suit yourselves," Wayne said. He reached into his pocket, pulled out a little baggie of weed gummies, and dangled it in front of Maddie. "Might help."

"Thanks. I'm good," she said.

"Vince?"

"Dude, put that away. We're in church. Jesus."

Wayne pointed to the crucifix. "Jesus," he repeated.

Maddie let out a single "Ha" before stifling her reaction, and then the tension inside of Vince's body released itself in the form of laughter, and Wayne joined in, pleased his nonjoke had landed.

They sat quietly for a minute, and then, without speaking, they all stood up to leave. Supporting his weight on the back of one pew and the front of another, Wayne swung his body into the aisle like a little kid. Maddie stepped out slowly. Vince genuflected and crossed himself before leaving, an unconscious habit, though this time he felt the odd sensation of performance, even though Maddie wasn't looking.

His mom had invited all the guys from Mahoney's to the reception, because she believed Mitch would have wanted them there, even though the old man had never invited them into their home while he was living. Vince tried to think of a way to discourage Wayne from showing up. If Maddie hadn't been there, he would have hung around with Wayne all day, but he did not want to mediate. He remembered feeling the same way when Woolf worked at the warehouse all those summers ago. Vince had always separated these worlds—his summers at Mahoney's and his peers' fancy internships, his father's drinking and the success of the business, the desire to stay close to home and the ambition that kept him away. But with Maddie and Wayne in the same room, he felt like he had to identify with one or the other, and neither felt like where he belonged.

Walking down the church steps, Maddie stopped abruptly, turned to Wayne, and asked, "How well did you know Woolf?"

Wayne shrugged. "How well does anybody know anybody?"

"You said he never mentioned he had a sister."

Throwing his arm around Vince's neck, Wayne pulled him in tight. "For one glorious summer, we were like this." He crossed his fingers in front of Vince's face. "Moving boxes all day long was like a tour in Iraq." Wayne was too dense to think twice about comparing the transportation of fruits and vegetables to the grueling atrocities of war.

Vince grabbed his wrist and pulled it forward, ducking to get out from under his arm. He said to Maddie, "They barely knew each other."

Winking, Wayne said, "He definitely wanted more, but Vince always tried to keep us apart."

"More of what?" Maddie asked.

Wayne posed like a bodybuilder, one scrawny arm curled up to flex an invisible muscle. "More of this," he said, adding, "Not in a gay way or anything."

Maddie shook her head, exasperated. Then she asked the question she wanted him to answer. "Did he ever buy drugs from you?"

Vince thought, *This must be what it's like to be in a deposition with her. First, you get a few soft questions, and then—bam!—"Answer the question now, you piece of shit." So you do.*

"Nah," Wayne said. "Woolf was way too uptight." He looked at

Vince and laughed. "Remember when I tried to pass him the joint?" He was referring to Woolf's first day on the job, in the empty lot behind Mahoney's.

Wayne took a step down and stood directly in front of Maddie, facing her with his back to the street. Below her on the steps, he reached out and placed his hands on her waist, which, to Vince's surprise, she allowed, as Wayne told her what she wanted to hear, which, in his reptilian mind, was the same as flirting.

"If you want to know what I think, I'll tell you. Woolf did not kill himself. That story was bullshit. The police couldn't figure out who did it, and everybody wanted answers, so they came up with something easy to believe. A hockey player hooked on painkillers." He pantomimed a yawn, placing his palm over his mouth for effect. "Case closed as far as they were concerned. They didn't know where he got the drugs, or why he was injecting them instead of swallowing pills like every other rich kid, but they were like, 'Choose your own adventure: suicide or accident.' So the idiot cops were all like, 'Probable suicide, blah blah blah.' People assumed Woolf's mom—*your* mom—was crazy. And she was a little crazy. It didn't help that she kept insisting it was the girlfriend, who everybody thought was far too pretty to kill anybody."

Maddie pushed his hands off her waist as soon as he brought up her mom. Wayne was rambling, but there were elements of truth in what he was saying. People did think Mo Whiting was crazy, and she had always been a little too attached to Woolf.

Then Wayne brought up something Vince hadn't anticipated, because it was the first he'd heard of it. "You want to know who did buy from me?"

"Who?" Maddie asked.

Wayne looked at Vince, raising his eyebrows. "Dude, this is going to blow your mind. Are you ready?"

Vince nodded.

"Danny fucking Perone. He came by twice. Asked for me at the front desk. The first time, he was there to warn me: 'Don't sell dope to my players, or else.' Then, like a week later, he came back. He bought enough pills to put down an elephant. 'Personal use,' he said. 'Bad back.'"

"What kind of pills?"

"Painkillers: oxy. Didn't look like a person in pain, though. He was walking fine."

Maddie dropped her bag on the steps and put both hands on Wayne's shoulders. She wanted him to focus. "How did the police not know Woolf's coach was buying painkillers illegally?"

"No one knew," Wayne said. "It was only the one time. He wasn't a regular."

Vince thought about the night Coach Perone had made him confess where he got his drugs.

"Why didn't you come forward?" Maddie asked, though she surely knew the answer.

"I couldn't exactly roll up to the police station and tell them I was dealing, now, could I?"

"They would have given you immunity for information related to the case," Maddie said.

"How could I have known that? Anyway, I did think about it, but what was the point of blowing up my life? I mean, it was a coincidence. Maybe he did have a bad back. Coach needed Woolf to win hockey games. He wouldn't have risked getting him hooked on painkillers. No one had motive. Well, except maybe this guy . . ."

"Vince?"

Wayne doubled over in laughter. With the back of his hand, he tapped Vince on the stomach. "You took his spot at Notre Dame, no? Wanted his girl too."

Maddie fell silent.

When she finally looked at Vince, searching his face, he blurted out, "The scout was there to watch *me*!" A Notre Dame scout was in the bleachers the night Woolf died. Vince didn't know who he was, but he could feel the eyes on him, watching his glove hand, his depth, his ability to recover.

He knew the guy was there because Woolf had arranged his visit, which was funny, because later, when people clawed for a motive like crabs in the sand, they said Vince had wanted Woolf out of the game so the scout would focus on his goaltending—give the spot to him—as if they were competing. But Woolf had already signed a letter of intent, his scholarship settled, a done deal.

Vince hadn't even wanted to go to Notre Dame. He wanted to bury his head in books at some small New England college. But after Woolf died, not going to Notre Dame felt like spitting in the face of his best friend's ghost. Too late, he realized ghosts don't care about spit; it goes right through them.

Wayne continued, "Like I said, no reason to blow up my life. Or Vince's, for that matter." He stuck his finger in Vince's face. "You bought more drugs from me than Danny Perone ever did. Jeez, now I'm fucking sorry I brought it up."

Maddie had stopped responding. She was looking up at the sky, bewildered.

Vince picked up her bag from the steps. "Let's go for a drive," he said.

THEY PARTED WAYS with Wayne, church bells clanging behind them, high noon on a warm summer day, and drove to the St. Ignatius campus, the only place they could think to go. Vince never stopped noticing how the path inward traced the fragrant, manicured lawns, foliage in every direction, lush, wild, and, at the same time, deliberate. They passed a grove of Japanese maples on the left, before reaching the old oak on the right, big and hearty, the branches creating a natural canopy over the road.

School was out of session for the summer, and campus was quiet. Maddie parked in the faculty lot. They got out of the car and walked toward Carson Hall, which was now LEED certified and retrofitted with a tech hub in the basement, though it hadn't changed from the outside since they'd added the "new wing," which was twenty years old. The front door was locked, but Vince remembered the way in.

The night Woolf died, Vince had returned to campus after dropping Maddie at her house. He parked on the street outside the gates and walked up the hill. From across the quad, he could see the chapel, cordoned off with yellow tape, now a crime scene. A few police cars remained in front. But the rest of campus was deserted.

The windows in the basement of Carson Hall, accessible through a window well, were never locked. He didn't have a good way to remove the screen from the outside, so he busted out the flimsy metal frame with his elbow, trying not to make the damage too obvious.

As he flushed the drugs he'd been keeping in his locker down the toilet, Vince imagined what it felt like to die. When the task was done, he groped his way along the wall until he reached the stairs. The first floor was lit dimly by the outdoor lamps, which shone through the windows. He quickened his pace and exited through the front door. Turned out, nobody had bothered to lock it that night—he could have walked right in. He returned to his van without being seen, later remembering the silent campus as peaceful, though it could not have been.

Now, Vince and Maddie squeezed between two freshly trimmed bushes and jumped down into the window well. The old screen had been replaced long ago. They could no longer push through it.

"After Woolf died, did your dad regret writing *The Spirit on the Ice*?" Vince asked.

Vince had followed the careers of all three players profiled in the book. Albie Harris, the player whose heart had stopped on the ice, was the most famous of the three. A legend in Pittsburgh, he was still around, involved in multiple charities, a fixture on TV, an all-around great guy. His jersey number had been retired.

All the players profiled in the book had decade-plus runs in the NHL. Only one didn't live to thirty-five. Considered an enforcer in the league, Eric Westby was known for bare-knuckle fighting on the ice and community service off the ice. After his retirement, his wife began noticing changes in his personality. Violent outbursts. Confusion. Depression. He started wandering around their suburban neighborhood in the middle of the night. Eventually, he took his own life in his basement. His wife sent his brain to Boston, where he was diagnosed posthumously with CTE.

Westby's condition only briefly captured the media's attention. People might have questioned the message of *The Spirit on the Ice*, but the book had been out for ten years. No one thought about it. No one wanted to think about it. They wanted the game to go on. And anyway, death was inevitable. Death was acceptable. Death was nothing compared to the life force imbued in those three men by the spirit on the ice. The widow probably disagreed, but what did she know? She worshipped a different god.

Maddie thought before answering Vince's question. "He never wrote another book, so maybe he stopped believing his own bullshit. Hockey is just a bunch of guys skating around with a rubber disk, knocking each other out of the way."

She pulled a Swiss Army knife out of her purse, slid the blade under the screen, and popped it out from the bottom. The screen remained intact. Maddie was better than Vince at everything, even breaking and entering.

Once the screen was out, the window pushed open easily. They dropped down onto the basement floor.

The lights were off, but the window wells created a dim moody space, easily navigable. The walls were lined with lockers. Almost everything in the basement had been renovated, but the lockers remained, altered only by a fresh coat of paint. Vince walked through the cluster of tables and benches, where the freshmen and sophomores hung out, to the far corner of the room. He traced his finger on number 037, his old locker.

After Woolf died, people started calling Vince a drug dealer, but he wasn't really. He'd occasionally sold a little weed to some of his buddies from the team and a couple other kids he knew pretty well. No big deal. When the police started asking about drugs on campus, his name inevitably came up, even though he'd never dealt painkillers or any other kind of pill in his life.

They searched his locker, but there was nothing there. They pulled him out of class and searched his backpack and made him turn his pockets inside out. They didn't find any drugs. They also didn't find any customers, because no one admitted to buying weed from Vince or anybody else. Vince denied he'd ever smoked the stuff, let alone sold it. Even if he wanted to, he had told the police, he wouldn't have had the first idea where to get it.

With no drugs and no dealer and no customers, the cops only had rumors. They hit a dead end, which was where everybody wanted it to go—the headmaster, the president, the teachers, the parents, the lunch ladies, the custodians, and, obviously, the students. Nobody wanted to believe St. Ignatius had a drug problem.

"I remember when they searched your locker," Maddie said, "Everybody was talking about it. Why didn't you tell the police about Wayne?"

"Because I was a scared kid," Vince said.

"But Woolf was—"

"My best friend. I didn't think about where the drugs came from. I just knew *we* had nothing to do with it."

"We?"

"You, me, and Susanna."

"But Wayne—"

"Wayne barely knew Woolf. I didn't see a connection. I still don't—" He cut himself off. "It is surprising that Coach Perone went to see Wayne. Coach caught me with a little weed behind the hockey rink, but he didn't turn me in because he didn't want me to be suspended right before playoffs. Instead, he made me tell him where I got it, and then he threatened to tell my dad if he ever caught me again. So that's how *he* knew about Wayne. I figured that would be the end of it, because Wayne didn't go to St. Ignatius. What was Coach going to do? You know?"

Maddie sat on top of a table with her feet on a chair. She leaned back, supporting her weight with her hands, and looked at the ceiling. "It doesn't make sense that Coach would buy drugs illegally for his players. The doctor working with the team would have written scripts, right?"

"The police investigated the doctor," Vince said. "He'd been giving players Toradol, an anti-inflammatory. It wasn't even a secret. I saw the doctor giving the shots to Woolf, Walker, and McCabe. The parents okayed it. Father Michael knew about it."

"Coach Perone was fired, so he must have done something wrong," Maddie said.

"Resigned. But, yeah, once Coach was out, I never saw the doctor again. Guys on the team had to start going to regular doctors like everybody else."

"It has to be connected," Maddie said.

"Those shots helped Woolf play through some pretty serious pain," Vince said. "Maybe they weren't enough."

Maddie shook her head. "We're going in circles. I don't want to do this."

Vince didn't want to do it either, but he also didn't want to be at home with his mom and his sister, standing around while everyone talked about how Mitch was such a great guy. "Let's go upstairs," he said.

They climbed the stairs to the main level. The door to the headmaster's office was closed. The nameplate read CHAD CAMPBELL. The guy had been promoted after they graduated. Vince remembered him as a young, winsome English teacher. Father Michael had been the presumptive successor, but the board had decided, for some reason, that he was not the man for the job.

Down the hall to the right was the junior/senior lounge, behind glass doors. Outside of it, Vince and Maddie arrived at their bench. According to the placard, the bench was a gift from Mary Washington, whoever she was. Back in the day, they'd bantered about what it might take to get their names on a bench, or a room, or, say, the hockey rink (even Susanna did not know how much her dad had paid for Mercer Arena). The bench was where the four of them hung out. When Maddie, Woolf, and Vince were granted entry to the lounge their junior year, Susanna was still a sophomore. She might have been the prettiest girl in school, but even that was not enough to allow her to infiltrate the sacred space.

The four of them knew each other's rhythms. When Susanna was around, they clustered at the bench; when she was not, they hung out in the lounge with their classmates.

"Let's go in," Maddie said, opening the door.

The lounge had couches and armchairs around the perimeter, which had been updated. Tables with reading lights occupied the center of the room, which Vince had used more for flick football than schoolwork.

Maddie dropped her handbag on the floor and threw her body down on one of the couches. She kicked off her heels and crossed her feet, which were elevated on the armrest. "The furniture might be new," she said, "but this place smells exactly the same."

"Remember how we used to find Woolf in here, sitting at a table underlining passages in some book?" Vince said.

Maddie added, "It was usually something Susanna's dad told him to read."

Vince laughed, "We were all reading *The Great Gatsby*, and Woolf was reading *Good to Great*."

"God, he loved those stupid business books," Maddie said. "Once, he even said he wished Ray Mercer would write a book—and I quote—'to help the common man.'"

"The master and his protégé," Vince mused.

"You know that's why Susanna broke up with him, right? She said she couldn't see herself as Mrs. Woolf Whiting. Notre Dame. Married at twenty-two. A bunch of kids. The whole Catholic deal. But really, she didn't want to date her dad."

"Makes sense," Vince said.

"Do you still talk to her?" Maddie asked.

"I got a message from her a couple months ago, out of the blue. She'd gotten a letter from Ms. Northrup, and it reminded her of what we did for her, keeping her secret."

"She sent me something similar," Maddie said. "Her memory is like a Polaroid of us, barefoot with our arms around each other's necks."

Sometimes Vince imagined them that way too. It was always the four of them, though; Woolf was always alive.

"You miss your dad?" Maddie asked.

"I guess," he said.

"What kind of answer is that?"

"I don't know if I loved him," he said. "And that makes me feel guilty."

"I hear that," she said. Declan Whiting wasn't dead, but Vince could hear in her voice that he wasn't part of her life anymore.

Her hands were folded behind her head, elbows out. She looked over at him before closing her eyes and resting her cheek on her bicep.

"How is old Declan?" he asked.

"Big D's living his best life," she said. "He's a Realtor now. And he's got a new family."

"Seriously?"

"Remarried and had another kid," she said. "Must be five or six by now."

"Wow."

"He calls me once a month," Maddie said. "I think he feels guilty."

"For leaving?"

"I should have been the one who left. I thought Mo needed me here. Big D went to Florida and filed for divorce. He spent his time golfing and going on internet dates, and whatever else middle-aged divorced men do. It worked out for him, more or less."

"Did it work out for you?"

"When I decided to stay in Pittsburgh for college, he told me I was making a mistake. Mo would be all right, he said, or maybe she wouldn't, but either way, there was nothing I could do."

"But he was wrong? You needed to be here?"

"I did," she said, "But not for Mo, like I told myself. For a long time, I was just angry. I didn't even know it was anger, but it was."

"At Mo?"

"Mostly. Angry she never snapped out of it. Angry she devoted herself to her dead son, and not her living daughter. Angry I stuck around for it like some kind of self-flagellation."

"Are you still angry?"

"At some point, I realized she had no choice. Neither of us did. Then I blamed Big D for leaving. For accepting it. Woolf didn't kill himself. No one will ever convince me that he did."

"Not even by accident?"

She blinked a few times and then squeezed her eyes shut. "Woolf didn't make those kinds of errors. He was so measured. If he was dosing, it would have been the correct dose."

"But eventually, you did leave. You went to New York."

"I did," she said, opening her eyes for the first time since she'd closed them. Vince saw a single tear well at the bottom of her right eye, the one that wasn't pressed up against her arm. She flicked it away with her finger, sat up, and straightened her dress. "Look at us! A shrink and his patient. You're the one with the dead father. Your turn to lie down and spill."

Vince stood up and moved over to the couch. He was ready to recline at her instruction, but she stayed. He put his arm around her shoulder, and they leaned back together, two friends sitting side by side.

"What are you going to do with Mahoney's Produce?" she asked.

"Sell it, I guess," he said. "Mitch didn't exactly leave a succession plan."

"Why not take it over?" she suggested. "You know the business. Hell, you've probably learned a thing or two up in Vermont that might be of some value."

"I never really thought about moving back," he said.

"Seriously?"

"Not really."

"I think about it all the time," she said.

ALCOHOL HAD BEEN slowly killing Mitch Mahoney for years, but his death was sudden. He did have the foresight to set up a trust for Mahoney's Produce. He wanted the business to go to Vince. The house and all the other shared assets belonged to his mom and Laura. A week after the funeral, Vince returned to Vermont to pack up his things and tell his friends at the farm that he had business to attend to in Pittsburgh and he wasn't sure when he'd be back. Maybe not until the next growing season. Initially, he thought he could get everything in order quickly and sell the business.

Within a few months, he secured an offer from a private equity firm that would have set up him, his mom, and Laura for life. But once he had the term sheet, he couldn't go through with it.

For a long time, beginning with college and followed by a stint working on an organic farm in New Zealand and, later, settling in Vermont, Vince did what was expected of a St. Ignatius man. He left. It was conceivable that people from other cities—Cleveland, maybe— saw Pittsburgh as aspirational, but as a young man, Vince viewed returning to his hometown as a failure of ambition. As if the simple act of leaving made him James Bond.

He never returned to Vermont. He developed a plan to distribute produce from independent growers to local restaurants around Pittsburgh, while accelerating the business his dad had built with larger suppliers.

He bought a condo in the Strip District, flipped it, and then settled into a small house in Lawrenceville. Every Sunday, he drove to Sewickley and went to Mass with his mom and Laura, and then hung around the house for the rest of the day until they'd cleared their plates from the dinner table.

Laura was a St. Ignatius woman by then, a decent soccer player on the varsity team and a bassist in the jazz band. Vince attended her games and concerts. She thought he was there for her, but really, he liked being back on those idyllic grounds. St. Ignatius was still the place where his best friend died, but with Laura there, something shifted. A couple times, he even stopped by Father Michael's classroom and sat with him at his table.

Then when Laura was a senior, an underclassman who played trumpet in the jazz band, Colton Brooks, stepped in front of a train.

Suddenly, the sanctuary, or the illusion of it, vanished once again.

21

FACING THE DEADLINE, Shiv and I stayed up all night working on our long-form essay for Community Journalism. We debated what to include and what to leave out; we discussed what made a good story. In the end, we followed Dr. Zap's advice: Essential truth is in the details. *Nominatim non generatim.*

We hadn't solved the mystery. Maybe we would never know what happened during Woolf's final minutes in the chapel. But we knew enough: Woolf Whiting was connected to Kyle Murphy and Colton Brooks—and not just because they played hockey.

In his homily, days after Kyle took his own life, Father Michael had compared suicide to autoimmune disease. Shiv and I titled our essay "The Body Attacks Itself." Everything we had uncovered about Woolf's life pointed to our conclusion: His was not the body where the attack originated.

The body was St. Ignatius.

OUR COMMENCEMENT CEREMONY began with a procession led by an Irish bagpiper. Girls donned white dresses; guys sported white pants, navy-blue jackets, and ties. We lined up in front of the hockey rink, alternating male-female, and slowly made our way up the hill, past the chapel, around the Lawn, and onto the main quad, where our families sat in folding chairs, partially shaded by the canopy of trees in front of Carson Hall.

Barbara Bertrand was our valedictorian, beating me by an inch.

(I'd earned an A- in Physics sophomore year. One. A. Minus.) Barbara was invited to speak; I was not. She offered the usual platitudes one would expect from a commencement address (gratitude, the promise of our generation) and then added that the greatest threat facing us outside the gates will be our inability to prioritize information, much of which will be false. If we cede that function—to the government, to corporations, to religious institutions, to the media, to AI—innate, humanistic urges (empathy, for example) could be deprioritized without our consent. The ultimate outcome would be loss of sanity on a mass scale. I wondered: *Are we already there?*

She ended on a crescendo. "So we must never forget to love! Love each other. Love our moms and dads. Love our teachers. Our priests." She smiled at Father Michael. "Love friends. Love strangers. Love ourselves. Love this beautiful planet. And if we find ourselves staring down the barrel of a lie, ask: 'Is it love? Or hate?' And choose love. Always choose love. Class of 2023, I love you all!"

Everyone erupted in applause. I didn't know Barbara had it in her.

Father Michael gave the benediction. Recently, I've been thinking more about what he said. Gazing out upon our cadre of high achievers, he didn't thank God for our intellects, which we would use to seek truth. He didn't praise God for our virtue, which would drive us to make the world better. He said: It is easy for us to imagine the future, full of possibility. It is a little harder to turn to the past, which, at times, slips from the path of progress, with its odd sensation of déjà vu. But it is harder still to do what we are called to do, which is to contemplate life as God experiences it, in a state of eternal present. It is humbling to consider a world not governed by action and reaction, not fueled by wanton desire, not subject to economic and political manipulations, a world where birth and death and growth and decay operate in tandem. In this state, we see each other—see ourselves—not for what we've done at St. Ignatius and not for what we will do in the next chapter, but for who we are: a collective of individuals. Invoking the Taoist tradition, he said that witnessing humanity in a state of eternal present is the opposite of ambition. It is freedom. He wished that for us—one day, we'd be free.

Amen.

22

A WEEK AFTER graduation, Mom took Shiv and me to the cabin in the Poconos where we vacationed every summer. We had two weeks before I dropped Shiv off at her Hindu summer camp, where she was a counselor.

Our time together felt different than in years past—heavier and lighter, in the way of dreams. We knew it might be our last opportunity to do nothing together. After we started college, there would be summer internships and jobs and trips abroad, new friends and new passions. But for two brief weeks, we had only each other. (And Mom, who was happy to read her books and let us be.)

The camp was only about thirty minutes away from the cabin, so when it was time to drop Shiv off, Mom handed me the keys to her car.

"I've been thinking about Woolf," Shiv said. "Maybe we didn't want to believe it was suicide, so we missed the obvious."

When I didn't respond, she added, "Mental illness is genetic."

"I know."

"Or Woolf might have been fine. Like Maddie said, his investment approach was long-term. Did you ever show those documents to anyone?"

I shook my head. Shiv had wanted me to give the amulet and the papers we found under the cherub to Mo. When she'd brought it up a third time, I'd asked her to back off. I agreed Mo had a right to know we found the amulet, but I wasn't ready to meet my grandmother.

When we arrived, I got out of the car to hug Shiv goodbye. She grabbed her bag from the trunk and reached into the side pocket. She handed me a note, origami-folded so it was its own envelope.

"See you in a couple weeks," I said.

"Text ya tonight," she said, slinging her bag over her shoulder and walking away.

Every summer for as long as I'd known her, Shiv went to Hindu camp. She said her favorite activity was "group sharing," where they talked to each other about growing up Indian in America. They spent an hour each day on Sanskrit and an hour on philosophy, studying scriptures, gods, and stories. She ate vegetarian. She did yoga.

When she spoke about the camp, she didn't complain about religious education in the way Catholic kids did. She viewed Hinduism as guidance on how to live, which made sense to her. She never talked about reincarnation or nirvana. Once, I asked her what she believed, and she said something vague, like "Hinduism is a very accepting religion." According to Shiv, her mom grew up in a nontraditional family in India, and her grandfather was an outspoken atheist.

She also had an entire social life that revolved around her temple in Monroeville, which I experienced firsthand only once, when we were fourteen. Her arangetram was held in a large community hall adjacent to the main temple. She performed classical dance, solo on stage, for over two hours. On the drive home, my mom couldn't stop talking about it. The dedication. The memorization. The endurance. It was a side of Shiv she'd never seen before.

Shiv looked back once more to wave goodbye before disappearing through the door, and I thought about how she rebelled against almost everything growing up, but never her religion. She'd made the family wager. I had too. No matter how far I strayed, I'd always find myself, again, in a Catholic church with my mom.

I climbed back into the driver's seat and opened the folded paper. She'd written a MindTwister:

Two amateur sleuths turned over every stone (and literally, a cherub). They didn't solve the mystery, but they have the answer. What is it?

The answer was love. It was connection. Not just biological, though I had that, but also a more tenuous communion—St. Ignatius, Sewickley, maybe planet Earth. All we had to do was pay attention.

MOM DIDN'T CHECK her St. Ignatius email while we were in the Poconos. It wasn't until we returned to Sewickley that she opened her inbox to find Father Michael's resignation letter, bcc'd to her in the spirit of mutual understanding, and perhaps also as a final goodbye.

June 30, 2023
Dear Headmaster Campbell,
  I hereby resign my position on the faculty of St. Ignatius, effective immediately.
  Our beloved institution has changed. During my tenure, I have witnessed, and been party to, the insidious spiritual death of this community. What is suicide but spiritual death taken to finality? I don't mean to dismiss the very real, scientific facets of mental health, which are not my area of expertise. But it is obvious that suicide shuts the door on all worldly possibilities. It is the opposite of potential. Spirituality, on the other hand, is the act of opening oneself to infinite possibility.
  As the sole Jesuit entrusted with the spiritual lives of the students, I have failed them. When Woolf Whiting died, I was beside myself, shocked, unmoored, so I could not fully contemplate the circumstances surrounding his loss. People said his death was "unfathomable," but it was my job to fathom it. I could not, or would not.
  Coach Danny Perone had fulfilled his promise, delivering our hockey program to the national stage. He did so through relentless focus on the sport, at the expense of academics and other extracurriculars, not to mention spiritual life. After Woolf's death and Coach Perone's departure, interest in the hockey program did not abate. By recruiting the best players from around

the state, the team ascended yet again. The board commissioned a dormitory to house recruits who could not easily commute, necessitating the removal of Faculty Row. None of the teachers—myself included—complained. We had no power. Anyway, we were all having too much fun at the games.

When Colton Brooks died fourteen years later, I abdicated responsibility, because I did not know Colton personally. We had never spoken. And yet I should have acknowledged that he, too, was entrusted to my care. Now, we have lost a third young man, Kyle Murphy. Kyle never stepped into my classroom, but I knew him on the ice.

I confess that I limited our conversations to the subject of hockey. I saw a hockey player, not a human being. I never encouraged him in the art of contemplation. I never sat with him in silence. Could I have saved him? I don't know. My God, I don't know. But I denied him the possibility of a spiritual awakening that I was in the unique position to offer.

When I returned to the United States in the late '90s, having served in the foreign missions for nearly twenty years but still a young man, eager to be of use, Father Gregory enlisted me to carry on the Jesuit tradition at St. Ignatius. He insisted that the same Jesuit values that guided the establishment of St. Joseph's in Dhaka were, in fact, essential to the character of St. Ignatius, and he beseeched me to return my attention to the *Ratio Studiorum* and pray for guidance.

St. Ignatius has, in many ways, exceeded my expectations, in the curiosity of the students and the intellectual rigor of my fellow teachers, in the ineffable spirit of excellence that undeniably pervades the air we breathe, and, more recently, in the pursuit of civic-minded extracurriculars. However, I can no longer recognize St. Ignatius as a Jesuit school.

The newsletter once led with principles; it now leads with statistics. The best of our students used to dream of admittance into exceptional colleges, and each year, we sent a handful of them to the Ivies, Notre Dame, and other top liberal arts schools. Today, the parents of the entire senior class have expectations—not dreams—that their kids will attend these schools.

I was swept away, along with everybody else, with success—the success of the hockey team, of college admissions, and, not the least, though I am ashamed to admit it, of the associated attention and fanfare. It was William James who called success a "bitch-goddess," and I am inclined to agree. Priests are as susceptible as everyone else to such idols.

Though the winds blow against us, I hope I am replaced by another Jesuit, one who is more up to the task. I would be remiss if I did not acknowledge that I've loved my time at St. Ignatius, in the classroom and on the ice.

Sincerely,
Father Michael

When I looked up from Mom's laptop screen, she saw the tears in my eyes. She reminded me that Father Michael was a servant of God, and his regret would likely motivate him toward his next act of charity. Anyway, she claimed, he was never meant to stay at St. Ignatius for as long as he did. The foreign missions had called him once, and they would call again.

23

I SAT ON the documents for three months. I told myself they had no meaning. Boring spreadsheets. Monthly statements. I didn't have the guts to tell Maddie we'd dug up the secret hiding place she'd shared with her dead brother. Woolf's amulet might have remained hidden in the plastic folder forever, except for one final encounter with Ingo, the night before I left for Princeton.

He sat at my desk on the red roller chair. The door was open, and Mom was downstairs, so we were just shooting the shit. Poking around my desk, he realized that the depth of the drawer was too shallow, and he found the not-so-secret compartment. When he pulled out the folder, I didn't stop him.

He held out the stack of papers. "What's with these?"

"Shiv and I found them when we were working on our Community Journalism project. They belonged to Woolf."

Ingo corrected me. "Looks like they belonged to Raymond Mercer Capital."

"Shiv thought Woolf might have been planning some big investment."

Ingo ran his finger down the spreadsheet. After several minutes, I approached to look over his shoulder. "I don't think so," he said. "Look." He handed me a few papers. "These are statements for CDs. They specify the term and the guaranteed return on the deposit. These rates look high. We could look up historical rates to compare."

Ingo had started an investment club at St. Ignatius. His mom was a data scientist, and his dad was an attorney, which had apparently genetically predisposed him toward identifying anomalies. Still, the extent of his knowledge surprised me.

He shuffled another set of papers. "These are standard letters that go out at the end of each term. They basically say, if you take no action, your money will roll into another CD with the current rate."

"Sounds normal," I said.

"Yeah, but take a look at this." His voice lifted in pitch and volume. "It's a partial set of books. You can see the deposits here. You can also see outlays."

"What are outlays?"

"Money going out. Some of these line items are incomprehensible. But the losses are massive. The deposits were basically all gone."

"What do you mean 'gone'? I thought you said the CDs were guaranteed?"

"Unless the bank is insolvent," he said. "Then, theoretically, people could lose their money. If a bank is located in the US, deposits are insured by the government up to a certain amount, but these statements have an offshore address."

"At some point, there was a major injection of capital. See, here." He pointed to a single entry: SI ENDOWMENT FUND. "If depositors lose confidence and try to get their money out, then you have a run on the bank. The thing collapses. If they never lose confidence, more people put money in, and the bank is fine. So what I'm saying is, at least according to these documents, the bank never collapsed."

"But it almost did? Isn't it illegal to tell people their money is guaranteed and then turn around and lose all of it?"

He shrugged.

"Setting aside the law, setting aside ethics," I said, "what about morality?"

"Morality is just a construct," he said.

"Morality is the opposite of a construct!"

"Well, who is to say what is moral? The whole point of finance is to use money to make money. Aggressive strategies can get a little dicey."

"But real people deposited their money. What if it was their life savings? Or their kid's college fund? What if they need it to pay medical bills?"

"Last time I checked, Ray Mercer's name is still on the hockey rink. I'm guessing everything turned out fine."

"But what if it hadn't?"

"That's not really a question people in finance ask," he said.

If you're listening, people will always tell you who they really are. But the listening is hard, especially when you think you're in love.

"But why hide the documents? Did he get in over his head? Was he covering for someone? Was he planning to do something?"

"Guess he never got the chance," Ingo said.

I was so close, then. The truth was already in my possession. I just didn't know it yet. But it was there, subterranean, trapped in the strata of remembrance: Woolf's weekends alone in Ray Mercer's downtown office. His sudden distance from Susanna and her father. His decision to hide the documents with the amulet. Woolf intended to blow the whistle.

THE NEXT DAY, Mom and I loaded up the Subaru with all my stuff. She'd given me a leather shoulder bag for graduation, which she'd found at the consignment shop in town. It looked like something that might have been passed down from one generation to the next. I tucked the folder containing the documents and the amulet inside the bag. Then we made the six-hour trek across Pennsylvania into New Jersey.

The parents were ushered away quickly after drop-off at the dorm. Mom cried as she hugged me goodbye. Holding on to her embrace, I experienced an odd sensation of having arrived without the assurance of belonging. It was disorienting, standing on Princeton soil, feeling a deep and nagging fear that my achievement was not enough, that it would never be enough. Even though every external signal was validating, the internal one—the one inside my head—blinked red, indicating not that I had failed, but worse: that I had succeeded, but my success was irrelevant.

Mom adjusted the strap of the bag on my shoulder. I realized I'd been afraid to put it down, worried someone might walk off with a set of documents and a necklace that didn't belong to me.

MY ROOMMATE, WHO was from the Bronx, explained how easy it was to catch the Dinky train to Princeton Junction and take the train into the city. She offered to blow off orientation with me, but I told her I had to take care of something on my own, and not to worry. My aunt would be there to meet me. *Aunt* felt like a lie.

I left the following morning. According to Google Maps, Maddie's office was walking distance from Penn Station. I texted her from the train, informing her I would be there in an hour.

I'd been to New York City before, but never by myself. Stepping out onto the street, I felt alert in a way I had not when Mom dropped me off in New Jersey. Sewickley suddenly seemed utterly inconsequential. I understood why Maddie had chosen this place as her home, and I imagined Vince had felt the same way when he arrived on the farm in rural Vermont: a sense of immediacy, of reality, of, I suppose, departure. Of course, Vince chose to return to Sewickley. Maybe one day Maddie would too.

Maddie's law firm occupied ten stories of a high-rise in Midtown, all charm limited to the exterior. Inside, the walls and the carpets were shades of gray. This was the building where Maddie spent most of her waking hours.

When I got up to the thirty-seventh floor, the elevator opened to an enormous logo and a woman sitting behind a front desk wearing a headset. She stripped it off and greeted me. "You must be Frankie Northrup," she said, popping out from behind the desk.

I shook her hand, but I couldn't get out of my own head long enough to force a smile.

"I love your bag," she chirped.

Instinctively, I clutched the strap, as if she might snatch it off my body.

She led me to a waiting area with black leather chairs and *The Wall Street Journal*. "Can I get you a water? Madeline is on a call. I'll let her know you're here."

She returned with a miniature bottle of water, so I must have at least nodded. *Madeline*, I thought. *She goes by Madeline now.*

Fifteen minutes later, Maddie appeared. She was smiling, but in the way a person does when she doesn't know what to do with her face. We shook hands. Then she held my shoulders and stared into my eyes, as if she had to confirm I was real. She led me through a corridor to her office, which was small, and, like the rest of the building, gray. I'd expected mahogany, I guess, but the desk was laminate. The ergonomic chair, designed to hold her hostage, was pushed back and swiveled to one side, like she'd sprung up in a hurry. I didn't know if her world was depressing or simply normal.

A flood of guilt threatened to take us under:

"We should have done this sooner."

"I should have come to Sewickley. I can't believe you are actually here."

"It's okay," I said. "I'm glad we got to know each other first. I came to give you something."

Her phone rang. She stepped behind the desk and looked at the caller ID. "For some reason, Mo believes calling my office line is *less* intrusive," she said. "I'll be quick." She gestured for me to take a seat, which I did.

"What's up, Mo? I only have a minute."

I couldn't hear Mo's side of the conversation, but since I had a mom, it was easy to fill in the blanks.

"What box? . . . What box, Mo? . . . What box? Is it your laptop? . . . Is there a button on the box? . . . If the power is out, it doesn't matter if the cords are plugged in. The box must have a battery."

I wondered why the power was out in Sewickley and felt a pang of longing for my own mom.

Maddie hung up the phone without saying goodbye and rolled her eyes. "Something is beeping, and she doesn't know how to make it stop. She's going to call right back."

When the phone rang again, she picked up quickly.

"Mo, I'm telling you, there is a button on the box . . . Press it . . . I have to go."

Maddie gesticulated a circular motion, like she was doing everything in her power to wrap it up. She said, "Sure, Mo."

The look on Maddie's face shifted. Whatever Mo was talking about was apparently deeply annoying.

"Frozen eggs aren't embryos, Mo . . . The eggs don't have a *destiny*. It's *science* . . . So my old eggs can fulfill their destiny? . . . Was it written by a Catholic with six kids? . . . How do you know what Big D is dropping in the mail? . . . Dad bought a book about my eggs . . . I get it. What does 'talking again' mean? What happened to his Florida family? . . . I am a lawyer, Mo. I don't need to date one . . . Okay, send me the link . . . Just send the link, so I can click on it . . . Yeah, Mo, I get it . . . It just popped up on your screen? Or you and Big D talked about it and then you googled it? . . . I'm only in my mid-thirties . . . Why now? After all these years, why have you now decided to forgive Big D? . . . Fine, I promise I'll read it . . . Okay . . . Love you . . . Bye."

She hung up the phone. "I'm so sorry about that."

"I don't mind," I said.

"It's worse if I cut her off. She calls back. She wanted to talk about my 'ovarian reserve.' What a term! It sounds like an idea invented by Alan Greenspan. Like he explained the reserve requirement to some gynecologists, and they were like: 'That's it! Women should have a *reserve requirement*! We'll make them freeze a certain number of eggs by their early thirties to ensure sound fertility. But only if they can afford it. Because it's expensive. And painful. And there will be mood swings!' Mo really wants a *grandchild*," Maddie said, breaking the somber mood with a wink.

"What did she forgive your dad for?" I pried.

"Big D told the police Woolf might have secretly sought out illicit painkillers so he could keep playing through considerable back pain," Maddie said, expressionless. "It led to their divorce."

"Did he?" I asked.

"No, of course not," she said. "He took only what the doctor prescribed, what Coach Perone sanctioned. Woolf was just a kid."

"Kids can be addicts," I said softly.

"Woolf was not an addict." Her voice cracked. "The police questioned me without a parent present. Big D lost his mind. He couldn't stand the accusations. He couldn't listen to the rumors. My pain was unbearable for him."

"I'm sorry you had to go through that," I said.

"The police had already made up their minds about Woolf anyway. For years, Mo was angry at Big D. She blamed him for not being strong enough—for not believing I was strong enough."

"I have something that belongs to you—or, I guess, to Woolf, but I think he would have wanted you to find it." I handed over the folder.

She pulled out the St. Christopher amulet. Dangling it by the chain, she said, "Where did you get this?"

"It was under the cherub statue," I said. "Shiv and I dug it up with the documents."

"Oh my god, Woolf buried it," she said. "Before I moved out of that house, I looked everywhere. Tore apart his room. Sorted through his smelly hockey gear. Mo was convinced Susanna took it. How did you know to look under the statue?"

"Vince told me about the BB gun incident."

Maddie cracked a smile. "Great fucking story."

"True?"

"That I shot a little girl in the butt with a BB? Yep." She continued to stare at the amulet. "The funny thing about St. Christopher is that the church demoted him, because they could find no evidence he ever existed. When I heard that, I thought, 'When did the church start relying on evidence?' But Woolf loved this thing." She dropped it on her desk.

"Why would he have buried it?" I asked.

"No idea," she said. "Maybe he wanted me to find it. Or Vince. We were the only two people who knew about the hiding spot. It's so crazy that you found it! I've walked by that statue a million times, always thinking about Woolf, feeling his absence. But I never had the heart to move the cherub."

Maddie knew about our Community Journalism project, but she'd never asked to read the essay. When I learned she was my aunt, I understood that she didn't care about the project. She was just happy to be talking to me.

I explained everything: Shiv's reconnaissance, her conversations with Mo, our fight, digging up the cherub, finding the documents with the amulet, showing the documents to Ingo (who wasn't my boyfriend exactly). I told her I'd wanted to find out who I was before I left for college, but I still didn't know, and she said, "It's a process." I'm not even sure she was fully listening to everything I said, because her eyes were on the documents.

"I'm glad you found these," she said, and because I was so relieved to have transferred them to her possession, I didn't ask any follow-up questions.

She handed me the amulet on my way out. "Woolf would have wanted you to have it," she said. I put it over my head, allowing it to hang around my neck for the first time.

Maddie didn't believe St. Christopher had the power to protect anybody, and maybe I didn't either, but wearing the amulet made me feel closer to Woolf.

"Are you sure you don't want to give it to Mo?" I asked. But it was already mine.

24

AFTER THE US attorney for the Western District of Pennsylvania opened an investigation into Raymond Mercer Capital, the documents Shiv and I found under the cherub were leaked to the press. Maddie never confirmed or denied whether she was the source of the leak.

On late-night phone calls with Susanna, Maddie, and Vince, we did our best to piece together what happened. Shiv stayed in the loop too, weighing in from her dorm room in Evanston.

We surmised that the most likely scenario went something like this:

Woolf worked after school and on weekends at Raymond Mercer's office in downtown Pittsburgh. Often unsupervised, he had his own badge to enter and exit the building. Ray Mercer either trusted Woolf blindly or didn't think a high school kid had the wherewithal for forensic accounting. But at some point during his apprenticeship, Woolf discovered the proverbial *second set of books*.

In economics class, my freshman year at Princeton, the professor loved to say, "There's no such thing as a free lunch." It was his catchphrase. I was reminded of Susanna's story about Woolf before he discovered the truth. I pictured him utterly starstruck by his mentor's infallibility, drawing that upward sloping graph on the chalk wall in her bedroom. Perhaps Woolf should have known all along—earlier, certainly—but he was a kid, and all the adults seemed happy to stuff their faces with free lunches.

The CDs from Raymond Mercer's bank in Antigua, which promised safe, outsize returns to ordinary people—people who'd been saving their whole lives for retirement—were fiction. The funds were misappropriated for personal use and a series of risky bets, which resulted in considerable losses. New deposits were used to pay off withdrawals.

Woolf must have gone to Mr. Mercer with the evidence, once he figured it out. He had printed out spreadsheets, which detailed the losses, and client statements, which showed—falsely and to the contrary—guaranteed returns. He might have gone straight to the authorities, but he loved Susanna. Also, his parents had invested their nest egg with Raymond Mercer Capital, which, had he gone down, would have been lost. These factors would have given Woolf pause, but he would not have looked the other way. He was too good—too Catholic—with his rigid morality and his guilt.

Raymond Mercer had a little time, but not much. The scheme was about to implode. He needed a major influx of capital to continue the charade. Patricia Mercer secured this, and more, with the delivery of the St. Ignatius endowment. Once that money was in play, they needed a windfall.

Now, as I've duly noted, there is no such thing as a free lunch. Financial windfalls require tolerance for a great deal of risk. Everything was on the line. A loss would have meant ruin. But again, Ray Mercer had a solution. A sure bet: short selling a stock with insider information. But he needed a little more time to cash out. How foolish that he had let Woolf get so close!

He decided to eliminate the threat. He knew Woolf suffered from back pain, and everyone would believe he took powerful painkillers. So he called in a favor. He asked his oldest friend, Danny Perone, to purchase the drugs discreetly. I doubt he shared his intentions. Once Ray Mercer had the pills, he needed only to crush and dissolve them in water and draw the liquid into a syringe. He knew where to find Woolf alone before the game. Everybody did.

Woolf trusted his former mentor enough to let him approach from behind, and the element of surprise ensured that Mr. Mercer could inject the drugs without a struggle. The powerful synthetic opioids incapacitated Woolf quickly. Even if there had been time to call for help, he didn't have a phone on him.

We'll never know if he died on the steps to the altar or if Ray Mercer positioned him there. The police removed the body from the crime scene without adequate investigation.

The returns from the short were massive. The St. Ignatius endowment ballooned. Raymond Mercer paid off his debts. His depositors received their capital with interest when the CDs expired. They were disappointed only when he announced he would no longer take their money, and that, for the foreseeable future, he would manage only his own money through a family office. He finally did the thing he'd told Maddie he would have done all along if not for his altruistic nature: He retired.

Bon voyage, little people!

AFTER THE NEWS of the financial scheme broke, Wayne voluntarily came forward, telling police that, back in 2005, Danny Perone had purchased "enough painkillers to put down an elephant."

Woolf's death and the Toradol shots had been enough for St. Ignatius to force Coach to resign, but he was immediately hired to build a hockey program at a prep school in Indiana, where he coaches today. His team is number one in the state.

Danny Perone was interviewed by police at his home in Bloomington via videoconference. He claimed he had purchased the drugs from Wayne for personal use, because he suffered from chronic pain. There'd been no record of Coach ever seeing a doctor for pain, but no one could prove he'd given the drugs to Ray Mercer or anyone else.

Susanna and I continued to talk on the phone regularly, about once a week. Mostly, we spoke about me: my classes, my friends, my loud-typing roommate who stayed up until 4 a.m. Once, knowing that Susanna had become estranged from her father, I worked up the courage to ask if she believed he was capable of taking Woolf's life.

"I know he is," she said.

"How?"

She audibly pushed air out of her lungs and said, "He came to me in a dream."

"Woolf?" I asked.

"No," she said. "My father."

I found it interesting that her dad haunted her dreams, not Woolf. It made sense, of course.

She added, "Initially, I assumed my mother had to be involved. I pictured her crushing the pills into dust and preparing the syringe. I imagined her giving my father instructions: 'He'll be at the chapel alone before the game. Approach from behind.' But when I confronted her, she reminded me of something."

There was a long pause, and I thought the call might have dropped. "What?"

Susanna continued, "Mother was offended that I would consider her such a brute. Murder, in her mind, was a solution employed by the underclass. She looked me in the eye and said, 'If your father had come to me, which he should have, I would have handled Woolf the way we handle everyone. By giving him something he wanted.' What did Woolf want? He wanted to save his parents' little nest egg. He wanted Maddie to go to college on scholarship, and law school too, feeling like she'd earned it—a Raymond Mercer scholarship, awarded for academic merit. They could have announced it to the press, set aside an endowment for future recipients. When Mother described this fantasy, she looked out the window in the direction of the garden, and I saw the world as she saw it, bendable to her will. She was probably right: Woolf would have kept quiet; he would have done anything for his family, Maddie especially. Ironically, that made him more like a Mercer than a Whiting."

ULTIMATELY, THE US attorney told the Whitings that they were in an "Al Capone-type situation." They had no direct evidence connecting Raymond Mercer to Woolf's murder, and though the documents Woolf had buried clearly suggested a Ponzi scheme, which he was eventually able to exit only through insider trading, the statute of limitations on securities fraud had expired. Then he paused, before adding, "But don't worry, we'll get him."

One and done is not the modus operandi of the financial criminal. The US attorney assured the family: Raymond Mercer would go away for financial crimes, which was as good as a murder conviction.

Monica Whiting didn't think it was the justice her son deserved, but the system is not designed to ameliorate a mother's grief. "That's between you and God," the prosecutor told her. Maddie called him a dick.

More than a year went by before the US attorney brought a case, but he eventually did.

At the trial, Ray Mercer's attorneys argued that any prior bad acts, barred from prosecution due to the statute of limitations, were inadmissible, and furthermore, that his former investors had all made considerable returns on their investments. Everyone was happy.

The judge agreed: Violations of US securities laws committed by Raymond Mercer Capital in Antigua were out.

Instead, the jury examined a cornucopia of evidence uncovered from the last ten years—text messages and emails and witness testimony—revealing an ongoing pattern of insider trading. When Ray Mercer retired from managing other people's money, he began using insider information to multiply returns on his own fortune.

Juries have little sympathy for white-collar criminals. Ray Mercer was convicted of one count of wire fraud and four counts of securities fraud.

25

SEWICKLEY FEELS FAMILIAR—MOM waiting at the bottom of the escalator at the Pittsburgh airport, my unaltered room in our town house, texts from Shiv: *Meet me at Starbucks*—but also glitchy. I keep having the sensation that this isn't my real life. Maybe it's not anymore. I am a junior at Princeton now. We turned over our Community Journalism project to the US attorney over two years ago.

Today is Raymond Mercer's sentencing hearing. Susanna, Maddie, Vince, Shiv, and I sit at Eat'n Park, ready to roll deep to the courthouse and learn his fate.

Shiv and I are both home from college for winter break.

Susanna had suggested we go together to "observe our genetic legacy," as if it were an object that could be held in the palm of a hand and then locked into a vault, like an heirloom seed. I thought she was the one who needed support, given that her father is now a convicted felon, but then I remembered who would be in the gallery: Woolf's parents, both of whom I've now met multiple times, separately, and Susanna's mother, who has never made any attempt to contact me.

Maddie traveled from New York for the sentencing, as she'd done for the trial, which I missed because Mom thought my classes were more important than watching a guy with a quarter of my DNA go down for financial crimes.

Before Vince greets us, he puts his hand on Susanna's shoulder and says, "Yo, someone parked a Bentley in the Eat'n Park lot."

Susanna looks down at the table. "When they froze the assets, Mom was awarded three cars and access to the jet. So I borrowed the white one."

"Nice," Vince says. "Three Bentleys?"

"One Bentley," she says. "Mother is driving the Range Rover today."

Vince laughs. The image of the wife of a disgraced financier rolling up to the courthouse in a Range Rover is a little too cliché.

Shiv makes a bad joke about Ingo, how he was a CEO in high school, driving around in his mom's Range Rover. When we first arrived at college, Ingo and I texted regularly, then not so much, and by the end of first semester, not at all. We haven't spoken since.

Vince doesn't let it go. "Who is Ingo?"

I look out at the mostly empty restaurant. "Just a boy . . ."

"Doesn't matter," Susanna says, looking from me to Shiv. "One day, you two will be sitting at some diner—maybe even this diner. You'll each have a couple kids. Or not. But you'll have each other, and you'll look back at some boy you knew in high school, and he'll seem like nothing at all."

No one really thinks about it, but boyfriends are only blips. The blips might vary in intensity, but they have one thing in common: They are there, and then they are gone. Best friends, on the other hand, hang around for a lifetime.

Maddie and Vince are squished in the booth next to each other, so close they are almost touching. Vince should put his arm around her. In high school, he might have been so bold.

Maddie's mind is elsewhere. "Back then, we felt so guilty about the things we were hiding we forgot we were just kids." Maddie looks at me and Shiv when she says *kids*, which makes me feel immature, even though I know she's seeing her younger self. "Corruption is an adult game, and my brother's murder was corruption taken to finality. Maybe we were *being* corrupted or learning to *become* corrupt, but we *weren't* corrupt. Not back then. Not yet."

"And now?" Susanna asks.

"What the hell are we doing here?" Vince says.

"Chasing catharsis?" Maddie suggests.

"No, I mean here," Vince slams his hand on the table.

"Oh, you're too good for Eat'n Park now?" Maddie says.

"Never, but I'm too good to deny myself a drink," Vince says.

"It's not even noon yet. Try harder not to become your father," Maddie says.

At first, I think Vince is embarrassed, and I'm surprised Maddie would be so insensitive, but he flashes a smile and says, "Comparatively, my dad doesn't seem so bad anymore."

Susanna shakes her head, but she's smiling too.

Maddie says, "Sure, Mitch Mahoney is a great guy, now that he's dead."

I can't join their chorus. Not because I don't share their history, though I don't, but because I've never looked at my own parent and felt ashamed.

MADDIE CALLS SHOTGUN as soon as the Bentley is in view, as if Shiv or I would have jumped into the front seat otherwise.

The interior of the car is insane: tan leather seats accented by wood detailing on the center console and the dash. Susanna puts the car in reverse, and slowly backs out of the parking spot.

"Still can't drive a stick, eh?" Maddie says. The Bentley is an automatic.

Susanna puts the car in drive and looks over at her best friend. "Too bad I didn't have a better teacher, back in the day."

"A good teacher recognizes a lost cause."

"They don't even sell these things with manual transmissions anymore," Susanna says, releasing the wheel. "Practically drives itself."

"Tell it to take us somewhere else," Vince chimes in from the back.

Everybody goes quiet, all of us aware of the place we must go before we can go anywhere else.

AT THE HEARING, three letters—penned by a local farmer, a single mother, and a retiree—are read aloud, all in praise of Raymond

Mercer, for affording them the quality of life and financial security previously granted only to the privileged, never before accessible to working-class people like them. The farmer's letter demands a remedy to Raymond Mercer's "wrongful conviction."

A guy in the back shouts, "Let him go." Several people stand up and yell at each other.

A woman's voice rises above the rest. "Murderer! Raymond Mercer is a murderer! Lock him up. Lock him up. Lock him up." The chant becomes a chorus.

I look at Mo, expecting her to join in, but she sits still, silently weeping into a tissue. Declan is sitting next to her. They do not touch. He will fly back to his Florida family after the hearing. Mo has invited my mom and me for Christmas Eve dinner with her and Maddie. We plan to go.

The judge demands silence in her courtroom. Finally, she says, "The only thing that separates Raymond Mercer from the Bernie Madoffs and Allen Stanfords of the world is luck." Then she corrects herself. "Luck is too generous. Deceit is not luck."

Gramps is sentenced to fifty-five years in prison.

AS WE EXIT the courthouse, a reporter pushes a microphone in Maddie's face, and Maddie makes a brief statement. "Did you notice his own lawyers never used the term 'victimless'? They know he killed my brother."

Before the reporter can ask a follow-up question, Vince puts his arm around her, holding her head to his chest as they push forward.

I think the reporters might follow us to the parking lot, but they hang back by the courthouse, waiting for the prosecutor to emerge and give a statement. The man is a local hero. He might be the next mayor.

"Warm up the Bentley," Vince says. "Pittsburgh is cool now; did anybody tell you?"

"Let's pay our respects first," Maddie says.

I close my eyes and feel Woolf in the car. He is young, more like me and Shiv than the others, as if dying were a way of opting out: of a body, a group of friends, a generation. He is a beautiful boy with a big smile and so much heart—heart that beats for his family, for his girlfriend and his best friend, but mostly for the future, for all he is destined to achieve.

When I open my eyes, I feel his loss as Maddie must feel it. Part of me, my genetic complement, has been stolen, and my existence has been altered—not devastated, but cracked wide open. I am fundamentally concerned with who I am, not what I will or will not become.

Maddie instructs Susanna to drive to the rink.

Susanna stops the Bentley in front of the liquor store on Broad Street, a classic Sewickley drop-off—cutting the engine in the middle of the street, without looking in the rearview mirror to find out if we're holding up traffic.

Vince jumps out to buy whiskey.

THE MAIN ENTRANCE to the rink is open. Most of the campus is locked down for winter break, but the men's and women's hockey teams practice through the holidays. No rest for winners.

The ice is empty now, smoothed by the Zamboni, ready for blood and spit.

Maddie stops in front of the Woolf Whiting Memorial plaque and says to Susanna, "They'll take your dad's name off the arena."

"The Woolf Whiting Memorial Hockey Rink?" Susanna suggests.

"This school has been trying to forget about Woolf for years," Maddie says.

"Trying and failing," Vince says.

"Some idiot will pay top dollar to have his name on the rink," Maddie says.

"How about the Madeline Whiting Rink for the Wayward?" Vince suggests.

"Why would I want my name on a hockey rink?"

"Because it's the only building that really matters here," Shiv says.

"True enough," Maddie says. "But I don't have a boatload of dirty money sitting around, and, more importantly, I'm not that vain."

"Exactly," Shiv says. "Why should this place carry the name of some dude trying to compensate? Why shouldn't it have a woman's name? Why not your name?"

"I agree," says Vince, passing the whiskey bottle to Maddie. Looking around the arena, he adds, "She's a lady all right."

"Me or the rink?" Maddie asks.

"Both," he says.

"You guys should just get married already," Susanna says, prompting Vince to get down on a knee in front of Maddie. She pulls him up and pushes him away.

Susanna looks over at me and winks conspiratorially, as if we've sanctioned the flirtatious banter, which, yes, please, we have. I marvel at the warmth of her gesture, and how natural it feels to receive it.

Breaking a surprisingly comfortable silence, Vince asks, "What are you studying at Princeton?"

"Religion."

Maddie smirks. "By the time you graduate, religion will be obsolete."

"Didn't you know, Frankie? Bridge released a premium add-on, Save Your Soul. Only nine ninety-nine," Shiv jokes. She has finally come to terms with her dad's decision to join the Hare Krishnas, or maybe his leaving doesn't matter anymore, because we've left too.

Maddie looks at Vince, singling him out. "How are you still *so* Catholic?"

"After my dad died and I moved back to run the business, I started going to Mass again with Mom and Laura. For a while, I thought I was going for *them*, to be with them, to be a family. Then one Sunday, Mom and Laura were out of town, visiting colleges. I drove all the way to Sewickley to go to St. Mary's. I had nothing else to do and no one to see in Sewickley. After Mass, I drove straight home."

"Sounds like you need a drinking buddy," Maddie says.

Susanna shakes her head. "Please, Maddie. You're as Catholic as Woolf was. Baptized on the same day. Mass every Sunday, throwing elbows at each other in the pews."

"The church will be here in the bitter end," Vince says. "That's when people will need it."

Maddie gestures toward the group, her outstretched hand briefly suspended in the direction of Shiv. "I'm not just talking about Catholicism."

I think about what my mom said to Father Michael the night after Kyle Murphy died. "Spiritual famine," she called it. In my room at home, the crucifix I received at my First Communion ceremony hangs above my bed. Mom had suggested I take it when I left for college, but I didn't want anyone to make assumptions about me. How could they possibly know who I was when I didn't know myself? But when I pray at night in my dorm room, I look up at the blank wall.

"Remember how Sinéad O'Connor tore up the picture of the pope?" Susanna asks.

"We were kids," Maddie says. "But, yeah, I definitely heard about it."

"For years, everyone thought she tore up the picture because of the church," Susanna says. "But really she tore it up because it had belonged to her mother."

"Are you having a midlife crisis?" Maddie asks.

"I'm too young."

Shiv says, "The mid-decade crisis is the new midlife crisis. I don't remember if I had one at five, but at fifteen, I definitely did." She points at me. "We both did. And I'm pretty sure by twenty-five we're due for another, a big one, like everyone says: the quarter-life crisis." She stands up and looks toward Susanna, Maddie, and Vince, who are sitting three across. "You guys are thirty-five-ish." Stepping over the bench, she lifts the bottle from Vince's hand and pours a swig of whiskey down her throat. "So everyone you grew up with is probably—"

"We get it," Maddie says.

"What *happened* to us?" Susanna lobs the question to Maddie and Vince.

"What do you mean?" Vince asks, his tone earnest.

"I always believed Woolf was the best of us," Maddie says. "So his death seemed especially cruel."

"It was cruel," Vince says.

"Deep down, I believed it should have been me and not him. Or not that it *should* have been me, but everything would have been better if it had been me. Better for my parents. Better for his daughter." Maddie paused to look at me. "Better for the world, I guess."

Vince shakes his head, I assume in disagreement, but then I understand he relates to her—he has felt the same way.

"But that's not true," I say.

Maddie smiles to assure me she's okay. "It was never him or me. I know that now."

The day I gave Maddie the documents that Shiv and I dug up from under the cherub, I believed I was the central figure in the story, the big secret that bound them together. But I can see now: Maddie, Vince, and Susanna didn't experience it that way. Woolf's death was the seminal moment of their lives. Maddie's family fell apart. She became a corporate lawyer, which was probably her way of stepping into Woolf's shoes. Vince believed returning to Pittsburgh was a failure of ambition. Certainly, he'd have come home sooner if it hadn't been the place where he'd lost his best friend. And maybe Susanna would have been able to sustain a romantic relationship for longer than six months. In other words, Woolf was obviously the central figure. And finding out how he died—knowing who killed him—must have knocked them all sideways.

Finally, they are all starting to get back on their feet, forge a path forward, discover the way back to each other, because they need each other most of all. They have regrets, I know, but there is something else that connects them, something more powerful than a secret: a well of joy. I think it comes from their time at St. Ignatius, not what happened in the end, but what happened when they were all together: Woolf, Maddie, Vince, and Susanna.

I finish Shiv's thought. "We're all who we always were and becoming something else at the same time. Those two things go to war at least once a decade."

Everyone nods like we've solved the mystery of the universe, when really we are just drunk, or on our way to it. Everyone is listening, but I speak directly to Susanna. "You know my mom is seeing somebody?"

"Ms. Northrup is hot." Susanna puts her arms around Maddie and Vince, one on each side. "Maybe there's still hope for us too. Who's the lucky woman?" she asks.

"Haven't met her yet. Mom's taking it slow."

Vince has a big, dumb smile on his face. "Where'd they meet?"

"Blood pressure clinic at St. Mary's."

He laughs. "Not exactly a lesbian meet market."

"It's actually pretty cute," I say. "Mom volunteers there every month. Most of the people who drop in are older parishioners. Mom checks their blood pressure, and then they sit around for twenty minutes or more, for the conversation. It's open to everybody. Mom puts a sign out front: 'Free Blood Pressure Screening.' Sarah—that's her name—happened to drive by. She's only like forty, one of those people who never goes to doctors unless her appendix bursts or something crazy. Anyway, she saw the sign and thought, 'Maybe it's a *sign*.' So she went in and she walked up to Mom and said, 'Do I need to confess my sins first?' and they both laughed. And that was it. They knew they liked each other."

Shiv and I are a couple rows below the others, straddling the bleacher bench so we can look up at them.

"Are you studying any religion, in particular?" Vince asks.

I think about some of the classes I've been taking: Islam in the West, The English Reformation, Zen Buddhism, Dante's *Divine Comedy*. They all interest me, but none as much as what William James called "the overlapping things, the things in the universe that throw the last stone, so to speak, and say the final word."

I picture the blank wall above my bed in the dorm. That wall contains multitudes: The absent crucifix. My mom's devotion. Shiv's arangetram. The puja room in her house. Her dad, elsewhere, chanting Hare Krishna. What Maddie called "the Absence." Mass at St. Mary's. Kyle's funeral. A mother's grief. A mother's grief. A mother's grief.

There is that one second, maybe more, when a car levitated between bridge and water. Do I believe Kyle's car defied the laws of physics? Of course not. But for the witness, that moment was expansive, infinite even, like Dante's white light, or what Albie Harris saw when he died on the ice, before being brought back to life. Who could say what occupies one second, maybe more?

It is the state of eternal present that Father Michael talked about in his benediction. It is the opposite of achievement. It is all those overlapping things, pushed aside and forgotten in an onslaught of Bridge alerts.

There's something else. I am beginning to see the thing I was unable to comprehend at St. Ignatius: myself. But only as a blur, as if I've just woken up, and I'm grasping around at my bedside for a pair of glasses. I am on the wall too, a girl who finally knows her origin story, knows who her biological parents are, knows who her biological grandparents are, knows that (at least) one of them is a killer, but who also knows that her life is predicated on a couple of decisions that might be mistaken for fate but were really representative of the goodness of youth—the naïveté, sure, but also the stubborn wisdom of the young: Susanna's recognition of her history teacher as the right mother for me, and Maddie's decision to keep the secret of my birth from her own mother, who would have otherwise claimed me.

My story isn't about an accidental pregnancy, which might have been easily prevented, or even the decision to carry a baby to term. Had either gone the other way, I wouldn't be here. And in the grand scheme of our infinite cosmos, so what? But once I arrived and Susanna handed me to the nurse, and the nurse to the woman who would raise me, I was granted the authority to ask the questions I've been asking since Kyle died: Why am I here? Why is Kyle not? Why is Colton not? Why is Woolf not?

People want to talk about these *nots* as individual decisions, about serotonin receptors and impetuousness and greed, but they are connected. St. Ignatius. Sewickley. Pittsburgh. America. Who are these gods that govern us? Who tricked us into wanting the Ivy League? The Stanley Cup? The Range Rover? The first million? Billion? What will become of us when we achieve our goals and realize they mean nothing? Will we double down? Drive off a bridge? Maybe, we'll give it all away. Move to a commune in West Virginia. Chant.

"I want to study secularism," I say.

"So, not religion?" Susanna asks.

"I dunno, I think maybe it is," I say.

Nobody responds.

"Shiv, tell them about the family wager."

"Heh." Shiv's tipsy, so she willingly explains that there are two choices, you can either love your parents or hate them, and there are two eventualities, either you will find out they are worthy of love or not. If you love them and you come to understand their choices—even if you don't agree with them, you know they did the best they could—you reap the rewards of family. If you hate them, whether they deserve it or not, you gain nothing. But if you hate them and you find that they deserved your love, you've already lost everything. You've lost your family.

"So, we choose to love them," Shiv says.

"Unless you're Sinéad O'Connor," Susanna says.

"Or Susanna Mercer?" The inflection in Maddie's voice suggests it's a question.

Susanna closes her eyes and shakes her head, as if she's trying to wake herself from a bad dream. I want to ask Susanna if she still loves her parents—my grandparents. Her mom, at least? I don't have the guts.

When I search Maddie's face, I see her youth. A stranger might guess we are sisters. Jaw clenched, she looks sad, but there are no tears. I move up one row, close enough to touch her. For my whole life, she cared about me without even knowing me. Not knowing me was her great act of love. "I don't know how much keeping Susanna's secret cost you," I say, "but I promise you, it was worth it."

She reaches out and cups her hands under my chin, smiles, and releases me.

"Come on," Vince says. "Let's go down on the ice."

Shiv and I stay up in the bleachers, watching Vince walk ahead of Susanna and Maddie. He steps into the penalty box, which doubles as a sound booth. Music envelops the empty rink. The sound system is top-notch.

Woolf is the one who got away. Not romantically, though there is romance, but in the senseless way that God took everything from Job.

I can hold two things in my mind at once. One: If Woolf hadn't died, I might not have been raised by my mom. Two: The fact of his death is absurd and, therefore, crushing. My father was taken from me before I had the chance to know him. The more I learn about him, the more viscerally I understand that I will never hold his hand, never ask him for advice, never break away, never come back. Maybe I can love him—at least, I can love the idea of him—but I suspect that's not the same as what most daughters feel for their fathers.

Of course, Woolf wasn't just taken from *me*. Mo will always see me as the artifact of the son, rather than the granddaughter who is alive. Madeline will continue to work insane hours and earn insane money and sell part of her soul, but not all of it. I'm optimistic about her future. And the rest of the world: Who knows what Woolf could have offered it? As Father Michael said that night he came to see my mom, a lifetime ago now: Woolf was "pure potential."

Susanna and Maddie hold hands, shuffling on the ice. Vince joins them in the center circle. All three of them bob and funny-walk, slipping around. Vince pulls Maddie into him and twirls her out and pulls her back again. Susanna's hands levitate, caressing the cold air. If I didn't know them, from that distance I might think they are St. Ignatius students, messing around, free from burdens. Fine young people, all of them.

Acknowledgments

SAMANTHA SHEA AND Betsy Gleick: How I landed with both the world's best agent and editor—for this book and this writer—is as mysterious to me as all life's good fortune for which I am profoundly grateful. The industry needs editors like Betsy; the world needs them.

Jovanna Brinck and Madeline Jones made Algonquin feel like home in a time of change, which is precisely when one needs a home. Seeing the work perfected through Elizabeth Johnson's copyedits was pure joy—the Pittsburgh connection was a bonus.

I've had many wonderful teachers over the years, but my high school teachers at Shady Side Academy were the ones who changed my life. Stan Nevola spent his hard-earned nights and weekends taking our jazz combo on trips around the country and to charity gigs in Pittsburgh. Buddy Hendershot was both my English teacher and my soccer coach. Tom Murphy introduced me to Andre Dubus and made me believe I could be a writer. Mr. Ashworth, Dr. Sutula, and Ms. Belles taught math, philosophy and Latin with humor and grace. There is no way to adequately acknowledge what these individuals have done for me. I hope they are rewarded for their service with riches beyond our material world.

This book is dedicated to Leena Somani. Even as a dense adolescent, I understood how lucky I was to be in the presence of such humor and light. Nearly 30 years later, I still look to Leena for an example of how to live. I am also grateful for the friendship of Jessica Strelec and Noah Meyers, who made high school a little easier, and more joyful.

Lynne and Bill Bruno provided unconditional love, a fine liberal arts education, and most important of all, a spiritual inheritance. They never questioned my decision to study religion, however financially unwise, and gave me the will to believe in something bigger than myself, beyond this world.

I grew up watching my brother, Billy Bruno, play hockey—on the ice and on the street in front of our house. I don't need to say how much I love him. He already knows.

Tamara Kraljic read this novel in two days, while managing three boys, a big-time career, and a million other jobs women do to keep us all afloat. Knowing she believed reading fiction was the most important way to spend her nonexistent time was an inspiration.

Nancy Parker and Dwight Dobberstein made life as a writer possible with all kinds of support, from help building a house to teaching my boys how to create and garden and explore.

When I imagine my ideal life, it involves long, uninterrupted conversations about writing and writers with smart, funny women like Raquel MacKay, Jen Adrian, Katie Runde, and Sanjna Singh. The fact that this fantasy is real amazes me every day.

Jen Adrian, Sophia Lin, Christine Utz, and Maria Kuznetsova were my first and most generous readers. They are the great gifts of the Iowa Writers' Workshop. Friendly librarian, Leah Agne, explained how a library might preserve digital and microfilm archives from a defunct small-town press.

Kevin Brockmeier was my brilliant teacher at the Writers' Workshop. Years later, because he is kind, he read this novel when I was stuck. Without him, it might be in a drawer.

Forty Years in Bangladesh: Memoirs of Father Timm provided a detailed account of the life and mind of a priest who lived in service to others. The facts of Father Timm's life—and the notion that people like him exist in our modern world—blew my mind.

Dr. Somani's correspondence helped me understand Vedic tradition, the Hare Krishna people, and the decision to detach and serve God. He has given me a richer understanding of religious devotion.

One benefit of being part of the University of Iowa community is that I can randomly reach out to the classics department about a Latin motto. Rachel Rucker helped write the St. Ignatius motto, *Nominatim non generatim*, over a lengthy correspondence that she patiently carried on with wisdom, and because strangers are sometimes awesome.

Writing is hard and often demoralizing, but my two children, Jack and Hugo, make me feel like a rock star every single day.

And Parker, my love: If these are the hard years, you've made them seem easy. One day, you'll have long, lazy hours to slow cook meat on the grill, and we'll know we've made it.